XXXHolic Volume 3 is a work of fiction. Names, places, and incidents either are a product of the author's imagination or are used fictitiously.

A Del Rey® Book
Published by The Random House Publishing Group

Published in the United States by Del Rey Books, an imprint of The Random House Publishing Group, a division of Random House, Inc., New York, and simultaneously in Canada by Random House of Canada Limited, Toronto. First published in serialization and subsequently published in book form by Kodansha Ltd. Tokyo in 2003.

Del Rey is a registered trademark and the Del Rey colophon is a trademark of Random House, Inc.

www.delreymanga.com

Library of Congress Control Number: 2004091024

ISBN 0-345-47181-4

Translator and Adaptor—William Flanagan
Lettering—Dana Hayward
Cover Design—David Stevenson

Manufactured in the United States of America

8 9

First Edition: October 2004

Contents

Honorifics Explained

Throughout the Del Rey Manga books, you will find Japanese honorifics left intact in the translations. For those not familiar with how the Japanese use honorifics, and more important, how they differ from American honorifics, we present this brief overview.

Politeness has always been a critical facet of Japanese culture. Ever since the feudal era, when Japan was a highly stratified society, use of honorifics—which can be defined as polite speech that indicates relationship or status—has played an essential role in the Japanese language. When addressing someone in Japanese, an honorific usually takes the form of a suffix attached to one's name (example: "Asuna-san"), or as a title at the end of one's name or in place of the name itself (example: "Negi-sensei," or simply "Sensei!").

Honorifics can be expressions of respect or endearment. In the context of manga and anime, honorifics give insight into the nature of the relationship between characters. Many translations into English leave out these important honorifics, and therefore distort the "feel" of the original Japanese. Because Japanese honorifics contain nuances that English honorifics lack, it is our policy at Del Rey not to translate them. Here, instead, is a guide to some of the honorifics you may encounter in Del Rey Manga.

-san: This is the most common honorific, and is equivalent to Mr., Miss, Ms., Mrs., etc. It is the all-purpose honorific and can be used in any situation where politeness is required.

-sama: This is one level higher than "-san." It is used to confer great respect.

-dono: This comes from the word "tono," which means "lord." It is an even higher level than "-sama," and confers utmost respect.

-kun: This suffix is used at the end of boys' names to express familiarity or endearment. It is also sometimes used by men among friends, or when addressing someone younger or of a lower station.

-chan: This is used to express endearment, mostly toward girls. It is also used for little boys, pets, and even among lovers. It gives a sense of childish cuteness.

Bozu: This is an informal way to refer to a boy, similar to the English term "kid" or "squirt."

Sempai: This title suggests that the addressee is one's "senior" in a group or organization. It is most often used in a school setting, where underclassmen refer to their upperclassmen as "sempai." It can also be used in the workplace, such as when a newer employee addresses an employee who has seniority in the company.

Kohai: This is the opposite of "-sempai," and is used toward underclassmen in school or newcomers in the workplace. It connotes that the addressee is of lower station.

Sensei: Literally meaning "one who has come before," this title is used for teachers, doctors, or masters of any profession or art.

[blank]: Usually forgotten in these lists, but perhaps the most significant difference between Japanese and English. The lack of honorific means that the speaker has permission to address the person in a very intimate way. Usually, only family, spouses, or very close friends have this kind of permission. Known as *yobisute,* it can be gratifying when someone who has earned the intimacy starts to call one by one's name without an honorific. But when that intimacy hasn't been earned, it can also be very insulting.

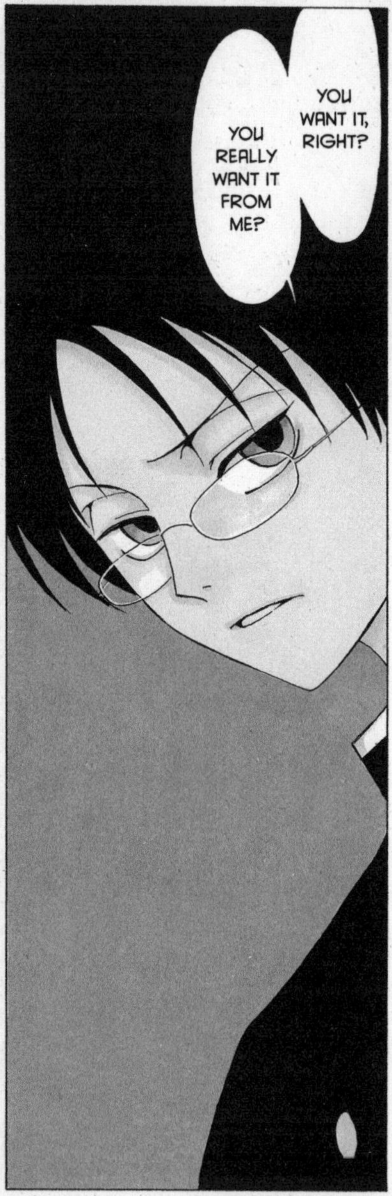
YOU WANT IT, RIGHT?
YOU REALLY WANT IT FROM ME?

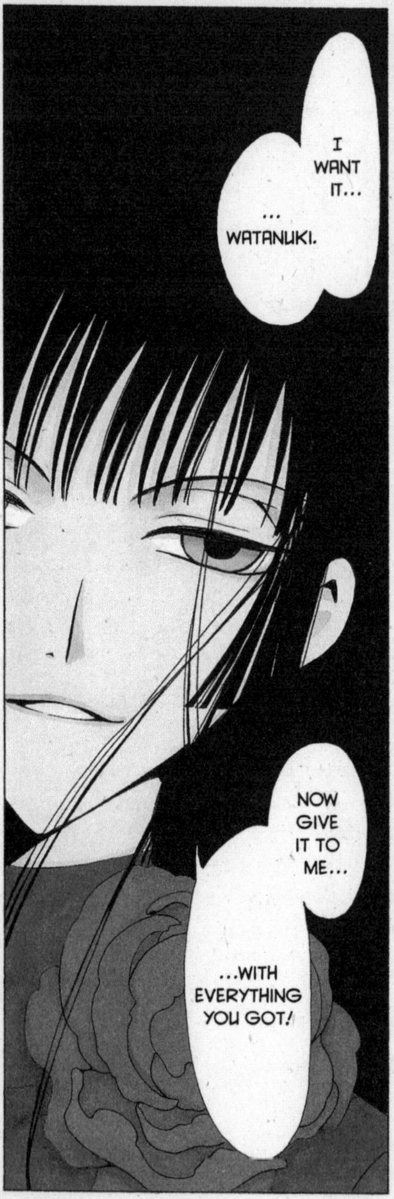
I WANT IT...
... WATANUKI.
NOW GIVE IT TO ME...
...WITH EVERYTHING YOU GOT!

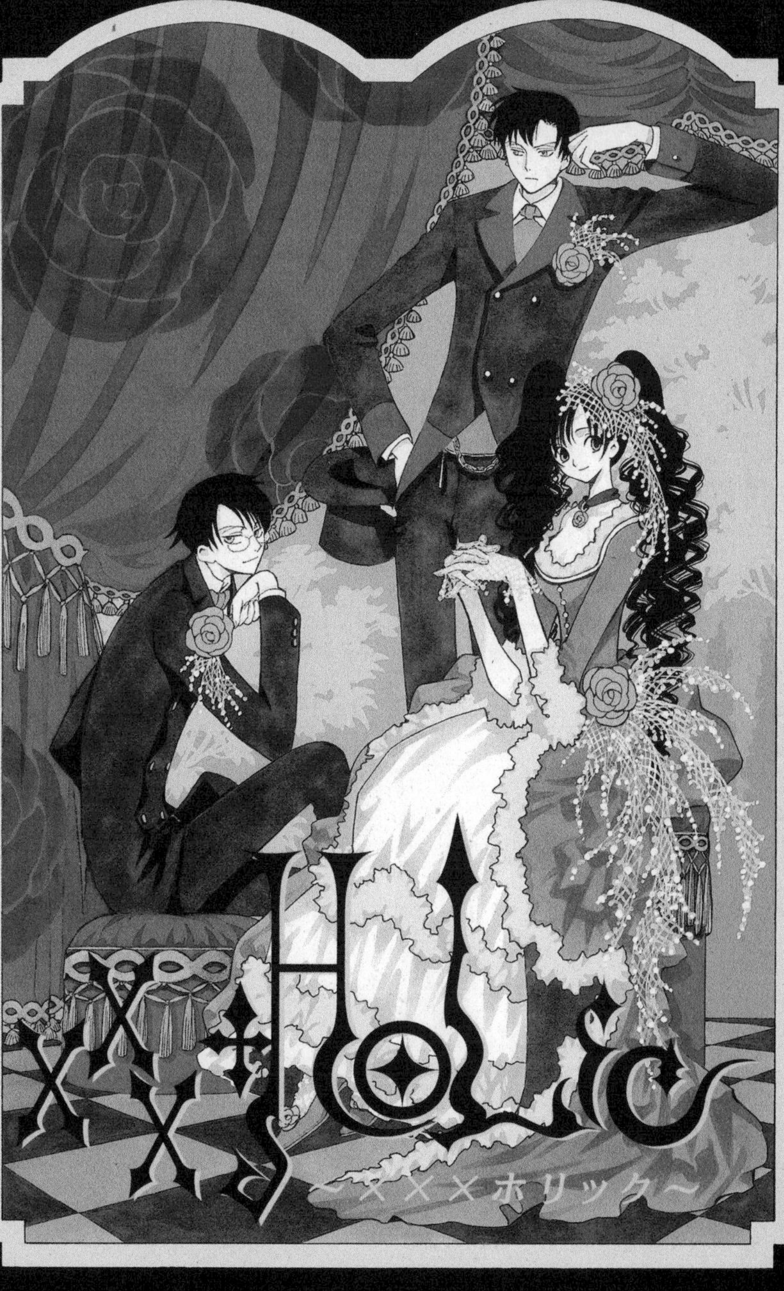
xxxHOLiC
〜×××ホリック〜

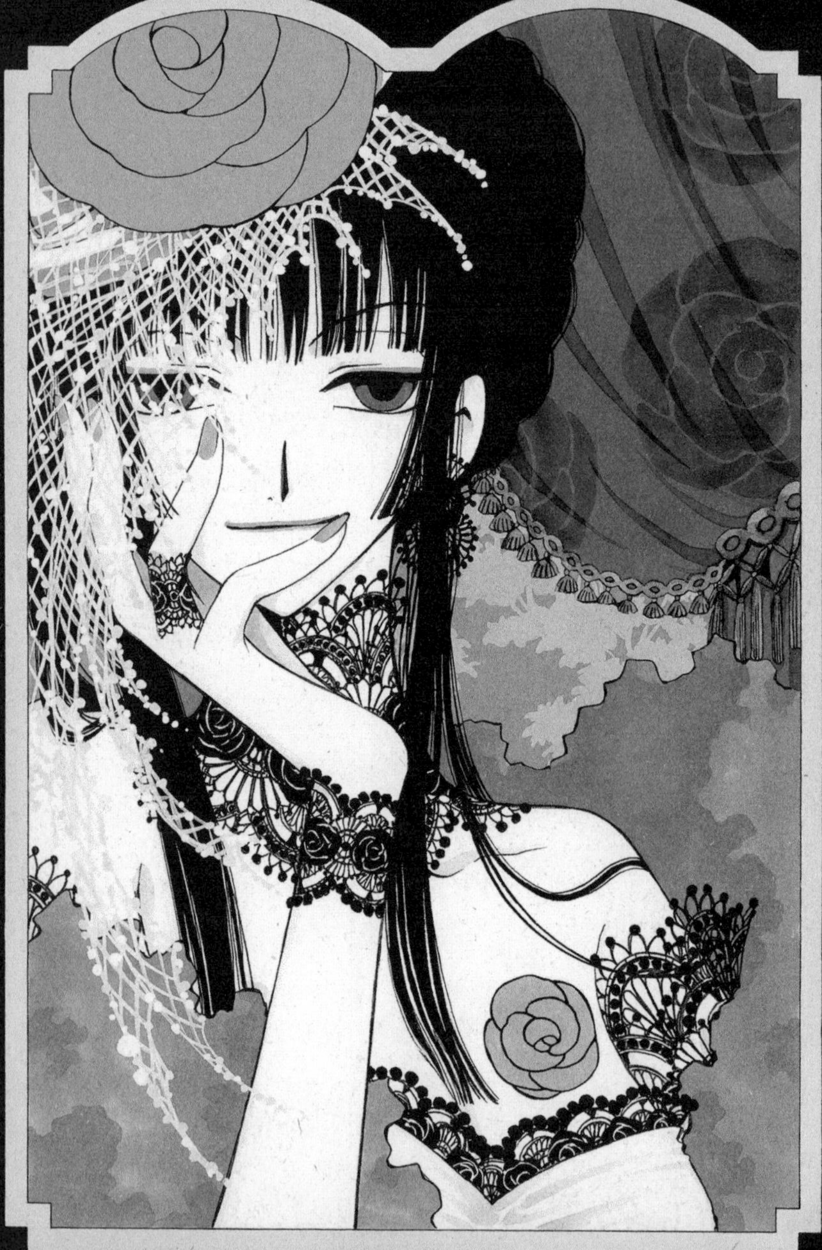

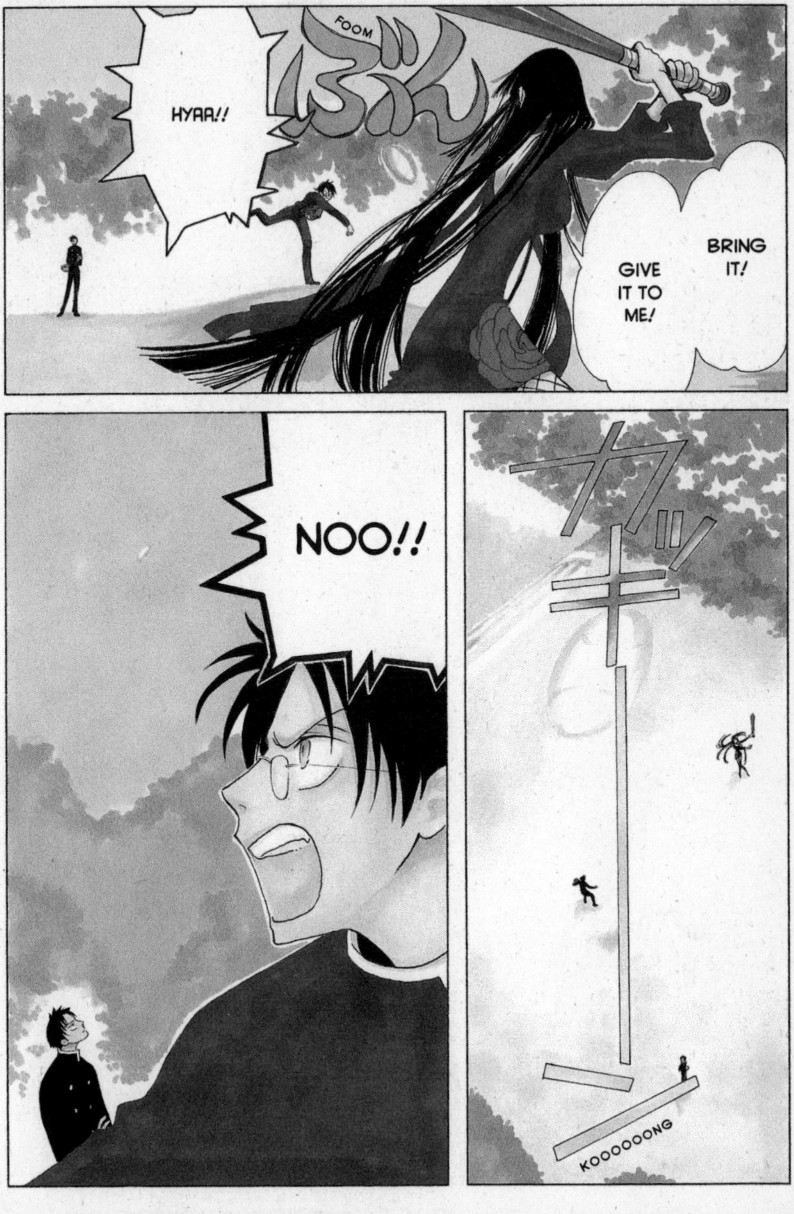
FOOM
BRING IT! GIVE IT TO ME!
HYAA!!
KOOOOOONG
NOO!!

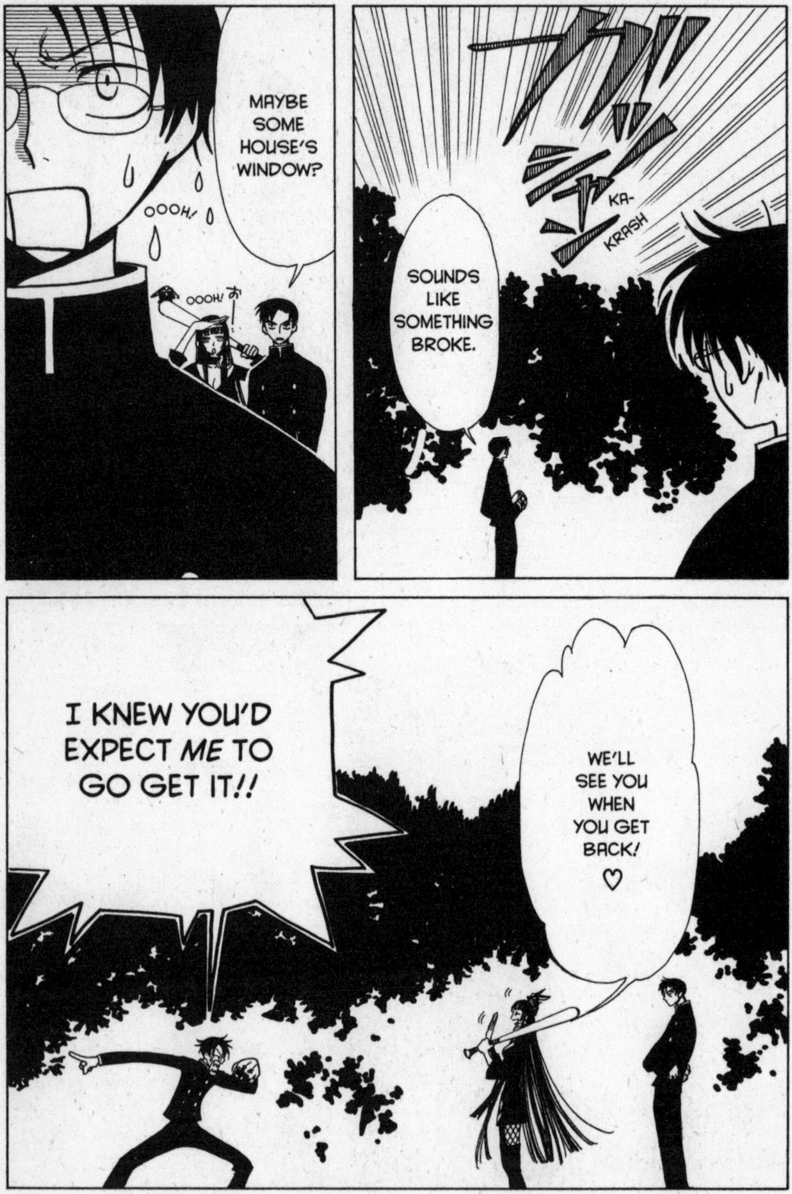

KA-KRASH
SOUNDS LIKE SOMETHING BROKE.
MAYBE SOME HOUSE'S WINDOW?
OOOH!
OOOH! お
WE'LL SEE YOU WHEN YOU GET BACK! ♡
I KNEW YOU'D EXPECT *ME* TO GO GET IT!!

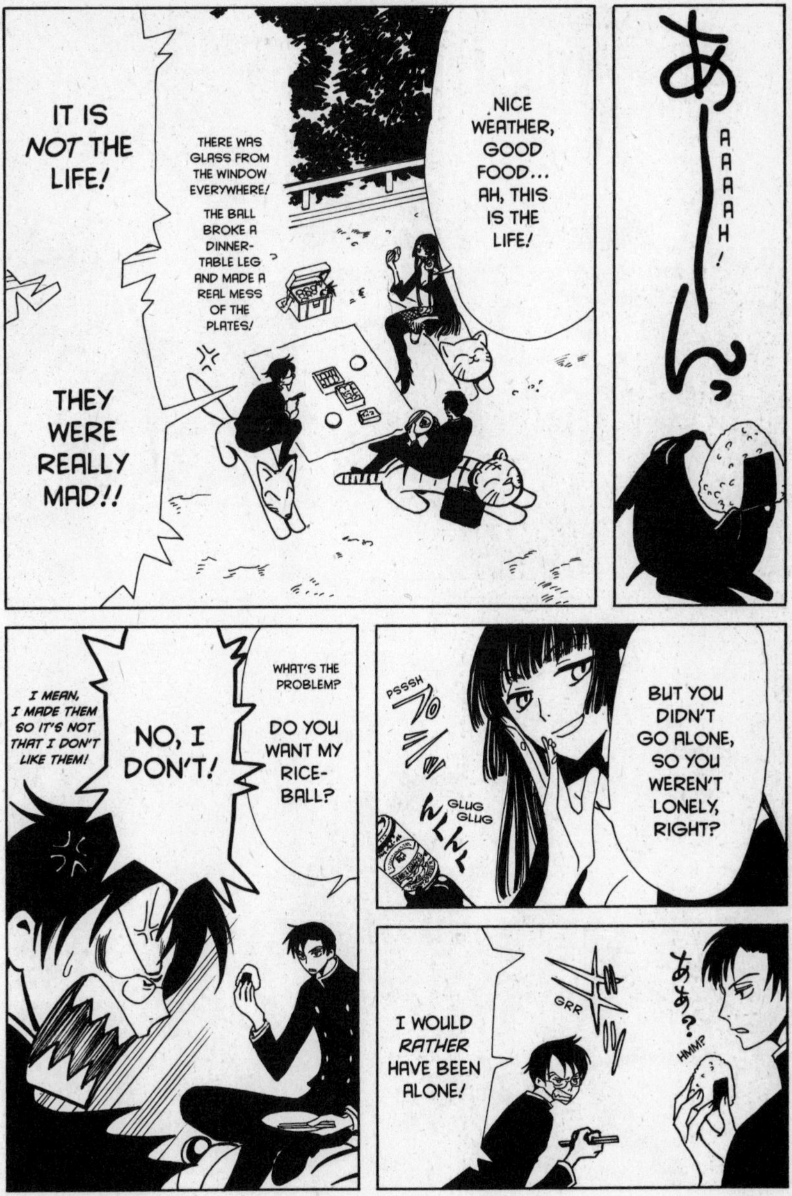
あーん
AAAAH!
NICE WEATHER, GOOD FOOD... AH, THIS IS THE LIFE!
THERE WAS GLASS FROM THE WINDOW EVERYWHERE!
THE BALL BROKE A DINNER-TABLE LEG AND MADE A REAL MESS OF THE PLATES!
IT IS *NOT* THE LIFE!
THEY WERE REALLY MAD!!
BUT YOU DIDN'T GO ALONE, SO YOU WEREN'T LONELY, RIGHT?
PSSSH
GLUG GLUG
ああ?
HMM?
GRR
I WOULD *RATHER* HAVE BEEN ALONE!
WHAT'S THE PROBLEM?
DO YOU WANT MY RICE-BALL?
NO, I DON'T!
I MEAN, I MADE THEM SO IT'S NOT THAT I DON'T LIKE THEM!

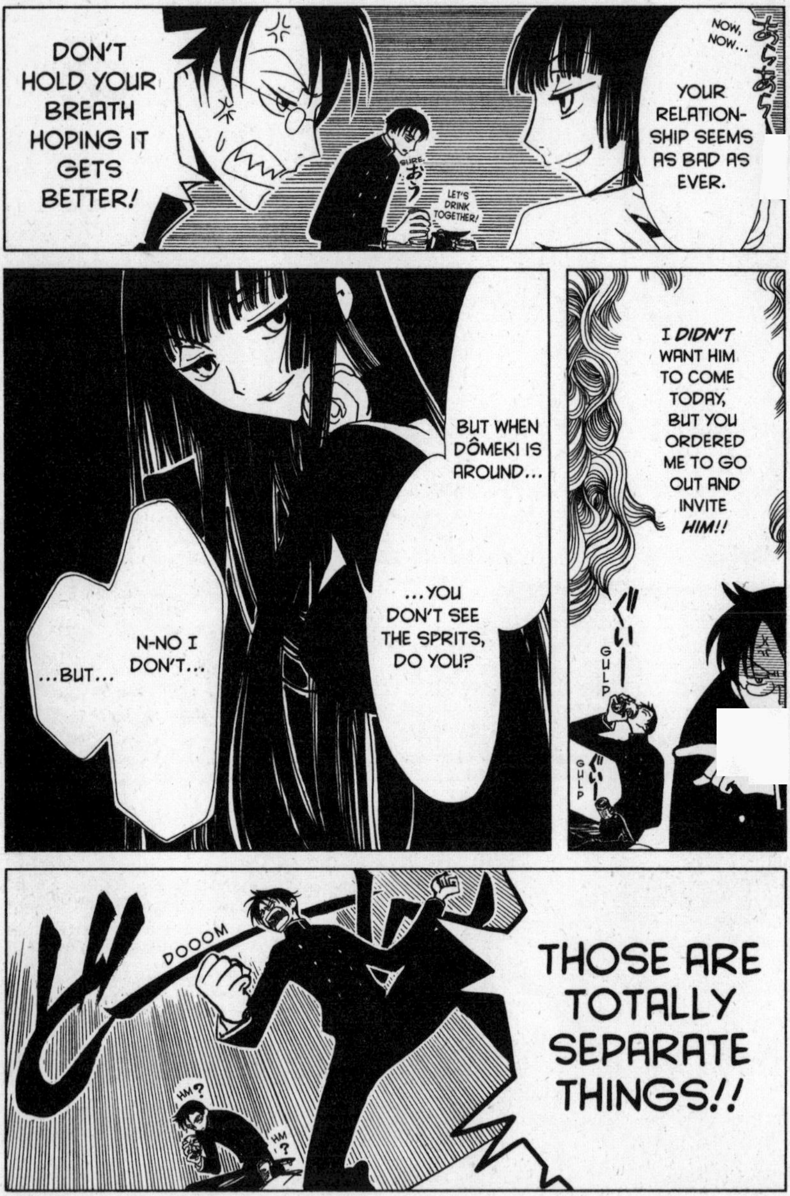
あらあら~
NOW, NOW...
YOUR RELATIONSHIP SEEMS AS BAD AS EVER.
SURE.
おう
LET'S DRINK TOGETHER!
DON'T HOLD YOUR BREATH HOPING IT GETS BETTER!
I *DIDN'T* WANT HIM TO COME TODAY, BUT YOU ORDERED ME TO GO OUT AND INVITE *HIM!!*
ぐいー
GULP
ぐいー
GULP
BUT WHEN DÔMEKI IS AROUND...
...YOU DON'T SEE THE SPRITS, DO YOU?
N-NO I DON'T...
...BUT...
THOSE ARE TOTALLY SEPARATE THINGS!!
DOOOM
HM?
HM?

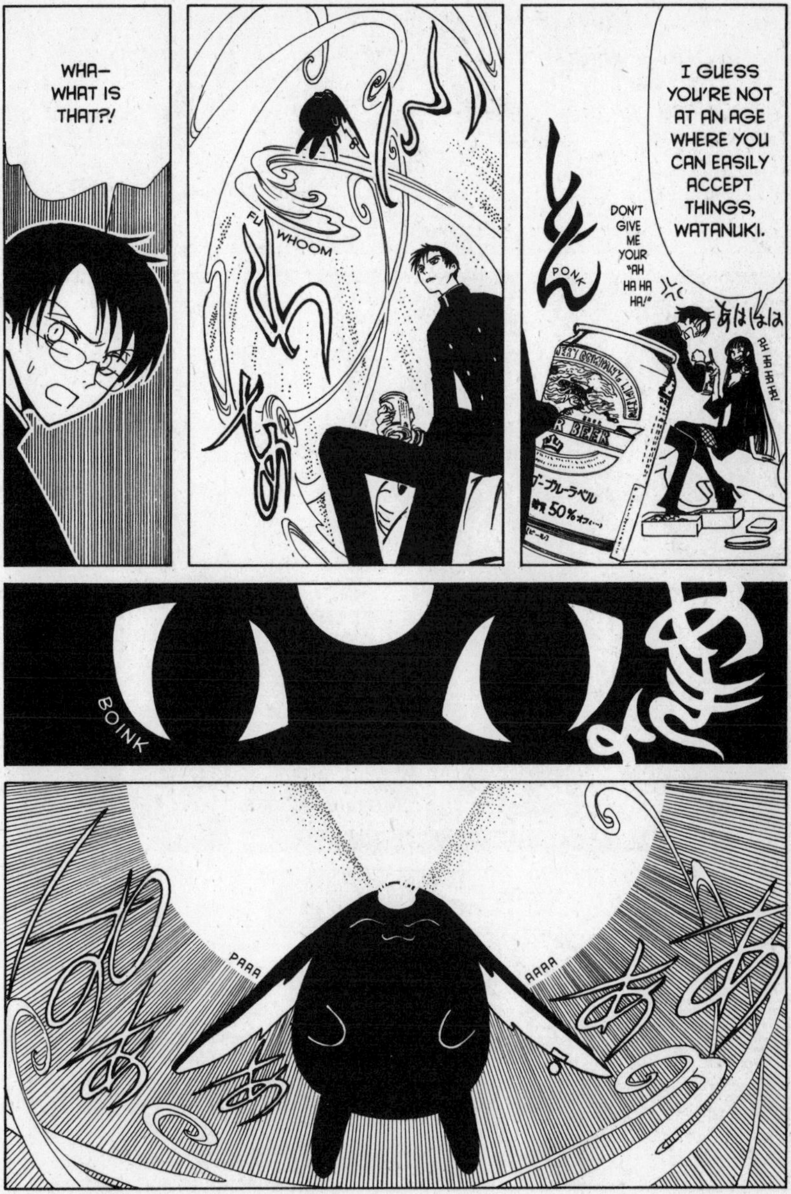
I GUESS YOU'RE NOT AT AN AGE WHERE YOU CAN EASILY ACCEPT THINGS, WATANUKI.
DON'T GIVE ME YOUR "AH HA HA HA!"
AH HA HA HA!
PONK
FU WHOOM
WHA— WHAT IS THAT?!
BOINK
PAAA
AAAA

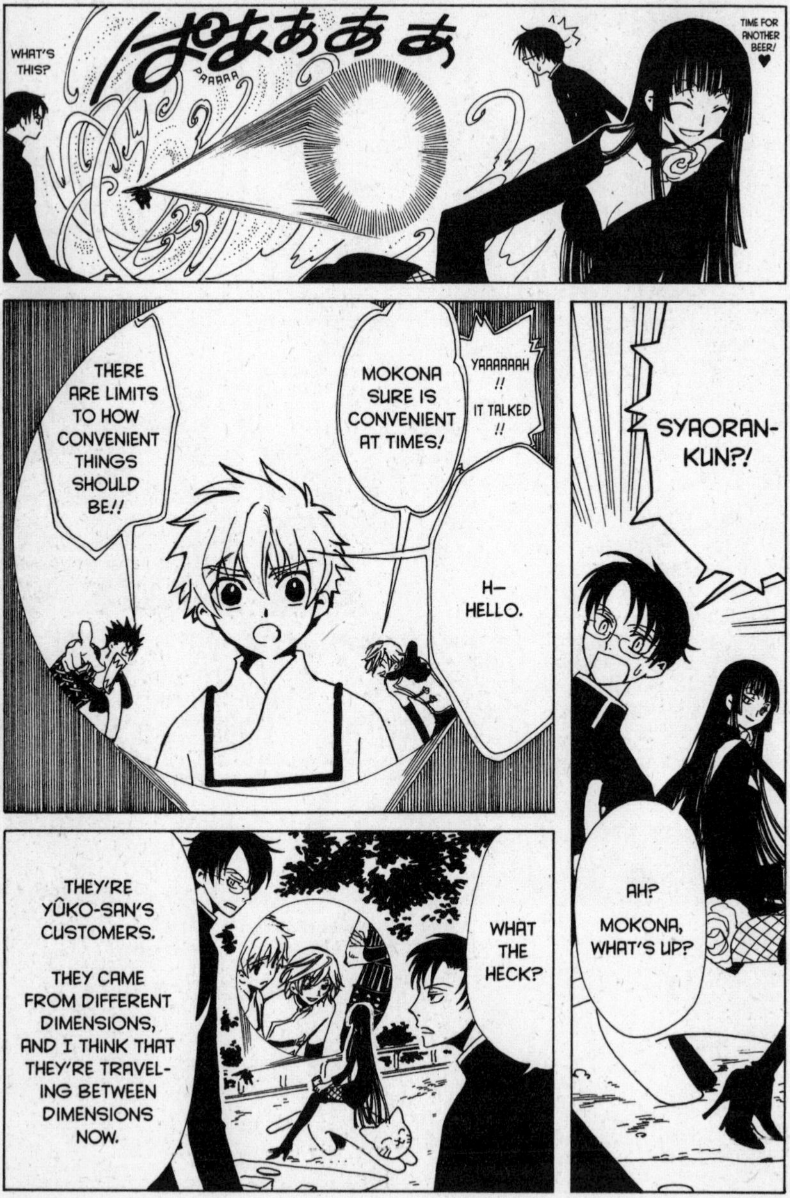
TIME FOR ANOTHER BEER! ♥
ぱあああぁ
PAAAAA
WHAT'S THIS?
SYAORAN-KUN?!
AH? MOKONA, WHAT'S UP?
YAAAAAAH!! IT TALKED!!
MOKONA SURE IS CONVENIENT AT TIMES!
H— HELLO.
THERE ARE LIMITS TO HOW CONVENIENT THINGS SHOULD BE!!
WHAT THE HECK?
THEY'RE YÛKO-SAN'S CUSTOMERS.
THEY CAME FROM DIFFERENT DIMENSIONS, AND I THINK THAT THEY'RE TRAVEL-ING BETWEEN DIMENSIONS NOW.

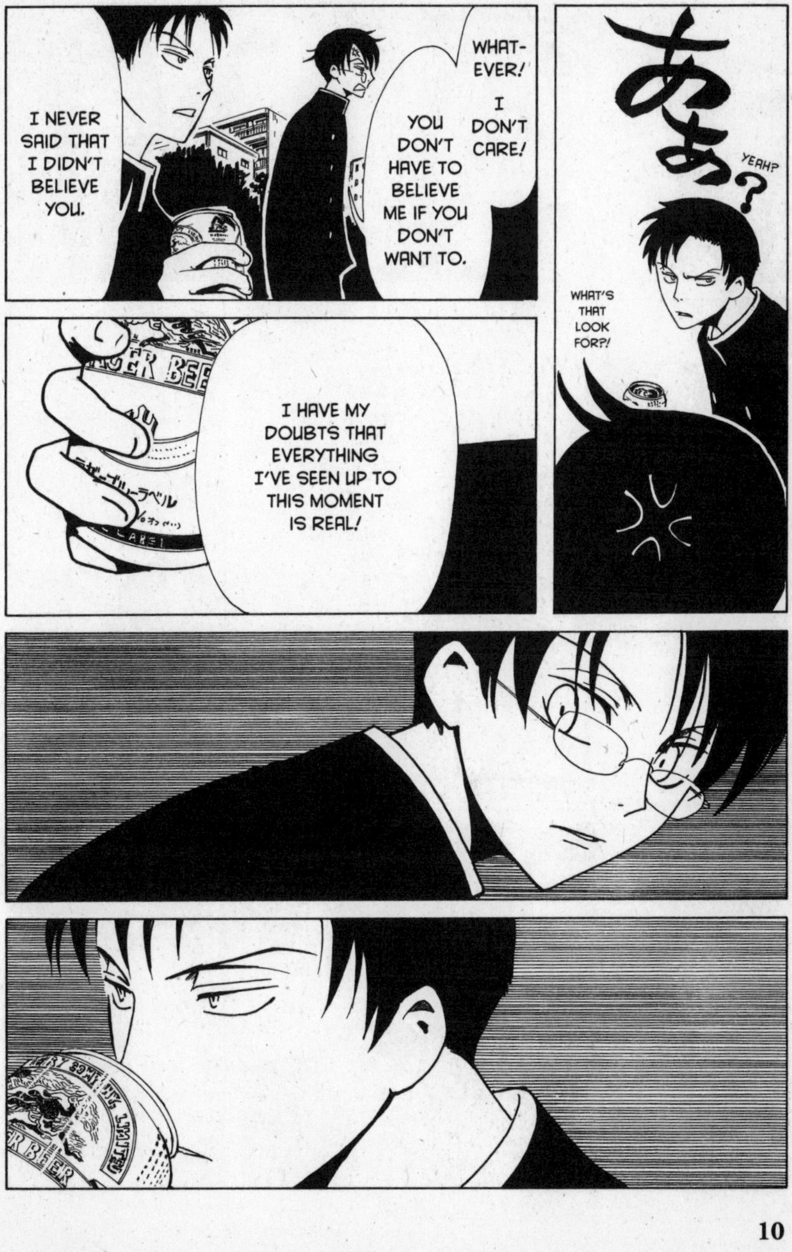
あぁ?
YEAH?
WHAT'S THAT LOOK FOR?!
WHAT-EVER! I DON'T CARE!
YOU DON'T HAVE TO BELIEVE ME IF YOU DON'T WANT TO.
I NEVER SAID THAT I DIDN'T BELIEVE YOU.
I HAVE MY DOUBTS THAT EVERYTHING I'VE SEEN UP TO THIS MOMENT IS REAL!

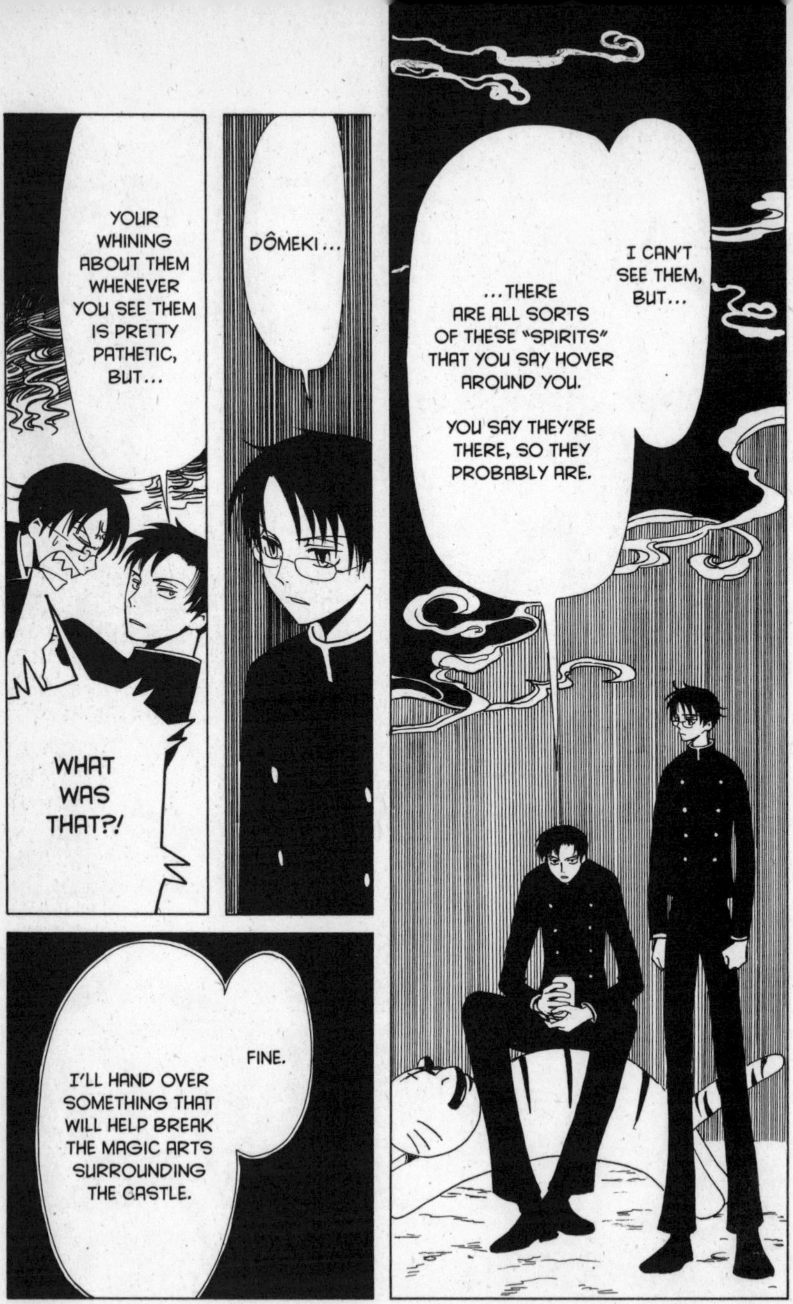
I CAN'T SEE THEM, BUT...
...THERE ARE ALL SORTS OF THESE "SPIRITS" THAT YOU SAY HOVER AROUND YOU.
YOU SAY THEY'RE THERE, SO THEY PROBABLY ARE.
DÔMEKI...
YOUR WHINING ABOUT THEM WHENEVER YOU SEE THEM IS PRETTY PATHETIC, BUT...
WHAT WAS THAT?!
FINE.
I'LL HAND OVER SOMETHING THAT WILL HELP BREAK THE MAGIC ARTS SURROUNDING THE CASTLE.

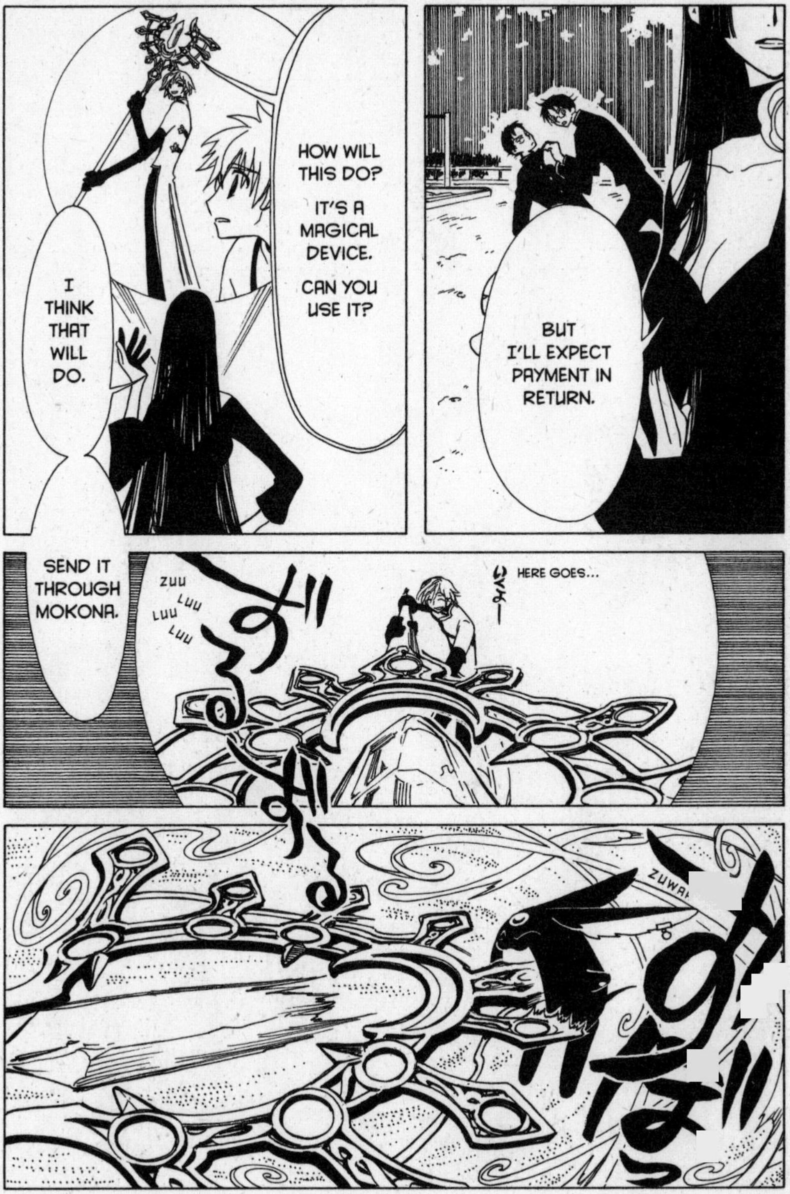
BUT I'LL EXPECT PAYMENT IN RETURN.
HOW WILL THIS DO?
IT'S A MAGICAL DEVICE.
CAN YOU USE IT?
I THINK THAT WILL DO.
いくよー
HERE GOES...
ZUU LUU LUU LUU
SEND IT THROUGH MOKONA.
ZUWA

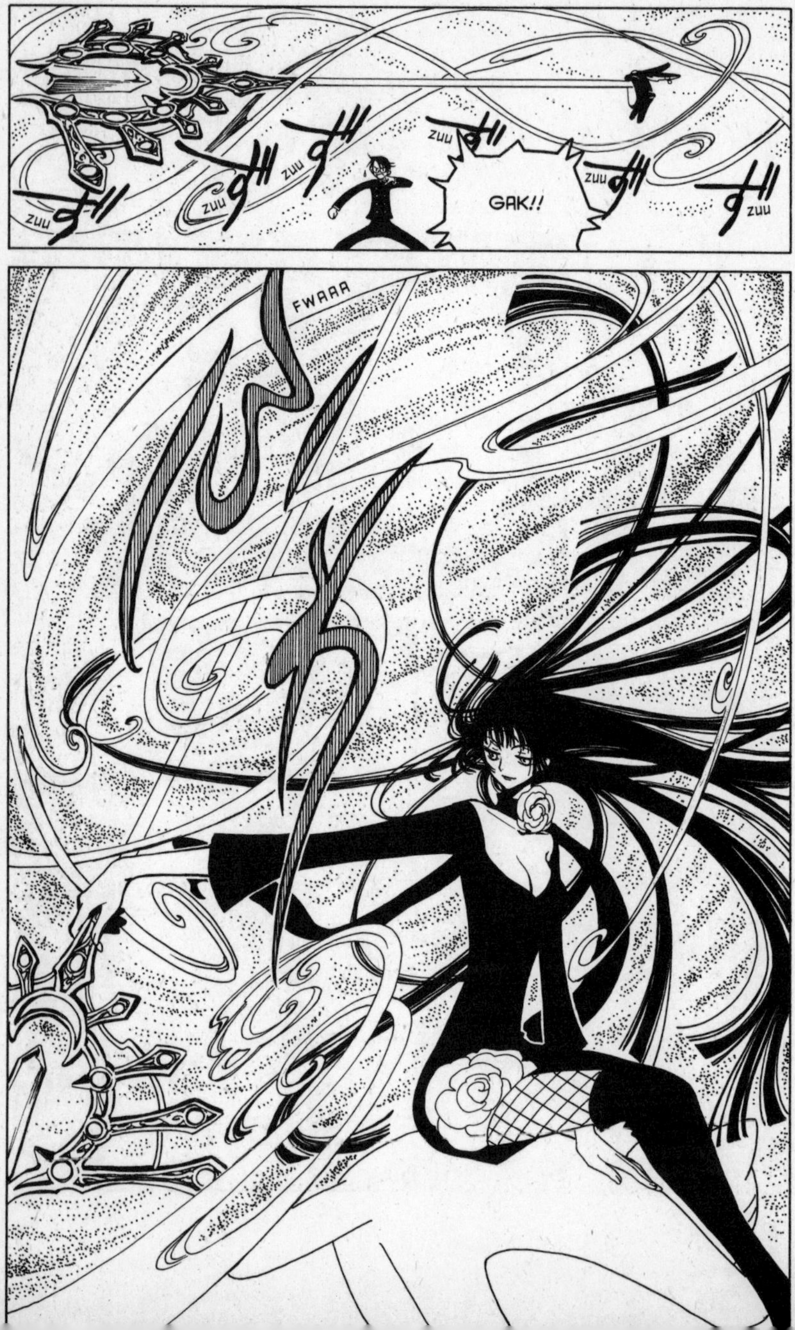
zuu
zuu
GAK!!
zuu
zuu
zuu
zuu
FWAAA

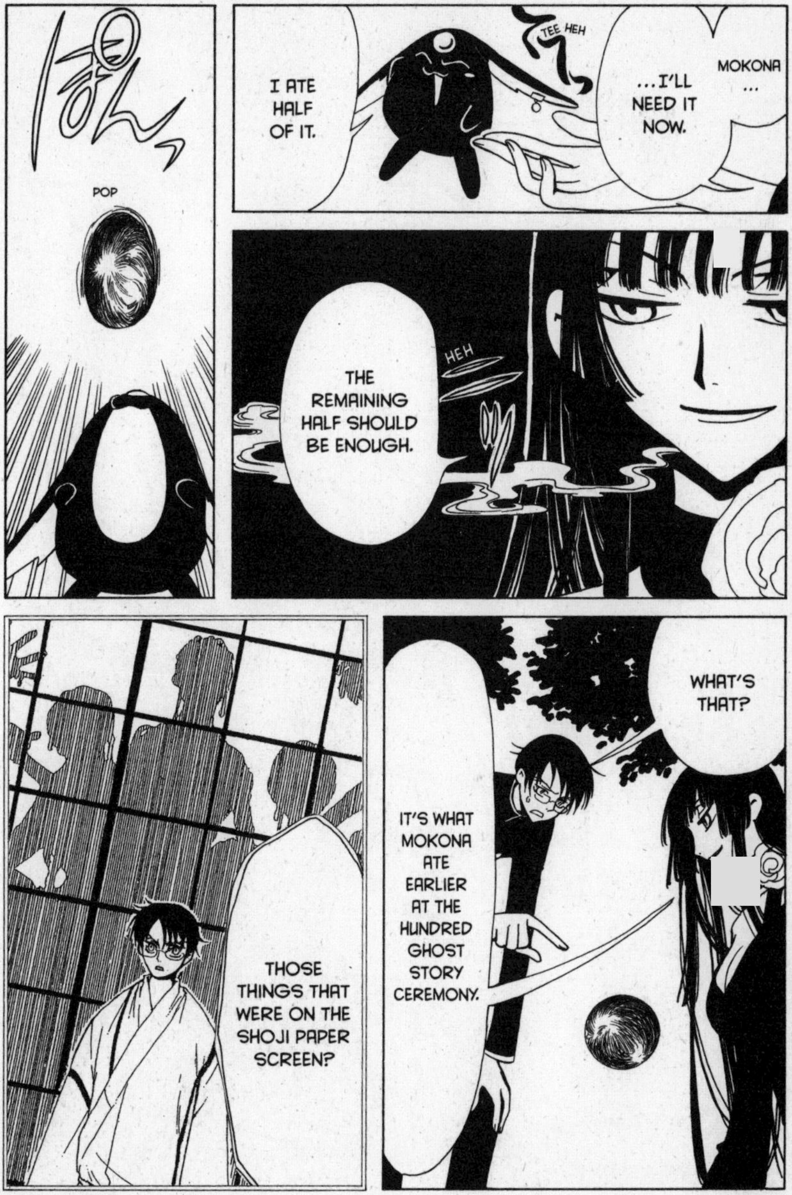
MOKONA ...
...I'LL NEED IT NOW.
TEE HEH
I ATE HALF OF IT.
HEH
THE REMAINING HALF SHOULD BE ENOUGH.
ぽん
POP
WHAT'S THAT?
IT'S WHAT MOKONA ATE EARLIER AT THE HUNDRED GHOST STORY CEREMONY.
THOSE THINGS THAT WERE ON THE SHOJI PAPER SCREEN?

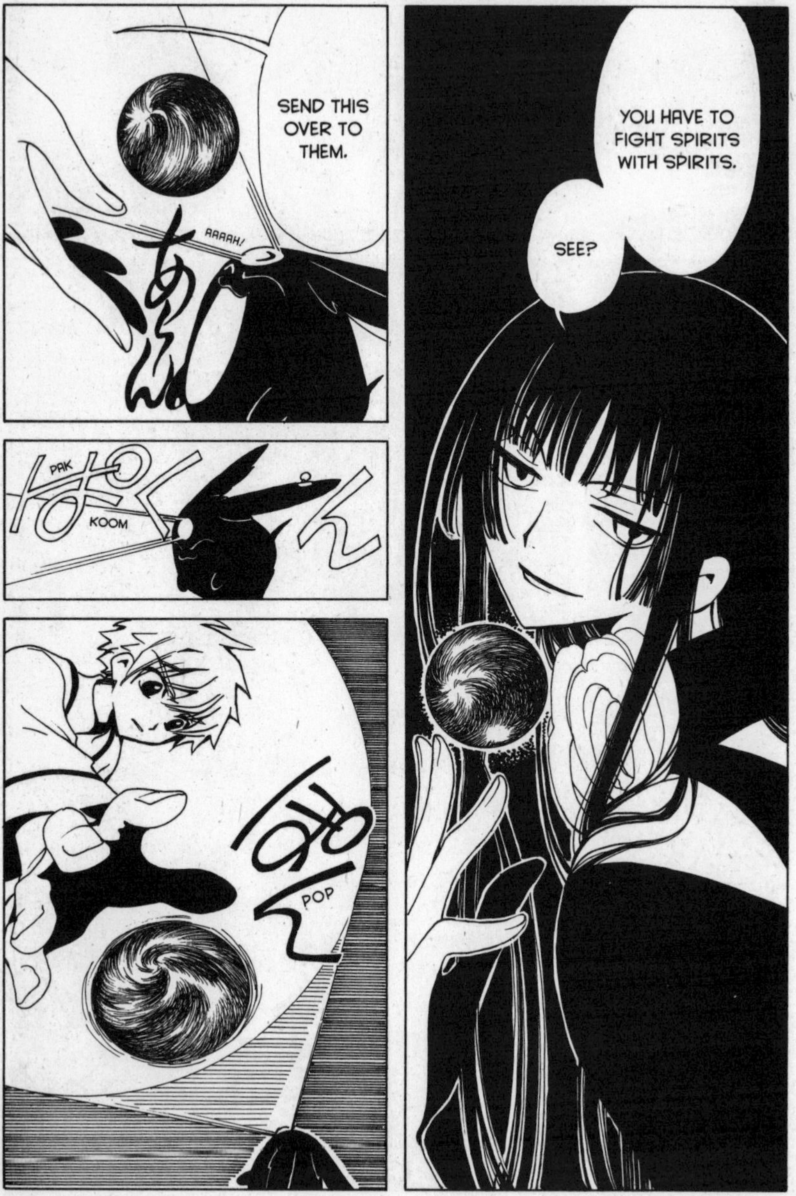
YOU HAVE TO FIGHT SPIRITS WITH SPIRITS.
SEE?
SEND THIS OVER TO THEM.
AAAAH!
PAK
KOOM
POP

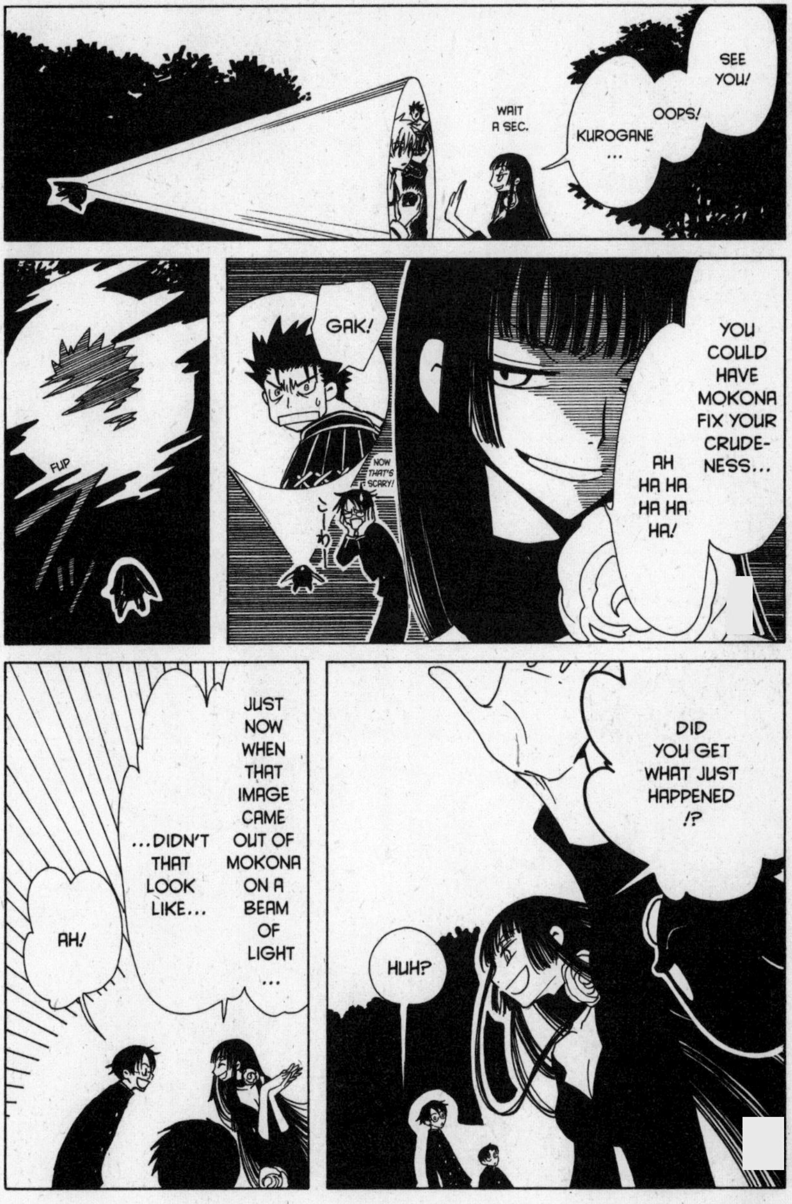
SEE YOU!
OOPS!
KUROGANE ...
WAIT A SEC.
YOU COULD HAVE MOKONA FIX YOUR CRUDE-NESS...
AH HA HA HA HA HA!
GAK!
NOW THAT'S SCARY!
FLIP
DID YOU GET WHAT JUST HAPPENED !?
HUH?
JUST NOW WHEN THAT IMAGE CAME OUT OF MOKONA ON A BEAM OF LIGHT ...
...DIDN'T THAT LOOK LIKE...
AH!

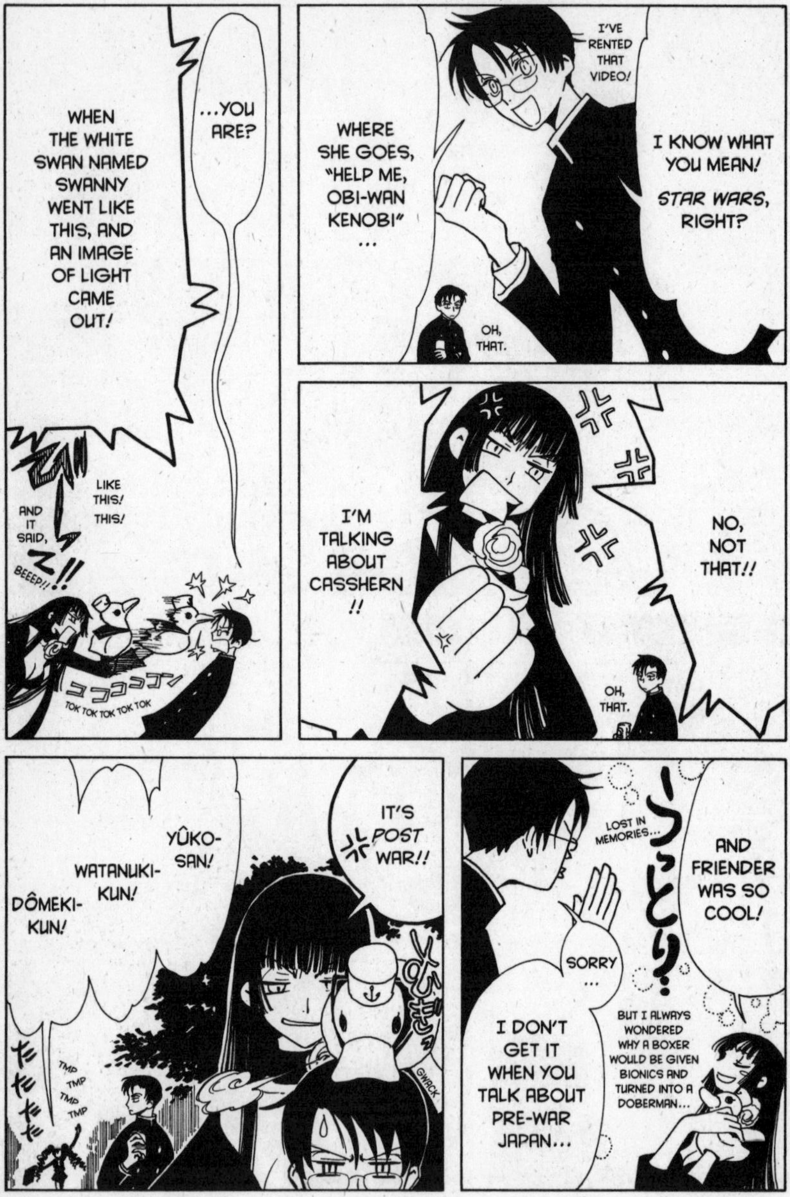
I KNOW WHAT YOU MEAN! STAR WARS, RIGHT?
I'VE RENTED THAT VIDEO!
WHERE SHE GOES, "HELP ME, OBI-WAN KENOBI"...
OH, THAT.
NO, NOT THAT!!
I'M TALKING ABOUT CASSHERN!!
OH, THAT.
...YOU ARE?
WHEN THE WHITE SWAN NAMED SWANNY WENT LIKE THIS, AND AN IMAGE OF LIGHT CAME OUT!
LIKE THIS! THIS!
AND IT SAID,
BEEEP!!
TOK TOK TOK TOK TOK
AND FRIENDER WAS SO COOL!
LOST IN MEMORIES...
BUT I ALWAYS WONDERED WHY A BOXER WOULD BE GIVEN BIONICS AND TURNED INTO A DOBERMAN...
SORRY...
I DON'T GET IT WHEN YOU TALK ABOUT PRE-WAR JAPAN...
IT'S *POST* WAR!!
YÛKO-SAN!
WATANUKI-KUN!
DÔMEKI-KUN!
GWACK
TMP TMP TMP TMP

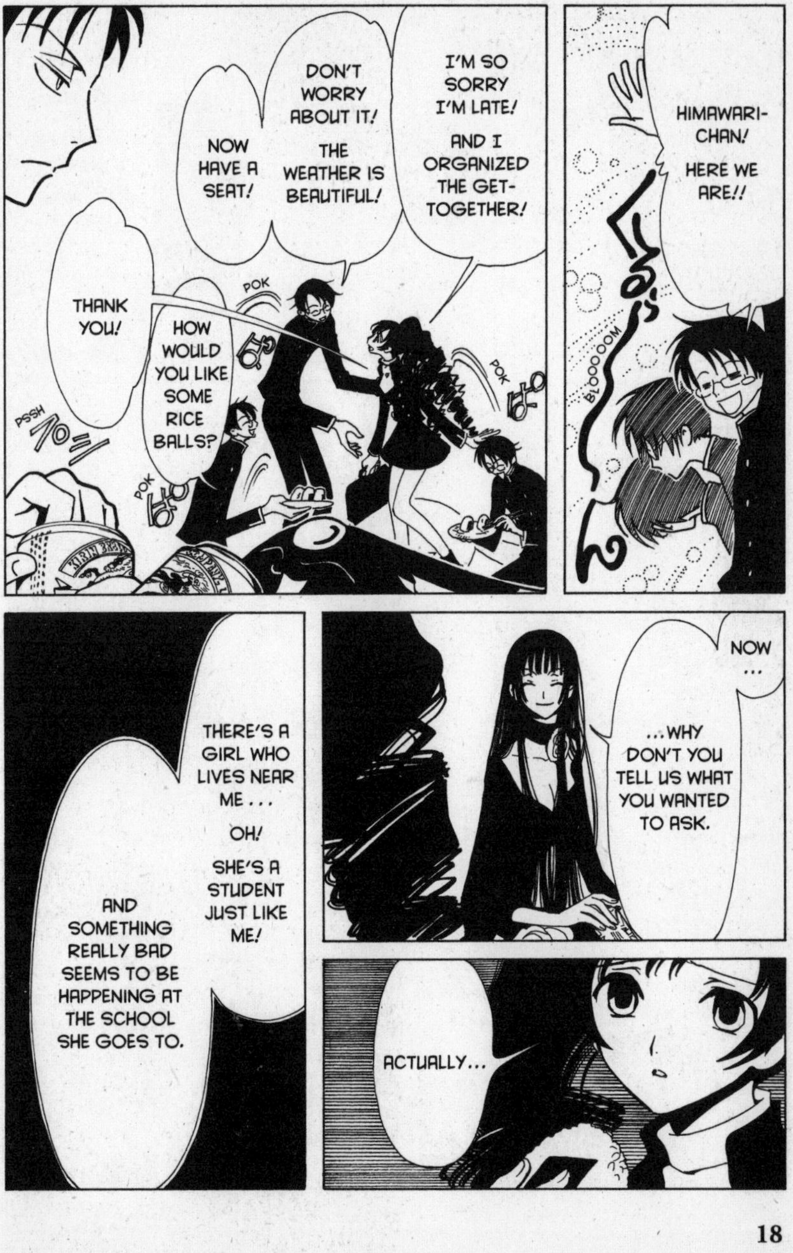
HIMAWARI-CHAN! HERE WE ARE!!
BLOOOOOM
I'M SO SORRY I'M LATE! AND I ORGANIZED THE GET-TOGETHER!
DON'T WORRY ABOUT IT! THE WEATHER IS BEAUTIFUL!
NOW HAVE A SEAT!
POK
POK
HOW WOULD YOU LIKE SOME RICE BALLS?
THANK YOU!
POK
PSSH
NOW ...
...WHY DON'T YOU TELL US WHAT YOU WANTED TO ASK.
ACTUALLY...
THERE'S A GIRL WHO LIVES NEAR ME . . . OH! SHE'S A STUDENT JUST LIKE ME!
AND SOMETHING REALLY BAD SEEMS TO BE HAPPENING AT THE SCHOOL SHE GOES TO.

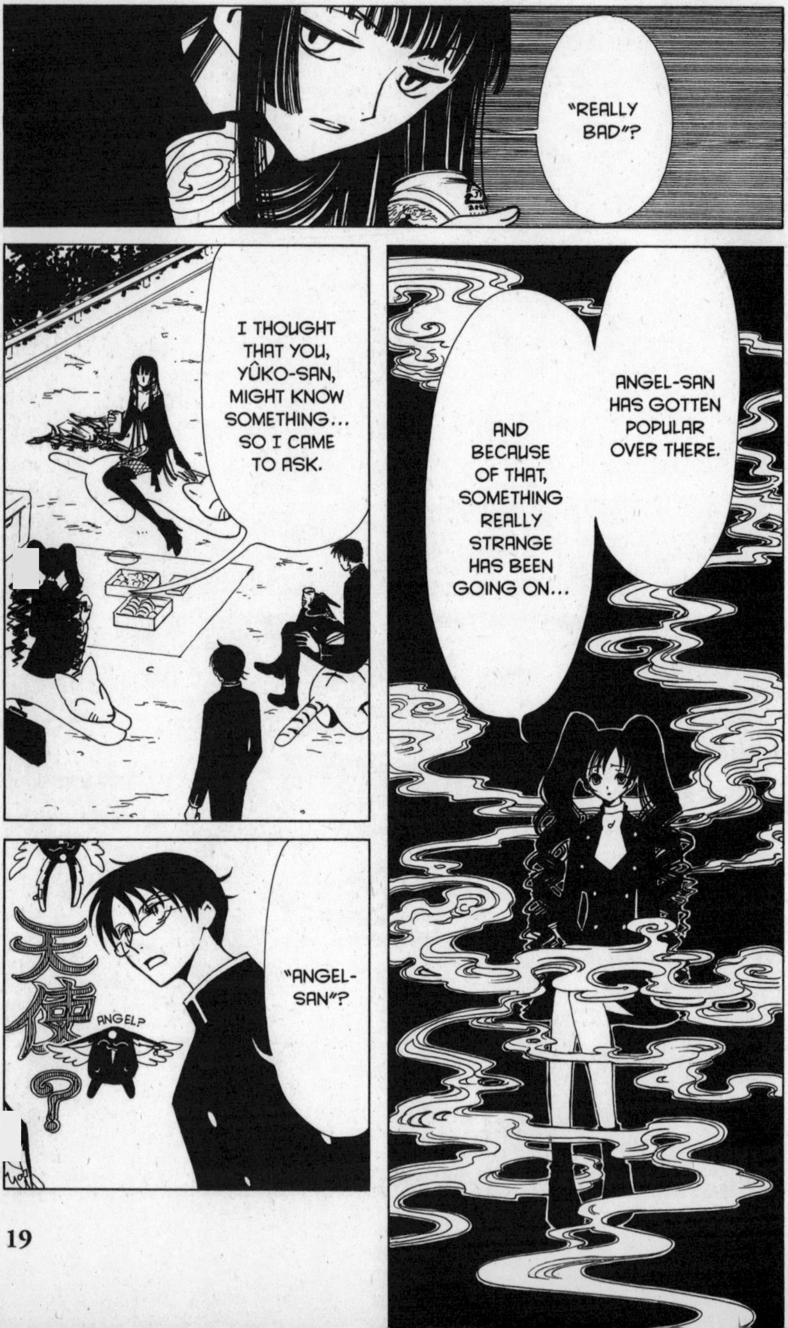
"REALLY BAD"?
ANGEL-SAN HAS GOTTEN POPULAR OVER THERE.
AND BECAUSE OF THAT, SOMETHING REALLY STRANGE HAS BEEN GOING ON...
I THOUGHT THAT YOU, YÛKO-SAN, MIGHT KNOW SOMETHING... SO I CAME TO ASK.
"ANGEL-SAN"?
天使?
ANGEL?

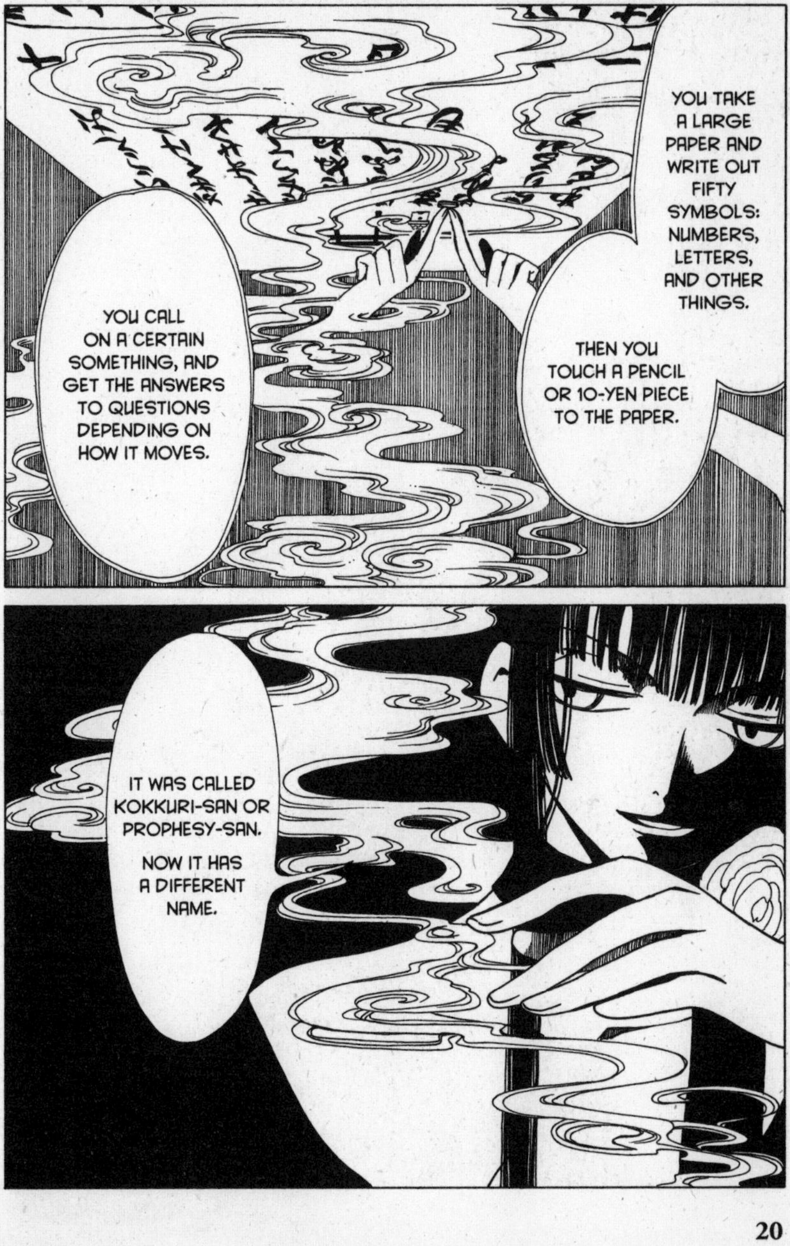
YOU TAKE A LARGE PAPER AND WRITE OUT FIFTY SYMBOLS: NUMBERS, LETTERS, AND OTHER THINGS.
THEN YOU TOUCH A PENCIL OR 10-YEN PIECE TO THE PAPER.
YOU CALL ON A CERTAIN SOMETHING, AND GET THE ANSWERS TO QUESTIONS DEPENDING ON HOW IT MOVES.
IT WAS CALLED KOKKURI-SAN OR PROPHESY-SAN.
NOW IT HAS A DIFFERENT NAME.

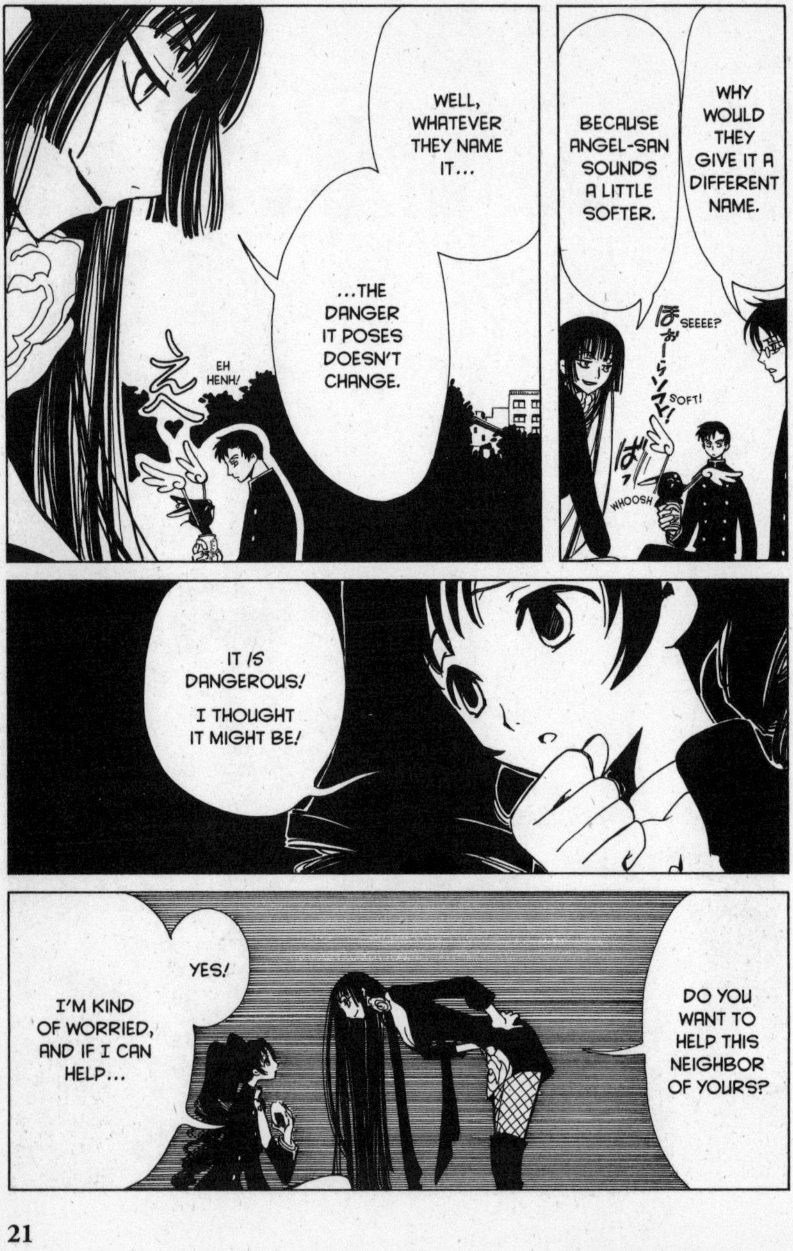
WHY WOULD THEY GIVE IT A DIFFERENT NAME.
BECAUSE ANGEL-SAN SOUNDS A LITTLE SOFTER.
SEEEE?
SOFT!
WHOOSH
WELL, WHATEVER THEY NAME IT...
...THE DANGER IT POSES DOESN'T CHANGE.
EH HENH!
IT IS DANGEROUS!
I THOUGHT IT MIGHT BE!
DO YOU WANT TO HELP THIS NEIGHBOR OF YOURS?
YES!
I'M KIND OF WORRIED, AND IF I CAN HELP...

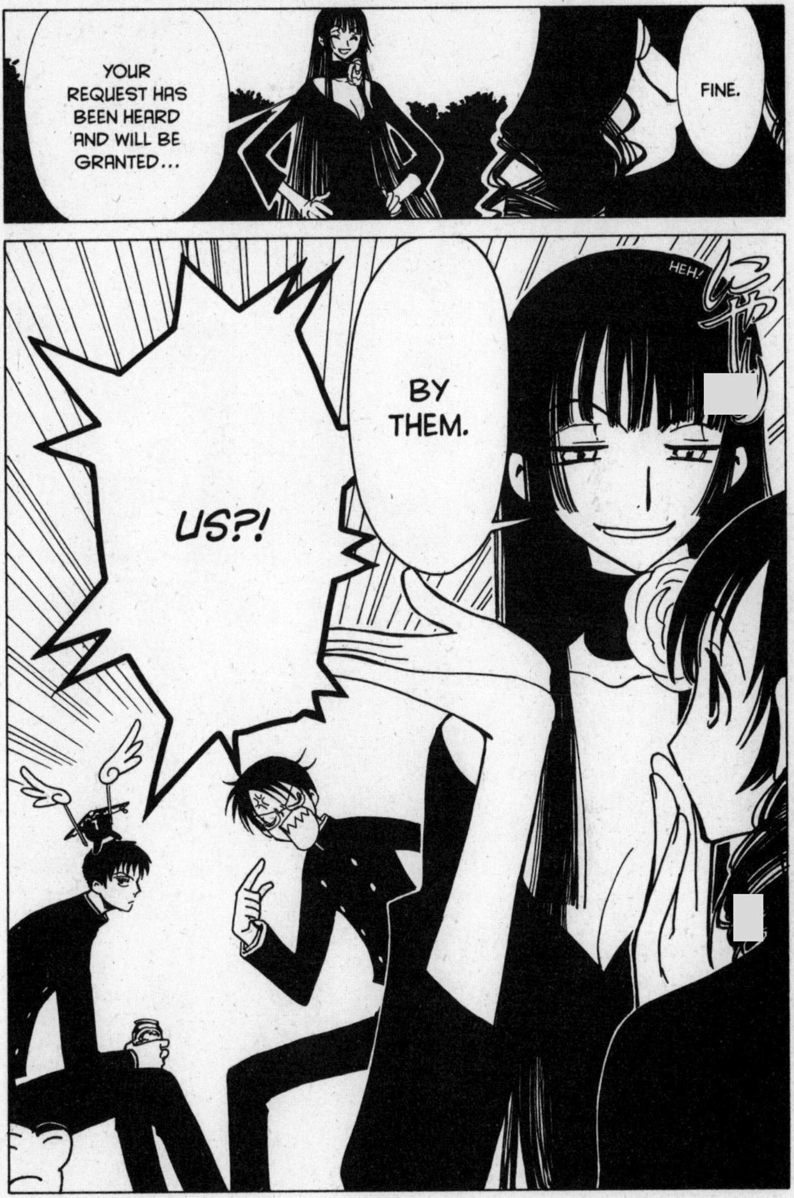
FINE.
YOUR REQUEST HAS BEEN HEARD AND WILL BE GRANTED...
HEH!
BY THEM.
US?!

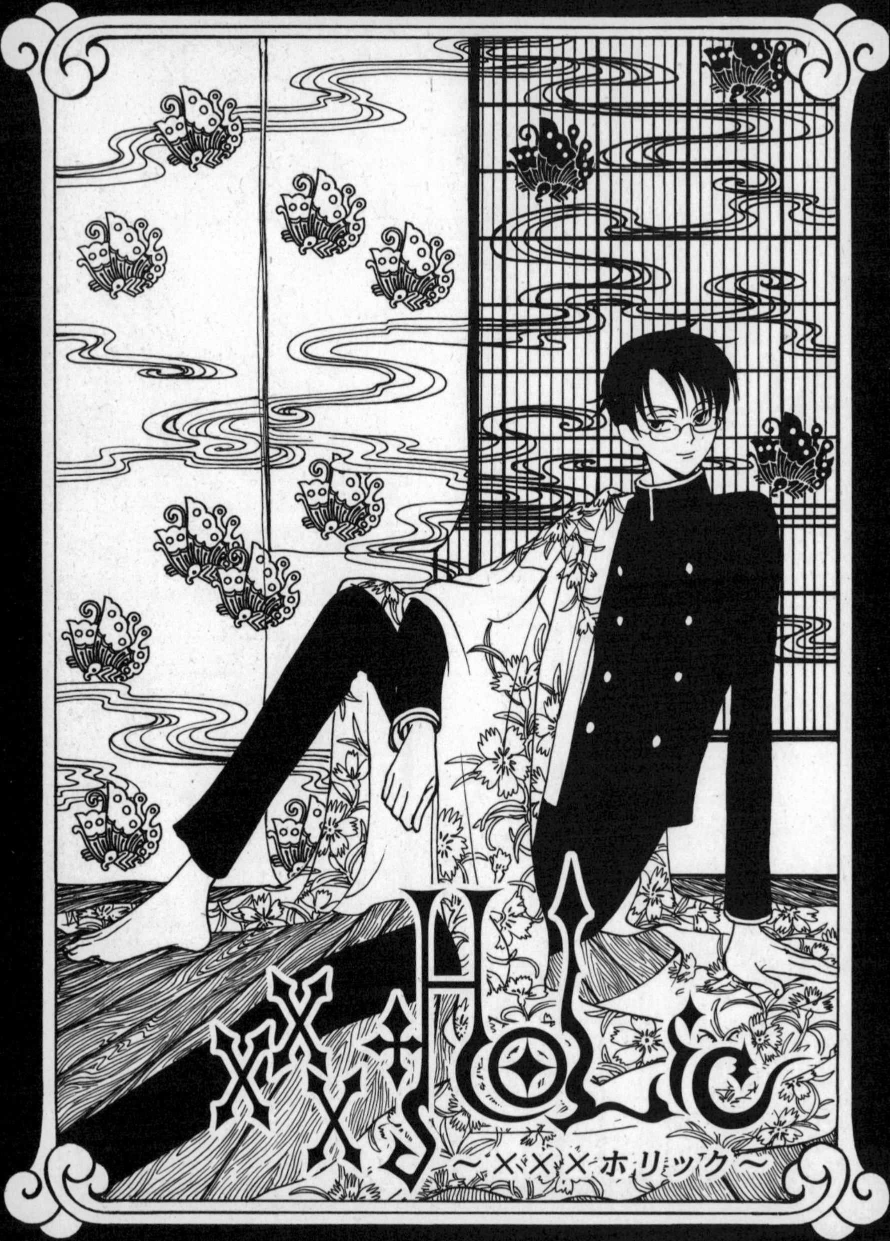
xxxHOLiC
～×××ホリック～

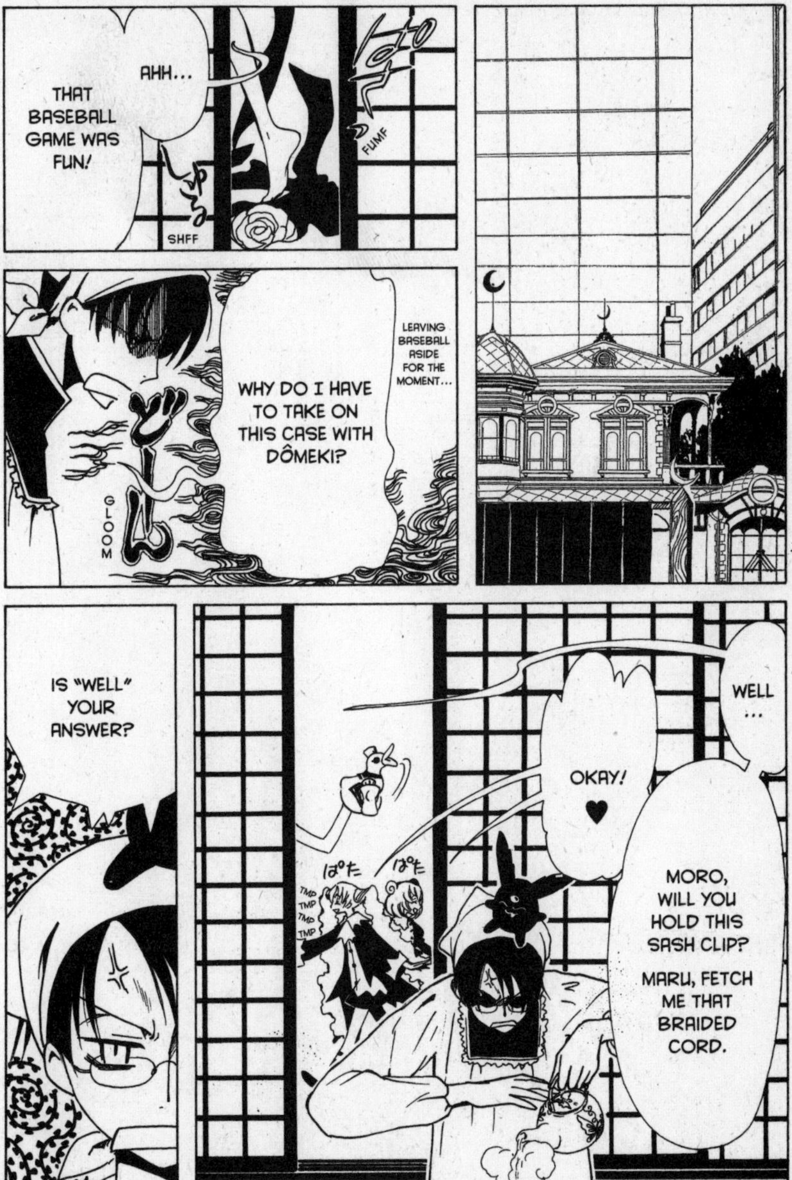
AHH...
THAT BASEBALL GAME WAS FUN!
FUMF
SHFF
LEAVING BASEBALL ASIDE FOR THE MOMENT...
WHY DO I HAVE TO TAKE ON THIS CASE WITH DÔMEKI?
GLOOM
WELL...
OKAY! ♥
MORO, WILL YOU HOLD THIS SASH CLIP?
MARU, FETCH ME THAT BRAIDED CORD.
TMP TMP TMP TMP
IS "WELL" YOUR ANSWER?

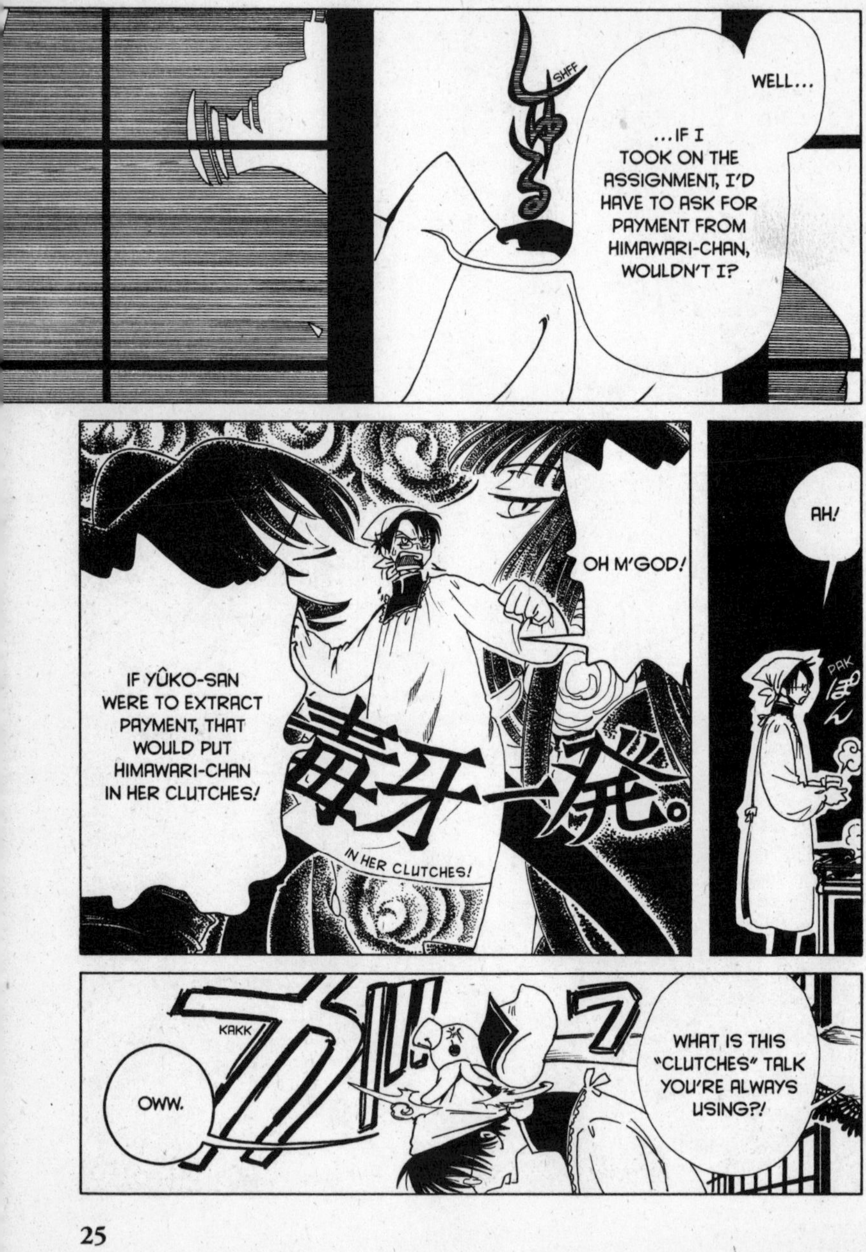
SHFF
WELL...
...IF I TOOK ON THE ASSIGNMENT, I'D HAVE TO ASK FOR PAYMENT FROM HIMAWARI-CHAN, WOULDN'T I?
AH!
PAK
OH M'GOD!
IF YÛKO-SAN WERE TO EXTRACT PAYMENT, THAT WOULD PUT HIMAWARI-CHAN IN HER CLUTCHES!
毒牙一発。
IN HER CLUTCHES!
WHAT IS THIS "CLUTCHES" TALK YOU'RE ALWAYS USING?!
KAKK
OWW.

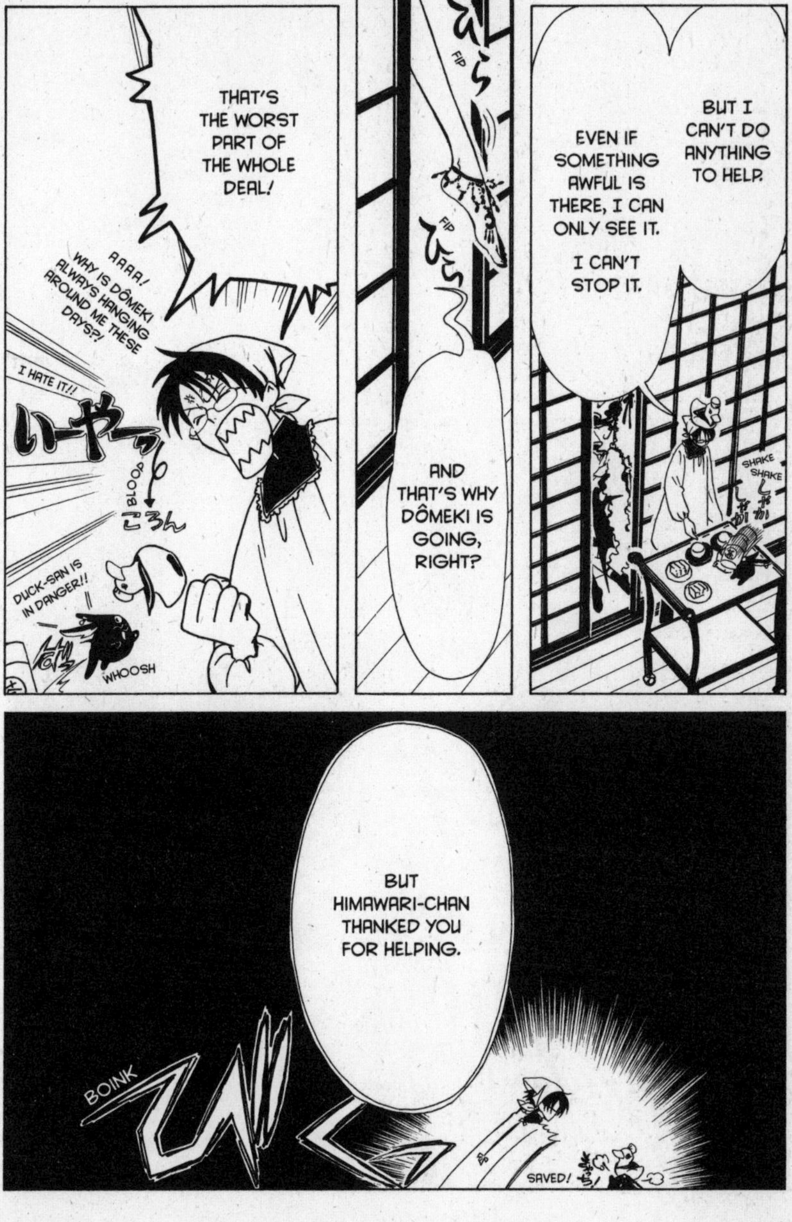
BUT I CAN'T DO ANYTHING TO HELP.
EVEN IF SOMETHING AWFUL IS THERE, I CAN ONLY SEE IT.
I CAN'T STOP IT.
SHAKE SHAKE
FIP
FIP
AND THAT'S WHY DÔMEKI IS GOING, RIGHT?
THAT'S THE WORST PART OF THE WHOLE DEAL!
AAAAA! WHY IS DÔMEKI ALWAYS HANGING AROUND ME THESE DAYS?!
I HATE IT!!
いやーっ
BLOOP
ころん
DUCK-SAN IS IN DANGER!!
WHOOSH
BUT HIMAWARI-CHAN THANKED YOU FOR HELPING.
BOINK
SAVED!

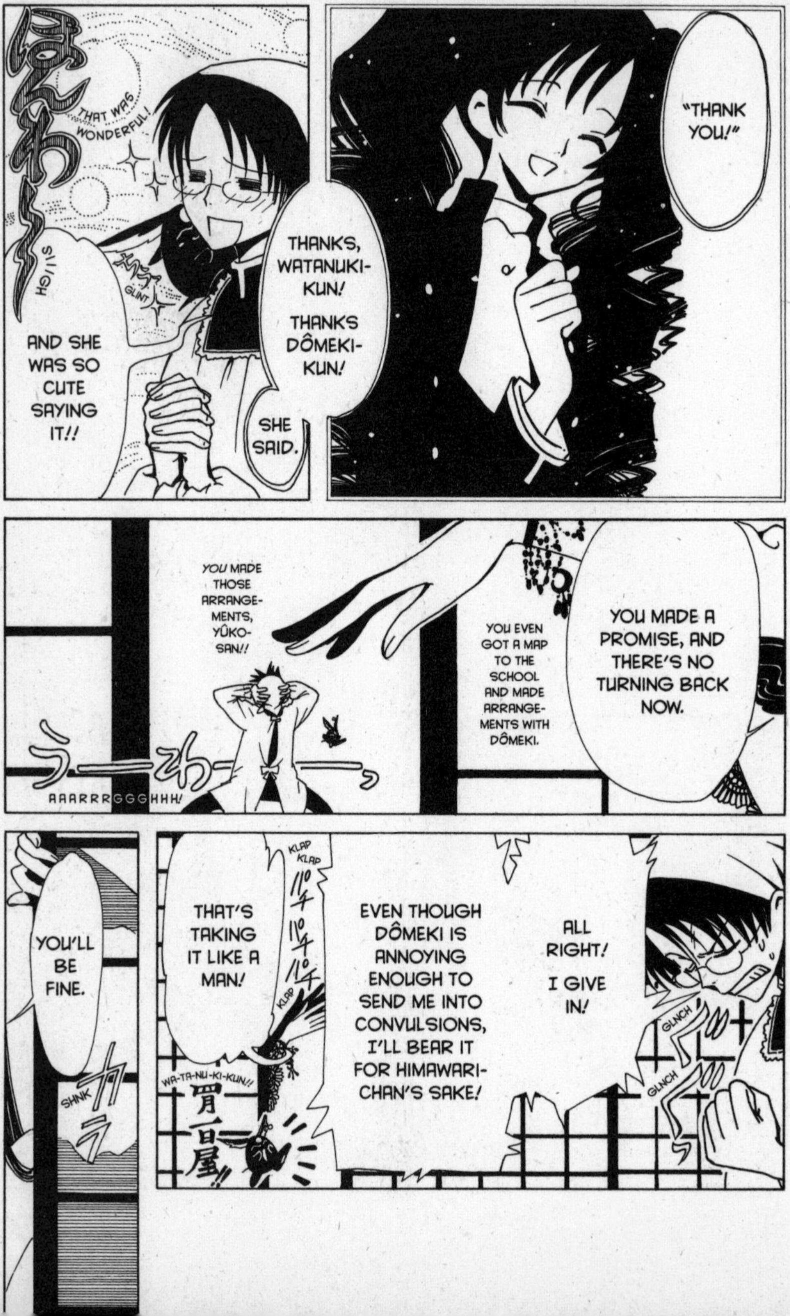
"THANK YOU!"
THANKS, WATANUKI-KUN!
THANKS DÔMEKI-KUN!
SHE SAID.
THAT WAS WONDERFUL!
GLINT
SIIIGH
AND SHE WAS SO CUTE SAYING IT!!
YOU MADE A PROMISE, AND THERE'S NO TURNING BACK NOW.
YOU EVEN GOT A MAP TO THE SCHOOL AND MADE ARRANGE-MENTS WITH DÔMEKI.
YOU MADE THOSE ARRANGE-MENTS, YÛKO-SAN!!
AAARRRGGGHHH!
ALL RIGHT!
I GIVE IN!
GLNCH
GLNCH
EVEN THOUGH DÔMEKI IS ANNOYING ENOUGH TO SEND ME INTO CONVULSIONS, I'LL BEAR IT FOR HIMAWARI-CHAN'S SAKE!
KLAP KLAP
KLAP
THAT'S TAKING IT LIKE A MAN!
WA-TA-NU-KI-KUN!!
YOU'LL BE FINE.
SHNK

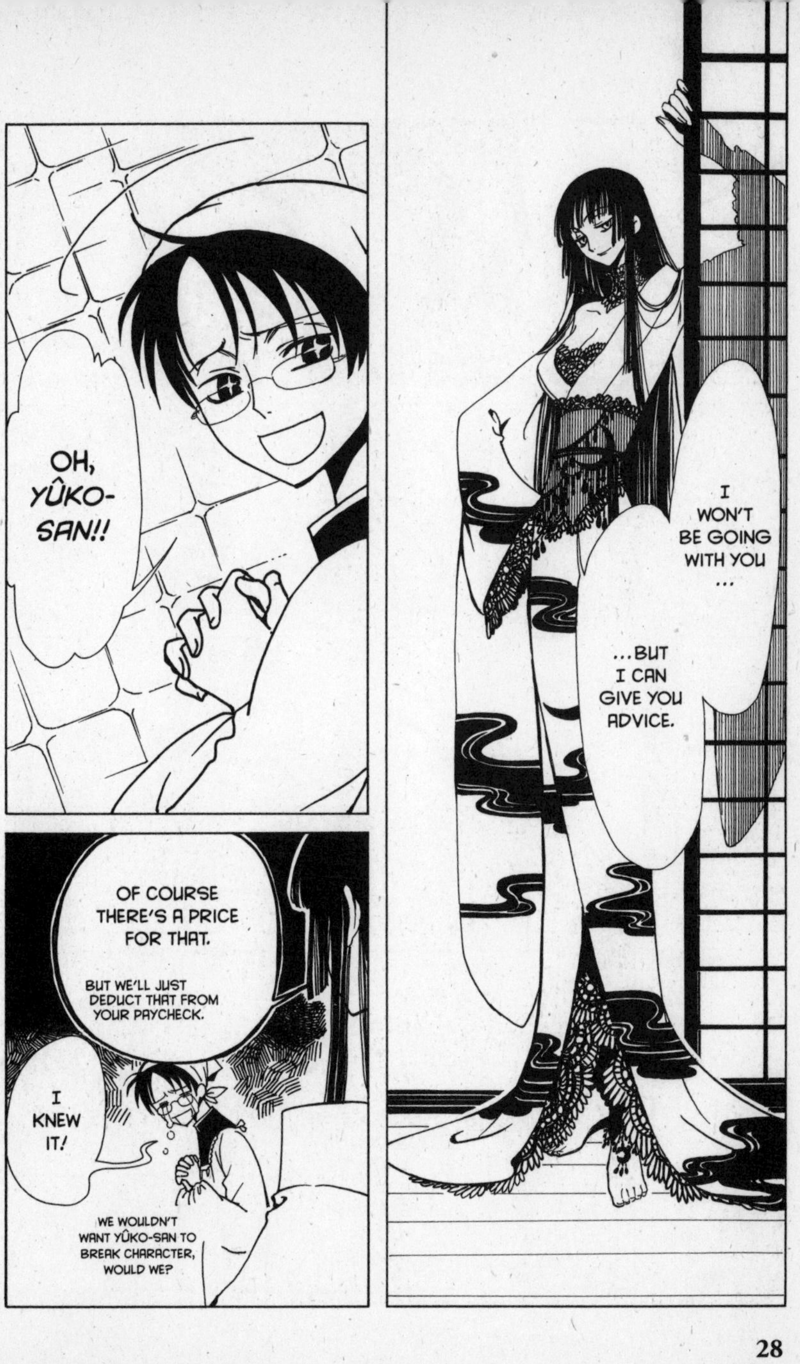
I WON'T BE GOING WITH YOU ...
...BUT I CAN GIVE YOU ADVICE.
OH, YÛKO-SAN!!
OF COURSE THERE'S A PRICE FOR THAT.
BUT WE'LL JUST DEDUCT THAT FROM YOUR PAYCHECK.
I KNEW IT!
WE WOULDN'T WANT YÛKO-SAN TO BREAK CHARACTER, WOULD WE?

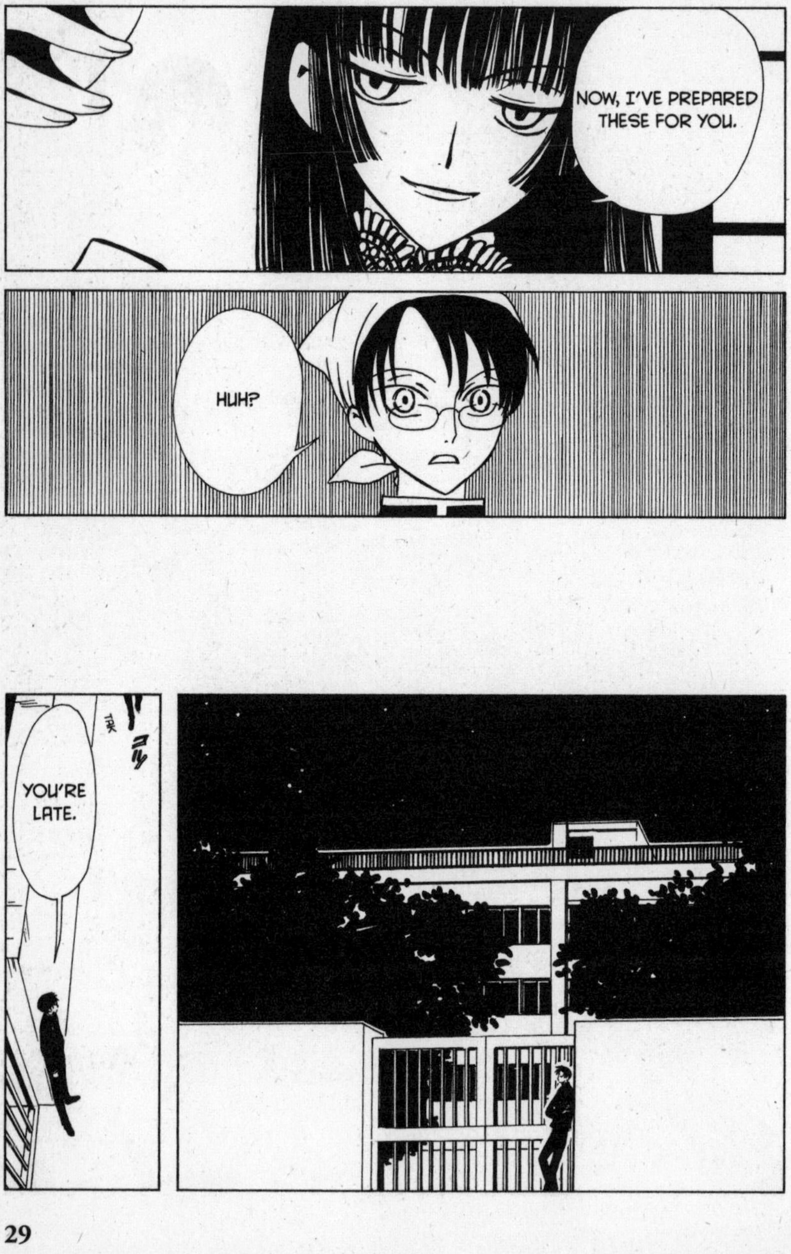
NOW, I'VE PREPARED THESE FOR YOU.
HUH?
TAK
YOU'RE LATE.

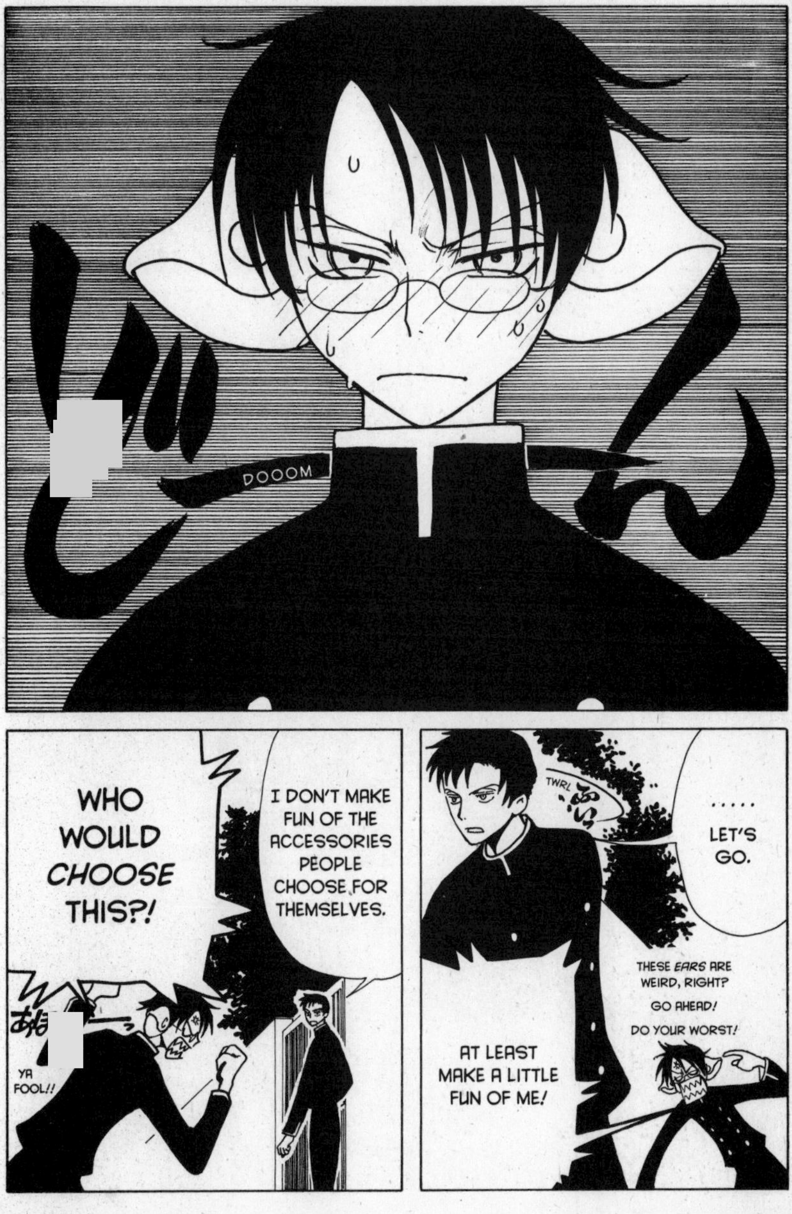
DOOOM
.....
LET'S GO.
TWRL
THESE EARS ARE WEIRD, RIGHT?
GO AHEAD!
DO YOUR WORST!
AT LEAST MAKE A LITTLE FUN OF ME!
I DON'T MAKE FUN OF THE ACCESSORIES PEOPLE CHOOSE FOR THEMSELVES.
WHO WOULD CHOOSE THIS?!
YA FOOL!!

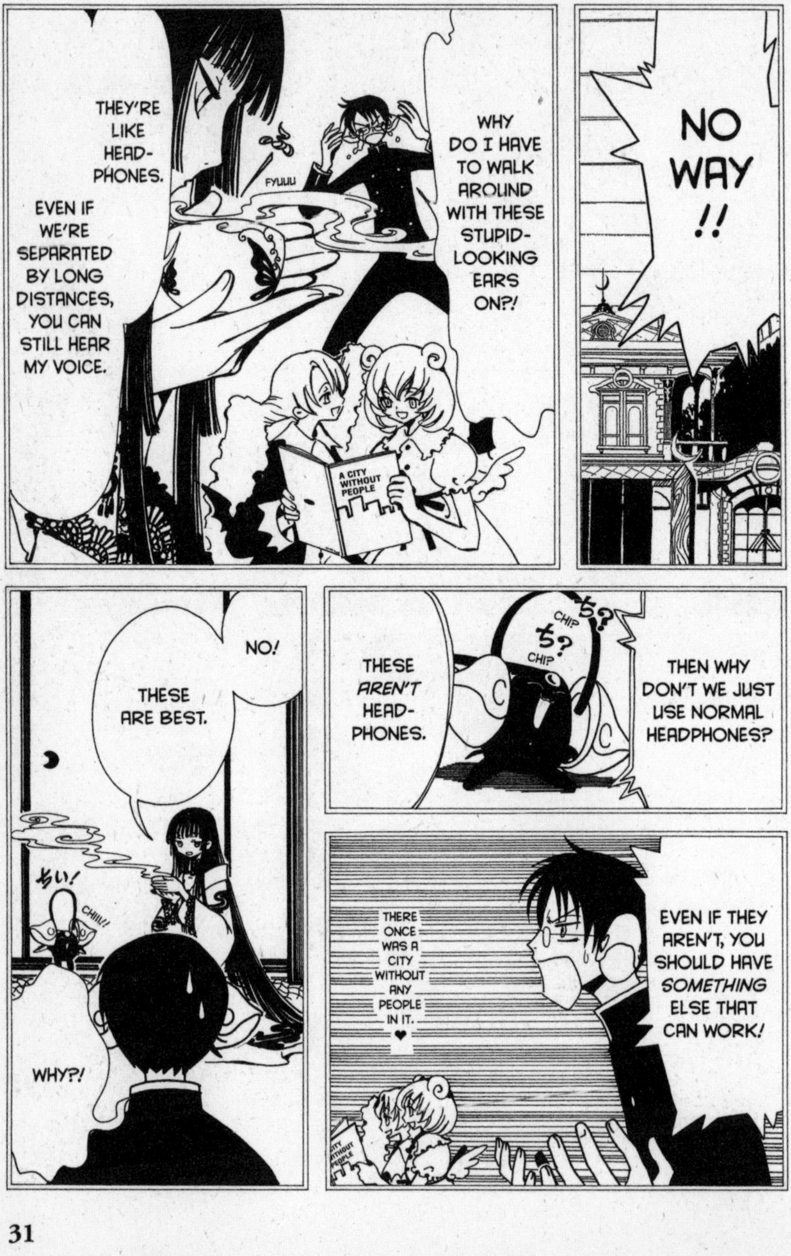
NO WAY!!
WHY DO I HAVE TO WALK AROUND WITH THESE STUPID-LOOKING EARS ON?!
THEY'RE LIKE HEADPHONES.
FYUUU
EVEN IF WE'RE SEPARATED BY LONG DISTANCES, YOU CAN STILL HEAR MY VOICE.
A CITY WITHOUT PEOPLE
THEN WHY DON'T WE JUST USE NORMAL HEADPHONES?
ち? CHIP
ち? CHIP
THESE *AREN'T* HEADPHONES.
EVEN IF THEY AREN'T, YOU SHOULD HAVE *SOMETHING* ELSE THAT CAN WORK!
THERE ONCE WAS A CITY WITHOUT ANY PEOPLE IN IT. ♥
CITY WITHOUT PEOPLE
NO!
THESE ARE BEST.
ちぃ! CHIII!!
WHY?!

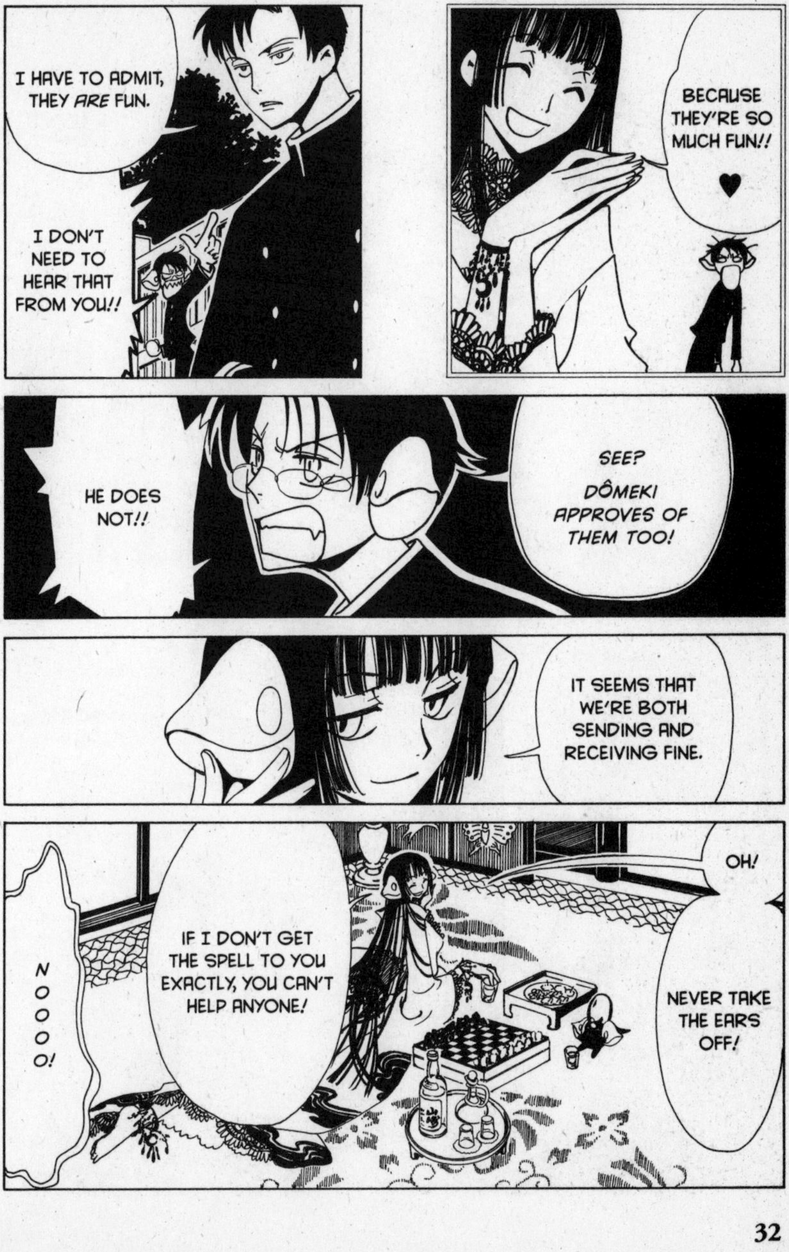
BECAUSE THEY'RE SO MUCH FUN!! ♥
I HAVE TO ADMIT, THEY *ARE* FUN.
I DON'T NEED TO HEAR THAT FROM YOU!!
SEE? DÔMEKI APPROVES OF THEM TOO!
HE DOES NOT!!
IT SEEMS THAT WE'RE BOTH SENDING AND RECEIVING FINE.
OH!
NEVER TAKE THE EARS OFF!
IF I DON'T GET THE SPELL TO YOU EXACTLY, YOU CAN'T HELP ANYONE!
NOOOOO!

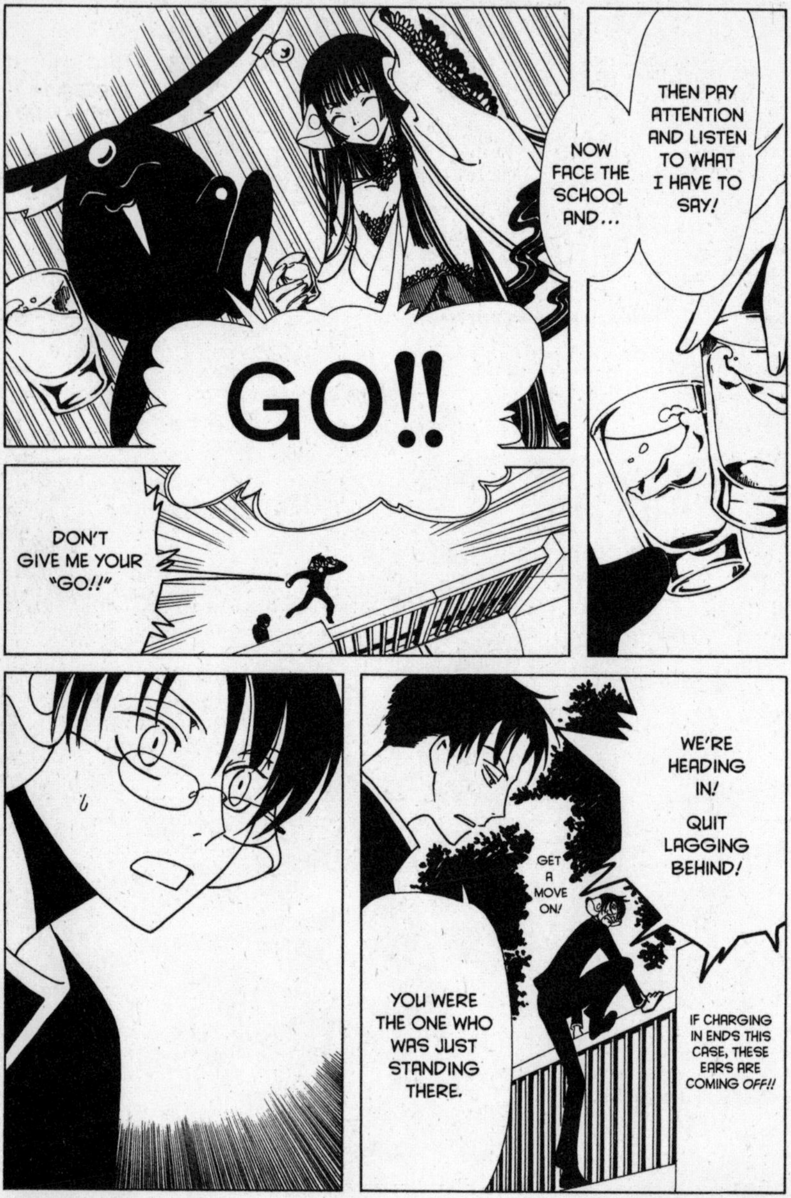
THEN PAY ATTENTION AND LISTEN TO WHAT I HAVE TO SAY!
NOW FACE THE SCHOOL AND...
GO!!
DON'T GIVE ME YOUR "GO!!"
WE'RE HEADING IN!
QUIT LAGGING BEHIND!
GET A MOVE ON!
IF CHARGING IN ENDS THIS CASE, THESE EARS ARE COMING *OFF!!*
YOU WERE THE ONE WHO WAS JUST STANDING THERE.

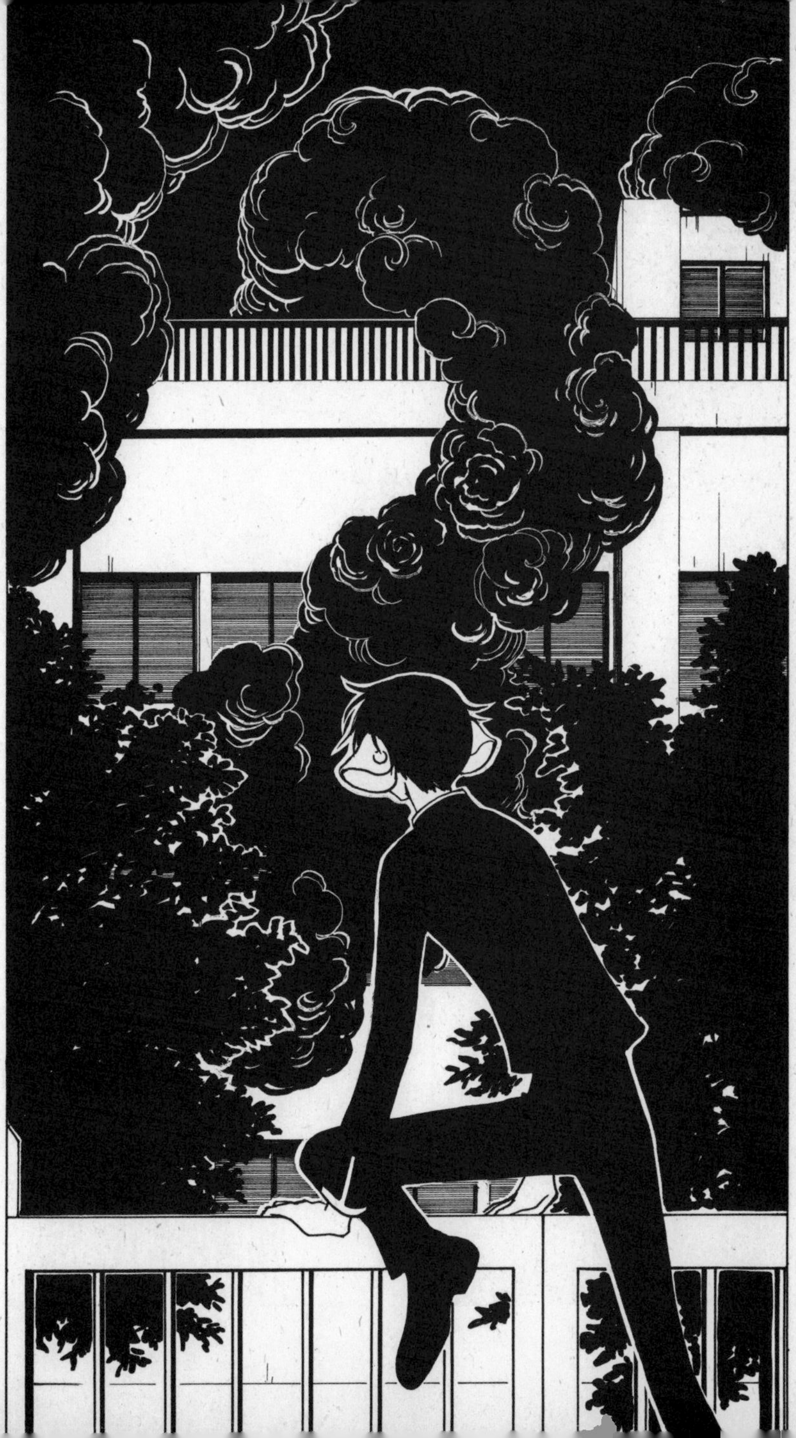

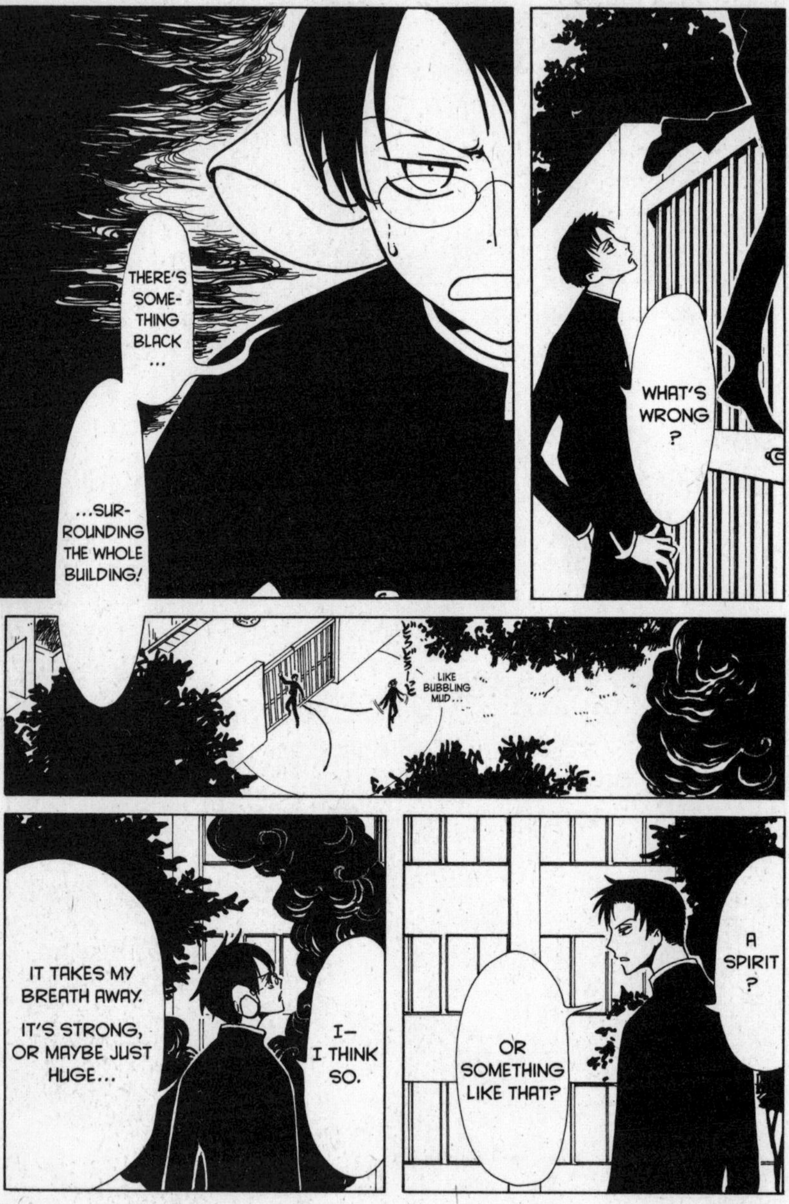
WHAT'S WRONG?
THERE'S SOME-THING BLACK...
...SUR-ROUNDING THE WHOLE BUILDING!
LIKE BUBBLING MUD...
A SPIRIT?
OR SOMETHING LIKE THAT?
I— I THINK SO.
IT TAKES MY BREATH AWAY.
IT'S STRONG, OR MAYBE JUST HUGE...

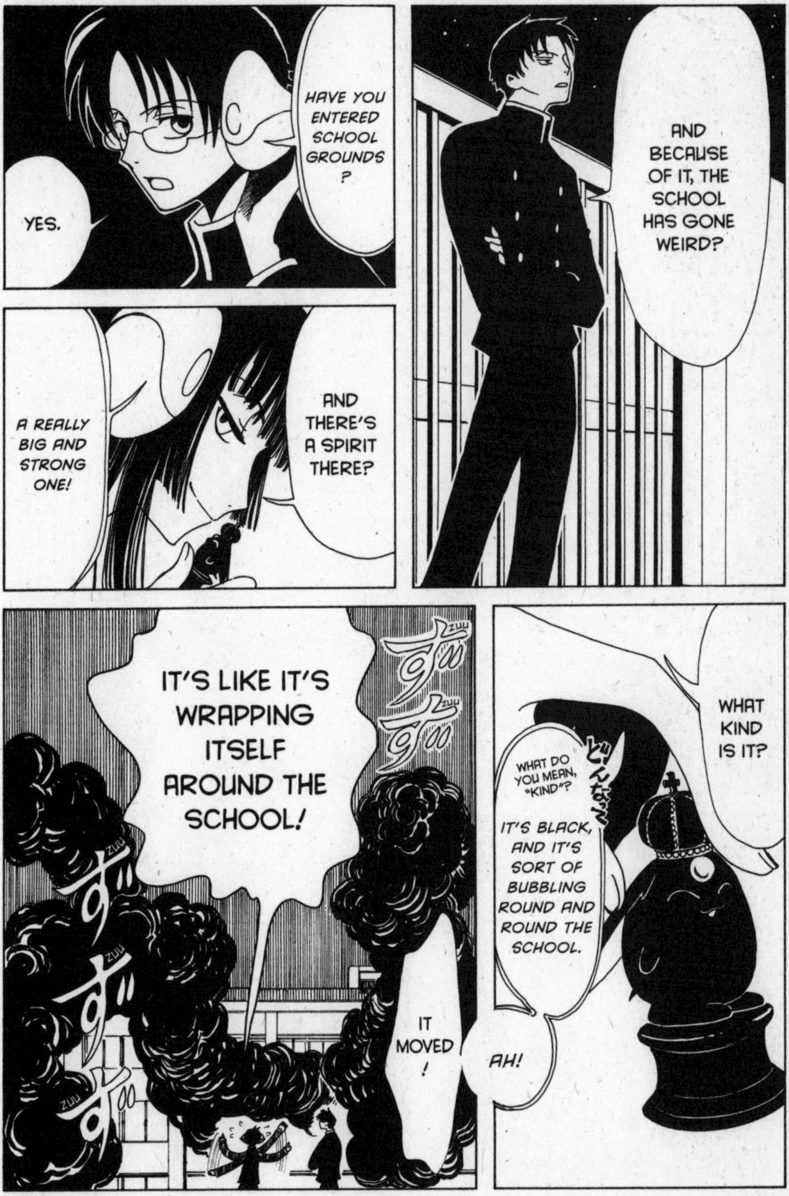
AND BECAUSE OF IT, THE SCHOOL HAS GONE WEIRD?
HAVE YOU ENTERED SCHOOL GROUNDS?
YES.
AND THERE'S A SPIRIT THERE?
A REALLY BIG AND STRONG ONE!
WHAT KIND IS IT?
WHAT DO YOU MEAN, "KIND"?
IT'S BLACK, AND IT'S SORT OF BUBBLING ROUND AND ROUND THE SCHOOL.
AH!
ZUU ZUU
IT'S LIKE IT'S WRAPPING ITSELF AROUND THE SCHOOL!
IT MOVED!
ZUU ZUU ZUU

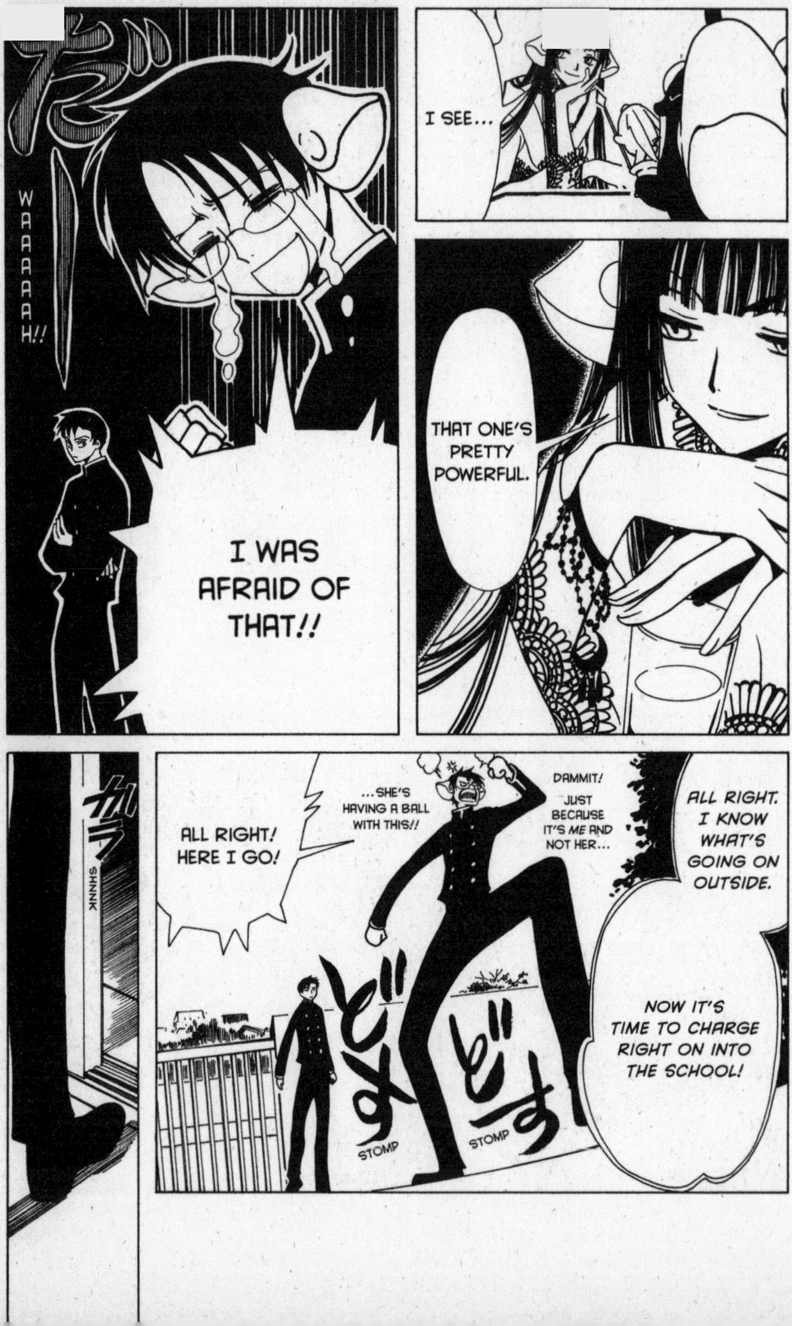
I SEE...
THAT ONE'S PRETTY POWERFUL.
WAAAAAAH!!
I WAS AFRAID OF THAT!!
ALL RIGHT. I KNOW WHAT'S GOING ON OUTSIDE.
NOW IT'S TIME TO CHARGE RIGHT ON INTO THE SCHOOL!
DAMMIT! JUST BECAUSE IT'S *ME* AND NOT HER...
...SHE'S HAVING A BALL WITH THIS!!
ALL RIGHT! HERE I GO!
STOMP
STOMP
SHNNK

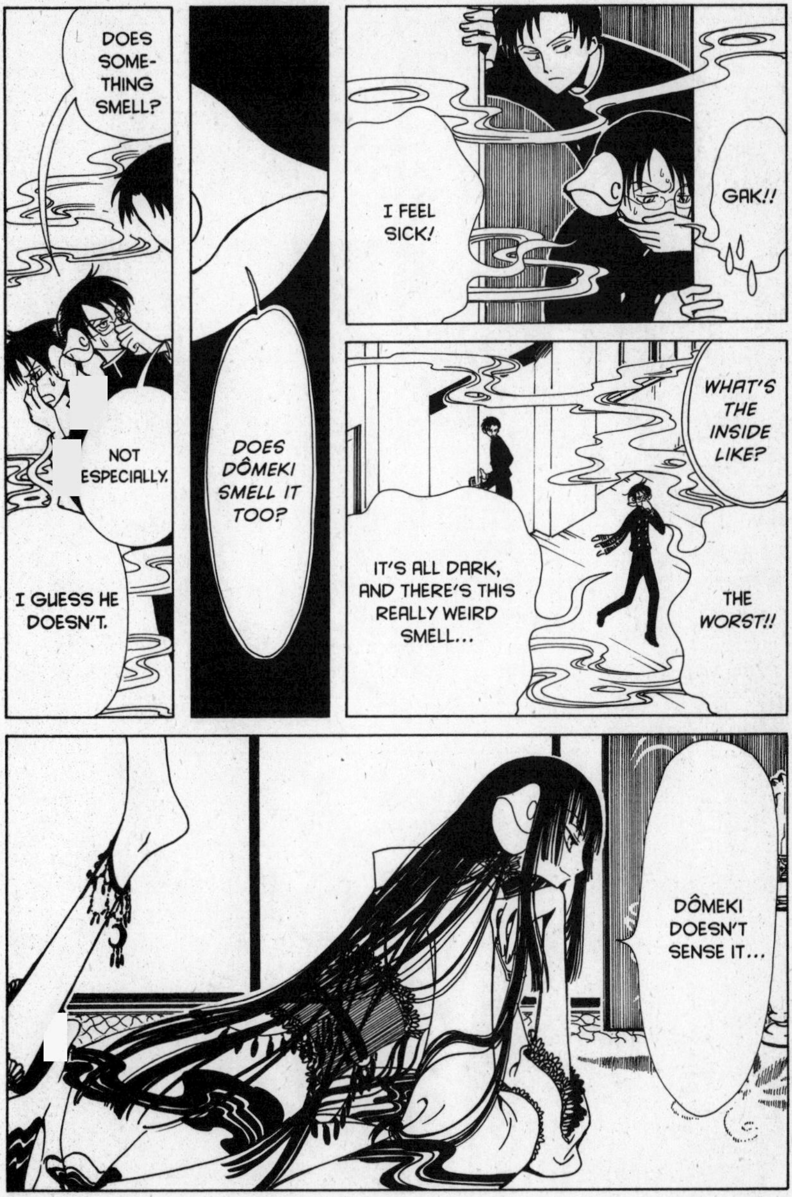
GAK!!
I FEEL SICK!
WHAT'S THE INSIDE LIKE?
THE WORST!!
IT'S ALL DARK, AND THERE'S THIS REALLY WEIRD SMELL...
DOES DÔMEKI SMELL IT TOO?
DOES SOME-THING SMELL?
NOT ESPECIALLY.
I GUESS HE DOESN'T.
DÔMEKI DOESN'T SENSE IT...

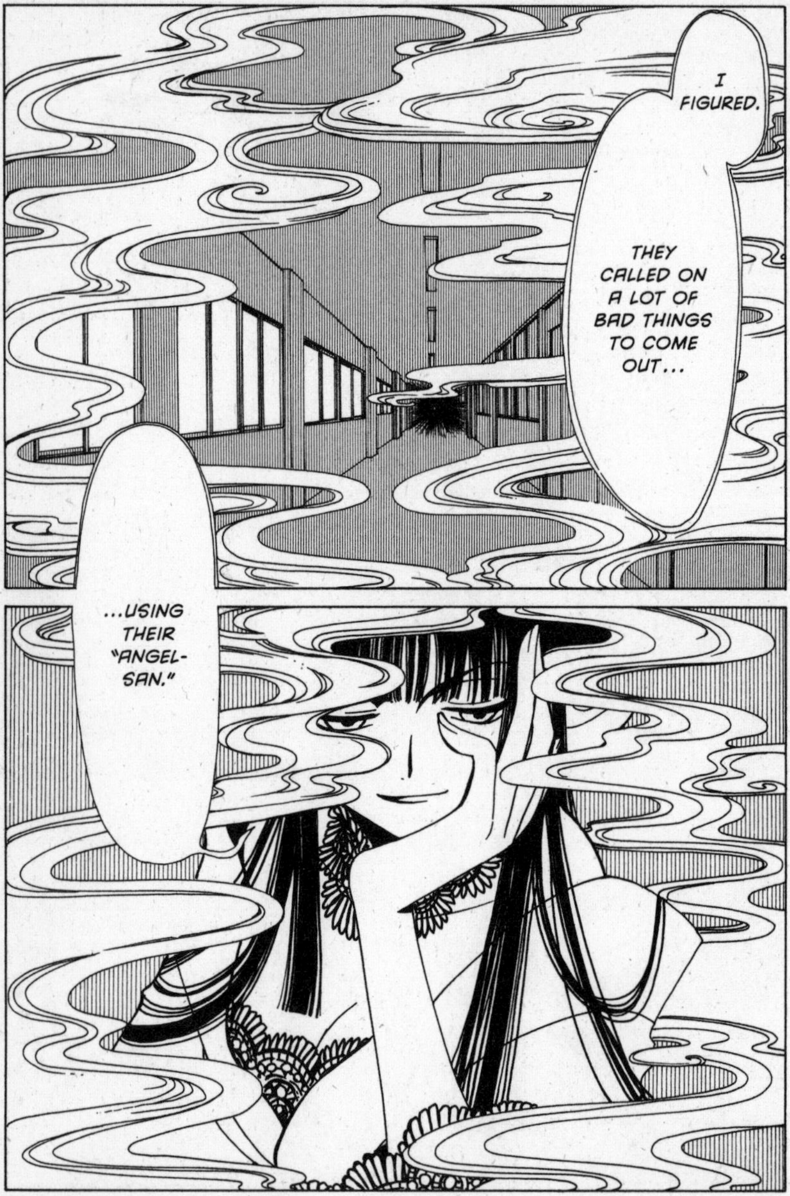
I FIGURED.
THEY CALLED ON A LOT OF BAD THINGS TO COME OUT...
...USING THEIR "ANGEL-SAN."

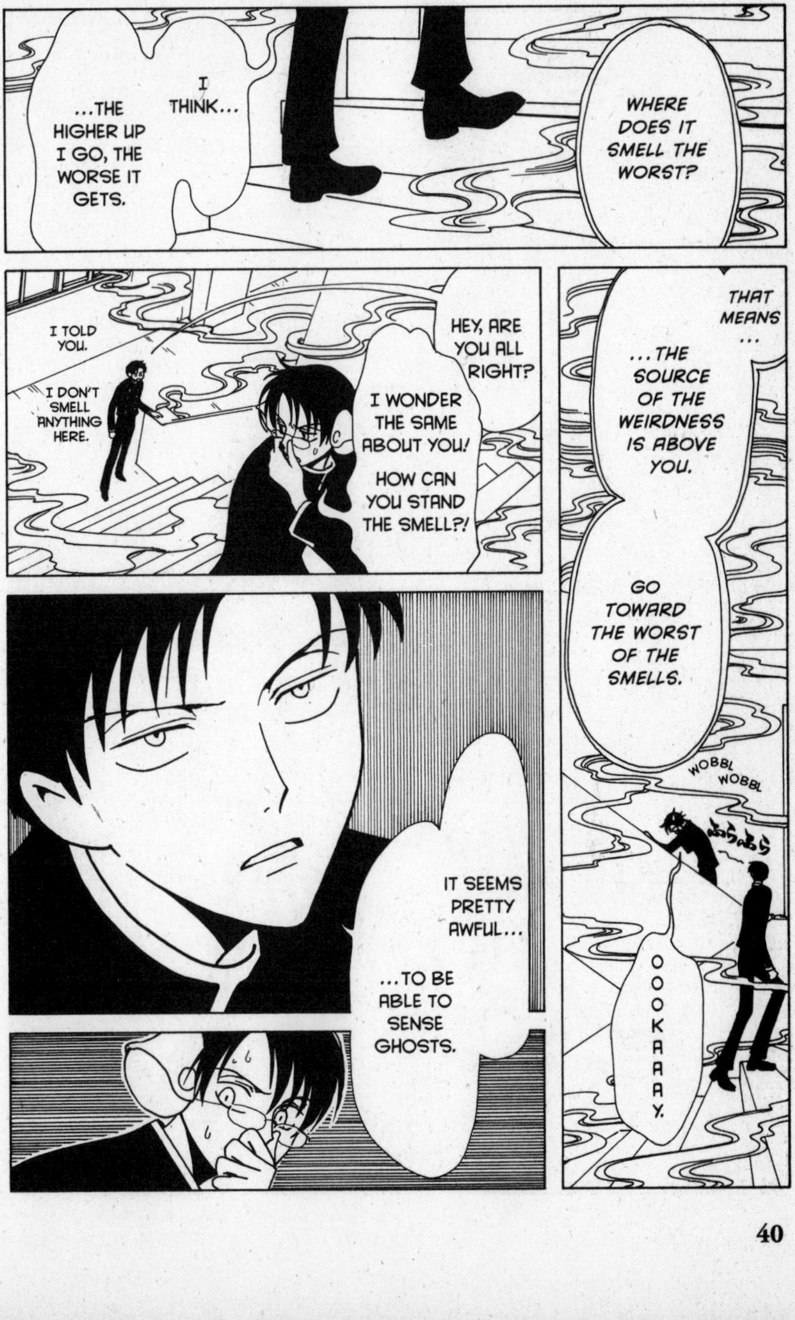
WHERE DOES IT SMELL THE WORST?
I THINK...
...THE HIGHER UP I GO, THE WORSE IT GETS.
THAT MEANS ...
...THE SOURCE OF THE WEIRDNESS IS ABOVE YOU.
GO TOWARD THE WORST OF THE SMELLS.
WOBBL WOBBL
ふらふら
OOOKAAAAY.
HEY, ARE YOU ALL RIGHT?
I WONDER THE SAME ABOUT YOU!
HOW CAN YOU STAND THE SMELL?!
I TOLD YOU.
I DON'T SMELL ANYTHING HERE.
IT SEEMS PRETTY AWFUL...
...TO BE ABLE TO SENSE GHOSTS.

BUT IT'S BETTER NOW THAN IT WOULD BE IF DÔMEKI WEREN'T HERE.
IF HE WEREN'T HERE, YOU WOULD HAVE COLLAPSED BY NOW, WATANUKI.
BE GRATEFUL TO DÔMEKI!
WHAT IS SHE SAYING TO YOU?
GRATEFUL ?!
WHEN I SEE THAT FACE...
WHEN I SEE IT...

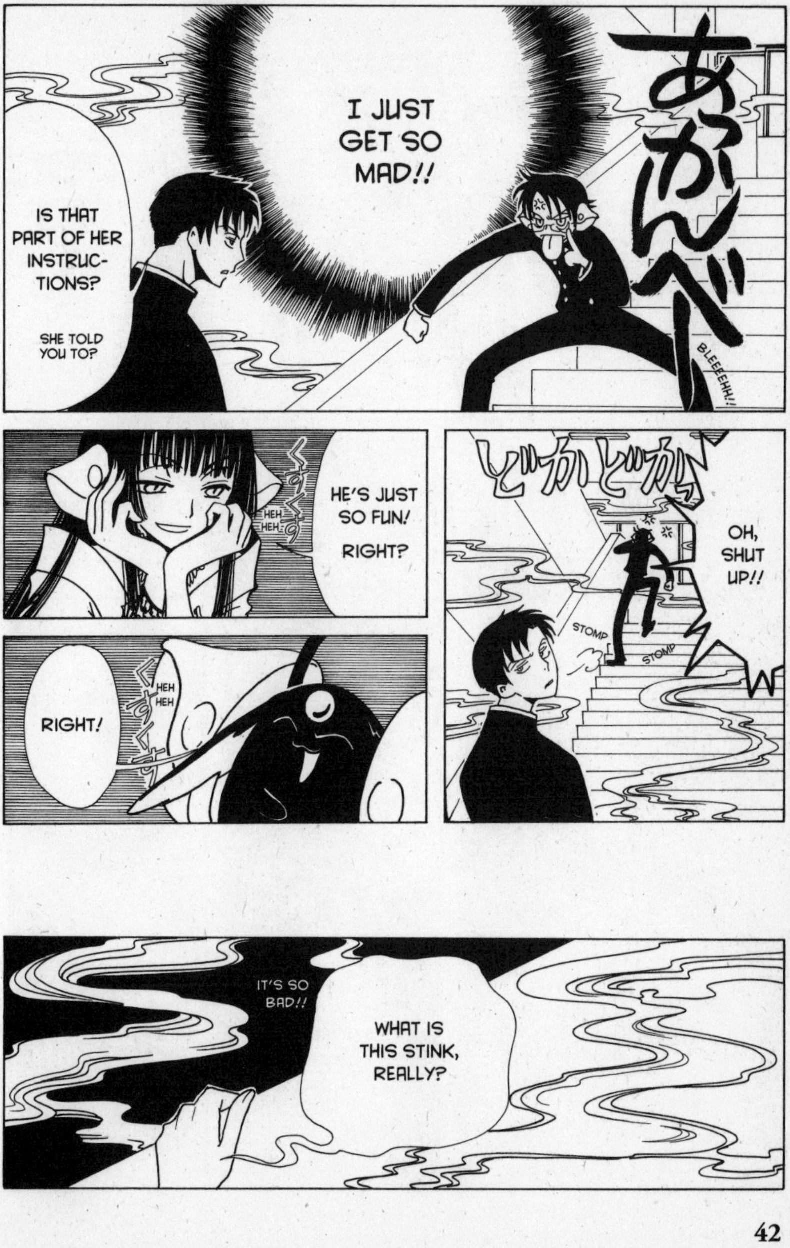

あっかんべー
BLEEEEHH!!
I JUST GET SO MAD!!
IS THAT PART OF HER INSTRUCTIONS?
SHE TOLD YOU TO?
どかどか
OH, SHUT UP!!
STOMP
STOMP
HE'S JUST SO FUN!
RIGHT?
くすくす
HEH HEH
くすくす
HEH HEH
RIGHT!
WHAT IS THIS STINK, REALLY?
IT'S SO BAD!!

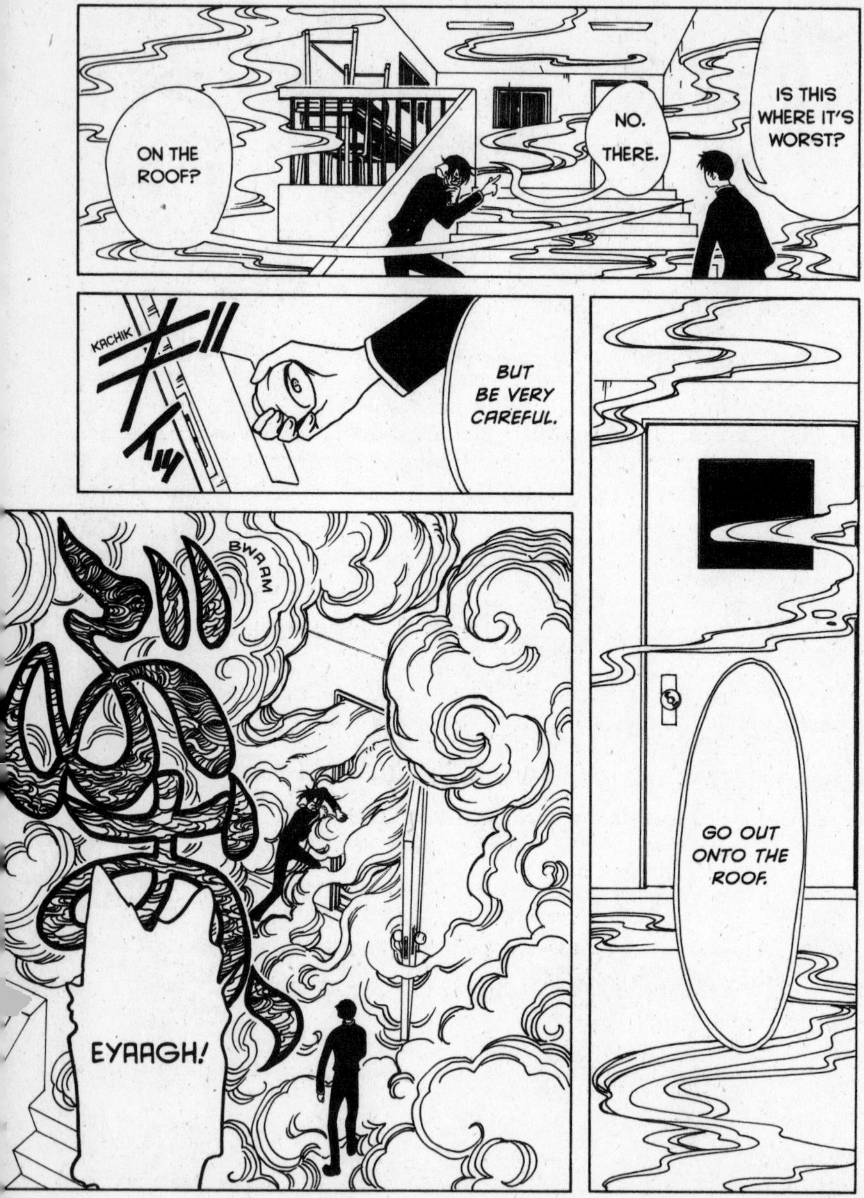
IS THIS WHERE IT'S WORST?
NO. THERE.
ON THE ROOF?
GO OUT ONTO THE ROOF.
BUT BE VERY CAREFUL.
KACHIK
BWAAM
EYAAGH!

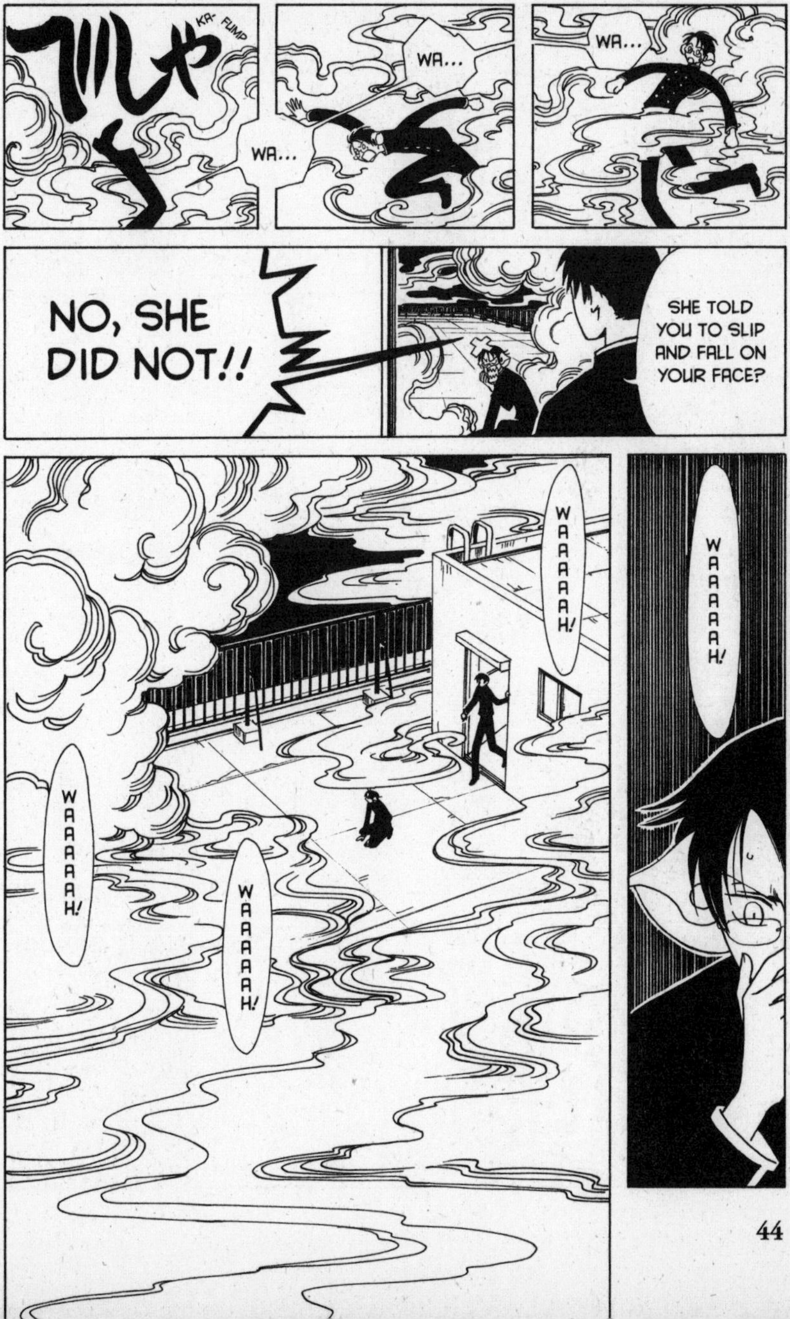

WA...
WA...
WA...
KA-FUMP
SHE TOLD YOU TO SLIP AND FALL ON YOUR FACE?
NO, SHE DID NOT!!
WAAAAAAH!
WAAAAAH!
WAAAAAAH!
WAAAAAAH!

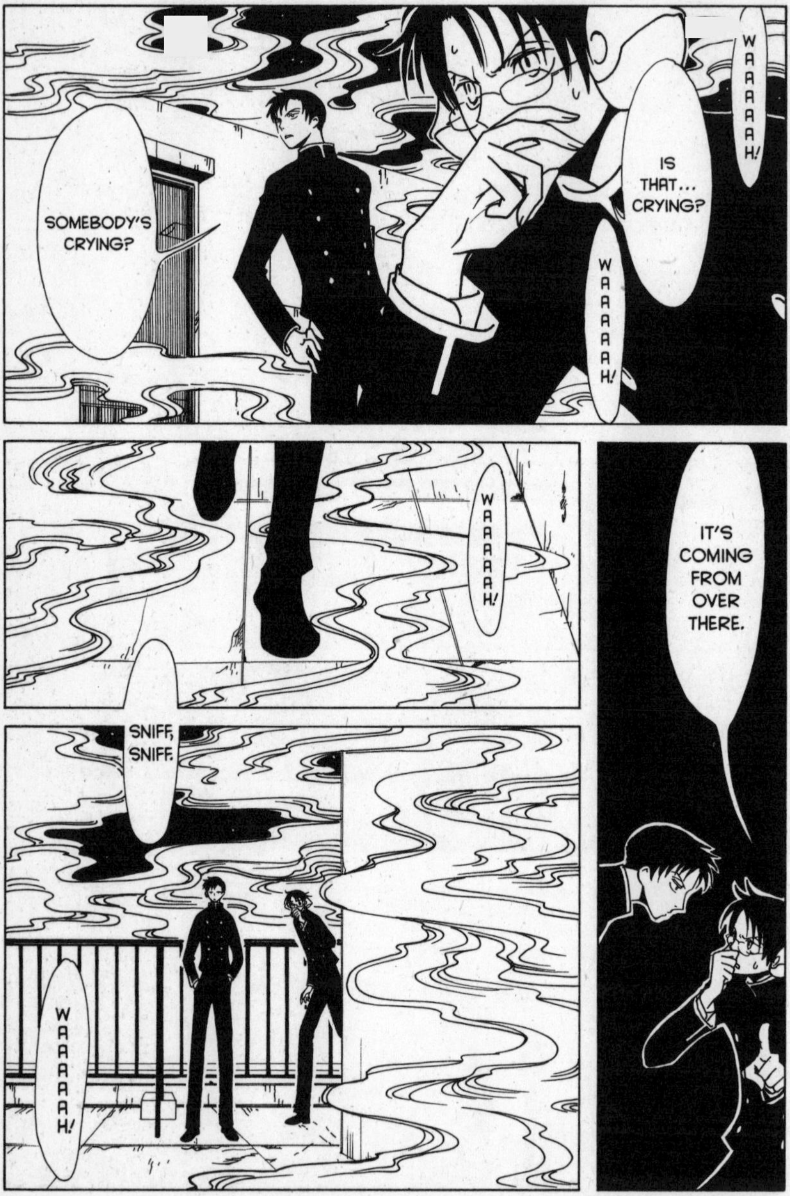
WAAAAAH!
IS THAT... CRYING?
WAAAAAAH!
SOMEBODY'S CRYING?
IT'S COMING FROM OVER THERE.
WAAAAAAH!
SNIFF, SNIFF.
WAAAAAAH!

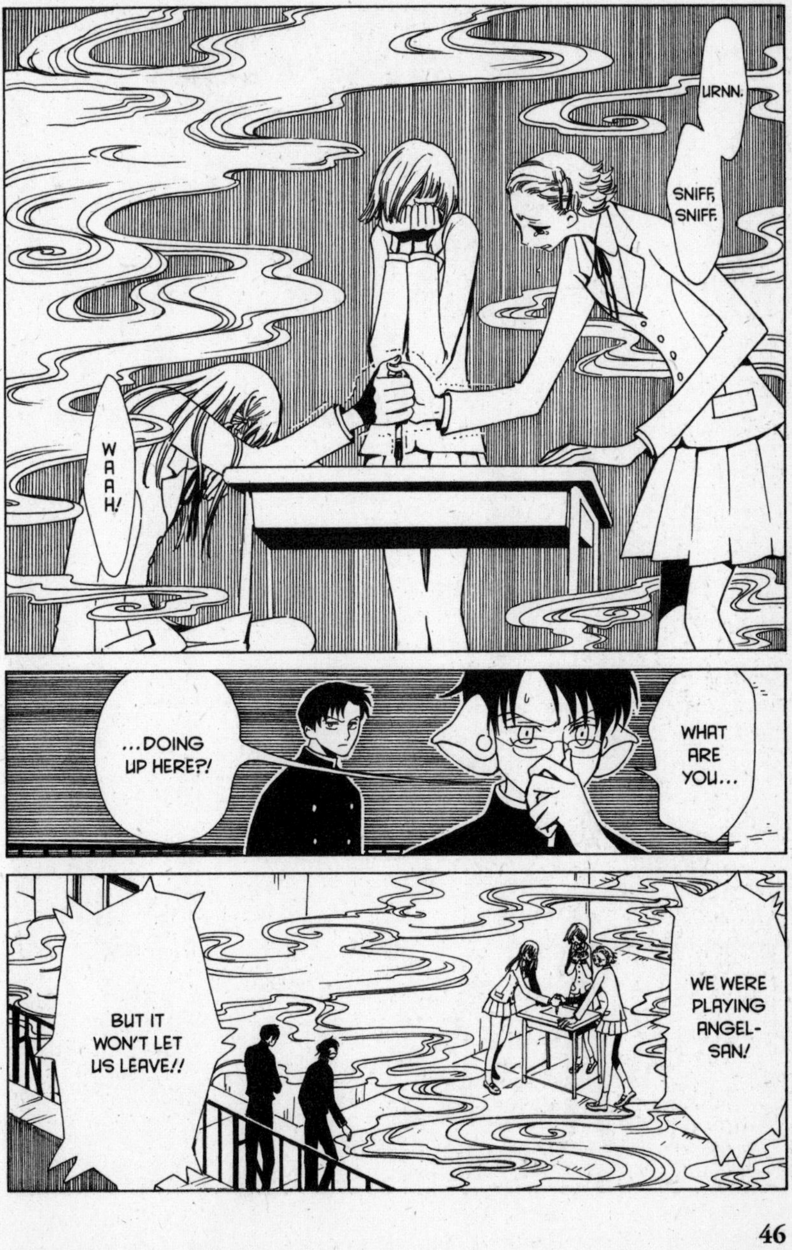
URNN.
SNIFF, SNIFF.
WAAAH!
WHAT ARE YOU...
...DOING UP HERE?!
WE WERE PLAYING ANGEL-SAN!
BUT IT WON'T LET US LEAVE!!

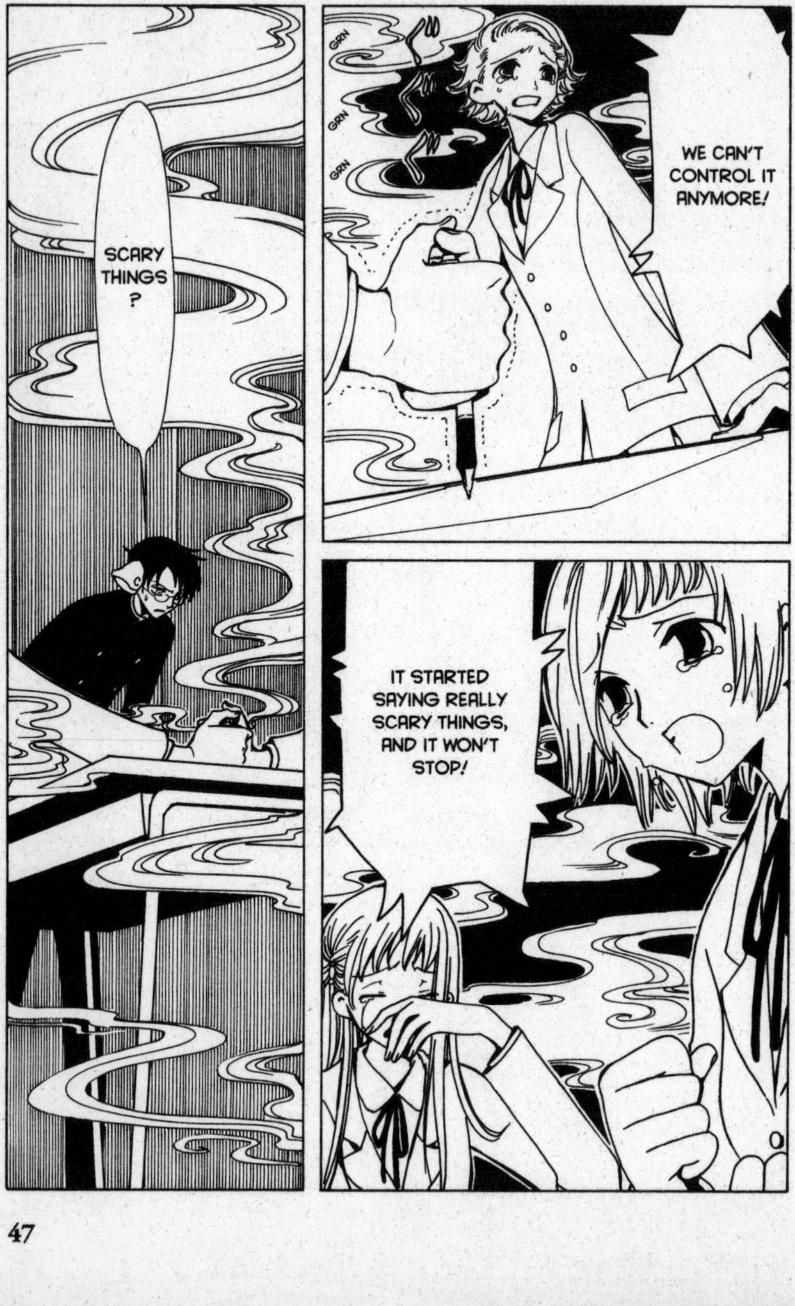
GRN GRN GRN
WE CAN'T CONTROL IT ANYMORE!
IT STARTED SAYING REALLY SCARY THINGS, AND IT WON'T STOP!
SCARY THINGS ?

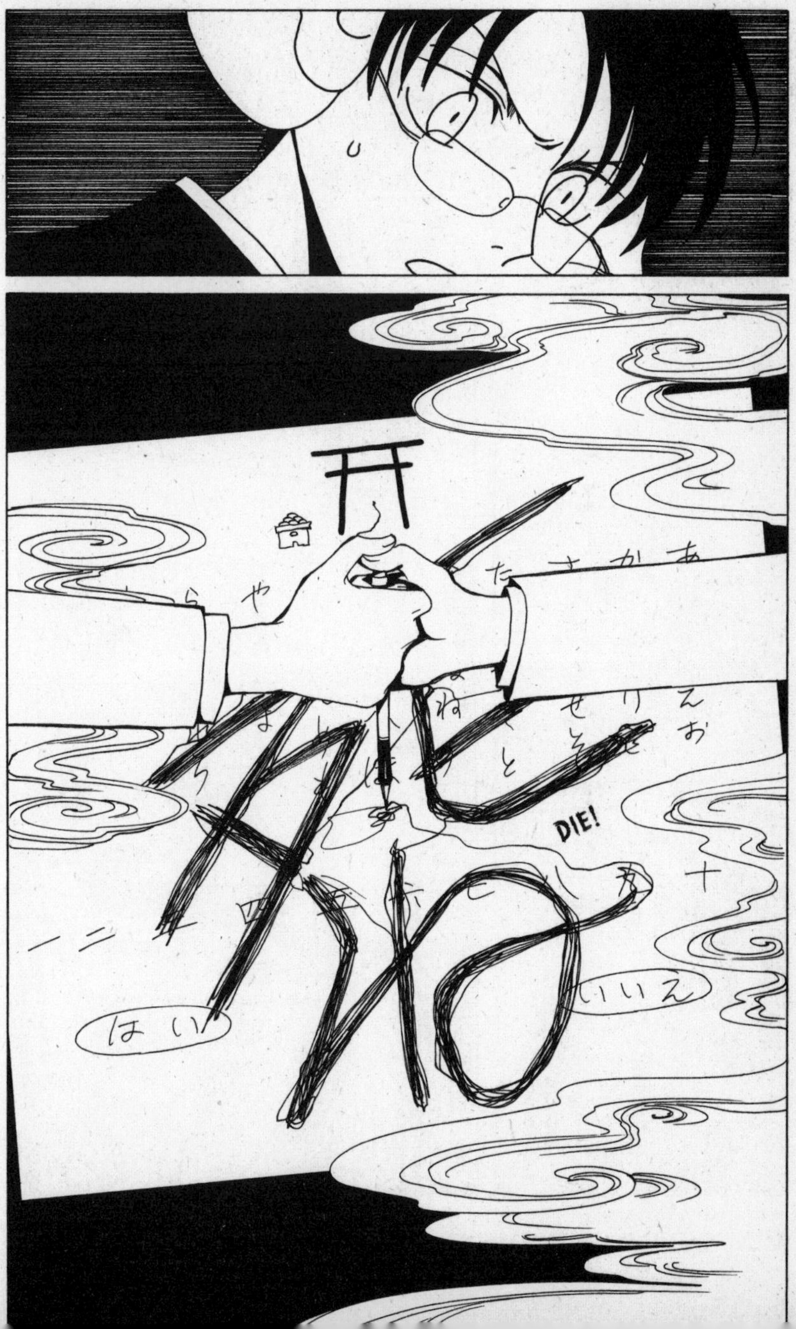
DIE!
いいえ
はい

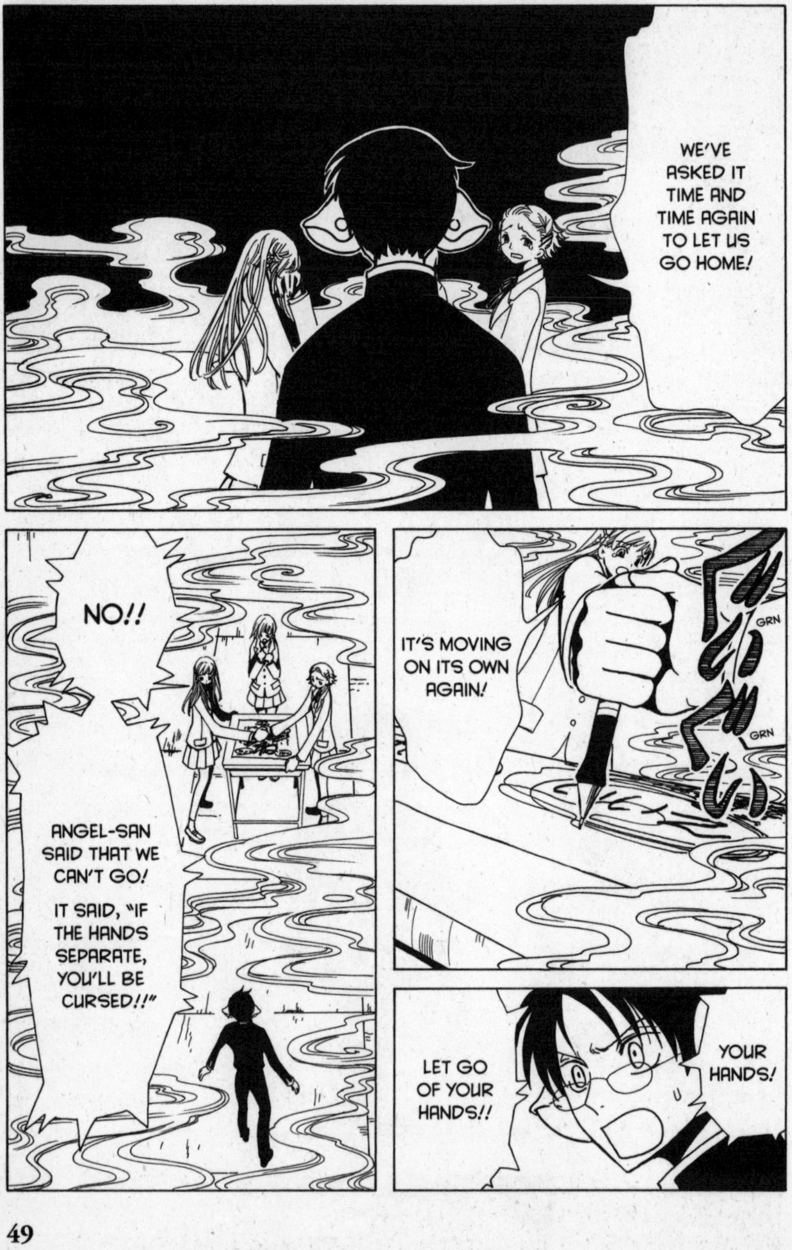
WE'VE ASKED IT TIME AND TIME AGAIN TO LET US GO HOME!
GRN
GRN
IT'S MOVING ON ITS OWN AGAIN!
YOUR HANDS!
LET GO OF YOUR HANDS!!
NO!!
ANGEL-SAN SAID THAT WE CAN'T GO!
IT SAID, "IF THE HANDS SEPARATE, YOU'LL BE CURSED!!"

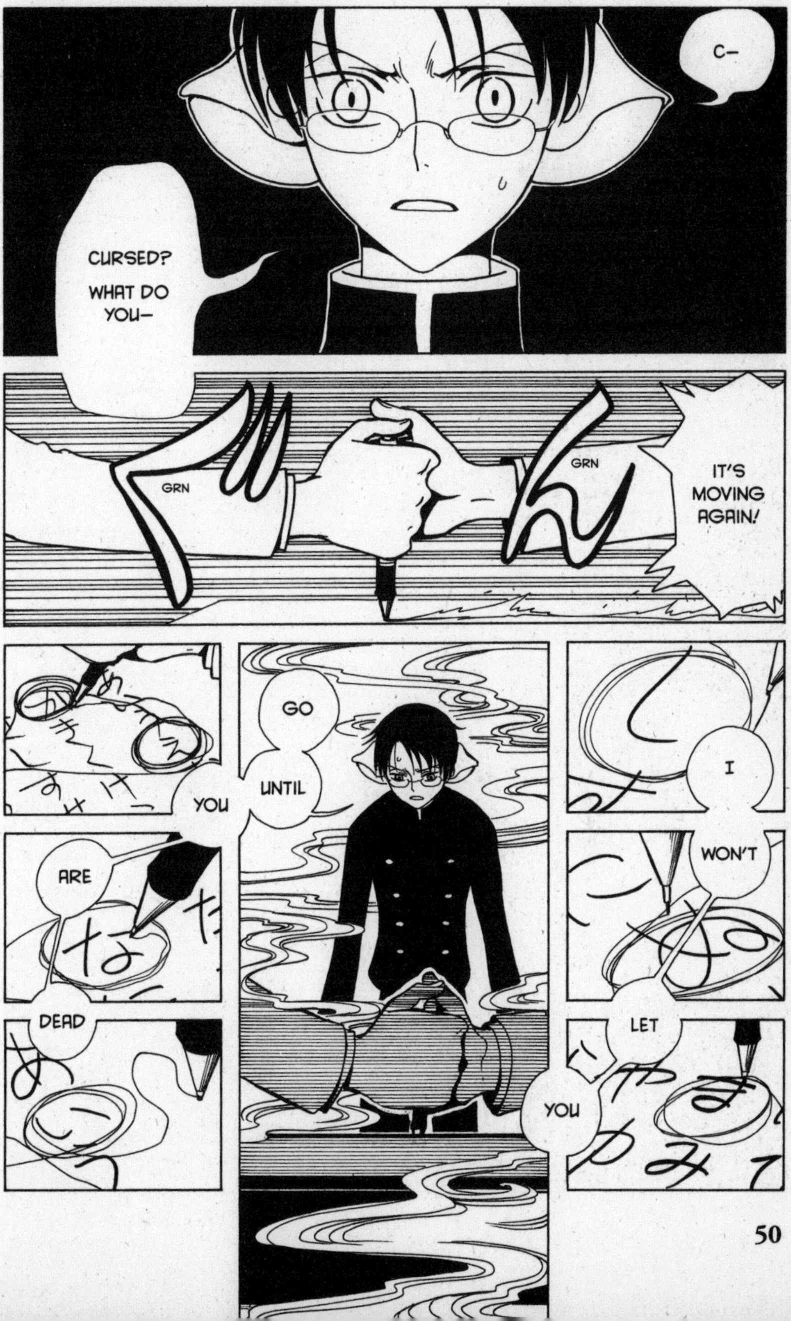

C–
CURSED? WHAT DO YOU–
IT'S MOVING AGAIN!
GRN
GRN
I
WON'T
LET
YOU
GO
UNTIL
YOU
ARE
DEAD

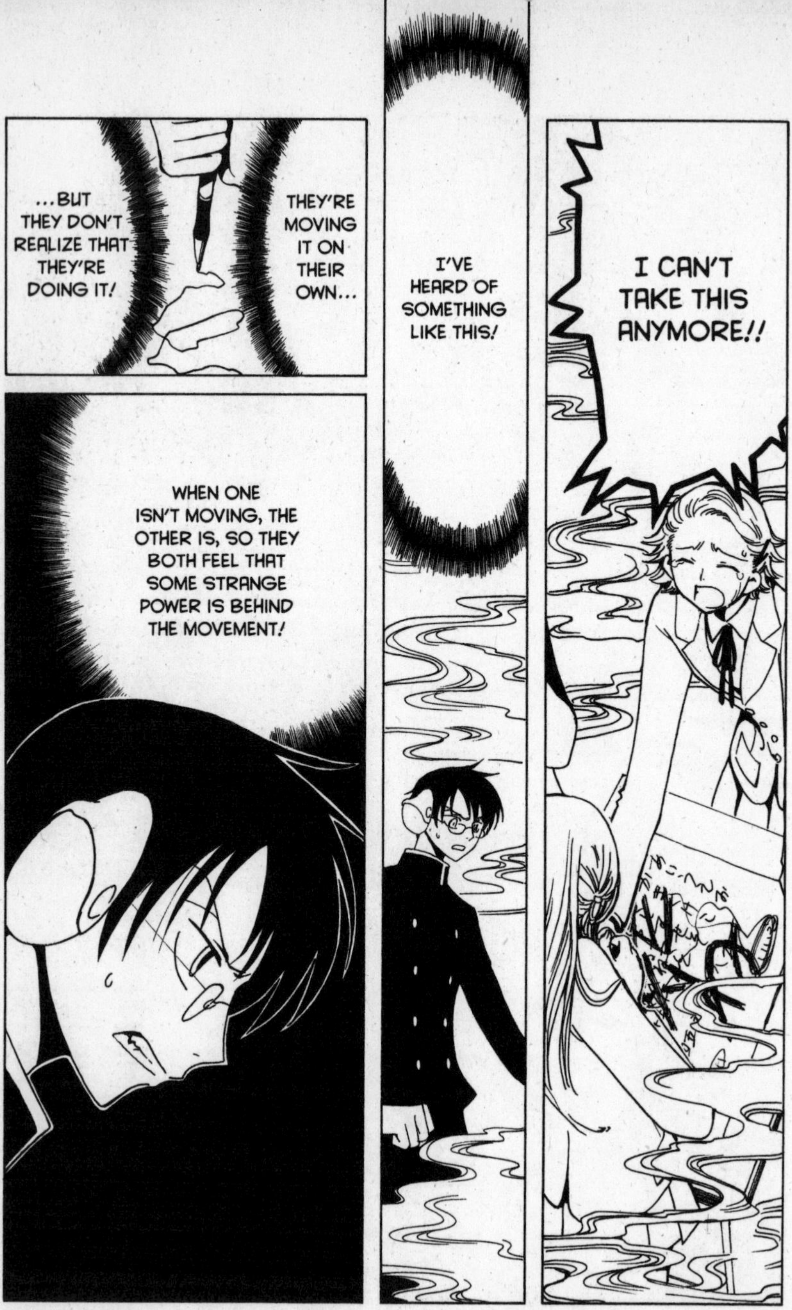
I CAN'T TAKE THIS ANYMORE!!
I'VE HEARD OF SOMETHING LIKE THIS!
THEY'RE MOVING IT ON THEIR OWN...
...BUT THEY DON'T REALIZE THAT THEY'RE DOING IT!
WHEN ONE ISN'T MOVING, THE OTHER IS, SO THEY BOTH FEEL THAT SOME STRANGE POWER IS BEHIND THE MOVEMENT!

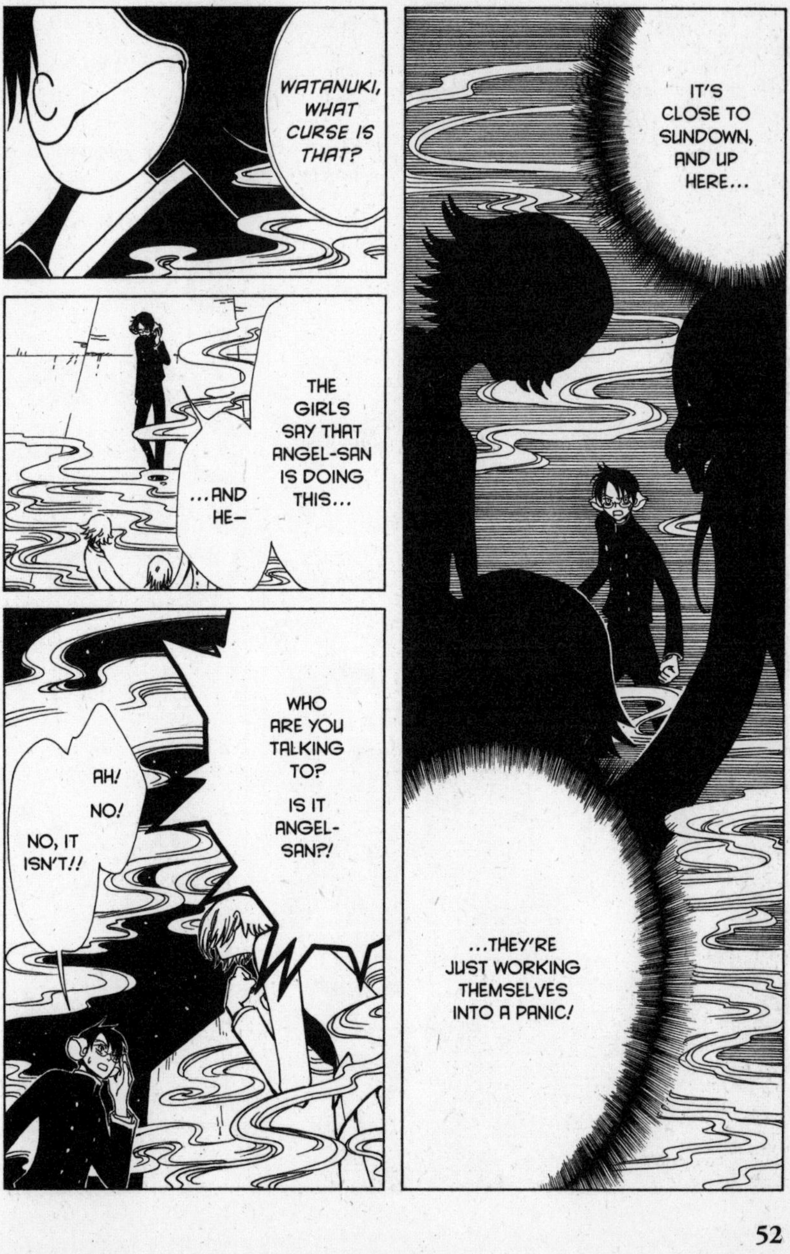
IT'S CLOSE TO SUNDOWN, AND UP HERE...
...THEY'RE JUST WORKING THEMSELVES INTO A PANIC!
WATANUKI, WHAT CURSE IS THAT?
THE GIRLS SAY THAT ANGEL-SAN IS DOING THIS...
...AND HE-
WHO ARE YOU TALKING TO?
IS IT ANGEL-SAN?!
AH!
NO!
NO, IT ISN'T!!

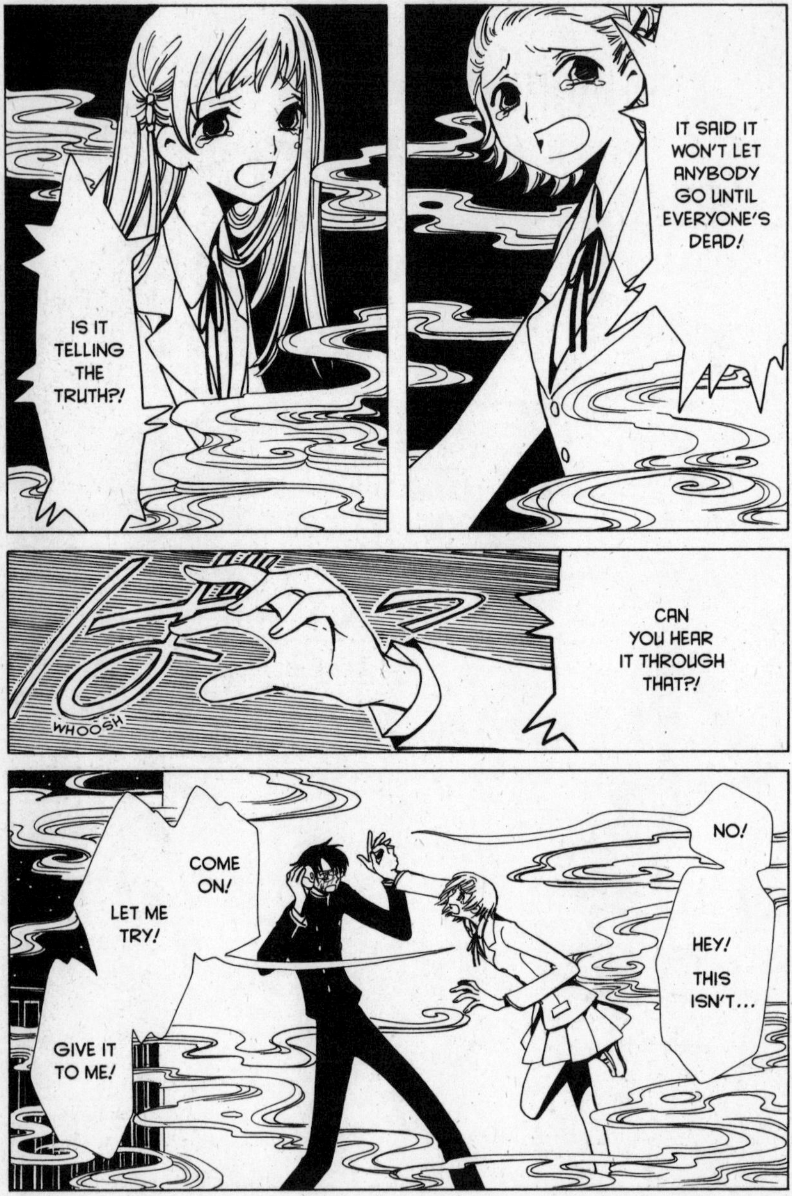
IT SAID IT WON'T LET ANYBODY GO UNTIL EVERYONE'S DEAD!
IS IT TELLING THE TRUTH?!
CAN YOU HEAR IT THROUGH THAT?!
WHOOSH
NO!
HEY! THIS ISN'T...
COME ON!
LET ME TRY!
GIVE IT TO ME!

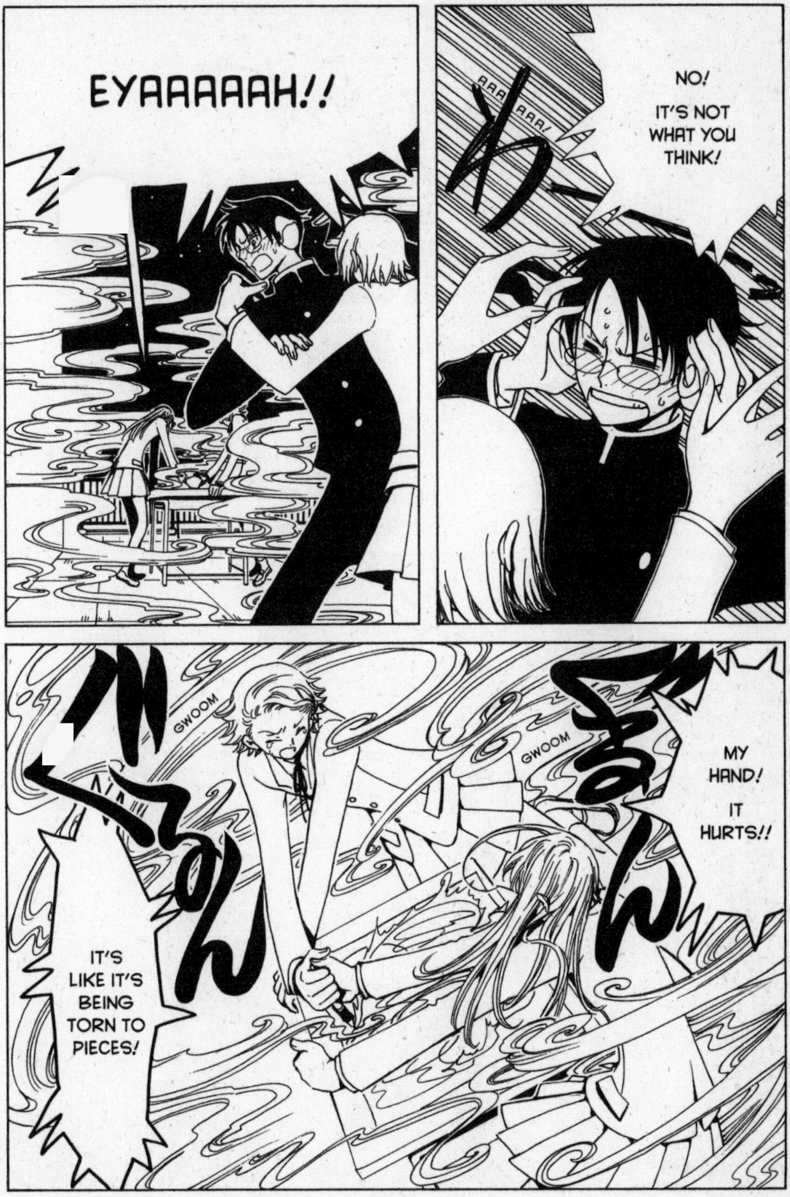
AAA AAA!
NO!
IT'S NOT WHAT YOU THINK!
EYAAAAAH!!
GWOOM
MY HAND!
IT HURTS!!
GWOOM
IT'S LIKE IT'S BEING TORN TO PIECES!

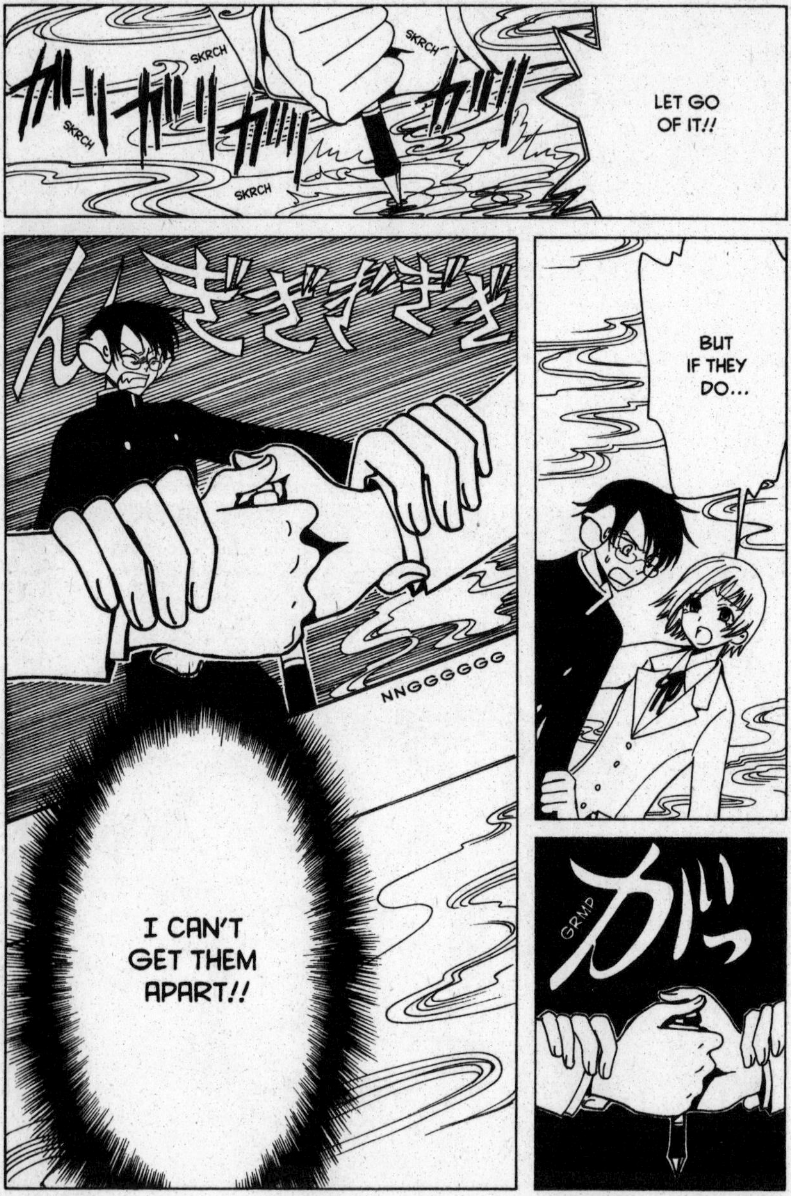
LET GO OF IT!!
SKRCH
SKRCH
SKRCH
SKRCH
BUT IF THEY DO...
GRMP
NNGGGGGG
I CAN'T GET THEM APART!!

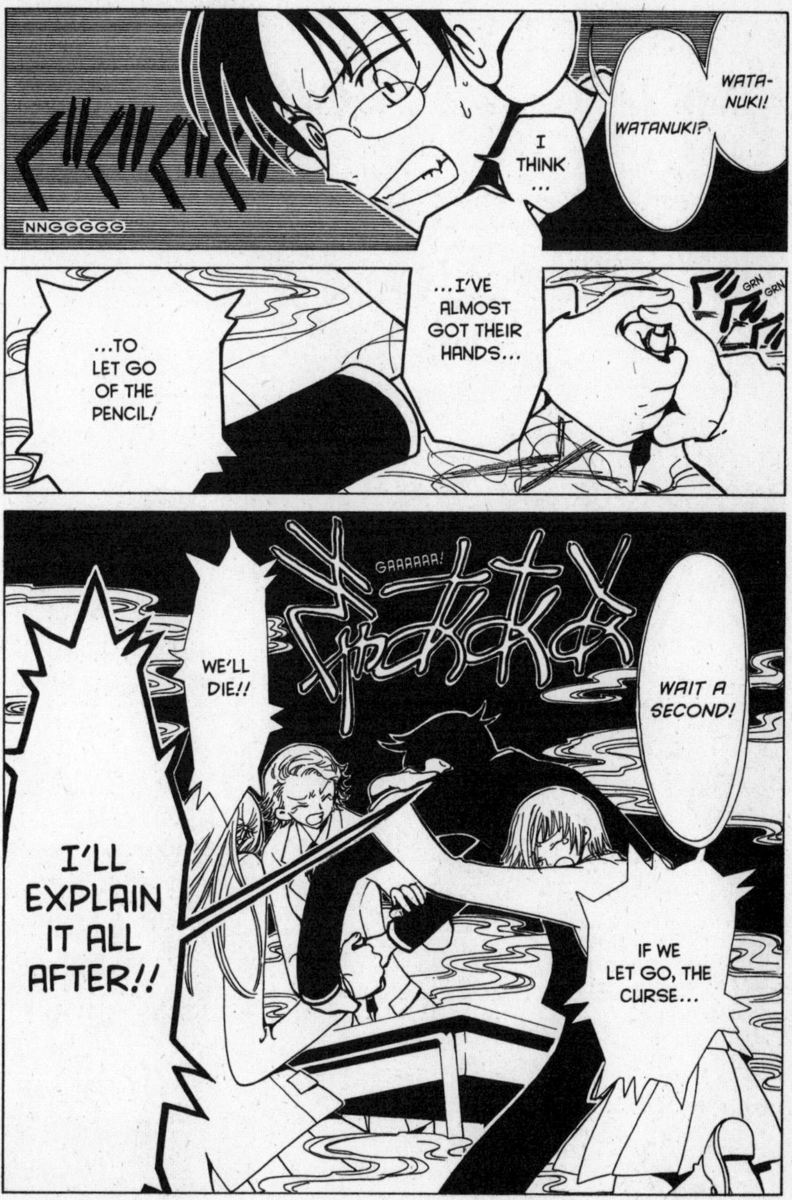
WATA-NUKI!
WATANUKI!?
I THINK...
NNGGGGG
GRN GRN
...I'VE ALMOST GOT THEIR HANDS...
...TO LET GO OF THE PENCIL!
WAIT A SECOND!
IF WE LET GO, THE CURSE...
GAAAAAAA!
WE'LL DIE!!
I'LL EXPLAIN IT ALL AFTER!!

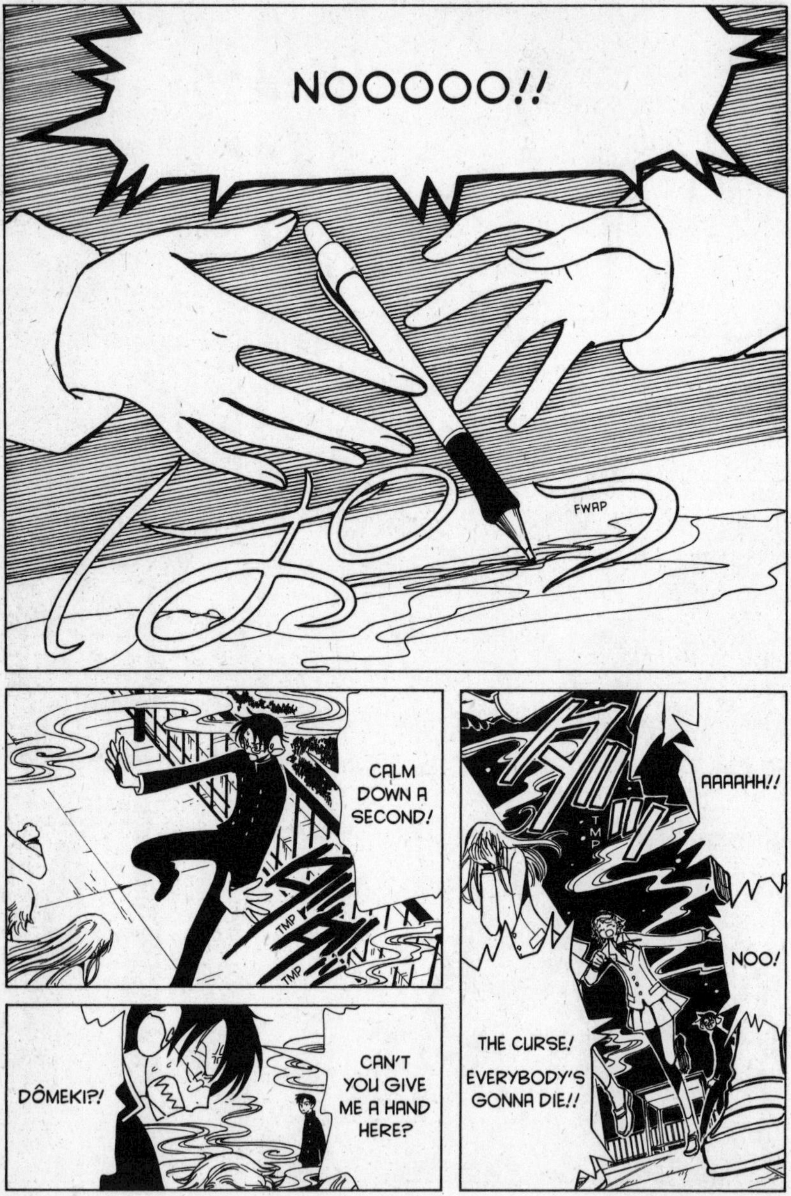
NOOOOO!!
FWAP
AAAAHH!!
TMP
NOO!
THE CURSE!
EVERYBODY'S GONNA DIE!!
CALM DOWN A SECOND!
TMP
TMP
CAN'T YOU GIVE ME A HAND HERE?
DÔMEKI?!

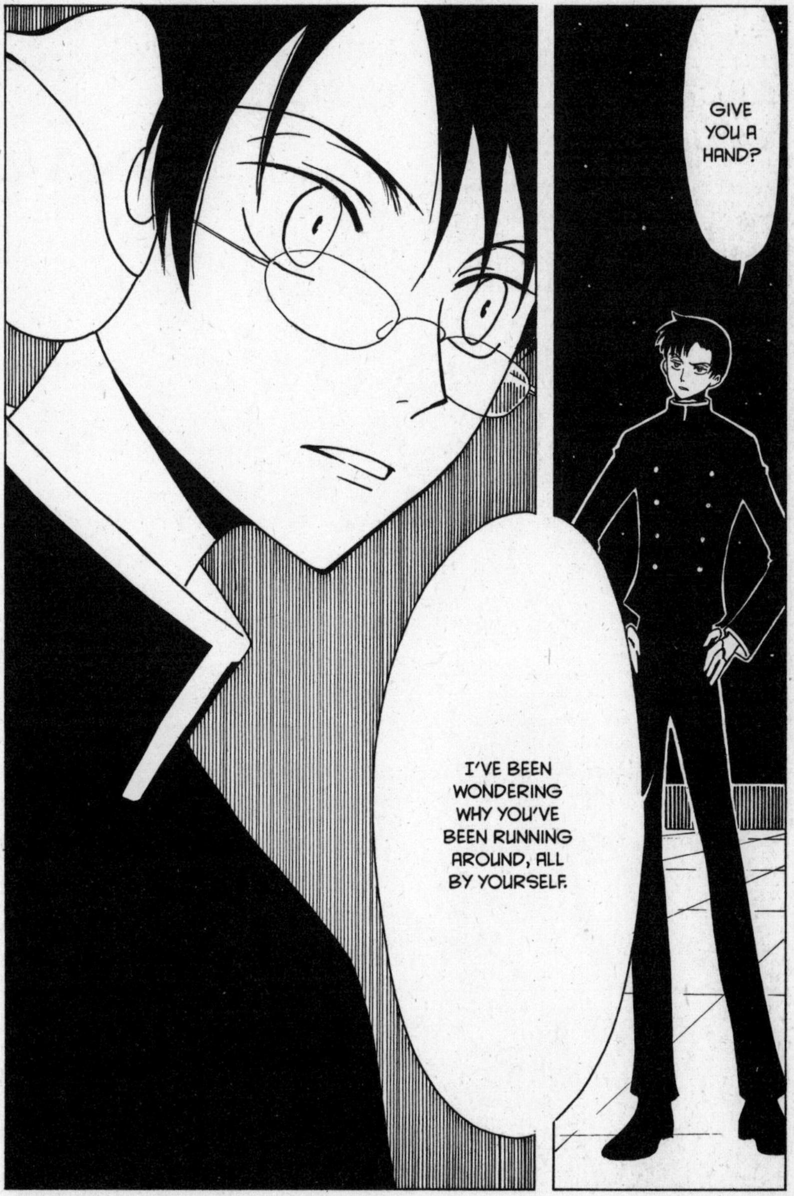
GIVE YOU A HAND?
I'VE BEEN WONDERING WHY YOU'VE BEEN RUNNING AROUND, ALL BY YOURSELF.

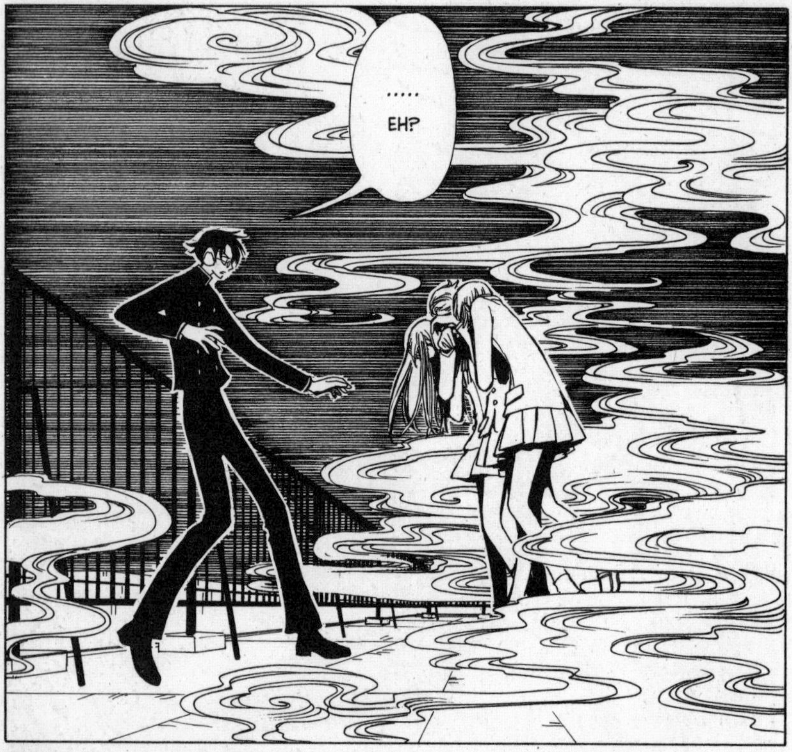
.....
EH?

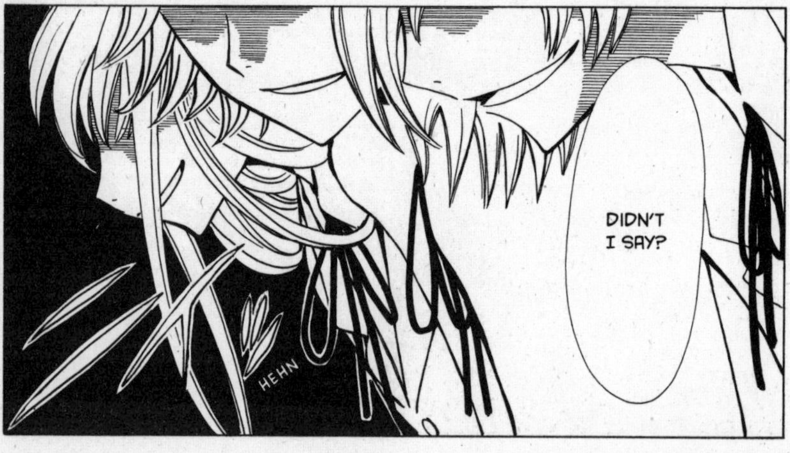
DIDN'T I SAY?
HEHN

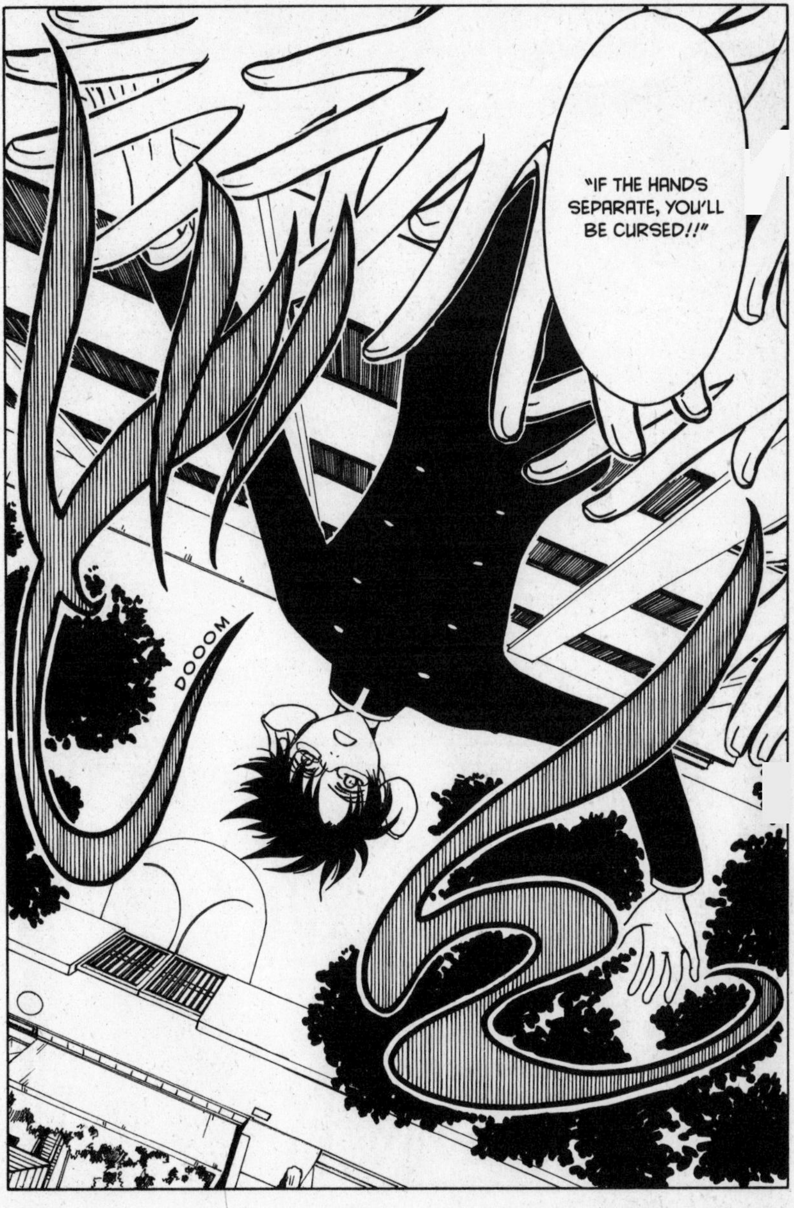
"IF THE HANDS SEPARATE, YOU'LL BE CURSED!!"
DOOOM

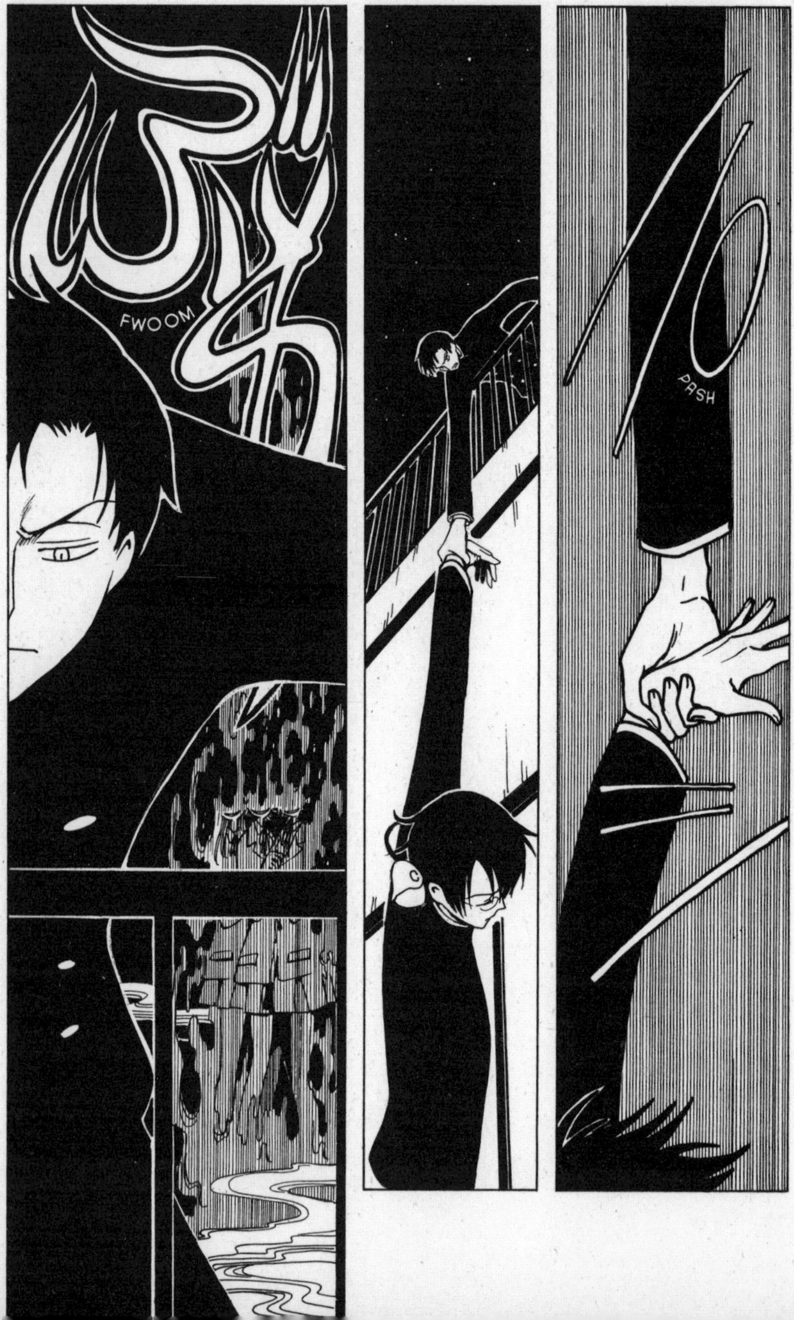
PASH
FWOOM

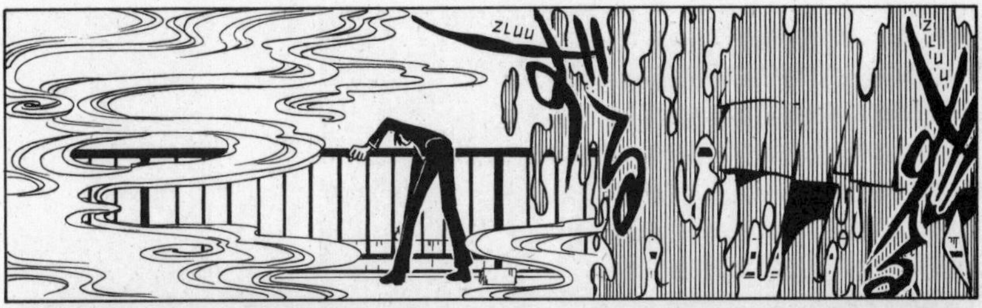
ZLUU
ZLUU
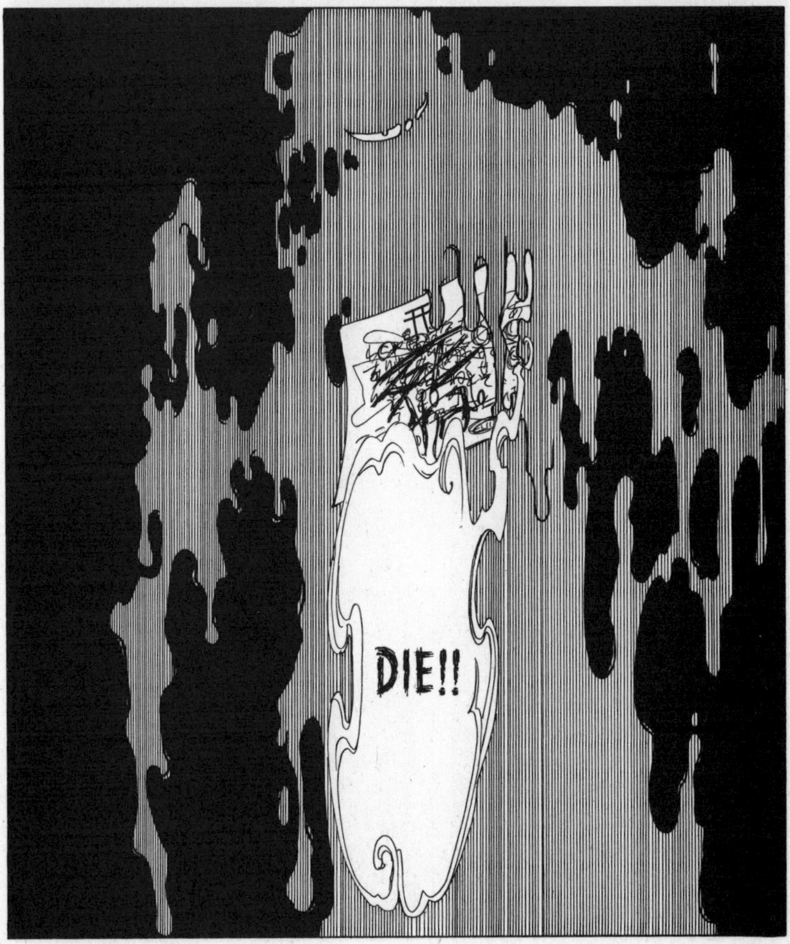
DIE!!

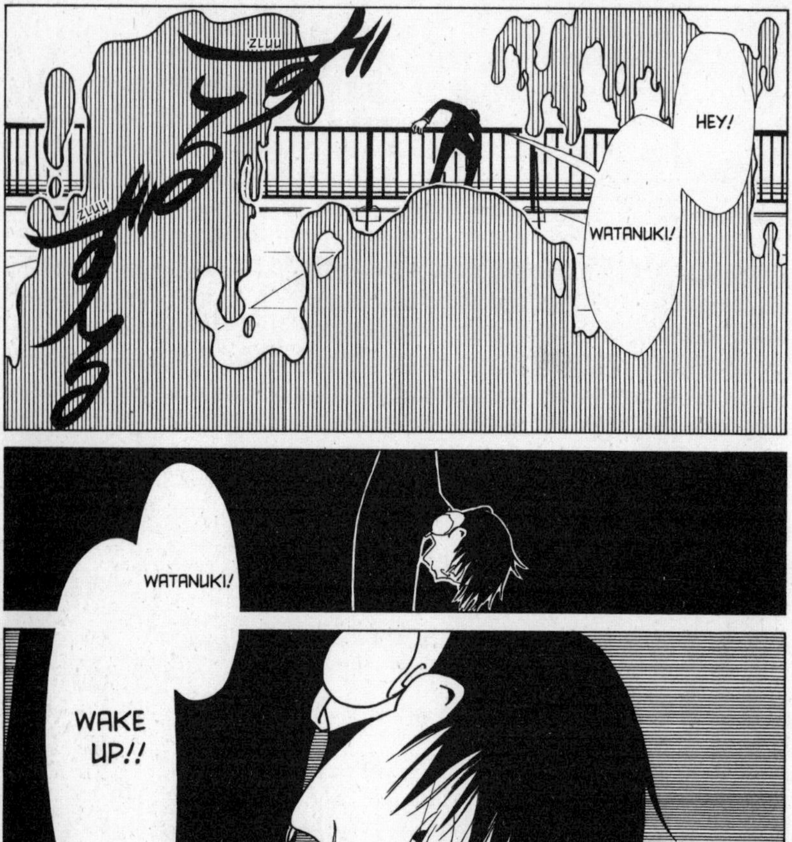
HEY! WATANUKI!
ZLUU
ZLUU
WATANUKI!
WAKE UP!!

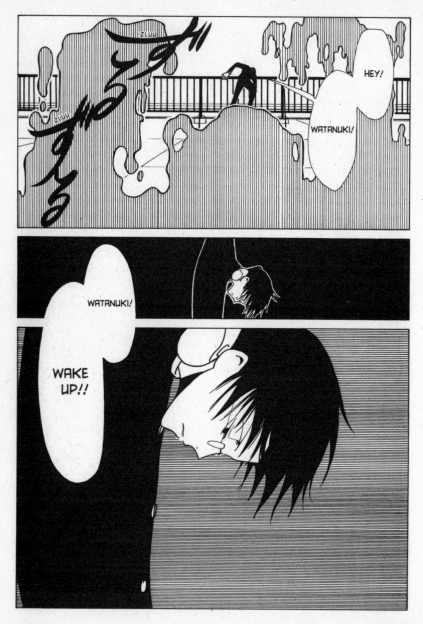

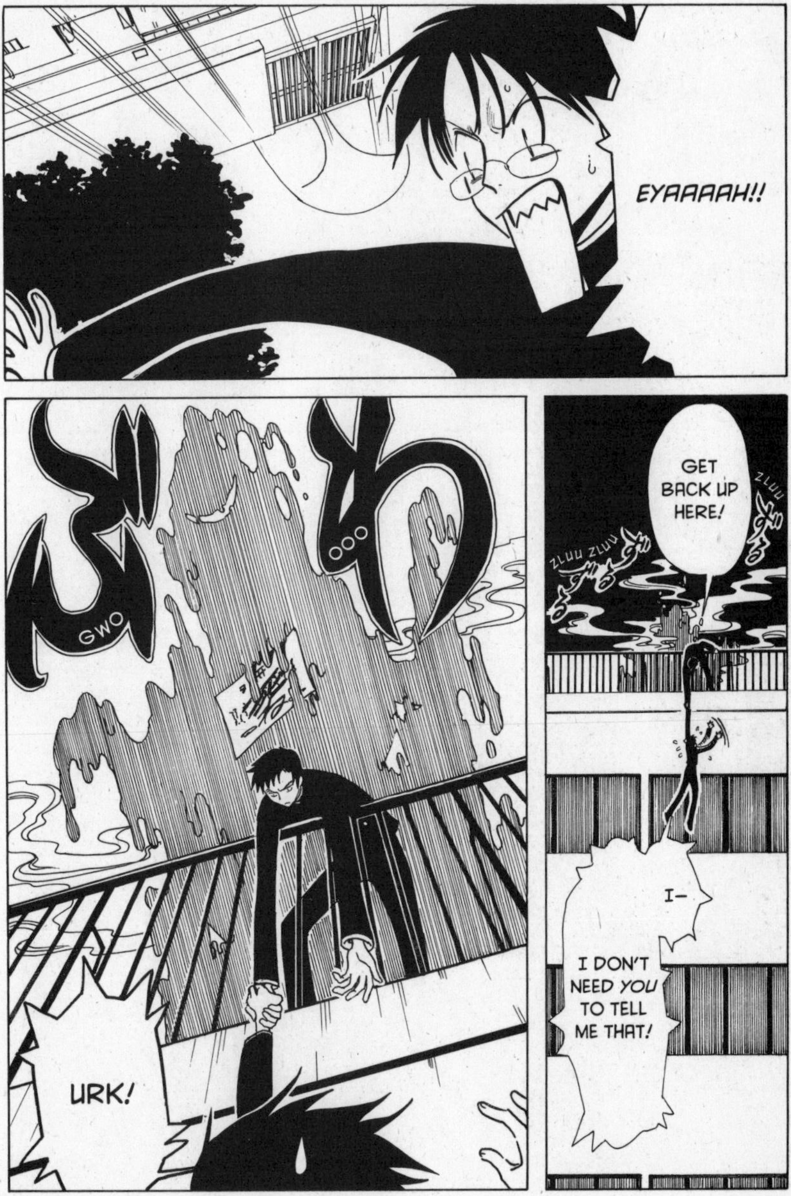
EYAAAAH!!
GET BACK UP HERE!
ZLUU
ZLUU ZLUU
I—
I DON'T NEED *YOU* TO TELL ME THAT!
GWO
URK!

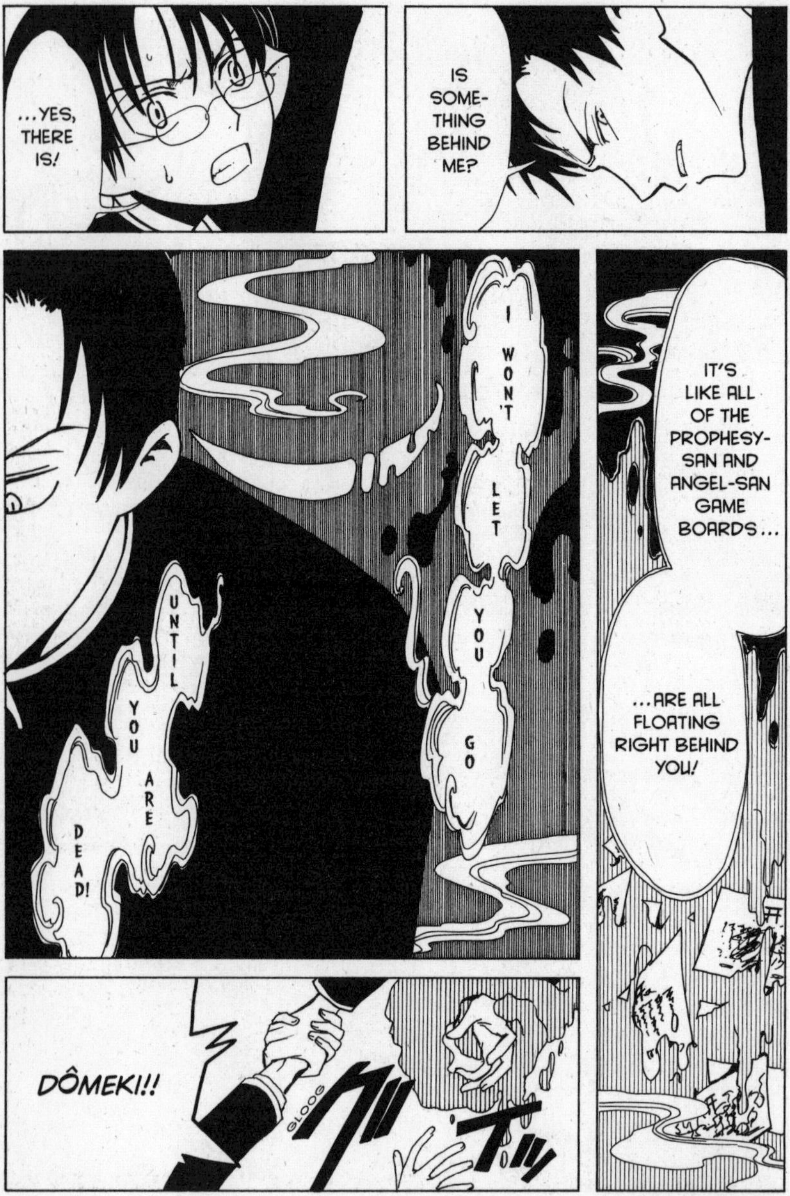
IS SOMETHING BEHIND ME?
...YES, THERE IS!
IT'S LIKE ALL OF THE PROPHESY-SAN AND ANGEL-SAN GAME BOARDS...
...ARE ALL FLOATING RIGHT BEHIND YOU!
I WON'T LET YOU GO
UNTIL YOU ARE DEAD!
GLOOG
DÔMEKI!!

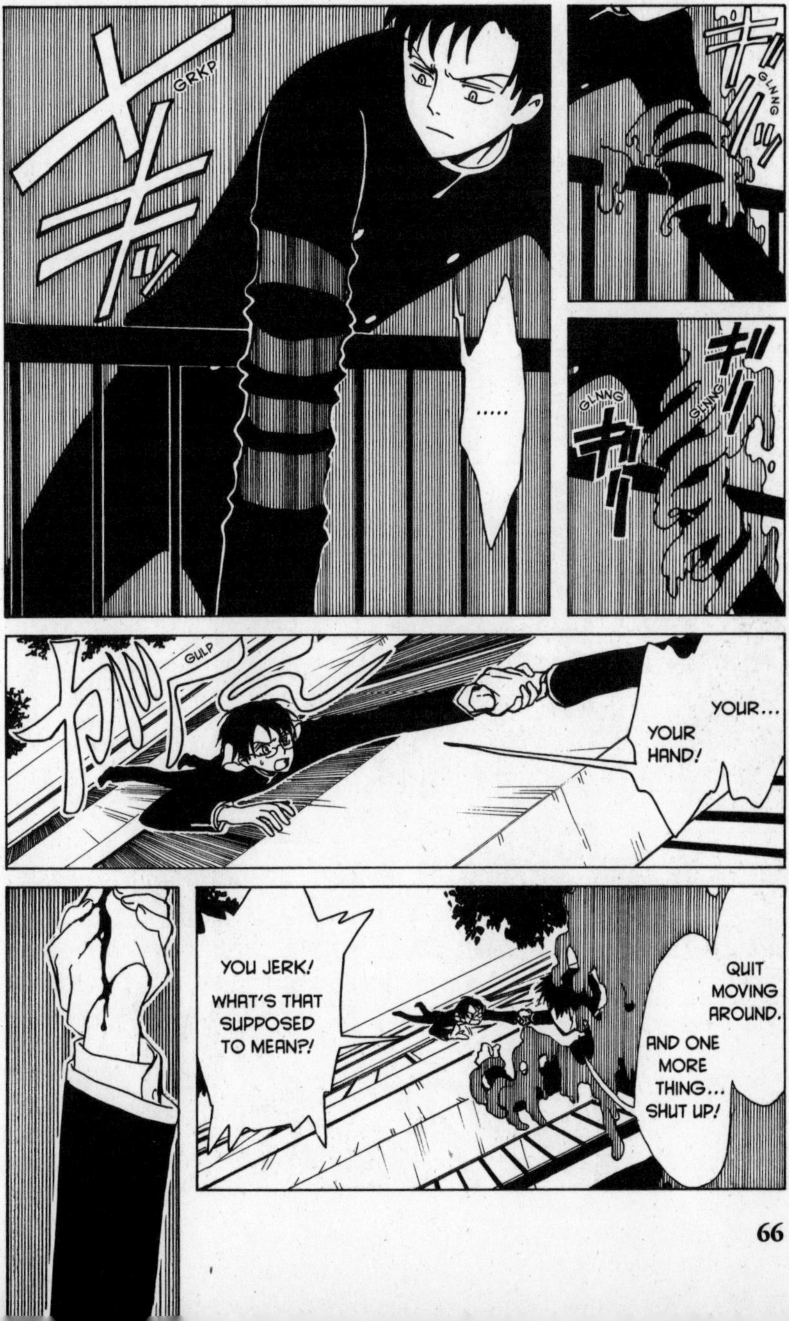
GLNNG
GLNNG
GLNNG
GRKP
......
YOUR...
YOUR HAND!
GULP
QUIT MOVING AROUND.
AND ONE MORE THING... SHUT UP!
YOU JERK!
WHAT'S THAT SUPPOSED TO MEAN?!

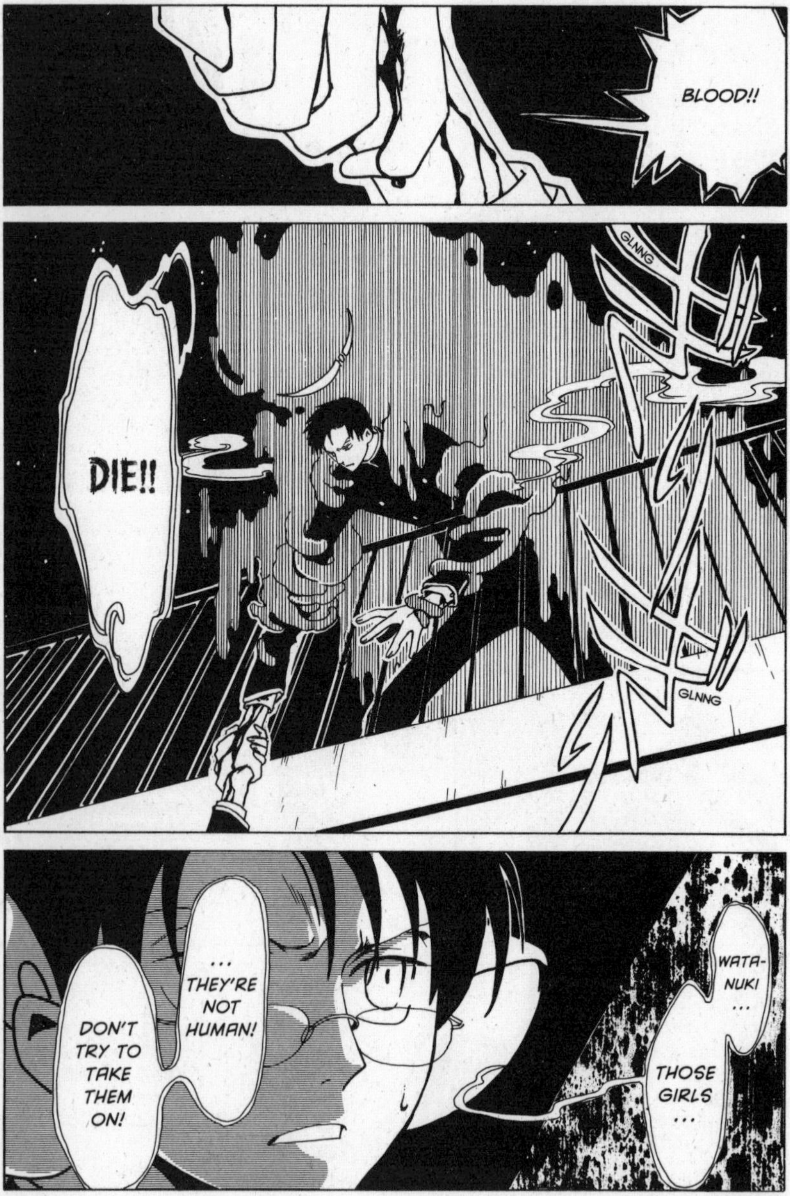
BLOOD!!
GLNNG
DIE!!
GLNNG
WATA-NUKI... THOSE GIRLS...
... THEY'RE NOT HUMAN!
DON'T TRY TO TAKE THEM ON!

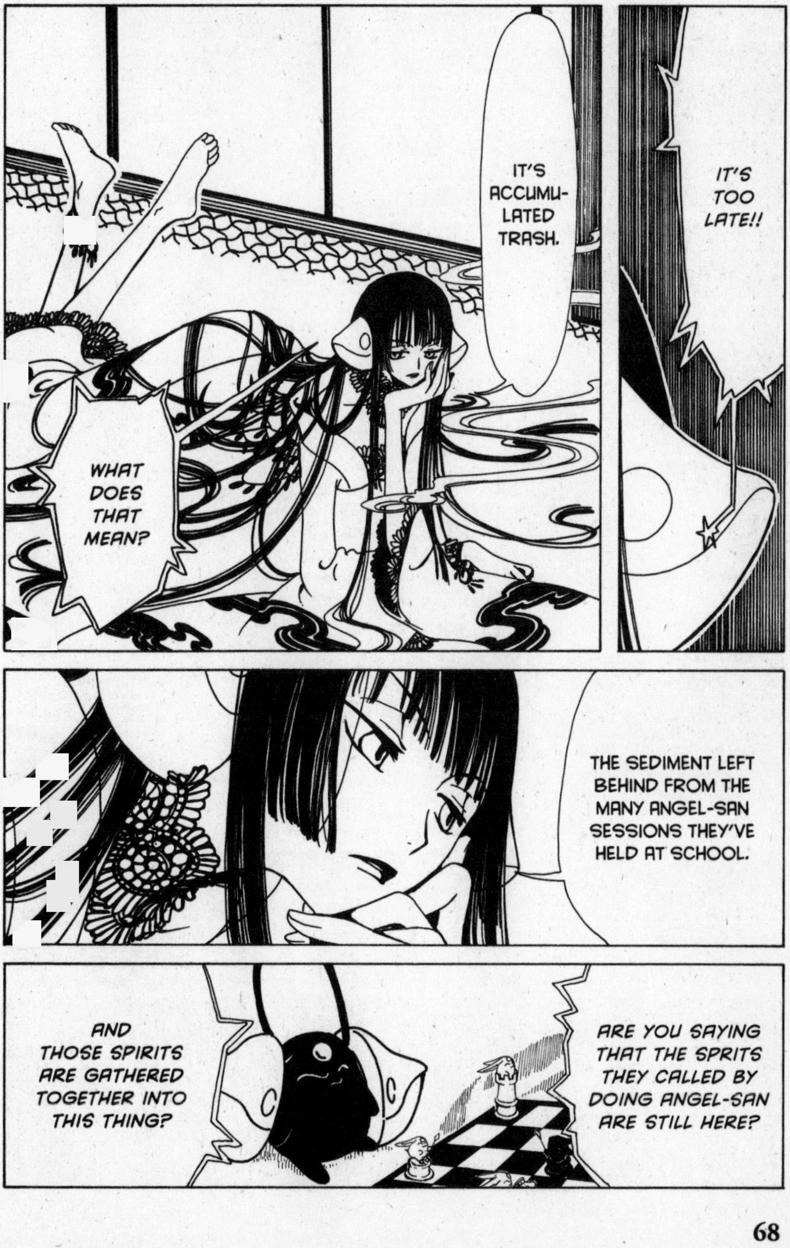
IT'S TOO LATE!!
IT'S ACCUMU-LATED TRASH.
WHAT DOES THAT MEAN?
THE SEDIMENT LEFT BEHIND FROM THE MANY ANGEL-SAN SESSIONS THEY'VE HELD AT SCHOOL.
ARE YOU SAYING THAT THE SPRITS THEY CALLED BY DOING ANGEL-SAN ARE STILL HERE?
AND THOSE SPIRITS ARE GATHERED TOGETHER INTO THIS THING?

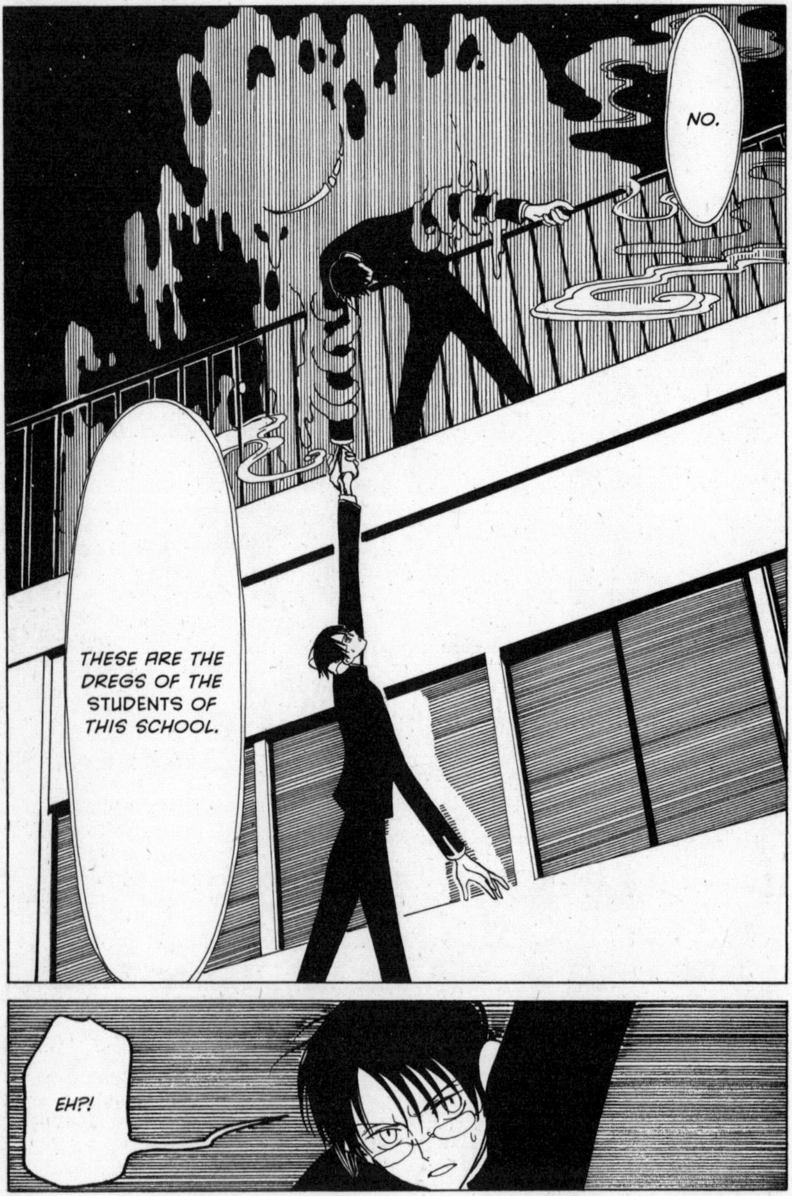
NO.
THESE ARE THE DREGS OF THE STUDENTS OF THIS SCHOOL.
EH?!

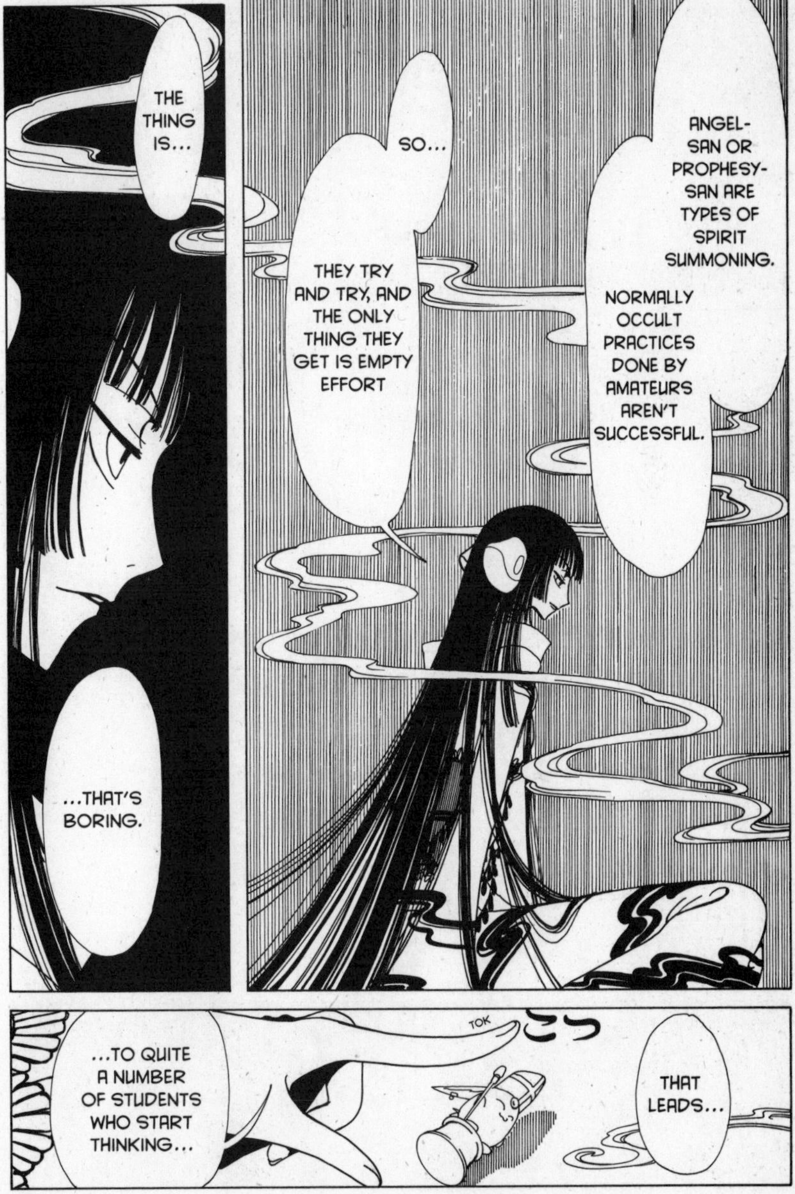
ANGEL-SAN OR PROPHESY-SAN ARE TYPES OF SPIRIT SUMMONING.
NORMALLY OCCULT PRACTICES DONE BY AMATEURS AREN'T SUCCESSFUL.
SO...
THEY TRY AND TRY, AND THE ONLY THING THEY GET IS EMPTY EFFORT
THE THING IS...
...THAT'S BORING.
THAT LEADS...
TOK
...TO QUITE A NUMBER OF STUDENTS WHO START THINKING...

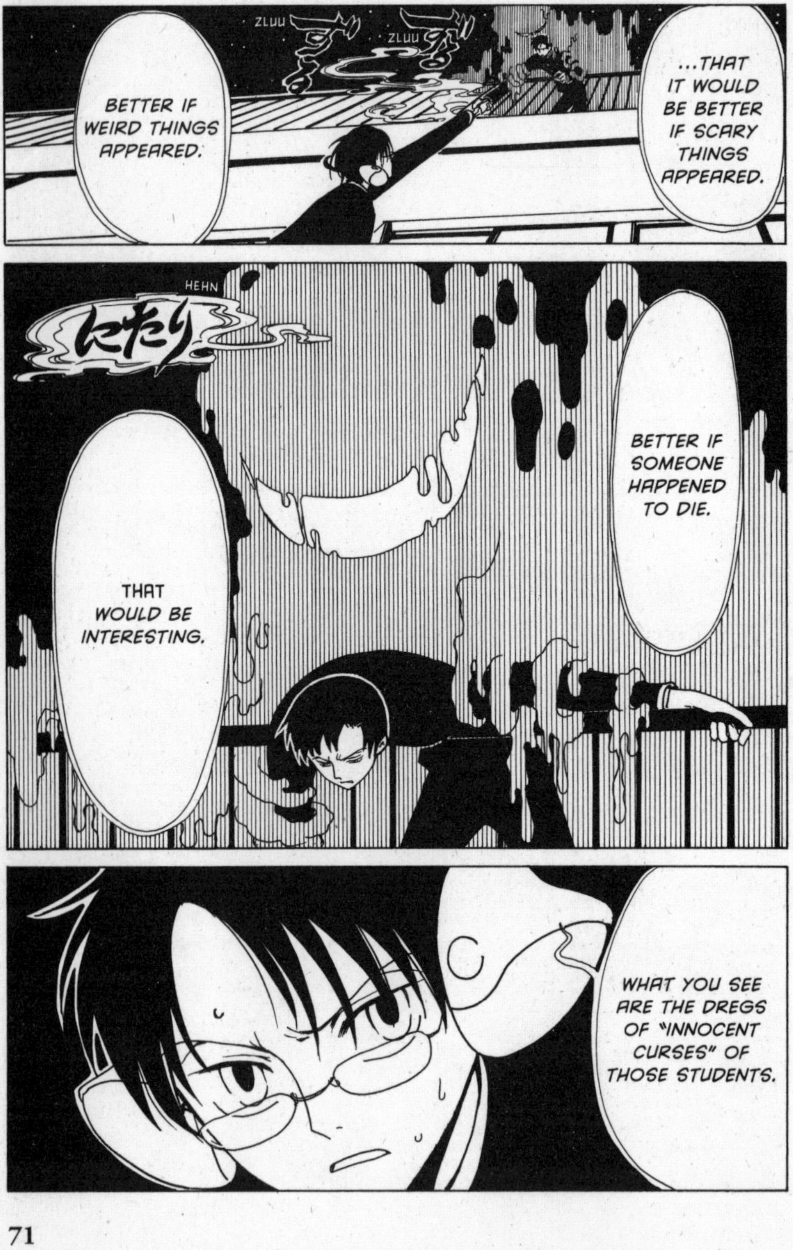
...THAT IT WOULD BE BETTER IF SCARY THINGS APPEARED.
ZLUU
ZLUU
BETTER IF WEIRD THINGS APPEARED.
BETTER IF SOMEONE HAPPENED TO DIE.
HEHN
にたり
THAT WOULD BE INTERESTING.
WHAT YOU SEE ARE THE DREGS OF "INNOCENT CURSES" OF THOSE STUDENTS.

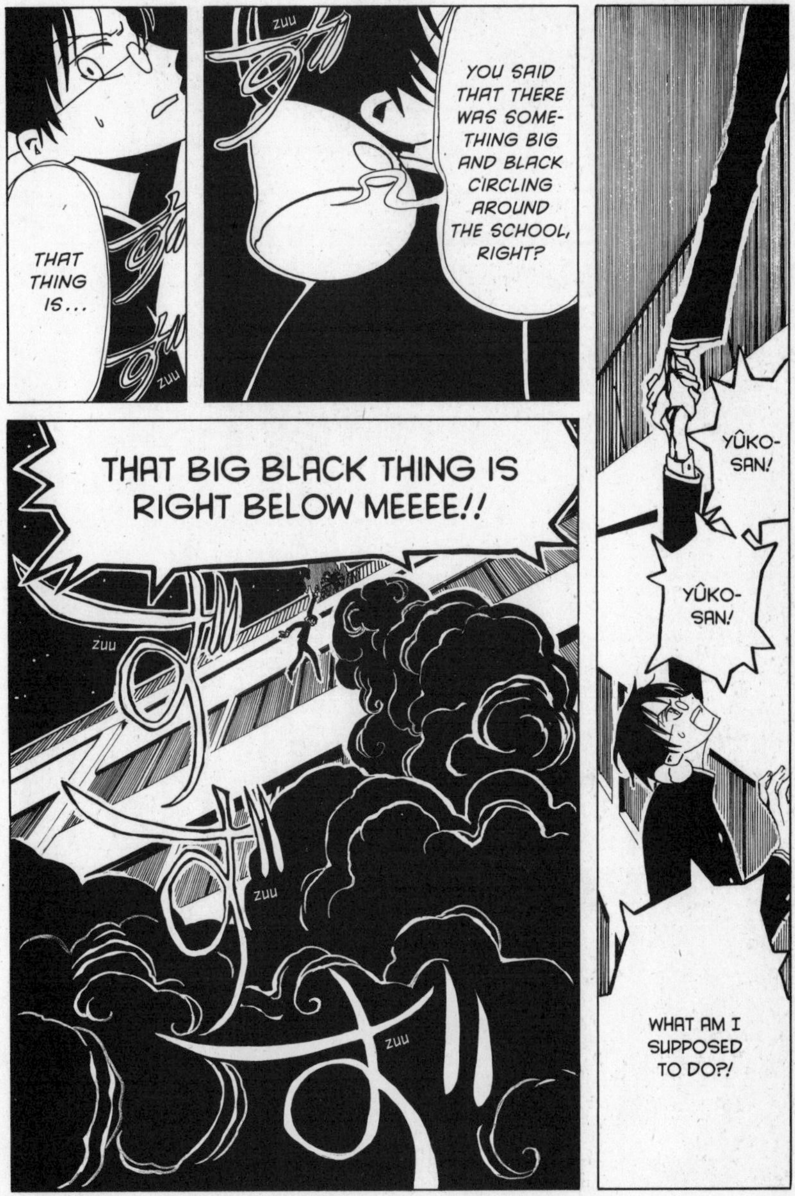
YÛKO-SAN!
YÛKO-SAN!
WHAT AM I SUPPOSED TO DO?!
ZUU
YOU SAID THAT THERE WAS SOMETHING BIG AND BLACK CIRCLING AROUND THE SCHOOL, RIGHT?
THAT THING IS...
ZUU
THAT BIG BLACK THING IS RIGHT BELOW MEEEE!!
ZUU
ZUU
ZUU

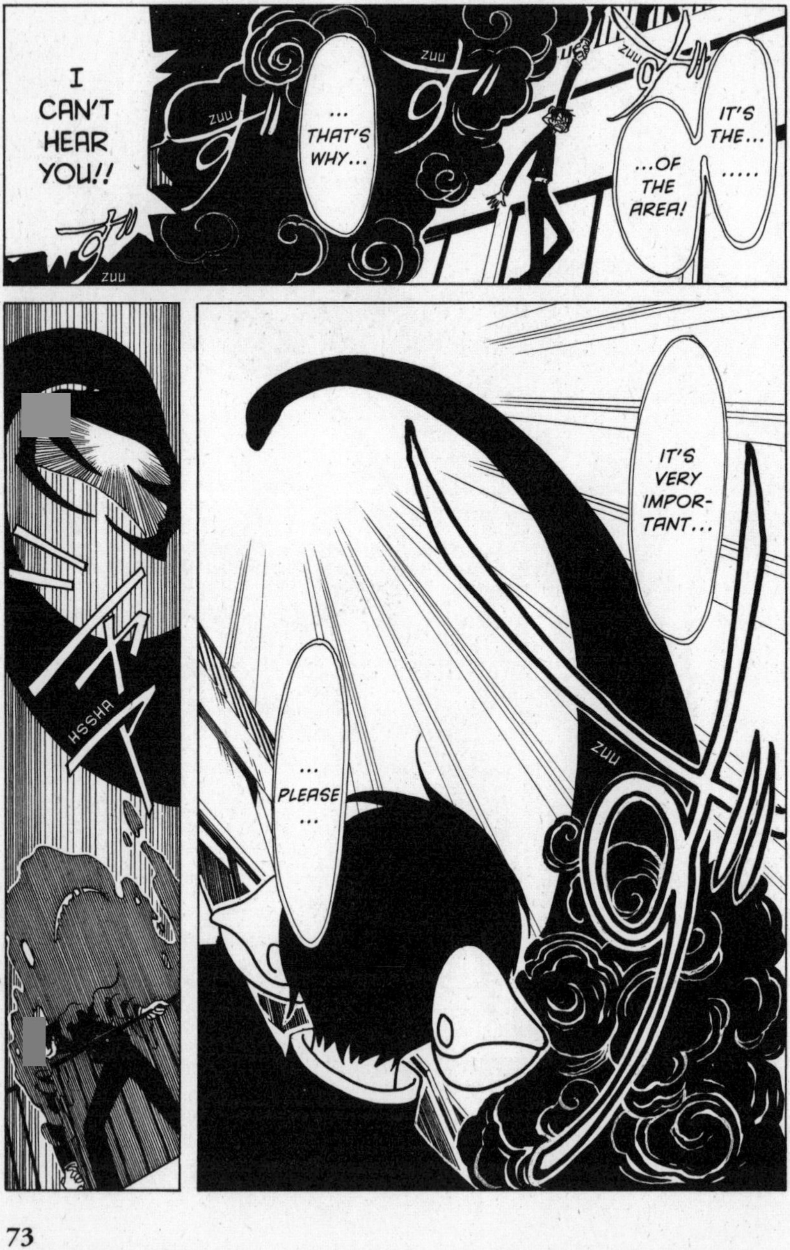
ZUU
IT'S THE... .....
...OF THE AREA!
ZUU
... THAT'S WHY...
ZUU
I CAN'T HEAR YOU!!
ZUU
IT'S VERY IMPORTANT...
ZUU
... PLEASE ...
HSSHA

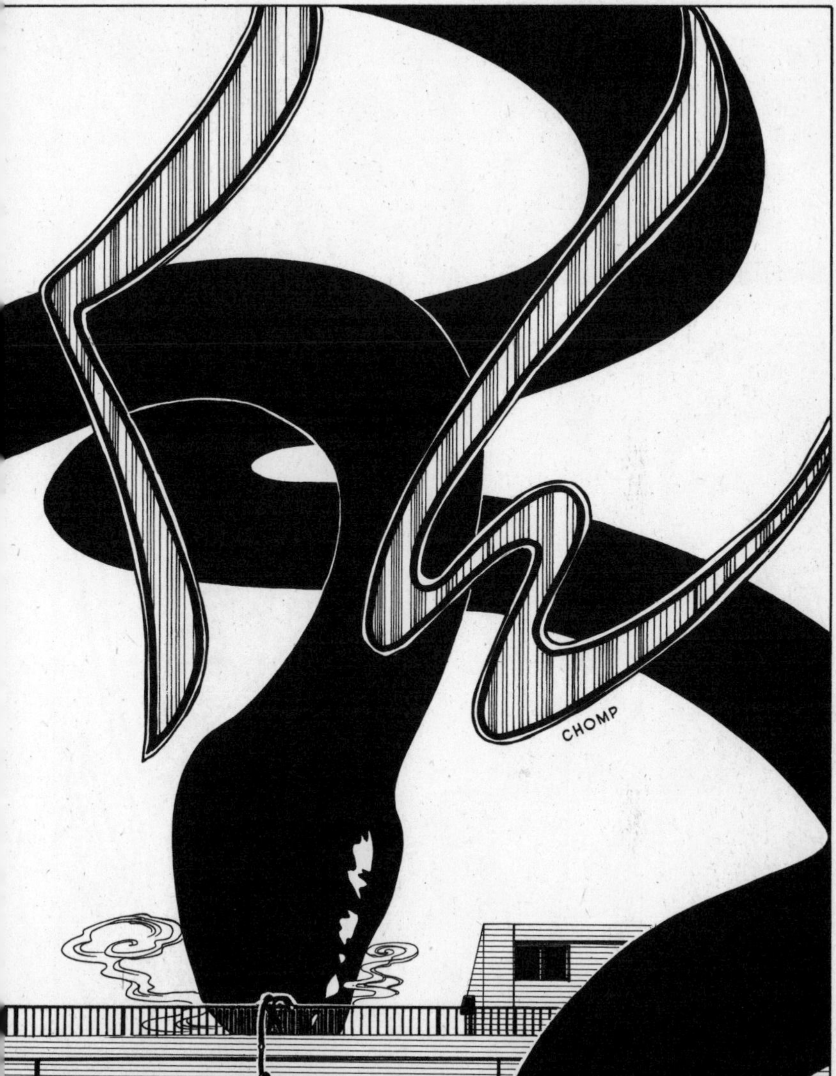
CHOMP

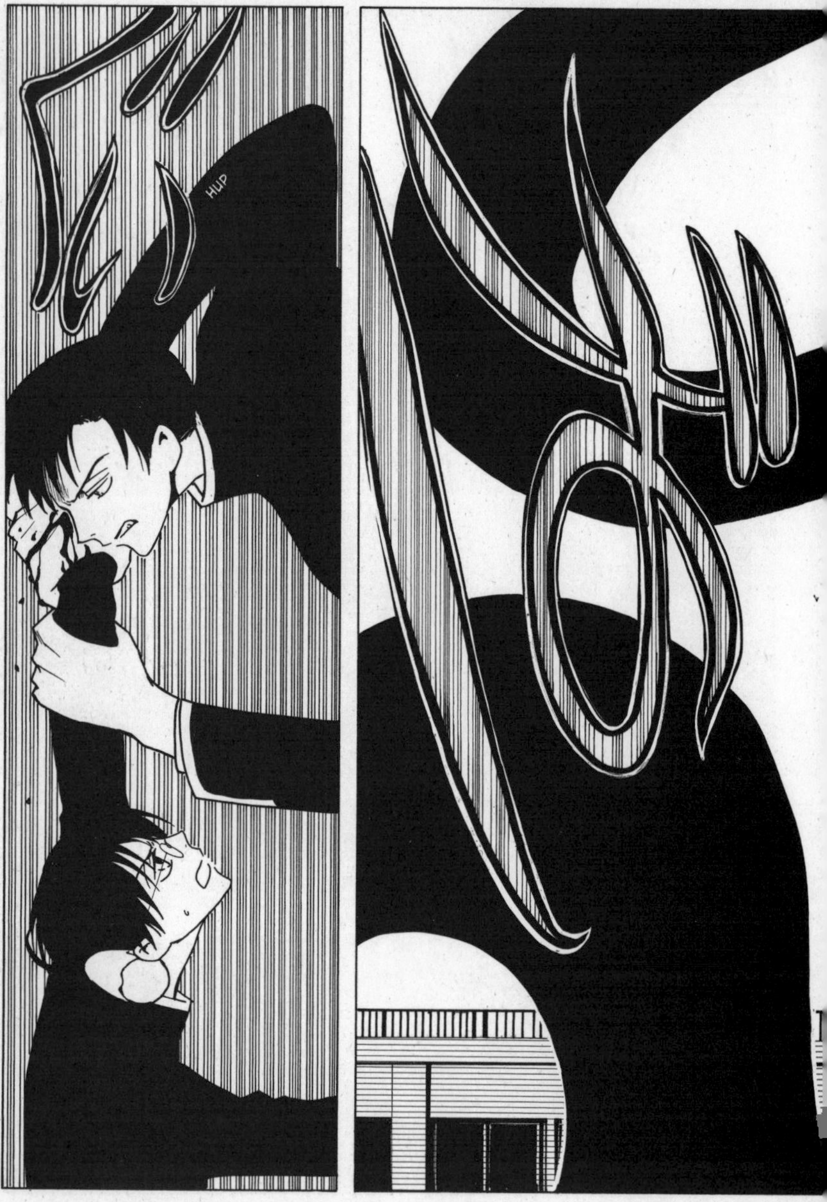
HUP

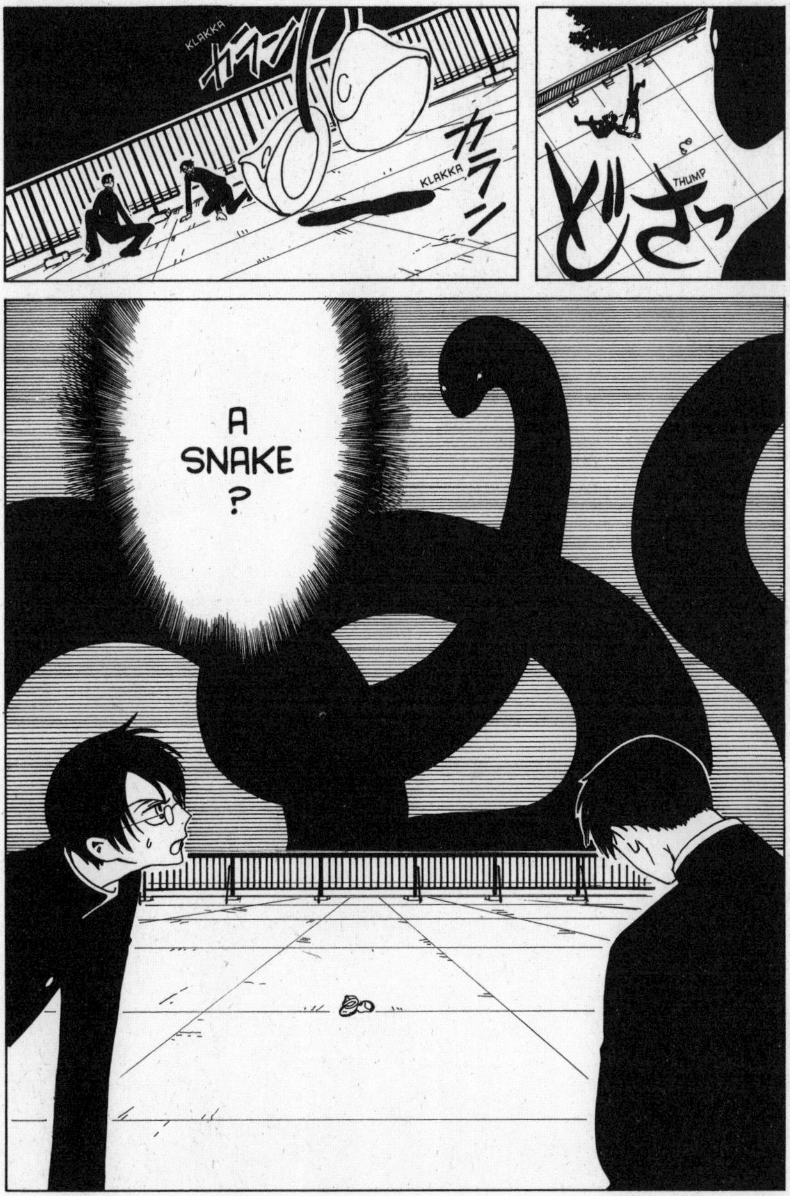
どさっ
THUMP
カラン
KLAKKA
カラン
KLAKKA
A SNAKE ?

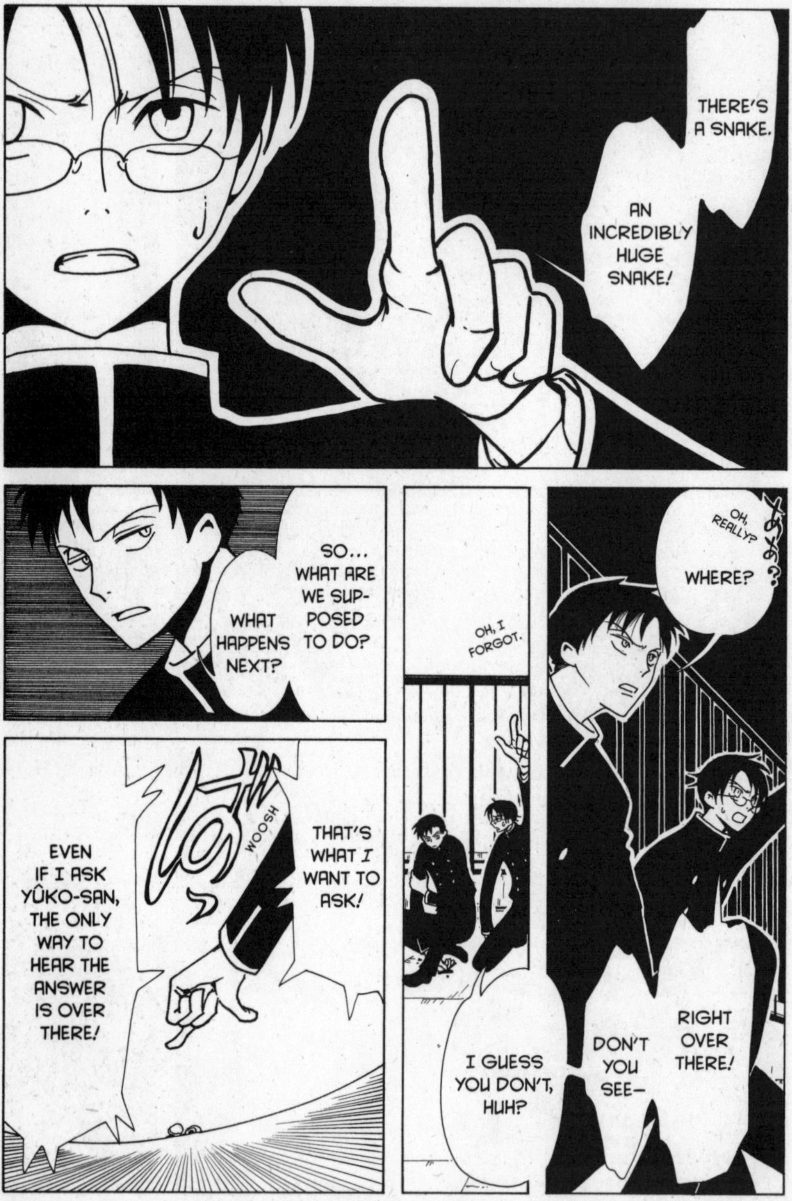
THERE'S A SNAKE.
AN INCREDIBLY HUGE SNAKE!
OH, REALLY?
WHERE?
RIGHT OVER THERE!
DON'T YOU SEE—
OH, I FORGOT.
I GUESS YOU DON'T, HUH?
SO... WHAT ARE WE SUP-POSED TO DO?
WHAT HAPPENS NEXT?
THAT'S WHAT *I* WANT TO ASK!
WOOSH
EVEN IF I ASK YÛKO-SAN, THE ONLY WAY TO HEAR THE ANSWER IS OVER THERE!

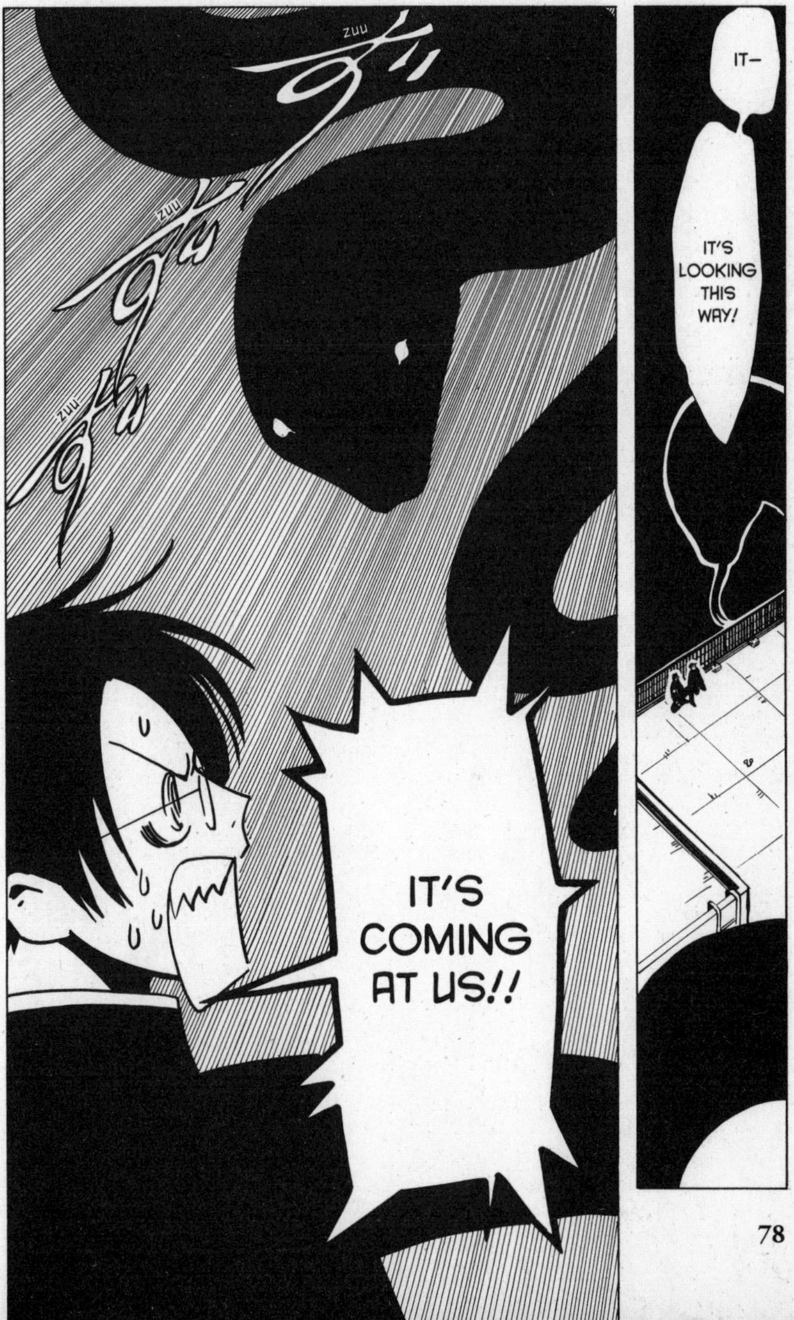
IT—
IT'S LOOKING THIS WAY!
ZUU
ZUU
ZUU
IT'S COMING AT US!!

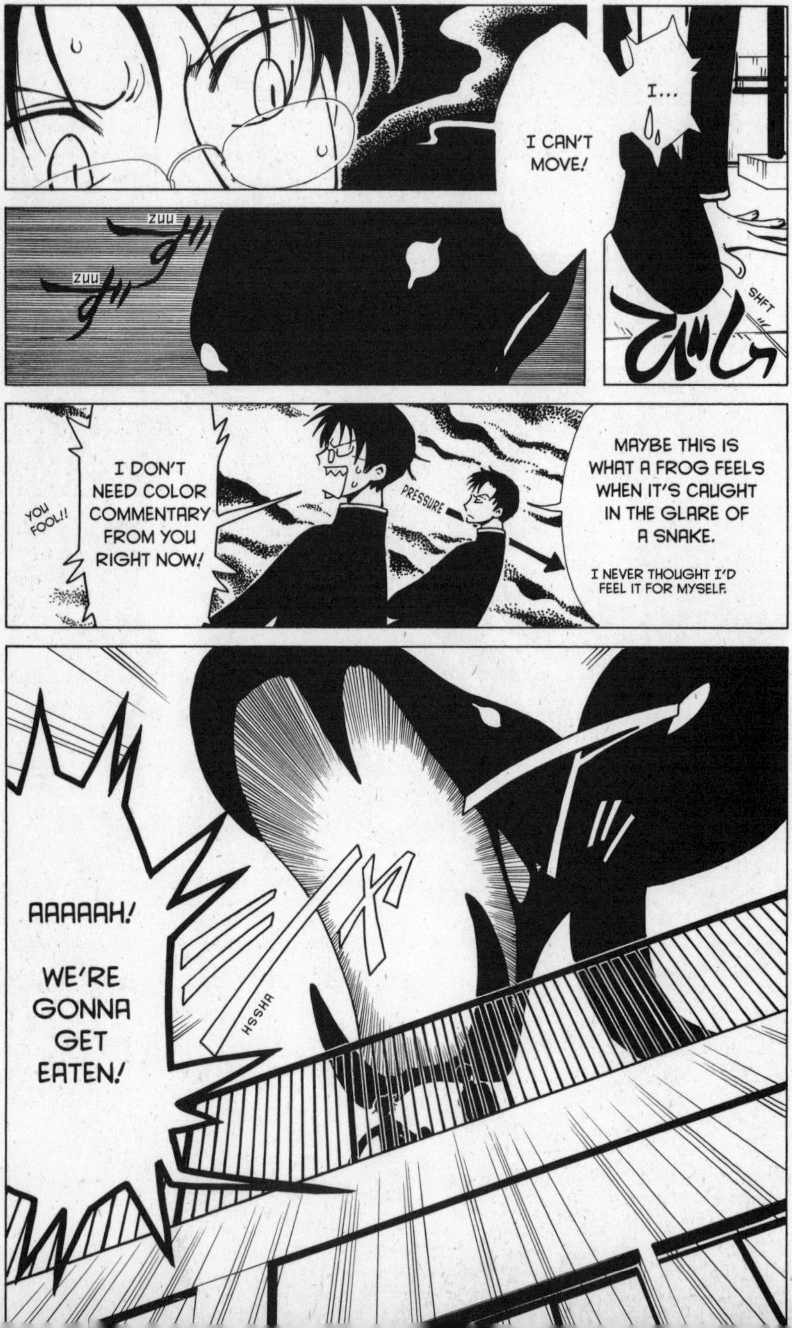
I...
I CAN'T MOVE!
SHFT
ZUU
ZUU
MAYBE THIS IS WHAT A FROG FEELS WHEN IT'S CAUGHT IN THE GLARE OF A SNAKE.
I NEVER THOUGHT I'D FEEL IT FOR MYSELF.
PRESSURE
YOU FOOL!!
I DON'T NEED COLOR COMMENTARY FROM YOU RIGHT NOW!
HSSHA
AAAAAH!
WE'RE GONNA GET EATEN!

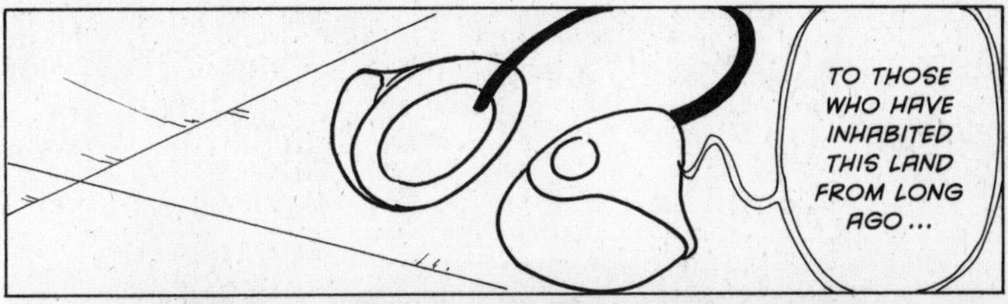
TO THOSE WHO HAVE INHABITED THIS LAND FROM LONG AGO...

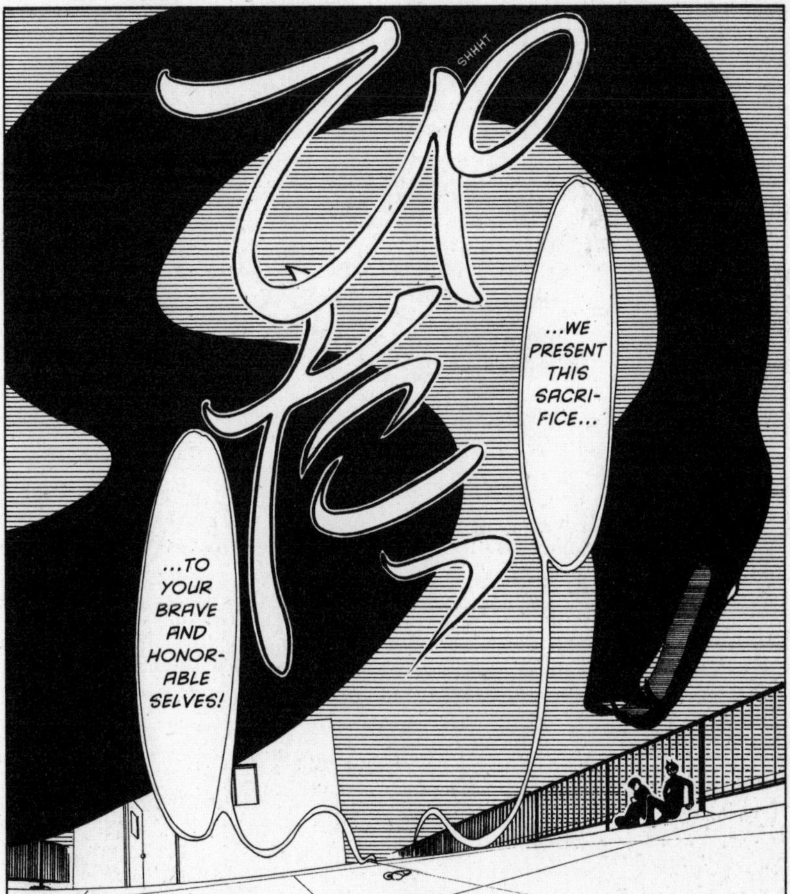
SHHHT
...WE PRESENT THIS SACRI-FICE...
...TO YOUR BRAVE AND HONOR-ABLE SELVES!

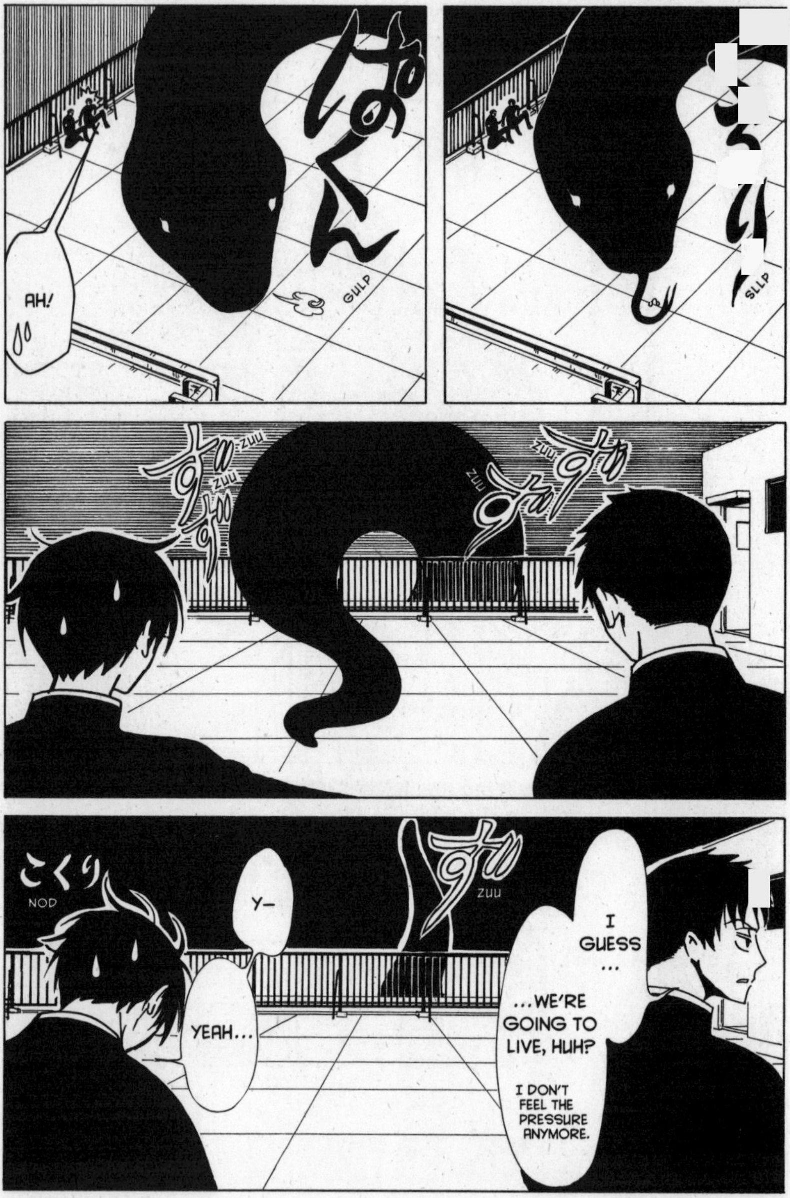
SLLP
ぱくん
GULP
AH!
ZUU
ZUU
ZUU
ZUU
I GUESS...
...WE'RE GOING TO LIVE, HUH?
I DON'T FEEL THE PRESSURE ANYMORE.
ZUU
Y—
YEAH...
こくり
NOD

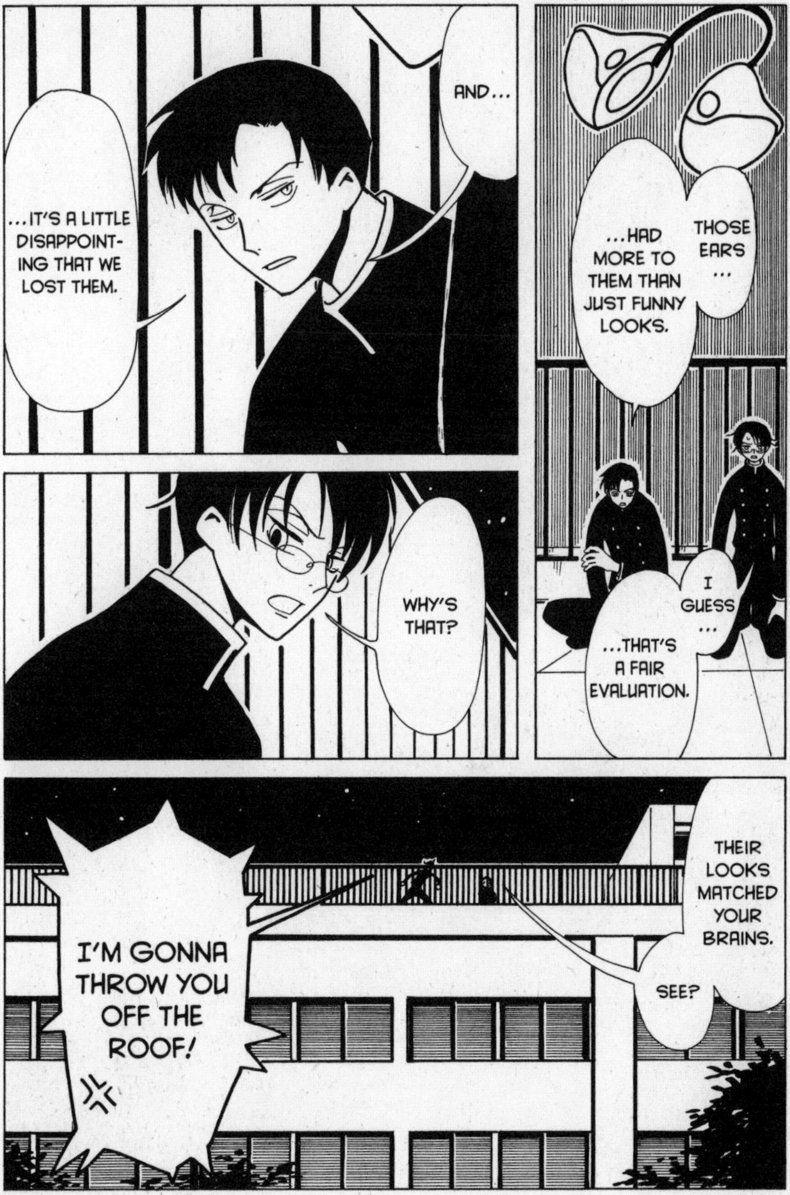
THOSE EARS...
...HAD MORE TO THEM THAN JUST FUNNY LOOKS.
I GUESS...
...THAT'S A FAIR EVALUATION.
AND...
...IT'S A LITTLE DISAPPOINTING-ING THAT WE LOST THEM.
WHY'S THAT?
THEIR LOOKS MATCHED YOUR BRAINS.
SEE?
I'M GONNA THROW YOU OFF THE ROOF!

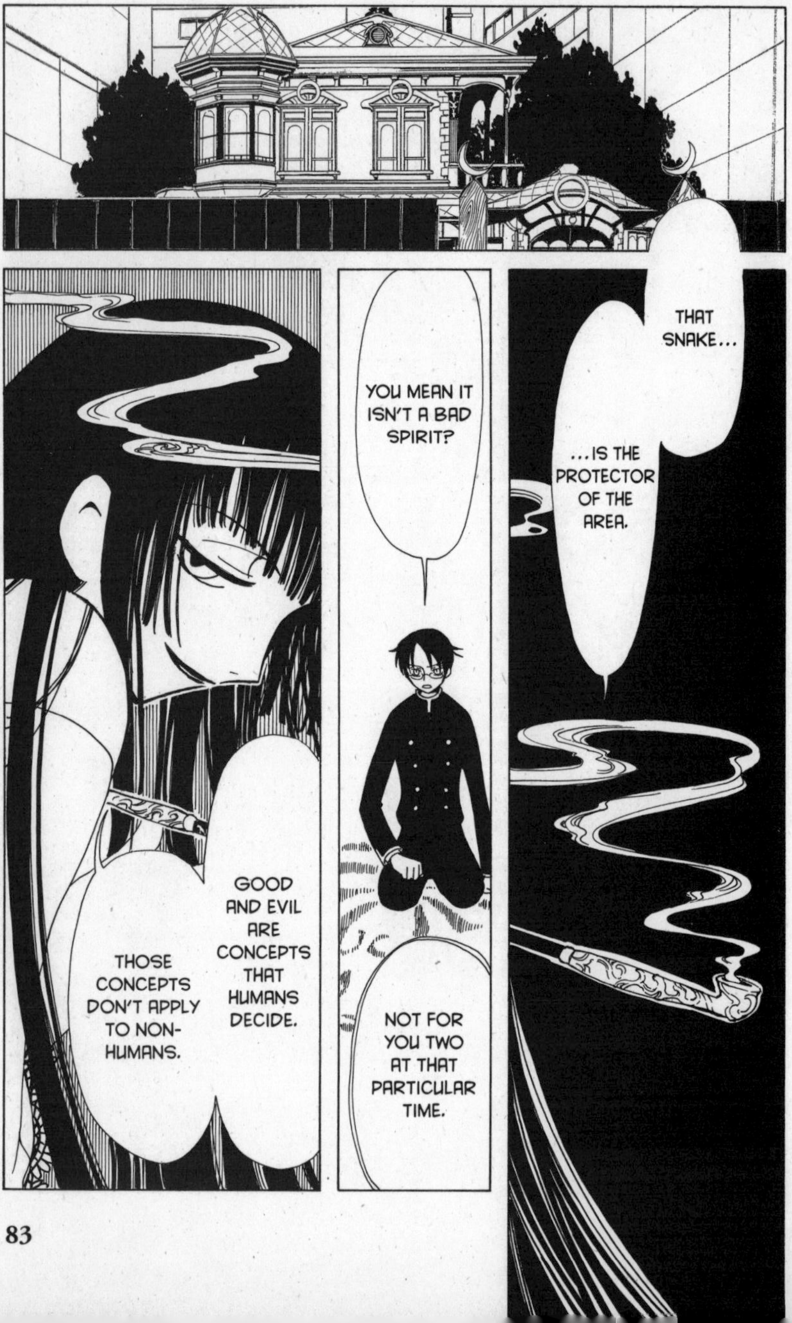
THAT SNAKE...
...IS THE PROTECTOR OF THE AREA.
YOU MEAN IT ISN'T A BAD SPIRIT?
NOT FOR YOU TWO AT THAT PARTICULAR TIME.
GOOD AND EVIL ARE CONCEPTS THAT HUMANS DECIDE.
THOSE CONCEPTS DON'T APPLY TO NON-HUMANS.

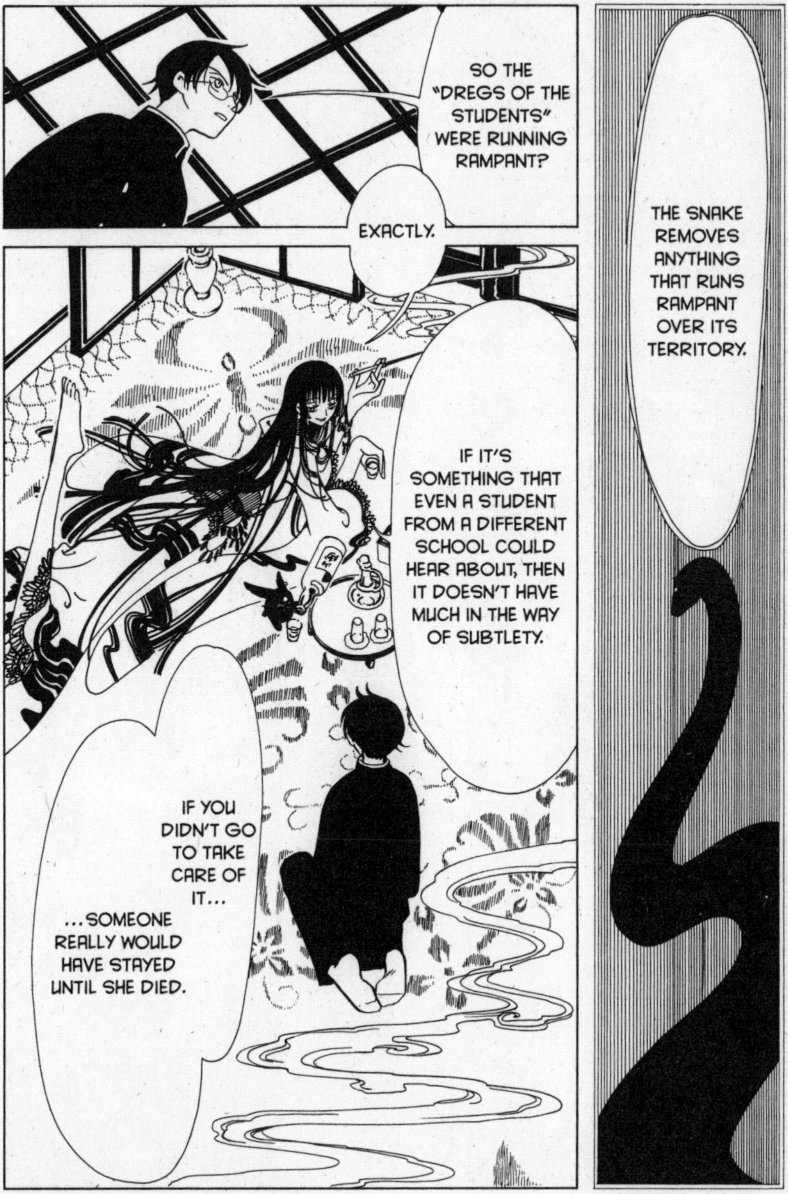
THE SNAKE REMOVES ANYTHING THAT RUNS RAMPANT OVER ITS TERRITORY.
SO THE "DREGS OF THE STUDENTS" WERE RUNNING RAMPANT?
EXACTLY.
IF IT'S SOMETHING THAT EVEN A STUDENT FROM A DIFFERENT SCHOOL COULD HEAR ABOUT, THEN IT DOESN'T HAVE MUCH IN THE WAY OF SUBTLETY.
IF YOU DIDN'T GO TO TAKE CARE OF IT...
...SOMEONE REALLY WOULD HAVE STAYED UNTIL SHE DIED.

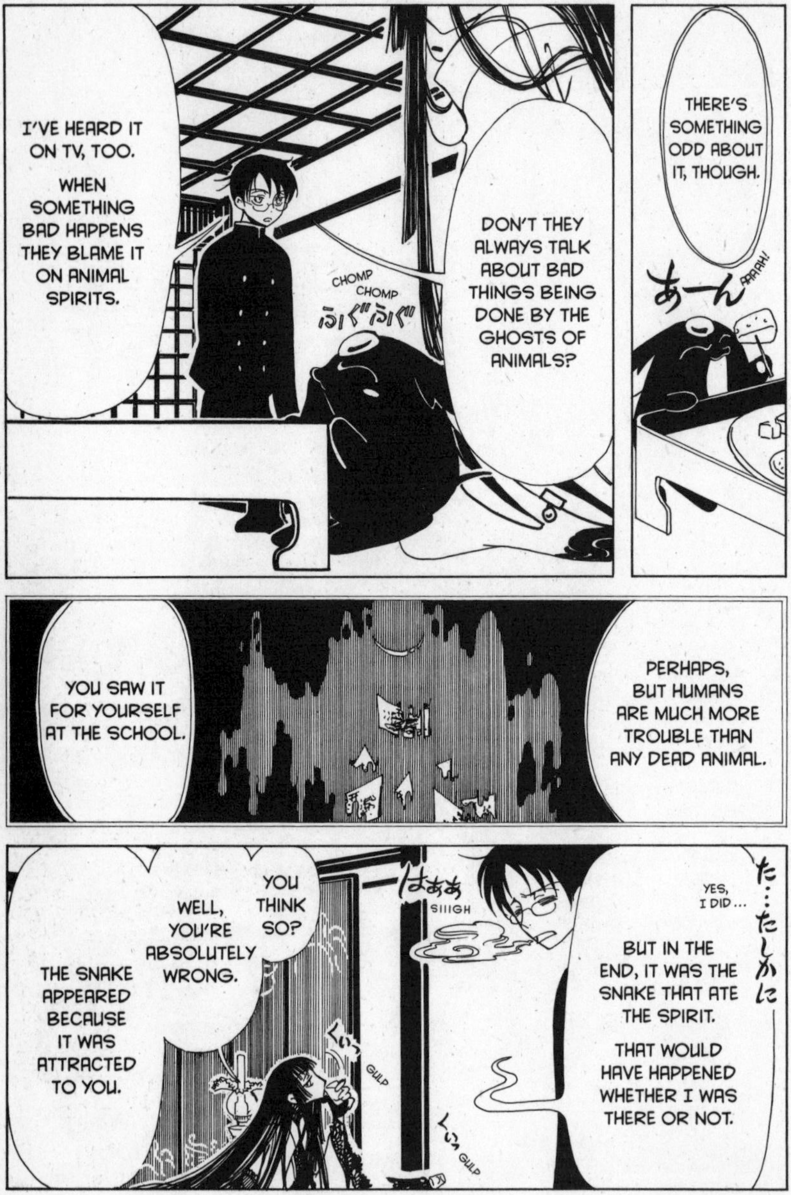
THERE'S SOMETHING ODD ABOUT IT, THOUGH.
あーん
AAAAH!
DON'T THEY ALWAYS TALK ABOUT BAD THINGS BEING DONE BY THE GHOSTS OF ANIMALS?
CHOMP CHOMP
ふぐふぐ
I'VE HEARD IT ON TV, TOO.
WHEN SOMETHING BAD HAPPENS THEY BLAME IT ON ANIMAL SPIRITS.
PERHAPS, BUT HUMANS ARE MUCH MORE TROUBLE THAN ANY DEAD ANIMAL.
YOU SAW IT FOR YOURSELF AT THE SCHOOL.
た…たしかに
YES, I DID...
BUT IN THE END, IT WAS THE SNAKE THAT ATE THE SPIRIT.
THAT WOULD HAVE HAPPENED WHETHER I WAS THERE OR NOT.
はぁあ
SIIIGH
YOU THINK SO?
WELL, YOU'RE ABSOLUTELY WRONG.
くいっ
GULP
THE SNAKE APPEARED BECAUSE IT WAS ATTRACTED TO YOU.
くいっ
GULP

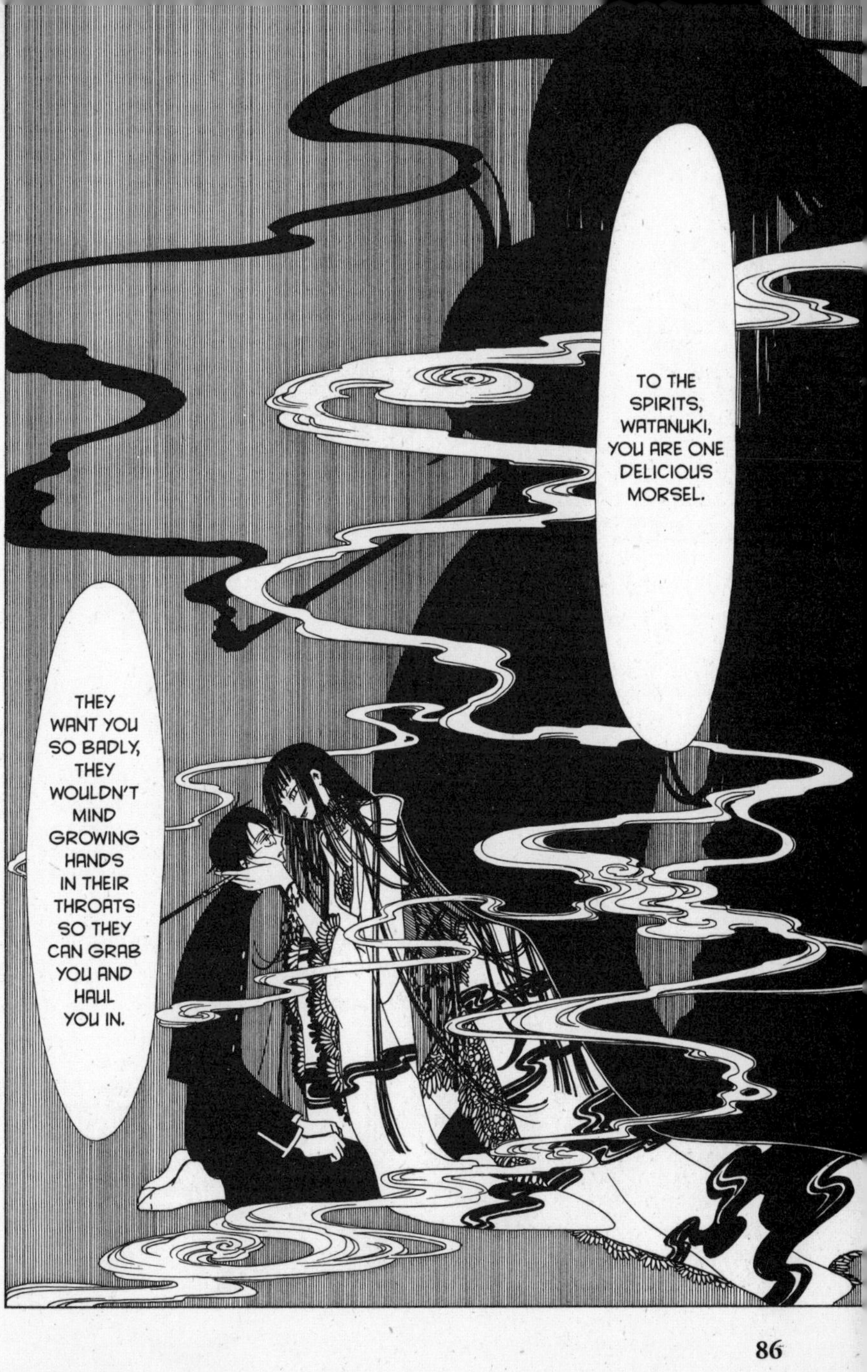
TO THE SPIRITS, WATANUKI, YOU ARE ONE DELICIOUS MORSEL.
THEY WANT YOU SO BADLY, THEY WOULDN'T MIND GROWING HANDS IN THEIR THROATS SO THEY CAN GRAB YOU AND HAUL YOU IN.

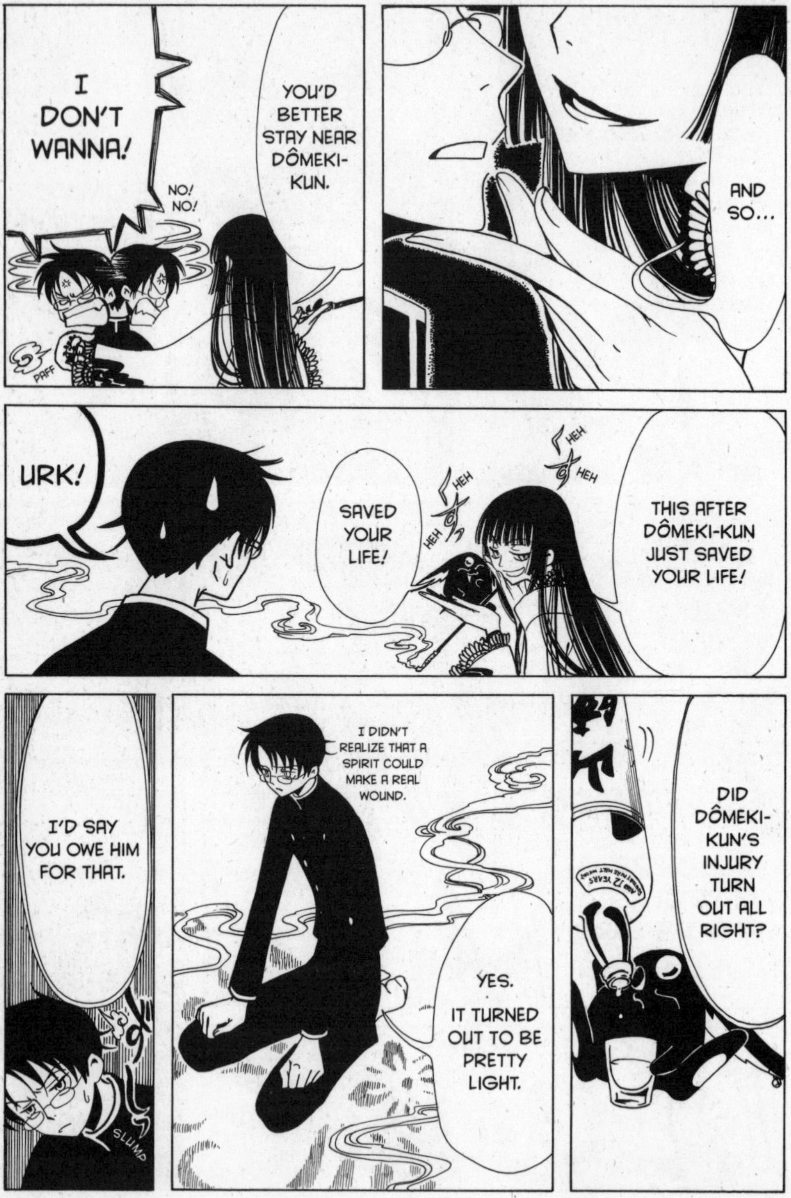
AND SO...
YOU'D BETTER STAY NEAR DÔMEKI-KUN.
I DON'T WANNA!
NO! NO!
PAFF
THIS AFTER DÔMEKI-KUN JUST SAVED YOUR LIFE!
HEH HEH
HEH HEH
SAVED YOUR LIFE!
URK!
DID DÔMEKI-KUN'S INJURY TURN OUT ALL RIGHT?
YES.
IT TURNED OUT TO BE PRETTY LIGHT.
I DIDN'T REALIZE THAT A SPIRIT COULD MAKE A REAL WOUND.
I'D SAY YOU OWE HIM FOR THAT.
SLUMP

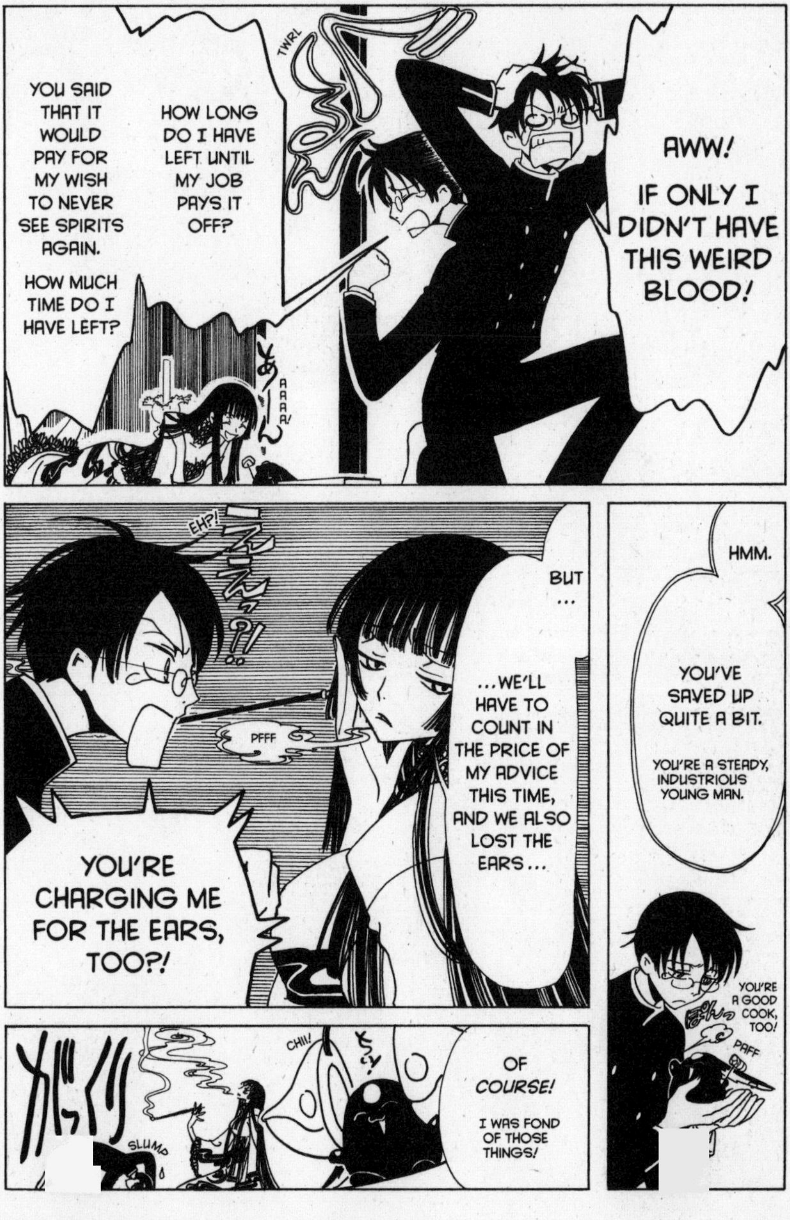
AWW!
IF ONLY I DIDN'T HAVE THIS WEIRD BLOOD!
TWRL
HOW LONG DO I HAVE LEFT UNTIL MY JOB PAYS IT OFF?
YOU SAID THAT IT WOULD PAY FOR MY WISH TO NEVER SEE SPIRITS AGAIN.
HOW MUCH TIME DO I HAVE LEFT?
AAAA!
HMM.
YOU'VE SAVED UP QUITE A BIT.
YOU'RE A STEADY, INDUSTRIOUS YOUNG MAN.
YOU'RE A GOOD COOK, TOO!
PAFF
BUT ...
...WE'LL HAVE TO COUNT IN THE PRICE OF MY ADVICE THIS TIME, AND WE ALSO LOST THE EARS...
EH?!
PFFF
YOU'RE CHARGING ME FOR THE EARS, TOO?!
OF COURSE!
I WAS FOND OF THOSE THINGS!
CHII!
SLUMP

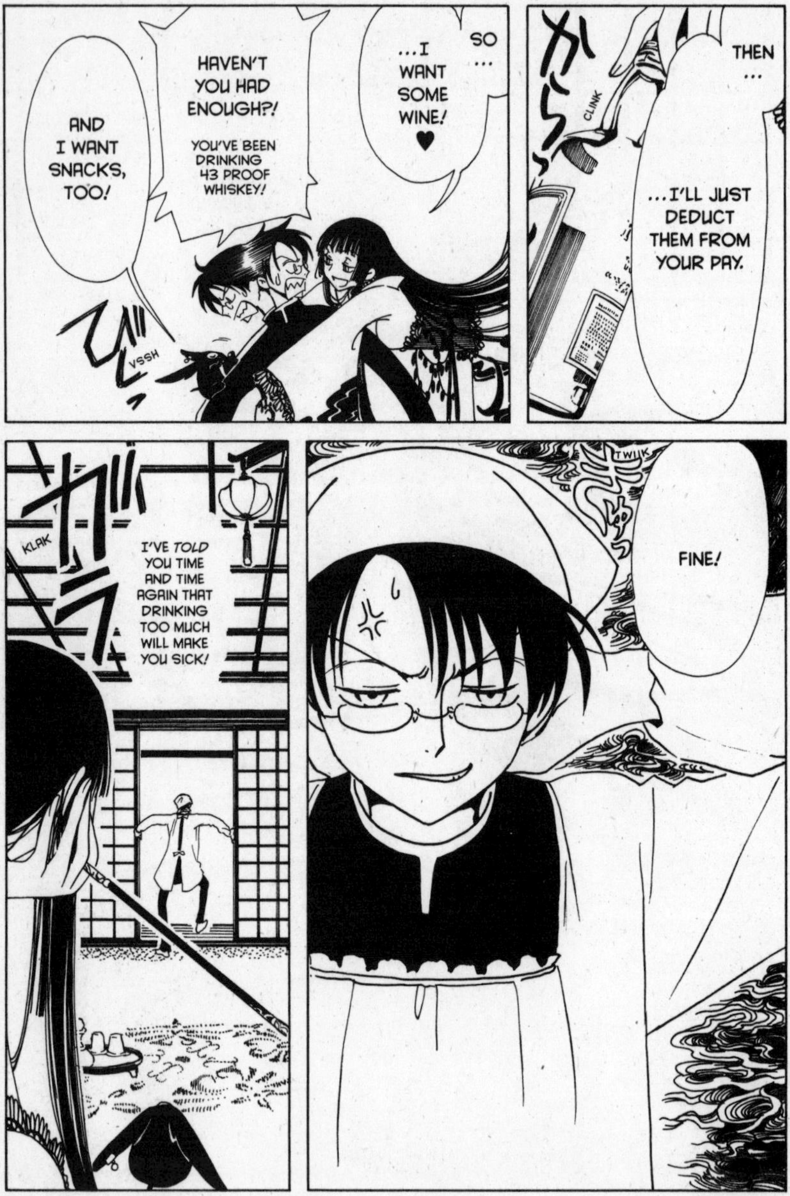
THEN ...
CLINK
...I'LL JUST DEDUCT THEM FROM YOUR PAY.
SO ...
...I WANT SOME WINE! ♥
HAVEN'T YOU HAD ENOUGH?!
YOU'VE BEEN DRINKING 43 PROOF WHISKEY!
AND I WANT SNACKS, TOO!
VSSH
TWIIK
FINE!
KLAK
I'VE *TOLD* YOU TIME AND TIME AGAIN THAT DRINKING TOO MUCH WILL MAKE YOU SICK!

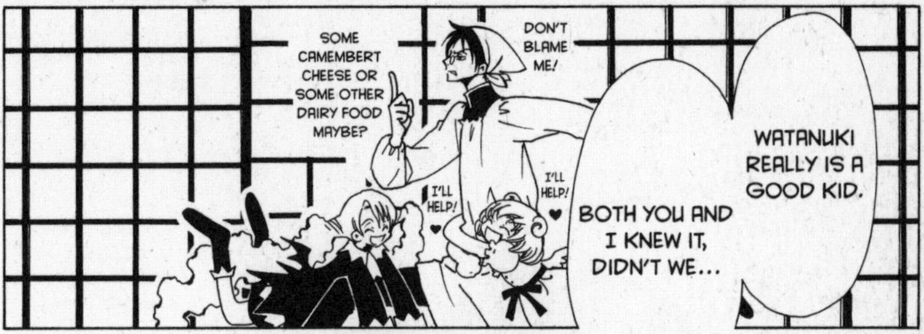
WATANUKI REALLY IS A GOOD KID.
BOTH YOU AND I KNEW IT, DIDN'T WE...
DON'T BLAME ME!
I'LL HELP!
I'LL HELP!
SOME CAMEMBERT CHEESE OR SOME OTHER DAIRY FOOD MAYBE?

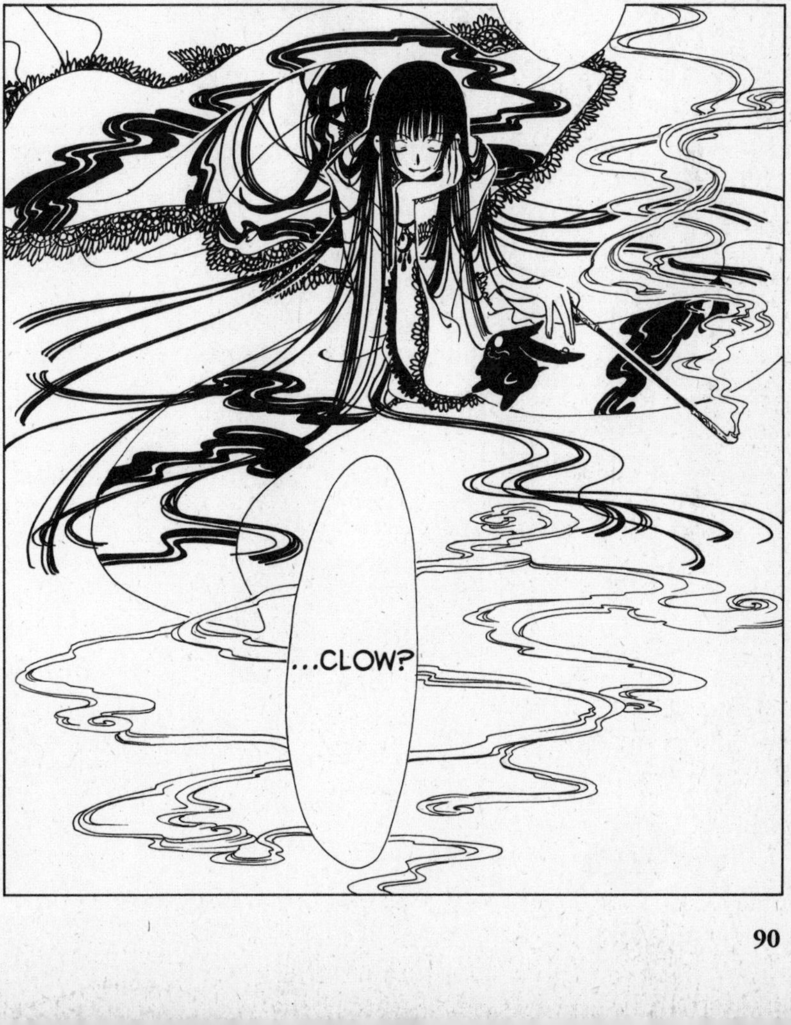
...CLOW?

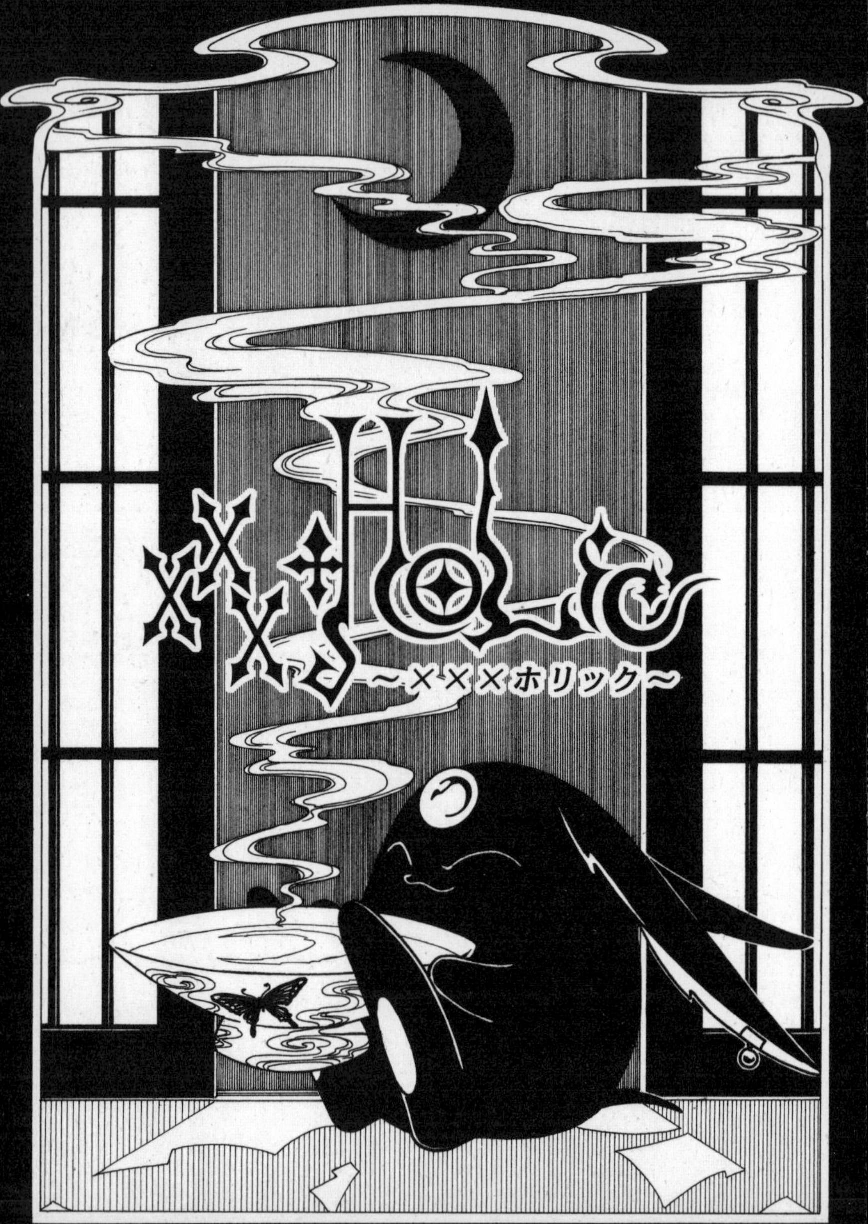
xxxHOLiC
~×××ホリック~

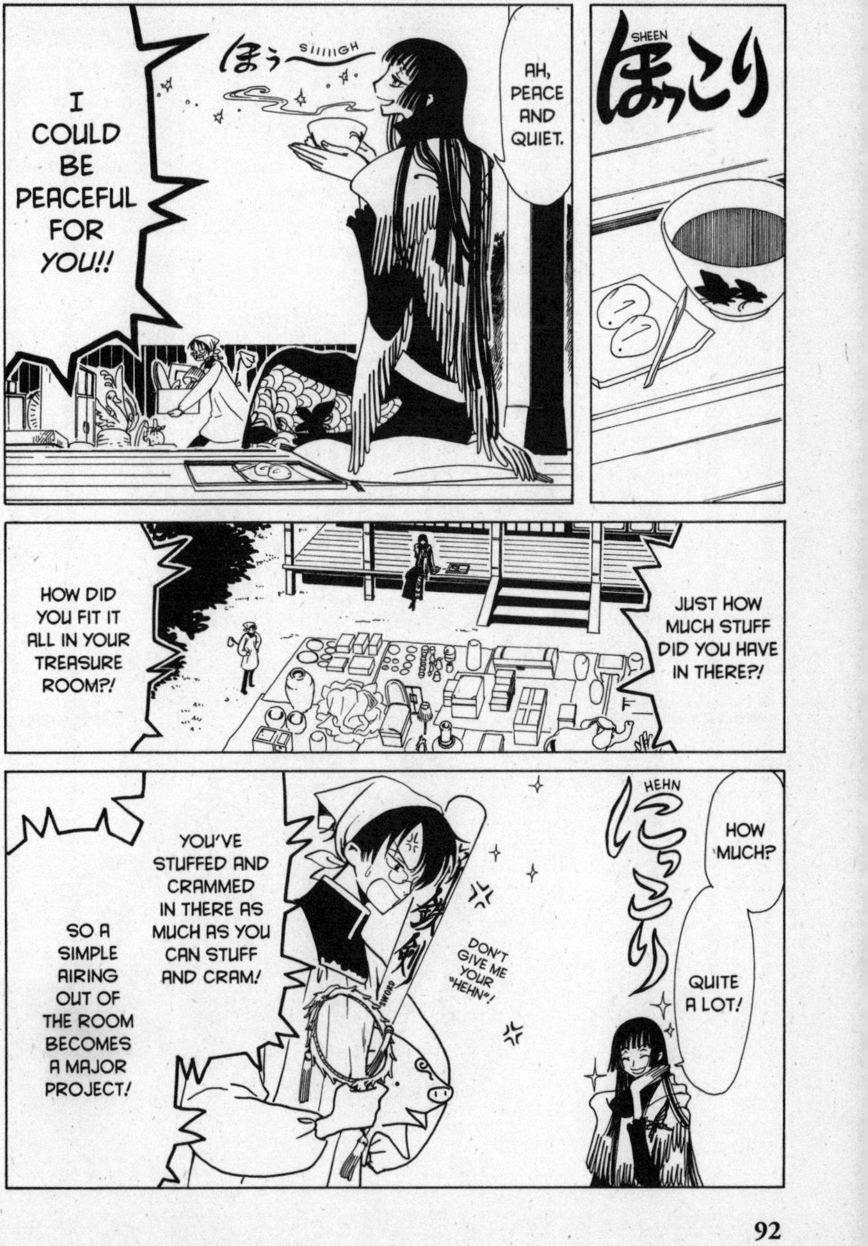
SHEEN
ほっこり
ほぅ~
SIIIIGH
AH, PEACE AND QUIET.
I COULD BE PEACEFUL FOR YOU!!
JUST HOW MUCH STUFF DID YOU HAVE IN THERE?!
HOW DID YOU FIT IT ALL IN YOUR TREASURE ROOM?!
HEHN
にっこり
HOW MUCH?
QUITE A LOT!
DON'T GIVE ME YOUR "HEHN"!
SWORD
YOU'VE STUFFED AND CRAMMED IN THERE AS MUCH AS YOU CAN STUFF AND CRAM!
SO A SIMPLE AIRING OUT OF THE ROOM BECOMES A MAJOR PROJECT!

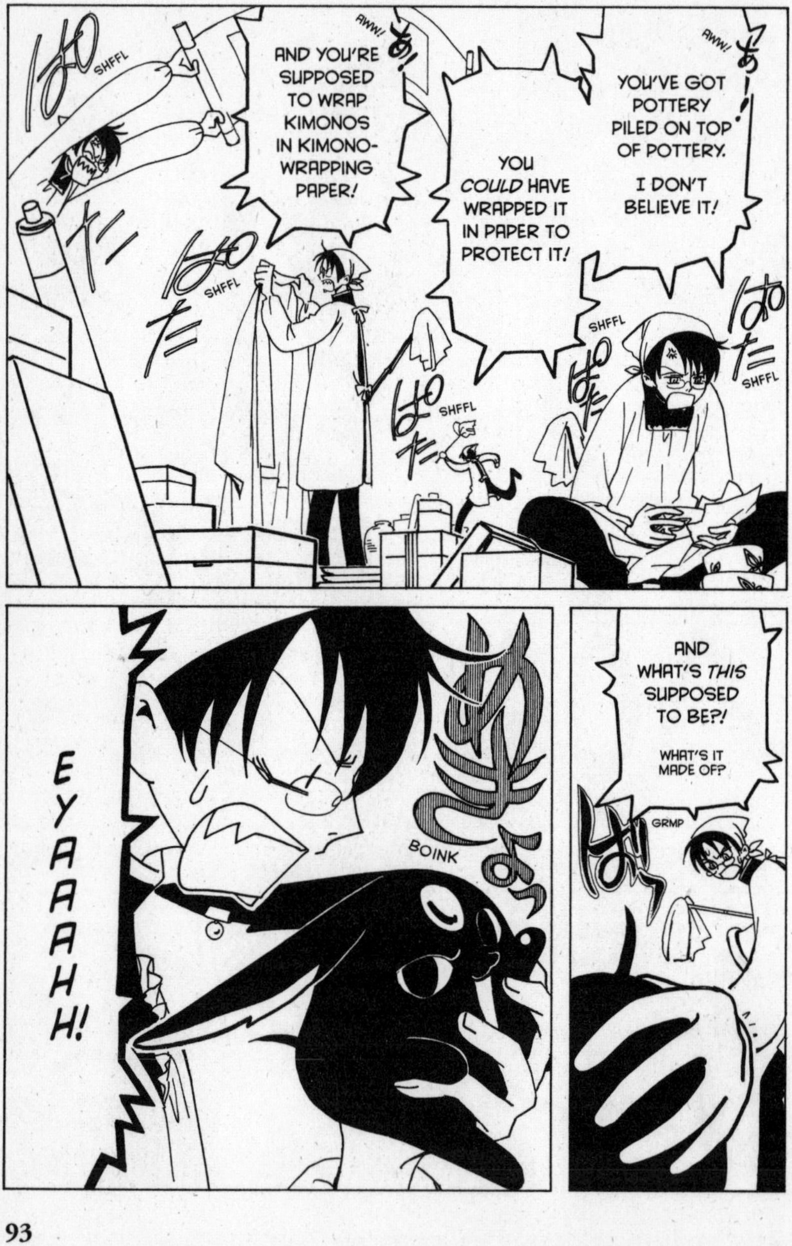
AWW!
YOU'VE GOT POTTERY PILED ON TOP OF POTTERY.
I DON'T BELIEVE IT!
YOU *COULD* HAVE WRAPPED IT IN PAPER TO PROTECT IT!
AWW!
AND YOU'RE SUPPOSED TO WRAP KIMONOS IN KIMONO-WRAPPING PAPER!
SHFFL
SHFFL
SHFFL
SHFFL
SHFFL
AND WHAT'S *THIS* SUPPOSED TO BE?!
WHAT'S IT MADE OF?
GRMP
BOINK
EYAAAAHH!

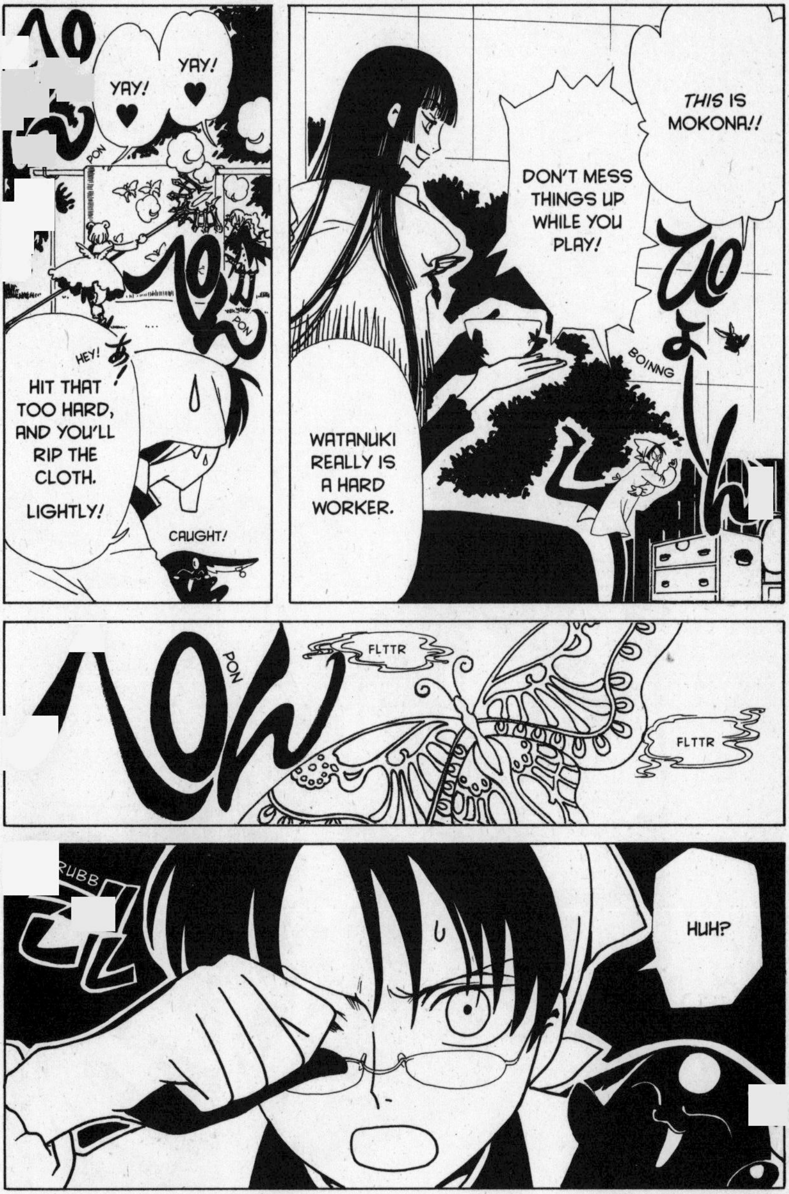
THIS IS MOKONA!!
DON'T MESS THINGS UP WHILE YOU PLAY!
BOINNG
WATANUKI REALLY IS A HARD WORKER.
YAY! ♥
YAY! ♥
PON
PON
HEY!
HIT THAT TOO HARD, AND YOU'LL RIP THE CLOTH.
LIGHTLY!
CAUGHT!
PON
FLTTR
FLTTR
HUH?
RUBB

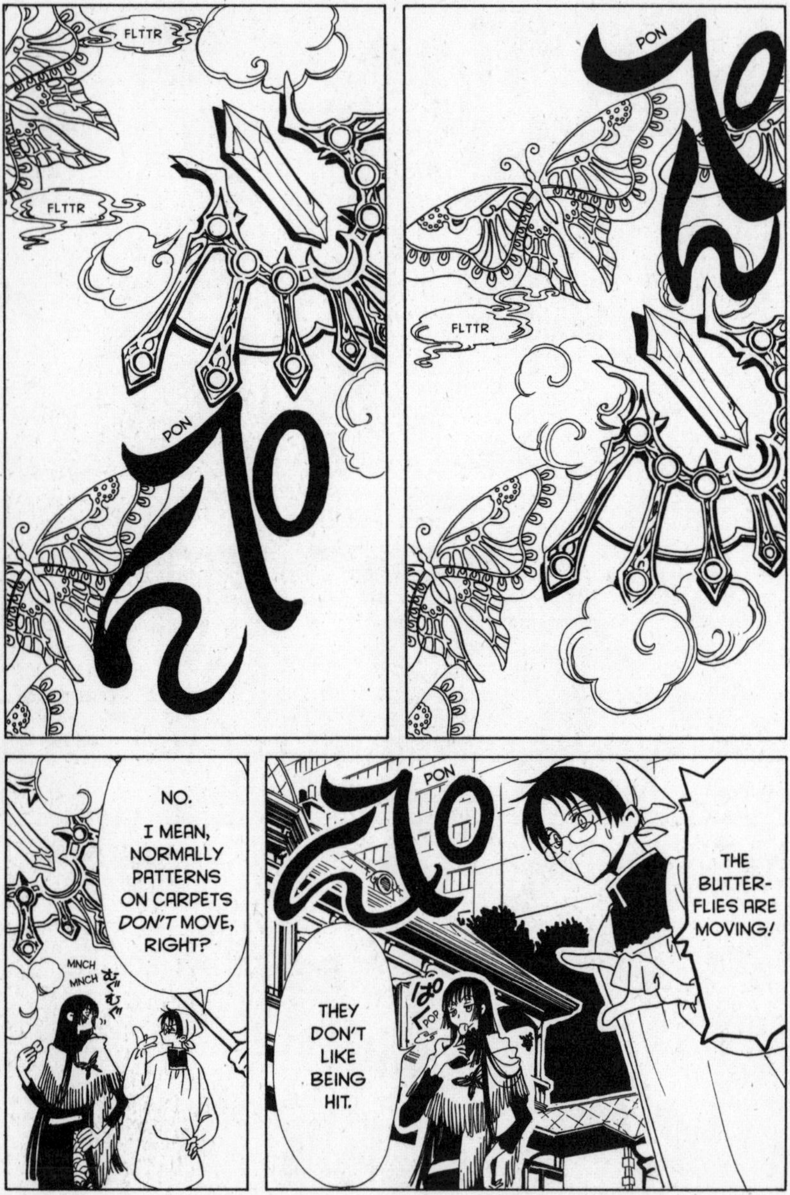
PON
FLTTR
FLTTR
FLTTR
PON
PON
THE BUTTER-FLIES ARE MOVING!
POP
THEY DON'T LIKE BEING HIT.
NO. I MEAN, NORMALLY PATTERNS ON CARPETS *DON'T* MOVE, RIGHT?
MNCH MNCH

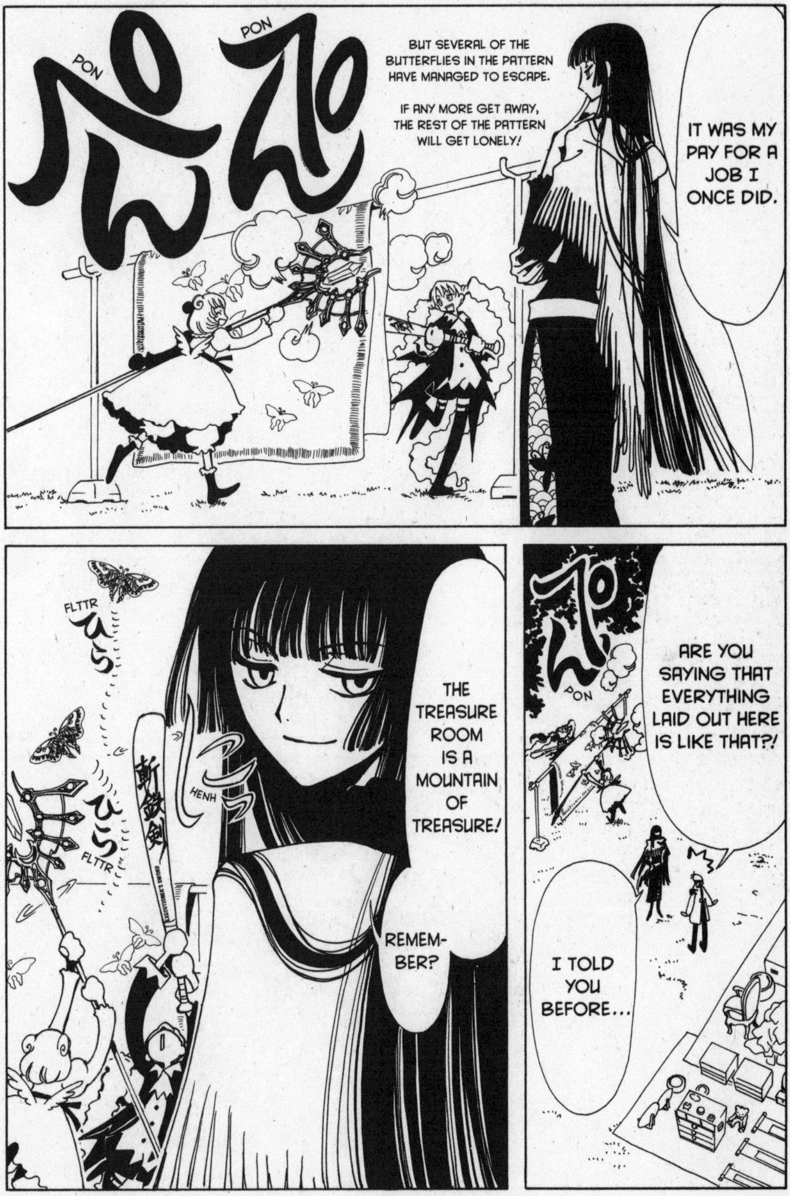
IT WAS MY PAY FOR A JOB I ONCE DID.
BUT SEVERAL OF THE BUTTERFLIES IN THE PATTERN HAVE MANAGED TO ESCAPE.
IF ANY MORE GET AWAY, THE REST OF THE PATTERN WILL GET LONELY!
PON
PON
PON
ARE YOU SAYING THAT EVERYTHING LAID OUT HERE IS LIKE THAT?!
I TOLD YOU BEFORE...
THE TREASURE ROOM IS A MOUNTAIN OF TREASURE!
REMEMBER?
HENH
斬鉄剣
FLTTR ひら
ひら FLTTR

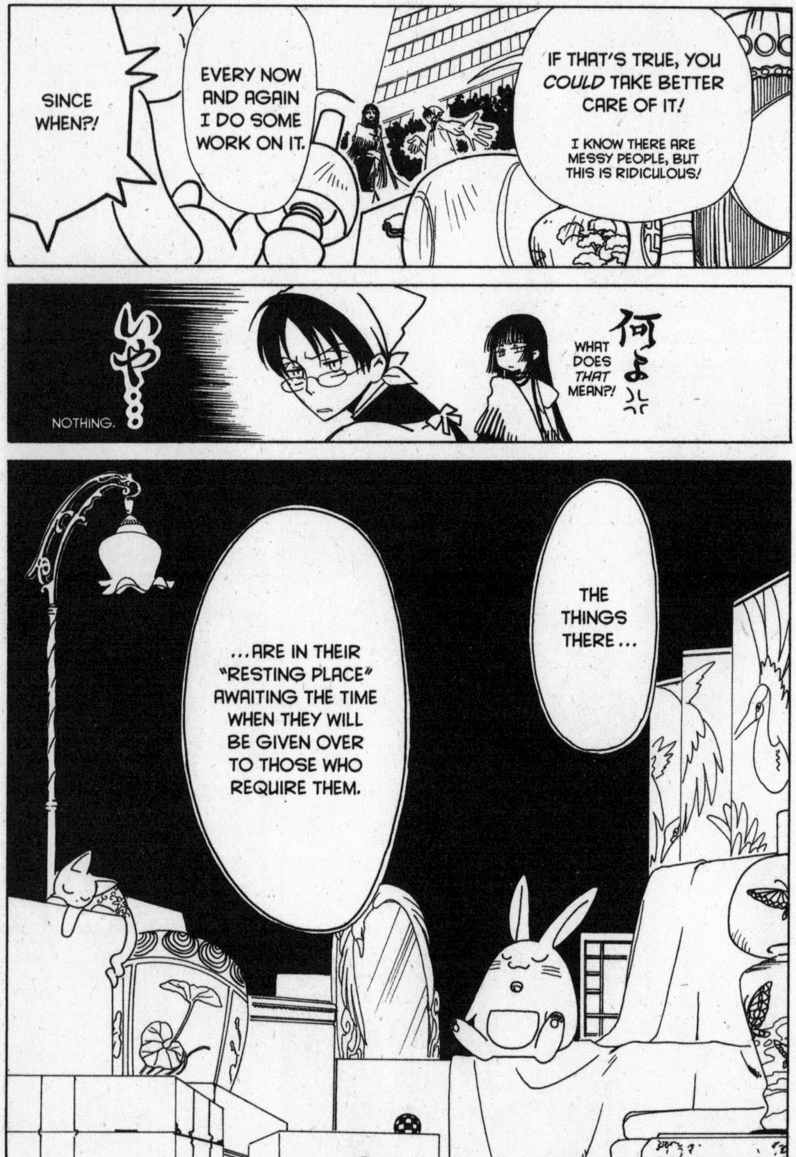
IF THAT'S TRUE, YOU *COULD* TAKE BETTER CARE OF IT!
I KNOW THERE ARE MESSY PEOPLE, BUT THIS IS RIDICULOUS!
EVERY NOW AND AGAIN I DO SOME WORK ON IT.
SINCE WHEN?!
何よ
WHAT DOES *THAT* MEAN?!
いや…
NOTHING.
THE THINGS THERE...
...ARE IN THEIR "RESTING PLACE" AWAITING THE TIME WHEN THEY WILL BE GIVEN OVER TO THOSE WHO REQUIRE THEM.

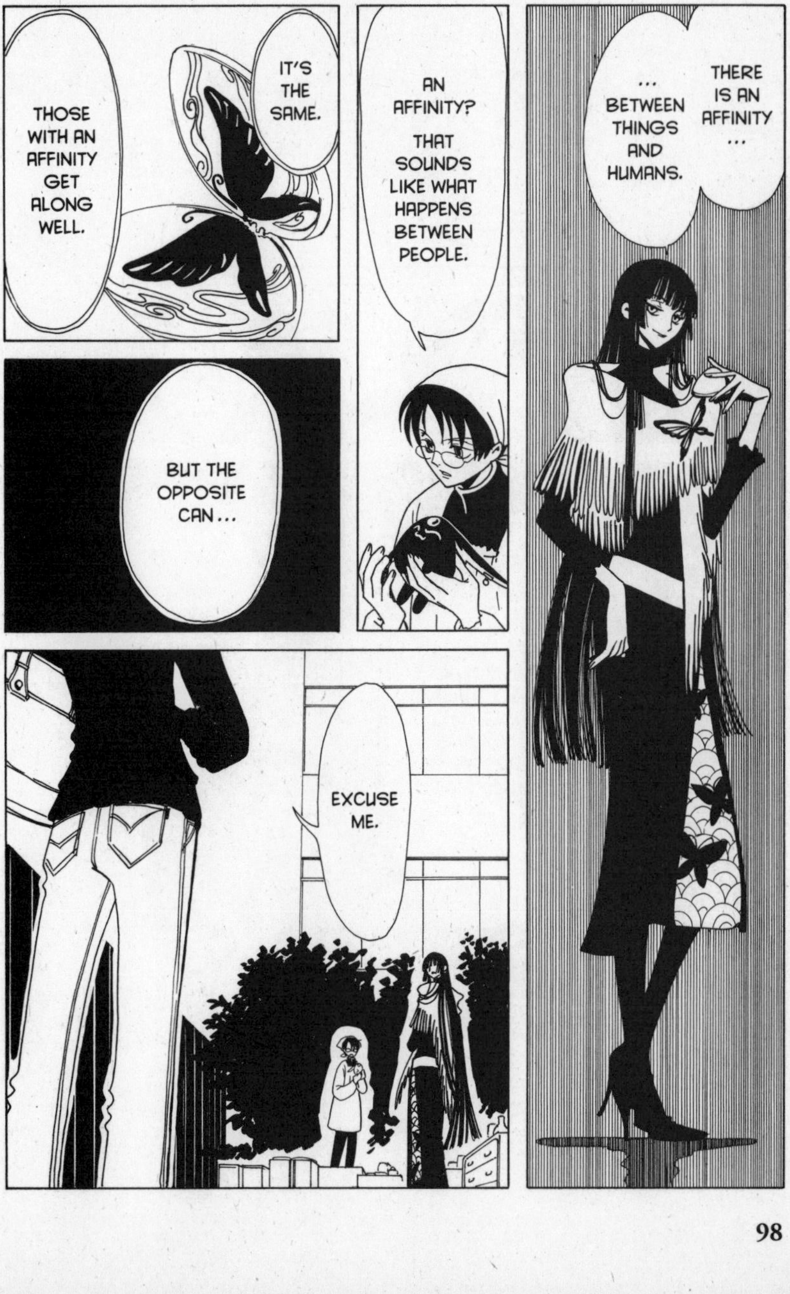
THERE IS AN AFFINITY ...
... BETWEEN THINGS AND HUMANS.
AN AFFINITY?
THAT SOUNDS LIKE WHAT HAPPENS BETWEEN PEOPLE.
IT'S THE SAME.
THOSE WITH AN AFFINITY GET ALONG WELL.
BUT THE OPPOSITE CAN ...
EXCUSE ME.

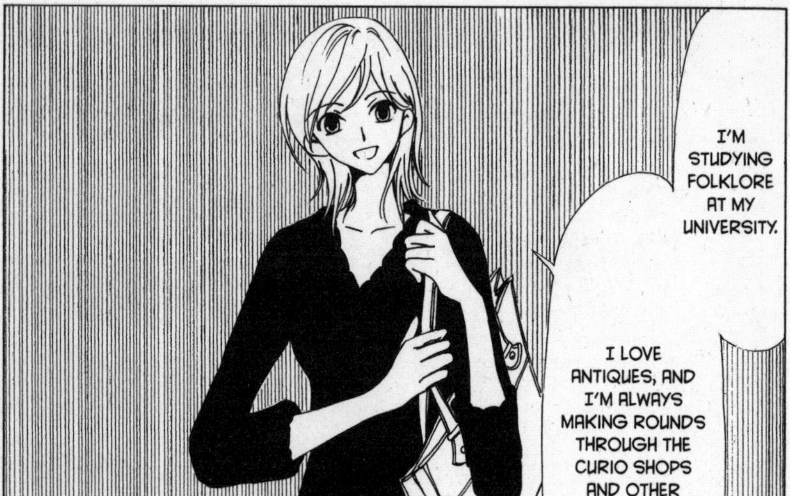
I'M STUDYING FOLKLORE AT MY UNIVERSITY.
I LOVE ANTIQUES, AND I'M ALWAYS MAKING ROUNDS THROUGH THE CURIO SHOPS AND OTHER COLLECTORS.

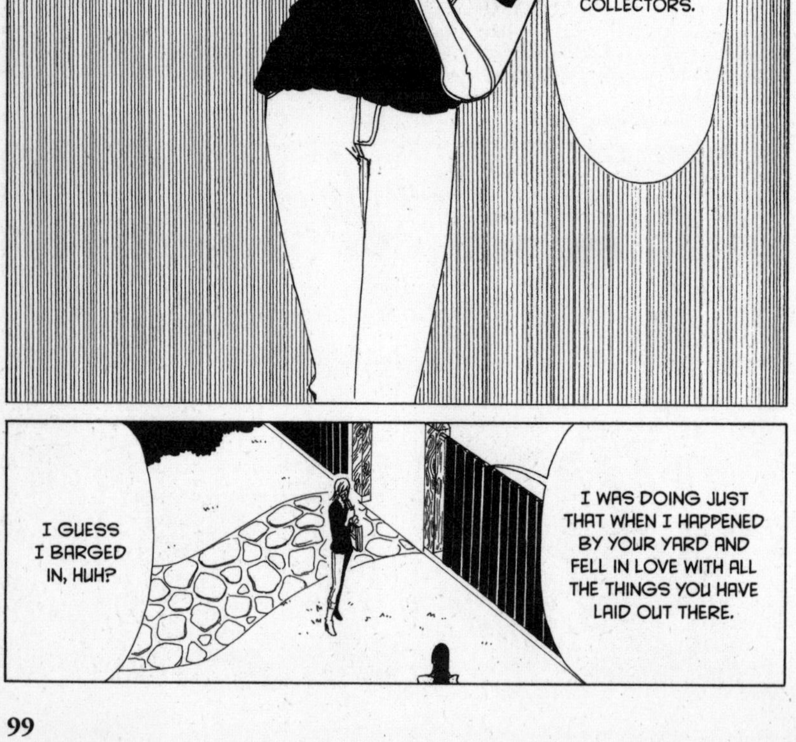
I WAS DOING JUST THAT WHEN I HAPPENED BY YOUR YARD AND FELL IN LOVE WITH ALL THE THINGS YOU HAVE LAID OUT THERE.
I GUESS I BARGED IN, HUH?

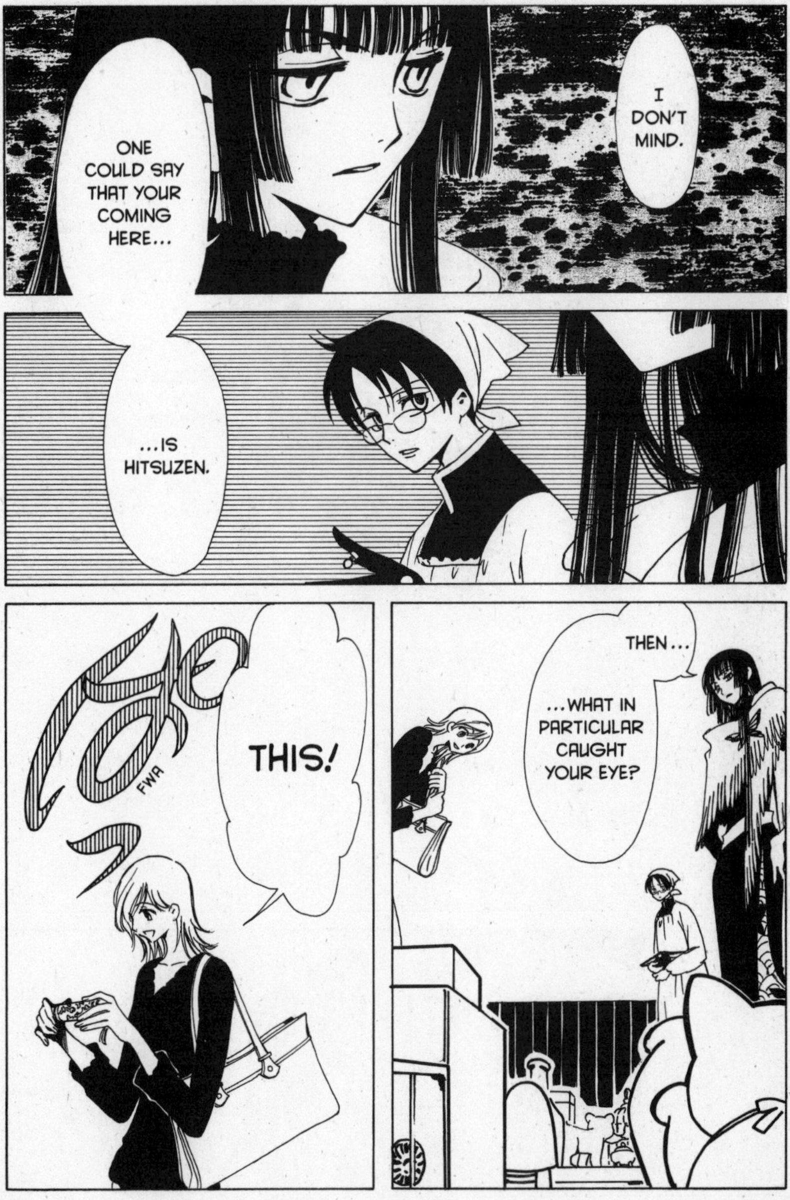
I DON'T MIND.
ONE COULD SAY THAT YOUR COMING HERE...
...IS HITSUZEN.
THEN...
...WHAT IN PARTICULAR CAUGHT YOUR EYE?
THIS!
FWA

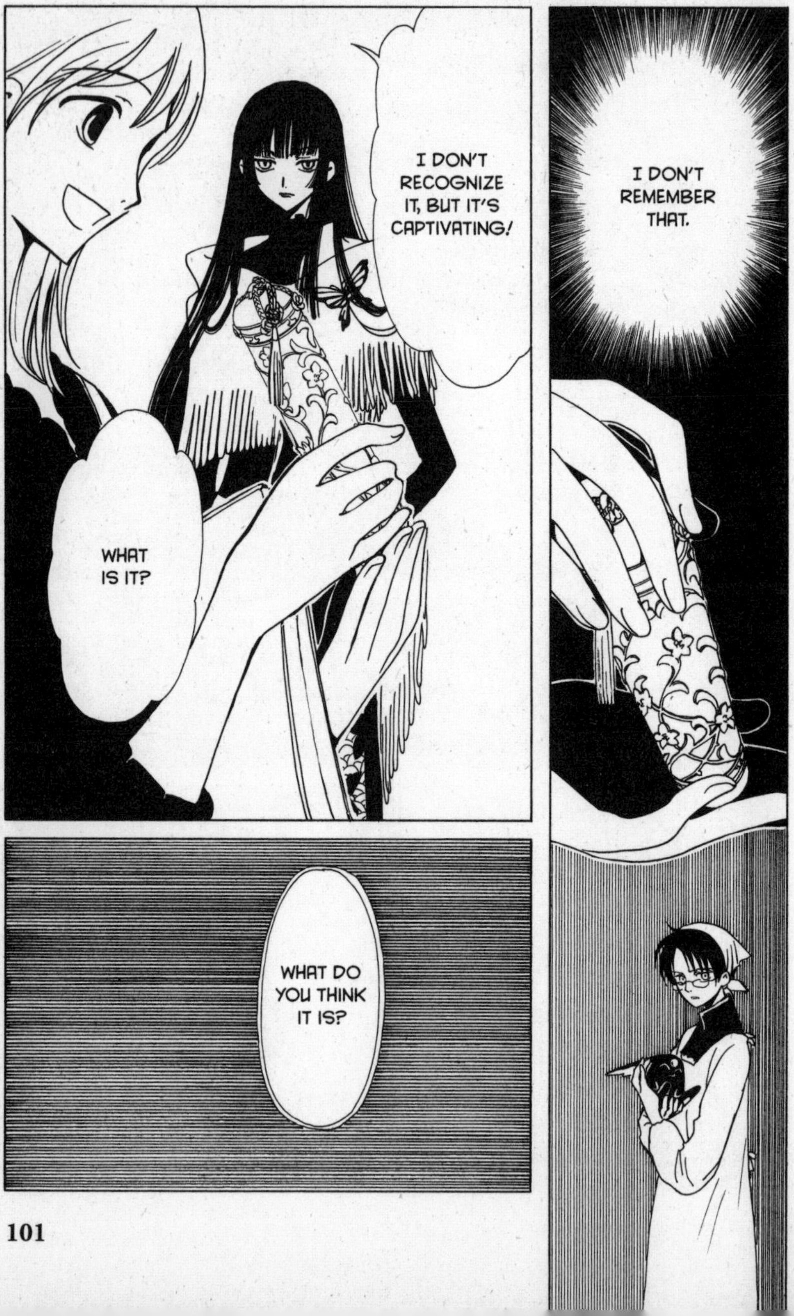
I DON'T REMEMBER THAT.
I DON'T RECOGNIZE IT, BUT IT'S CAPTIVATING!
WHAT IS IT?
WHAT DO YOU THINK IT IS?

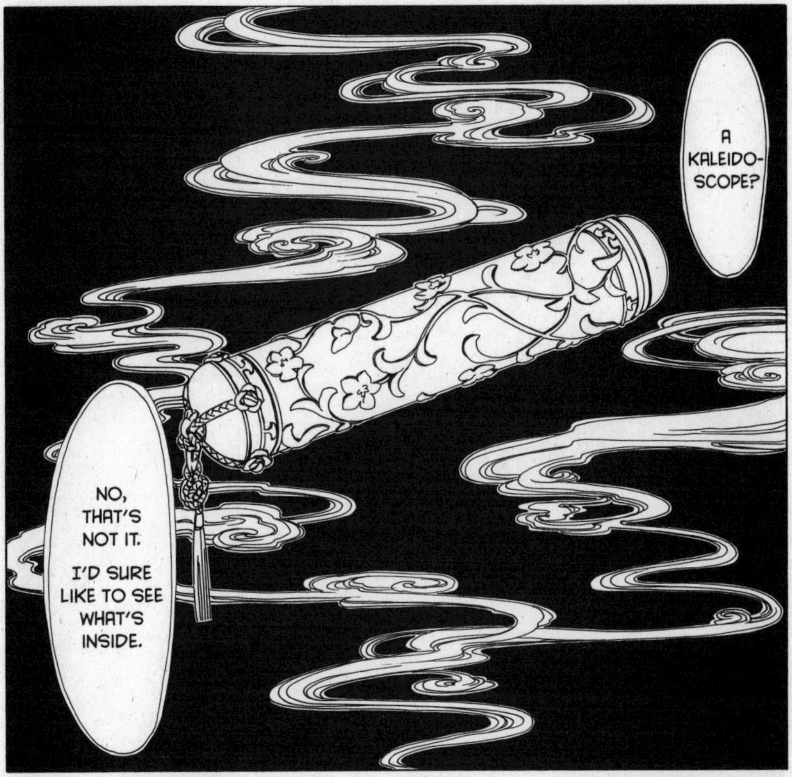
A KALEIDO-SCOPE?
NO, THAT'S NOT IT.
I'D SURE LIKE TO SEE WHAT'S INSIDE.
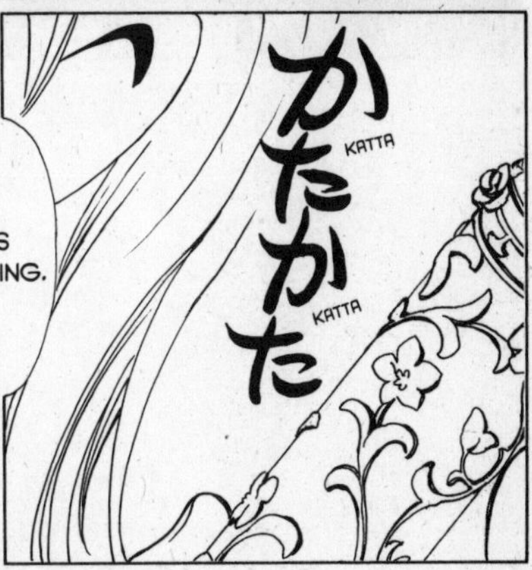
かたかた
KATTA
KATTA
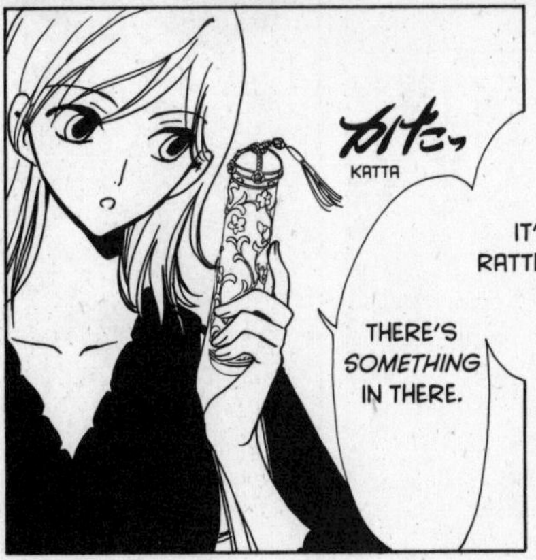
かたっ
KATTA
IT'S RATTLING.
THERE'S *SOMETHING* IN THERE.

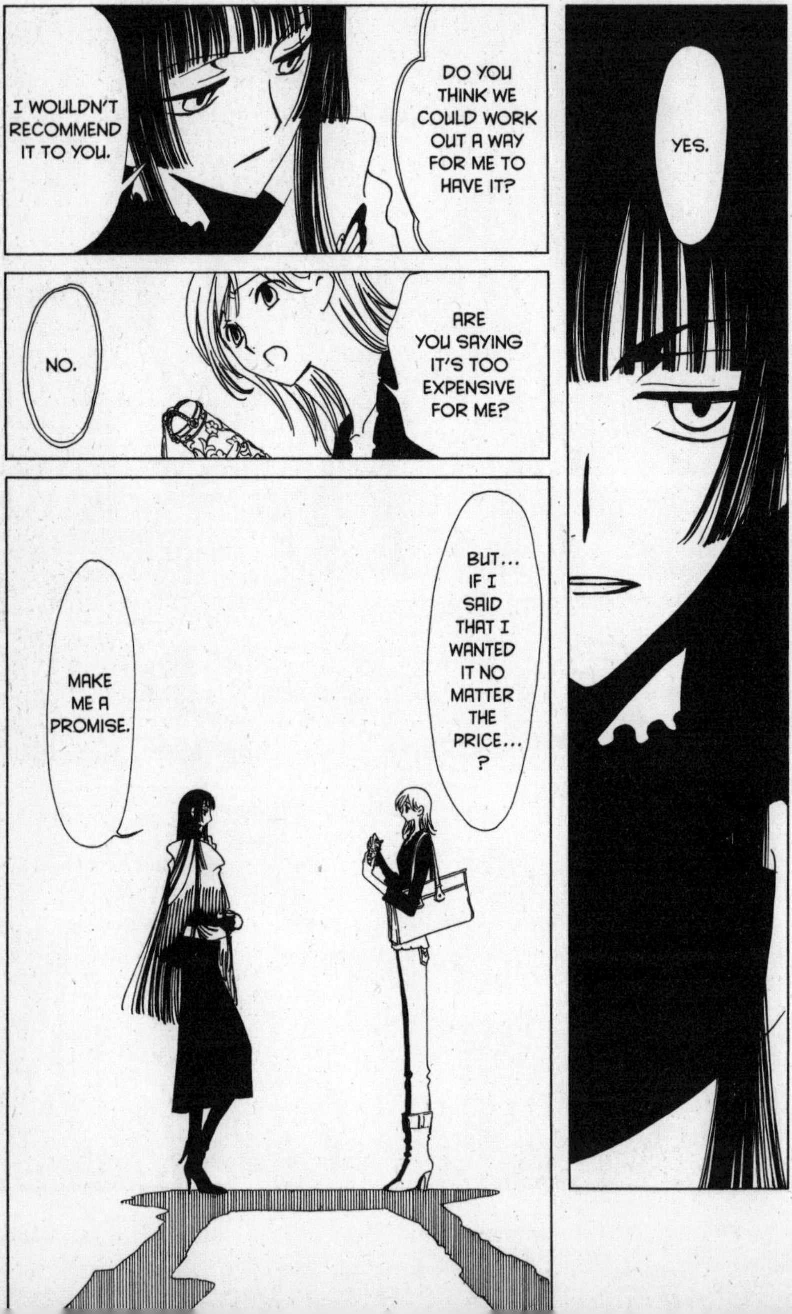
YES.
DO YOU THINK WE COULD WORK OUT A WAY FOR ME TO HAVE IT?
I WOULDN'T RECOMMEND IT TO YOU.
ARE YOU SAYING IT'S TOO EXPENSIVE FOR ME?
NO.
BUT... IF I SAID THAT I WANTED IT NO MATTER THE PRICE...?
MAKE ME A PROMISE.

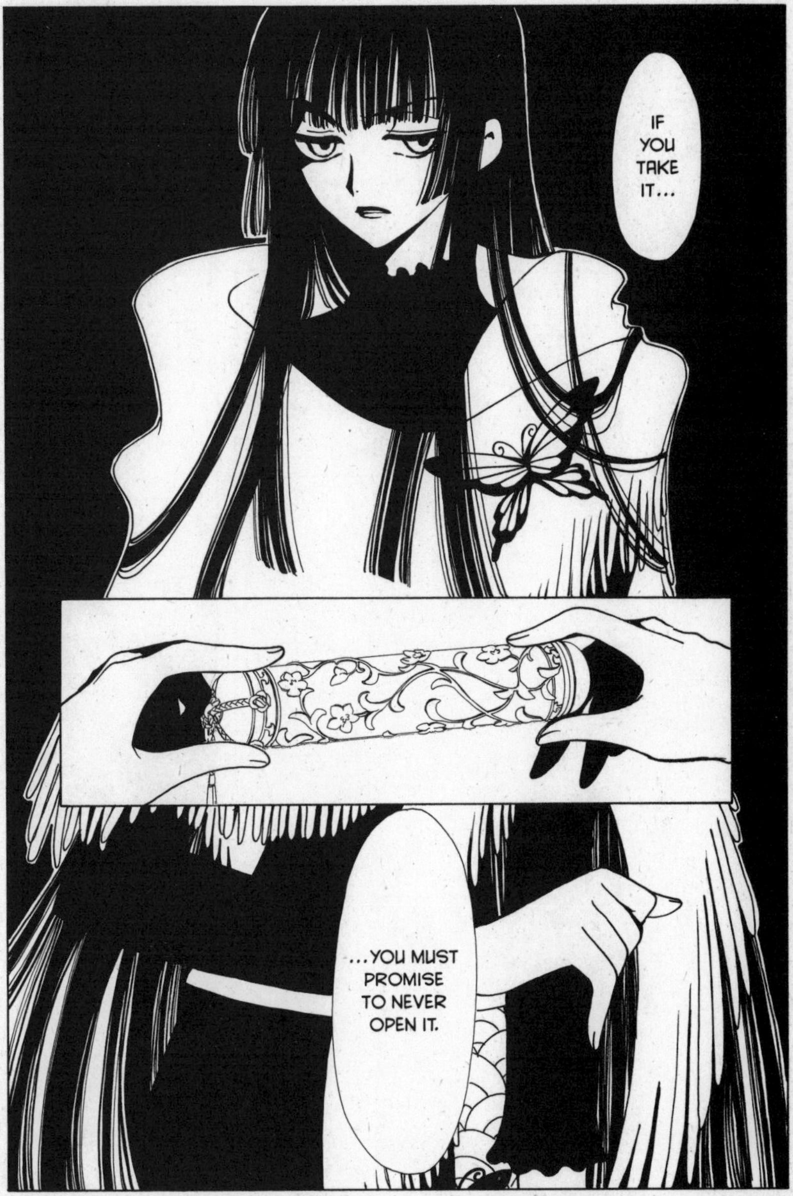
IF YOU TAKE IT...
...YOU MUST PROMISE TO NEVER OPEN IT.

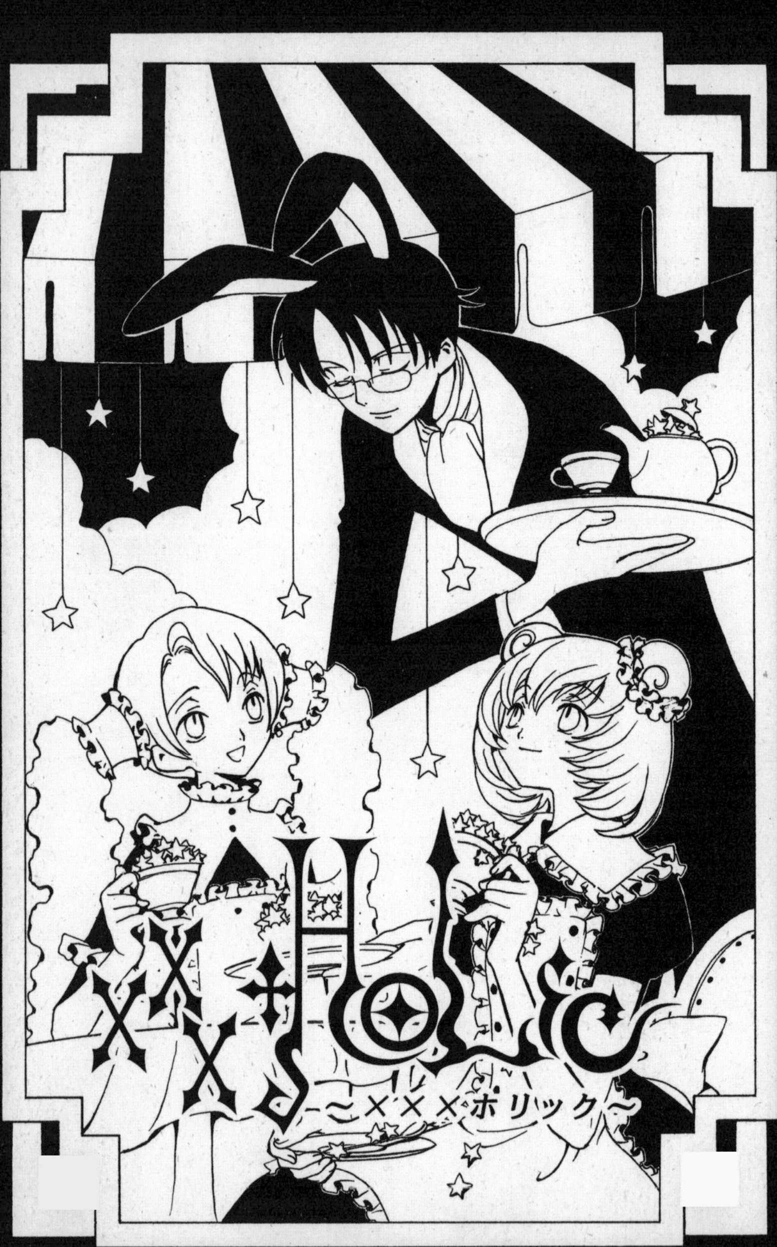
xxxHOLiC
～×××ホリック～

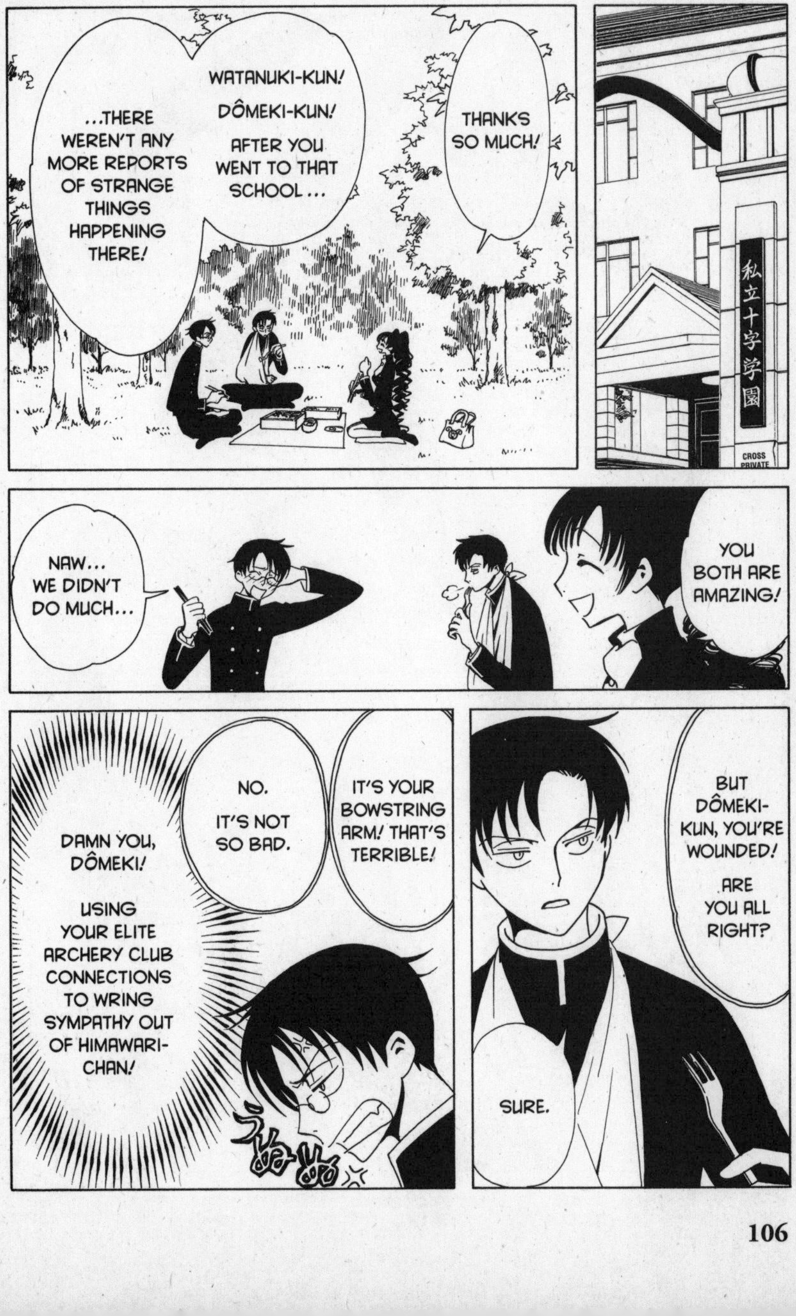
私立十字学園
CROSS
PRIVATE
WATANUKI-KUN! DÔMEKI-KUN! AFTER YOU WENT TO THAT SCHOOL...
...THERE WEREN'T ANY MORE REPORTS OF STRANGE THINGS HAPPENING THERE!
THANKS SO MUCH!
YOU BOTH ARE AMAZING!
NAW... WE DIDN'T DO MUCH...
BUT DÔMEKI-KUN, YOU'RE WOUNDED! ARE YOU ALL RIGHT?
SURE.
IT'S YOUR BOWSTRING ARM! THAT'S TERRIBLE!
NO. IT'S NOT SO BAD.
DAMN YOU, DÔMEKI! USING YOUR ELITE ARCHERY CLUB CONNECTIONS TO WRING SYMPATHY OUT OF HIMAWARI-CHAN!

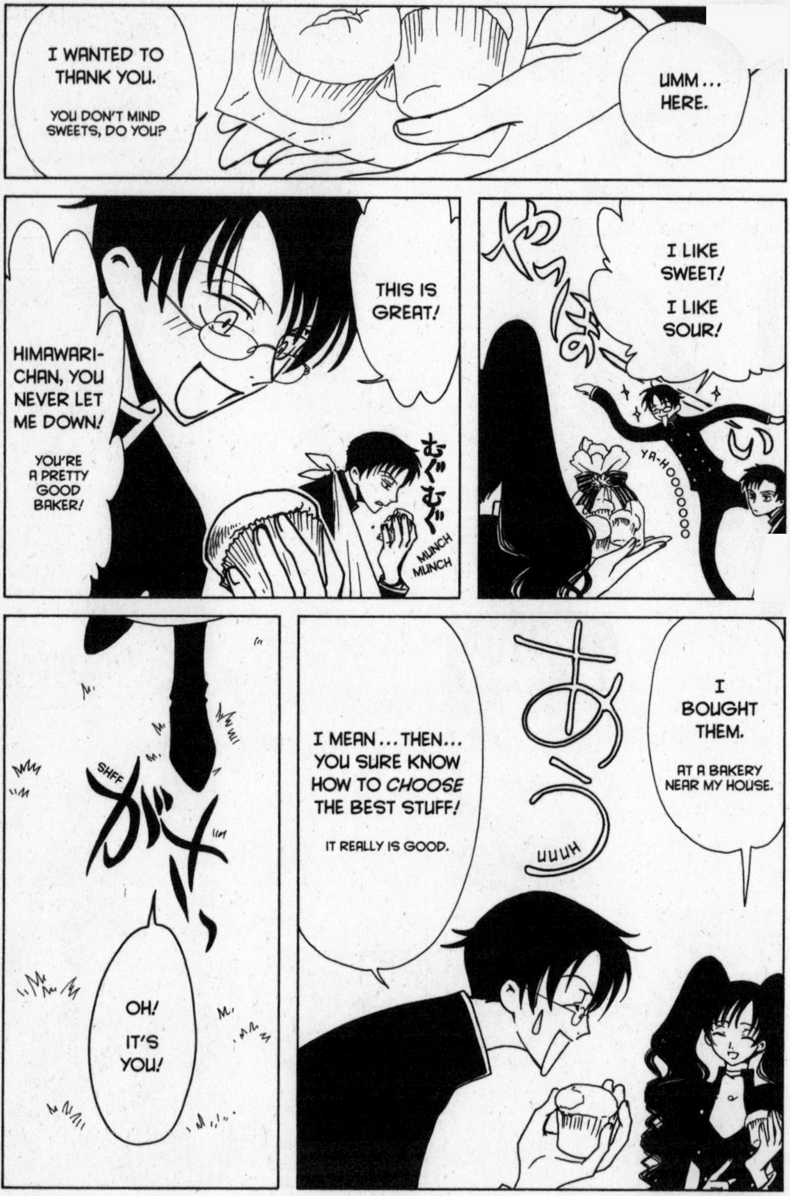
UMM ... HERE.
I WANTED TO THANK YOU.
YOU DON'T MIND SWEETS, DO YOU?
I LIKE SWEET!
I LIKE SOUR!
YA-HOOOOOOO
THIS IS GREAT!
HIMAWARI-CHAN, YOU NEVER LET ME DOWN!
YOU'RE A PRETTY GOOD BAKER!
MUNCH MUNCH
I BOUGHT THEM.
AT A BAKERY NEAR MY HOUSE.
UUUH
I MEAN ... THEN ... YOU SURE KNOW HOW TO CHOOSE THE BEST STUFF!
IT REALLY IS GOOD.
SHFF
OH!
IT'S YOU!

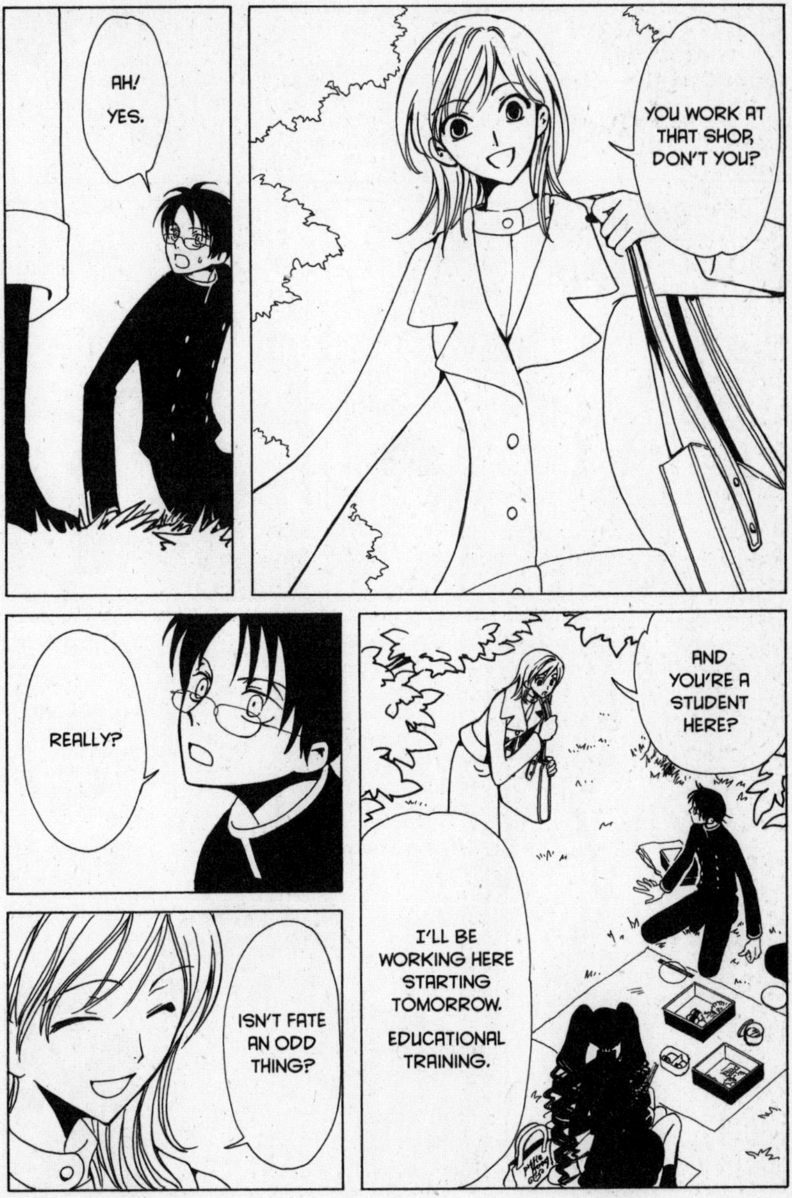
YOU WORK AT THAT SHOP, DON'T YOU?
AH! YES.
AND YOU'RE A STUDENT HERE?
I'LL BE WORKING HERE STARTING TOMORROW.
EDUCATIONAL TRAINING.
REALLY?
ISN'T FATE AN ODD THING?

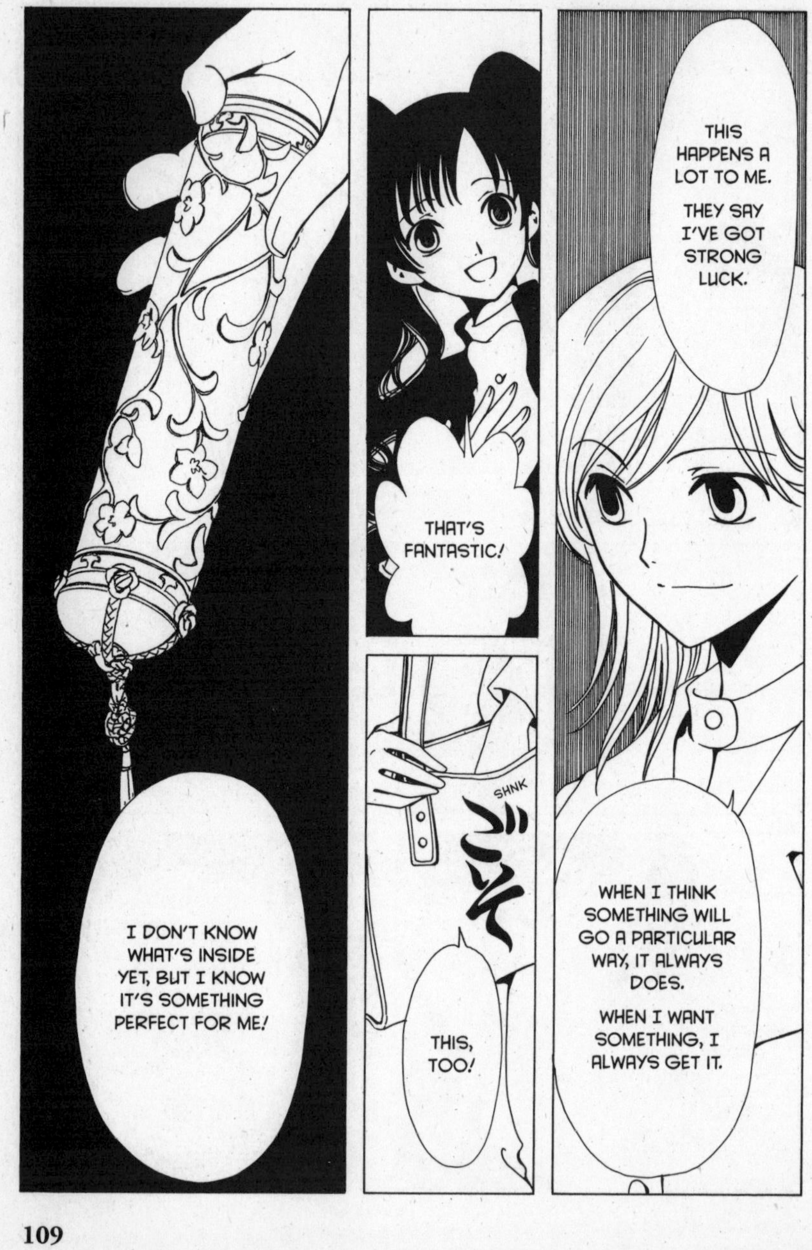
THIS HAPPENS A LOT TO ME.
THEY SAY I'VE GOT STRONG LUCK.
WHEN I THINK SOMETHING WILL GO A PARTICULAR WAY, IT ALWAYS DOES.
WHEN I WANT SOMETHING, I ALWAYS GET IT.
THAT'S FANTASTIC!
SHNK
THIS, TOO!
I DON'T KNOW WHAT'S INSIDE YET, BUT I KNOW IT'S SOMETHING PERFECT FOR ME!

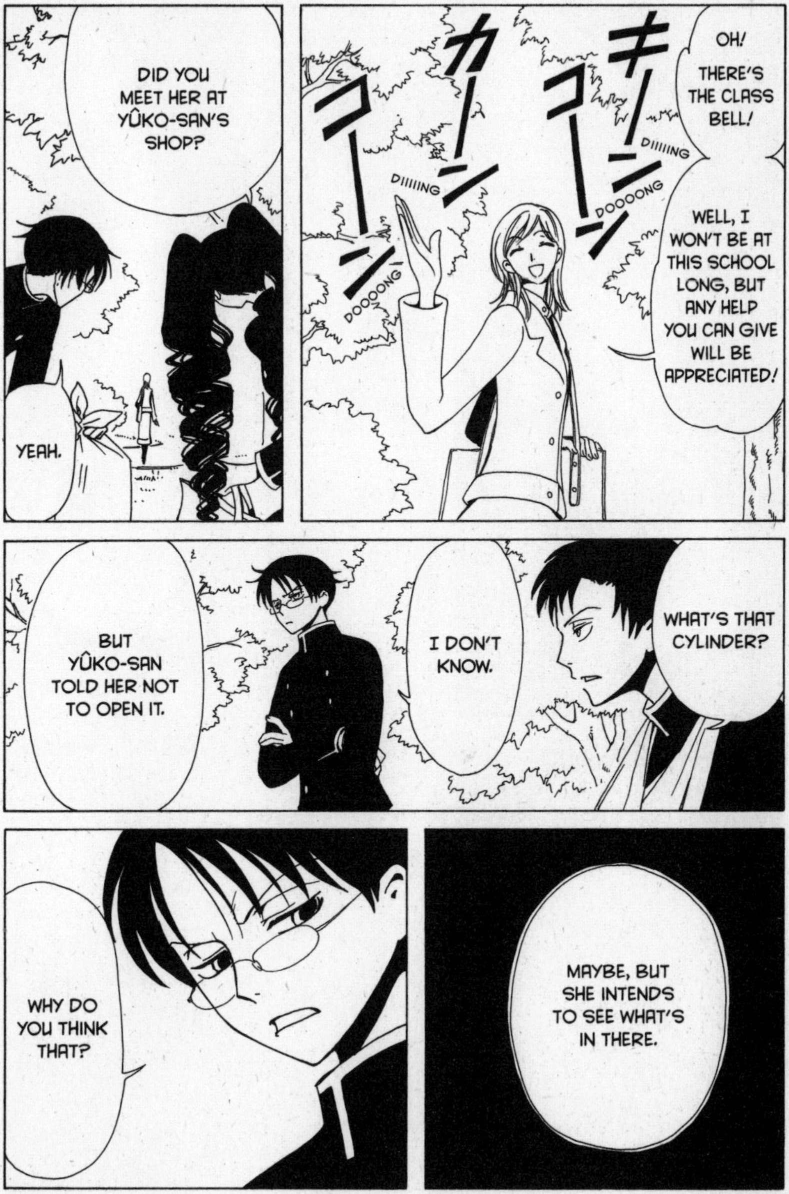

OH! THERE'S THE CLASS BELL!
キーンコーン
DIIIING
DOOOONG
カーンコーン
DIIIING
DOOOONG
WELL, I WON'T BE AT THIS SCHOOL LONG, BUT ANY HELP YOU CAN GIVE WILL BE APPRECIATED!
DID YOU MEET HER AT YÛKO-SAN'S SHOP?
YEAH.
WHAT'S THAT CYLINDER?
I DON'T KNOW.
BUT YÛKO-SAN TOLD HER NOT TO OPEN IT.
MAYBE, BUT SHE INTENDS TO SEE WHAT'S IN THERE.
WHY DO YOU THINK THAT?

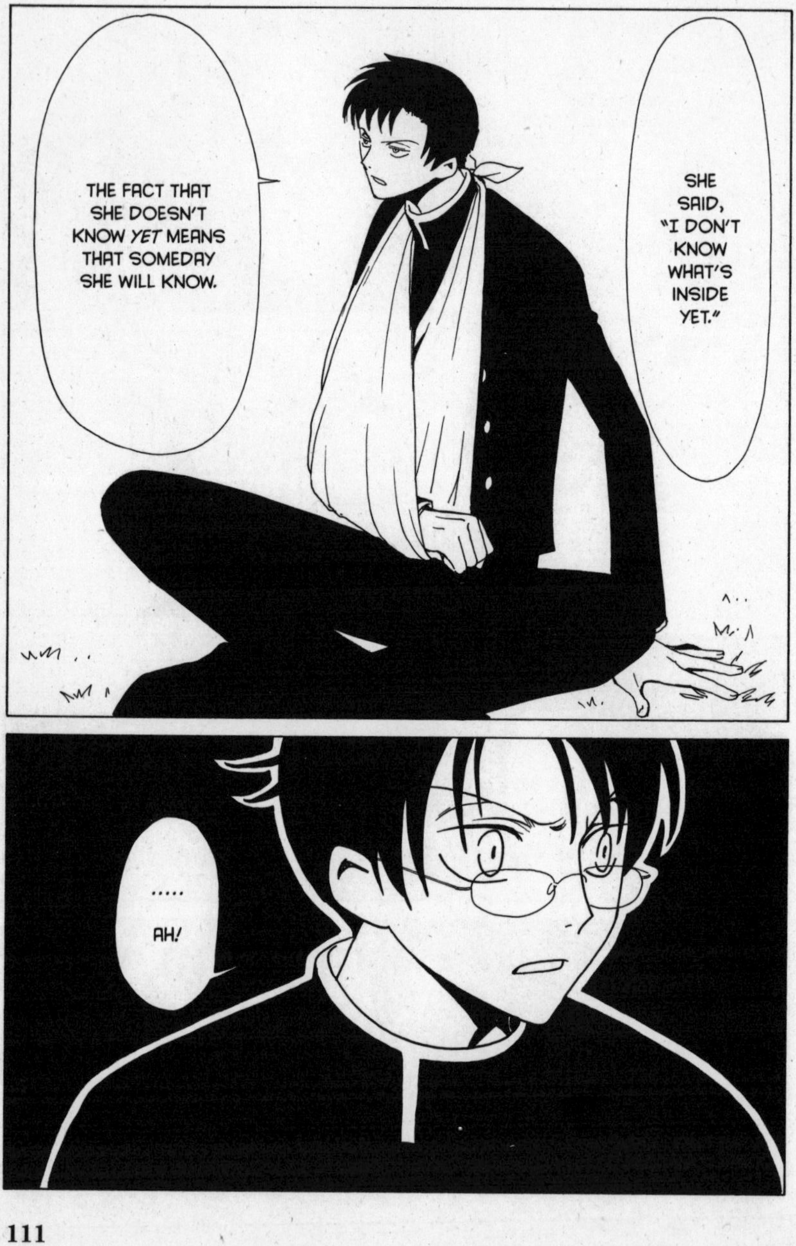
SHE SAID, "I DON'T KNOW WHAT'S INSIDE YET."
THE FACT THAT SHE DOESN'T KNOW *YET* MEANS THAT SOMEDAY SHE WILL KNOW.
.....
AH!

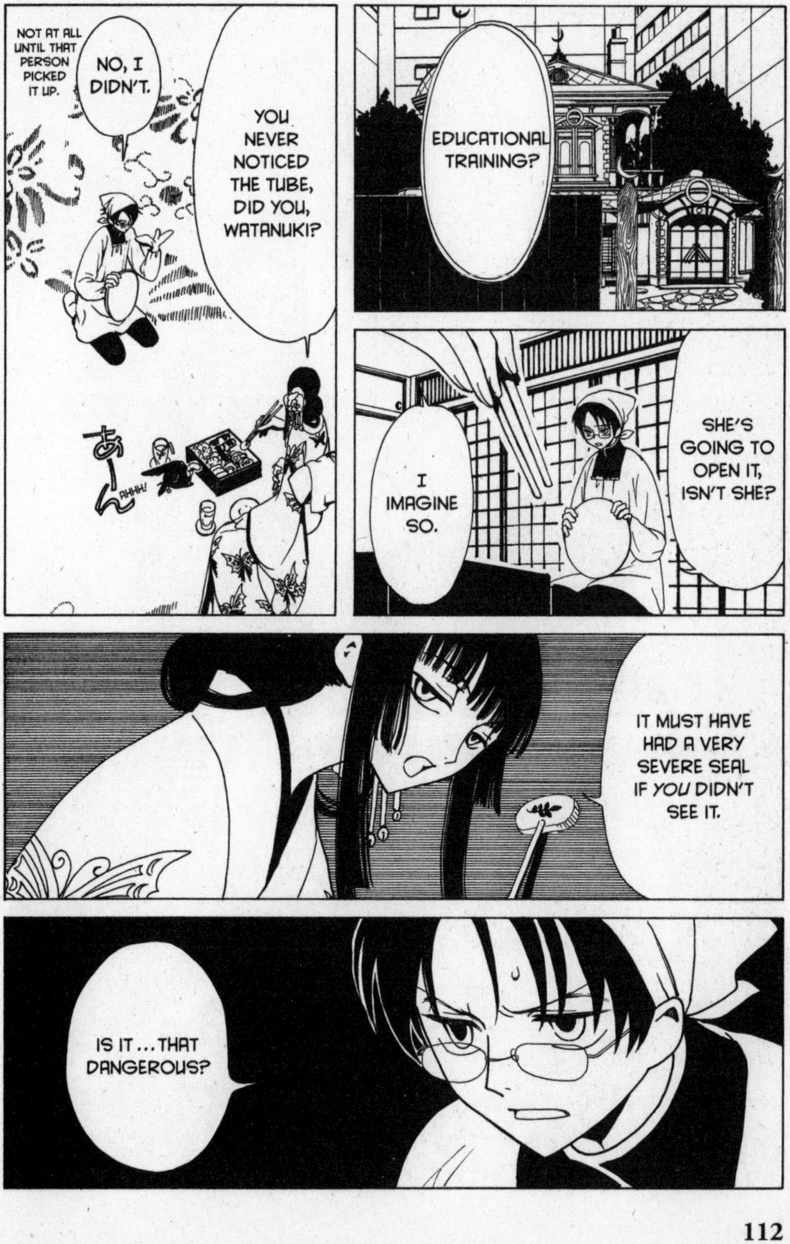
EDUCATIONAL TRAINING?
SHE'S GOING TO OPEN IT, ISN'T SHE?
I IMAGINE SO.
YOU NEVER NOTICED THE TUBE, DID YOU, WATANUKI?
NO, I DIDN'T.
NOT AT ALL UNTIL THAT PERSON PICKED IT UP.
あーん
AHHH!
IT MUST HAVE HAD A VERY SEVERE SEAL IF *YOU* DIDN'T SEE IT.
IS IT ... THAT DANGEROUS?

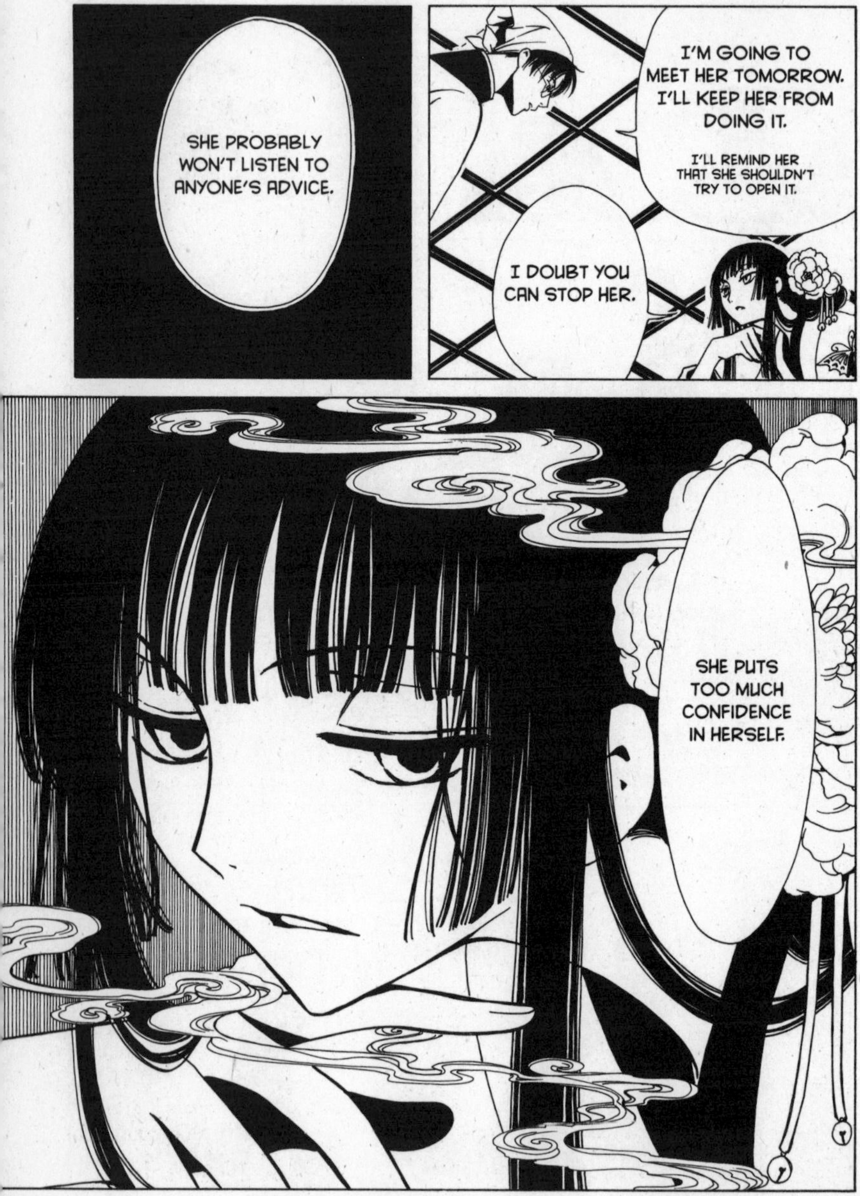
I'M GOING TO MEET HER TOMORROW. I'LL KEEP HER FROM DOING IT.
I'LL REMIND HER THAT SHE SHOULDN'T TRY TO OPEN IT.
I DOUBT YOU CAN STOP HER.
SHE PROBABLY WON'T LISTEN TO ANYONE'S ADVICE.
SHE PUTS TOO MUCH CONFIDENCE IN HERSELF.

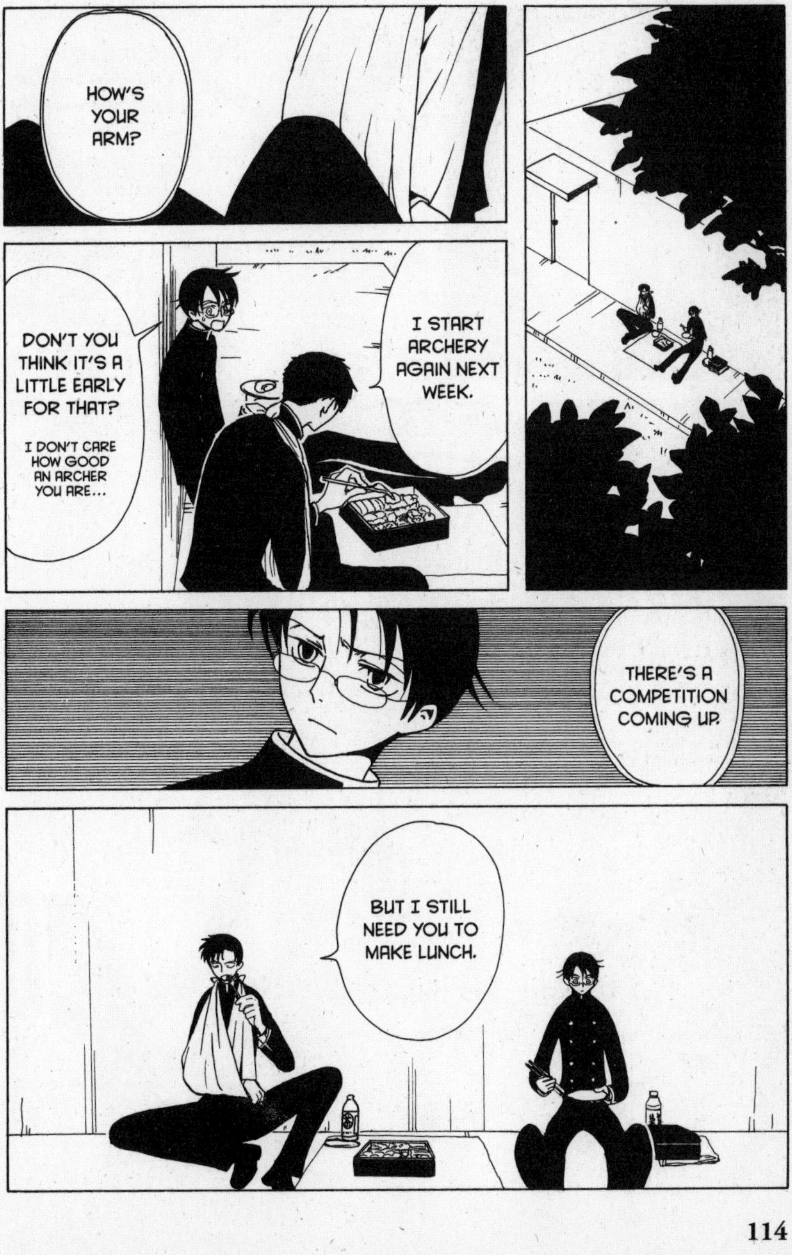
HOW'S YOUR ARM?
I START ARCHERY AGAIN NEXT WEEK.
DON'T YOU THINK IT'S A LITTLE EARLY FOR THAT?
I DON'T CARE HOW GOOD AN ARCHER YOU ARE...
THERE'S A COMPETITION COMING UP.
BUT I STILL NEED YOU TO MAKE LUNCH.

WELL, HE *DID* GET HIS INJURY WHILE HE WAS TRYING TO SAVE ME.
I GUESS MAKING HIM LUNCH AS PAYMENT ISN'T TOO BAD.
I'LL HAVE TO ASK YŪKO-SAN TO LEND ME THE BENTO BOXES FOR A LITTLE WHILE LONGER.
I THINK I'LL HAVE SOME FRIED CHICKEN BREAST TOMORROW.
I'M NOT TAKING YOUR ORDER HERE!!
IS THIS WHERE YOU'RE HAVING LUNCH TODAY?
UM...
THAT TUBE OF YOURS ...

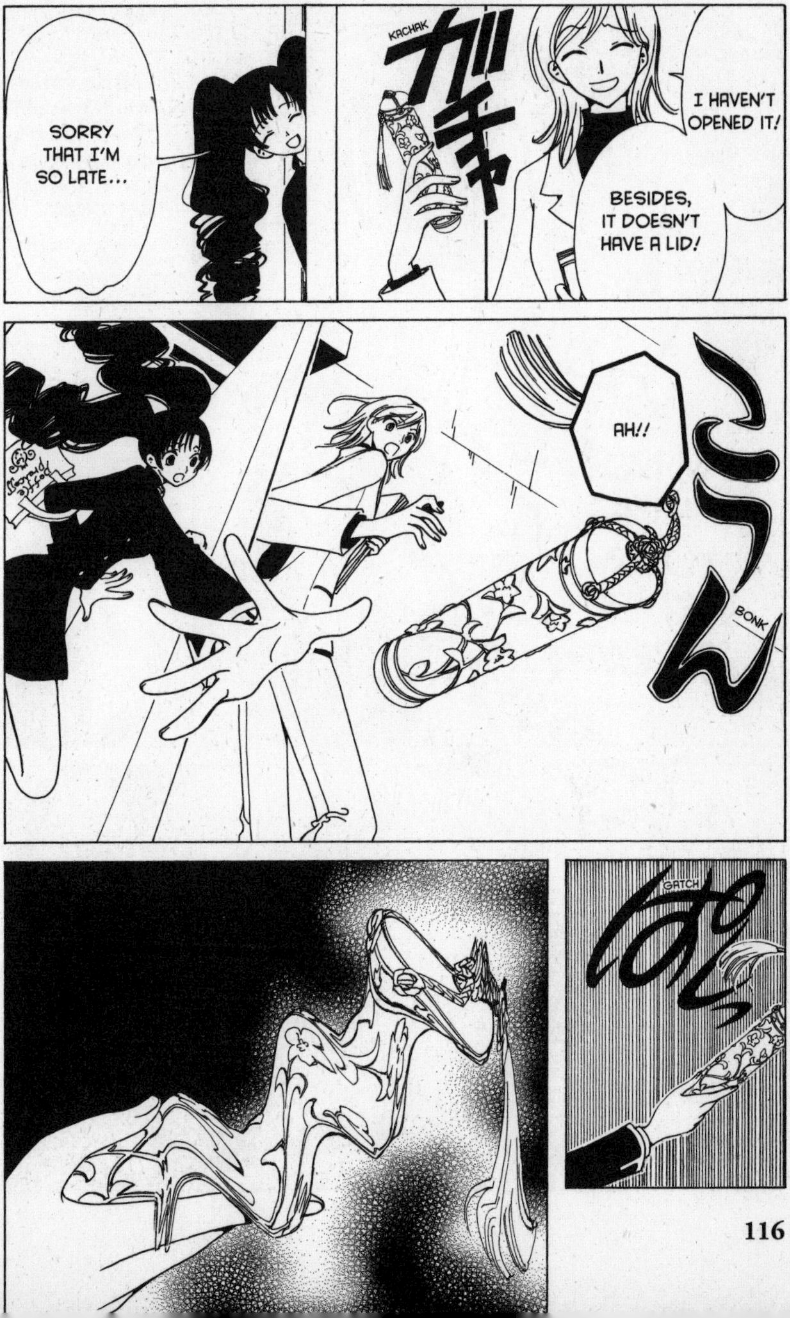
KACHAK
ガチャ
I HAVEN'T OPENED IT!
BESIDES, IT DOESN'T HAVE A LID!
SORRY THAT I'M SO LATE...
AH!!
BONK
GATCH

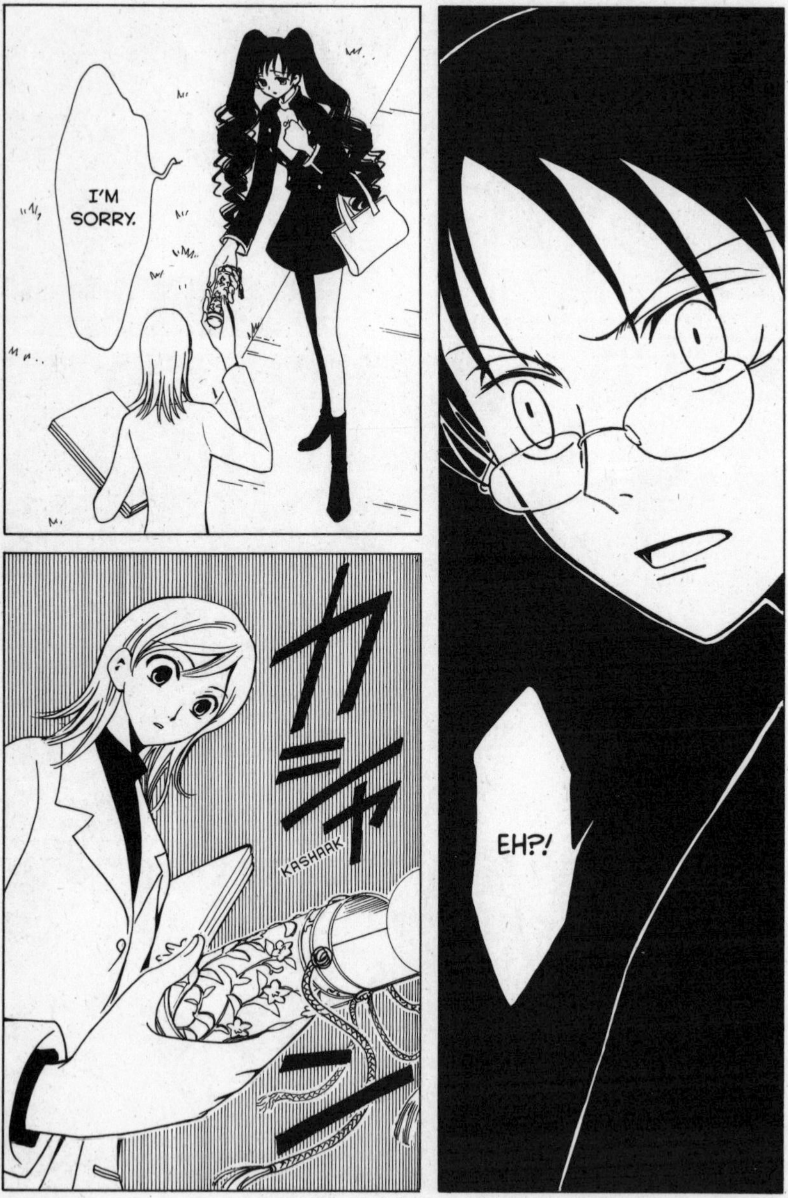
EH?!
I'M SORRY.
KASHAAK

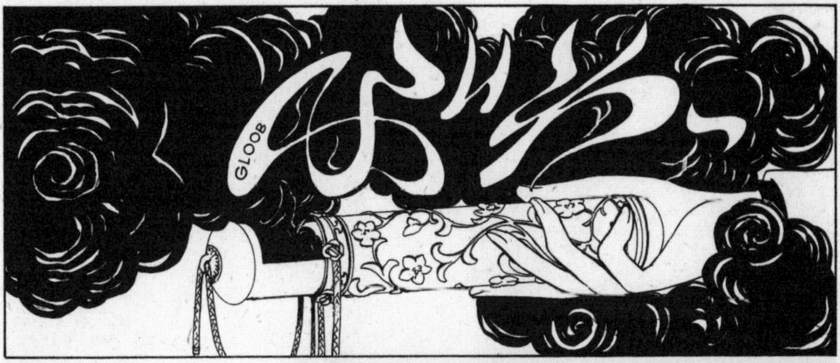
GLOOB
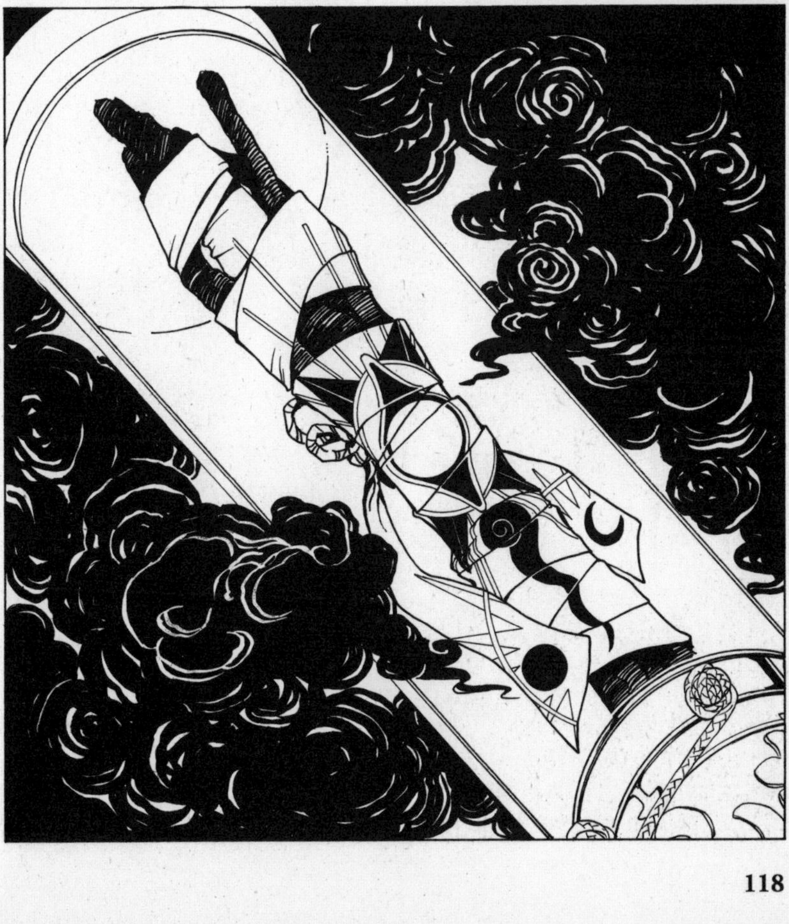

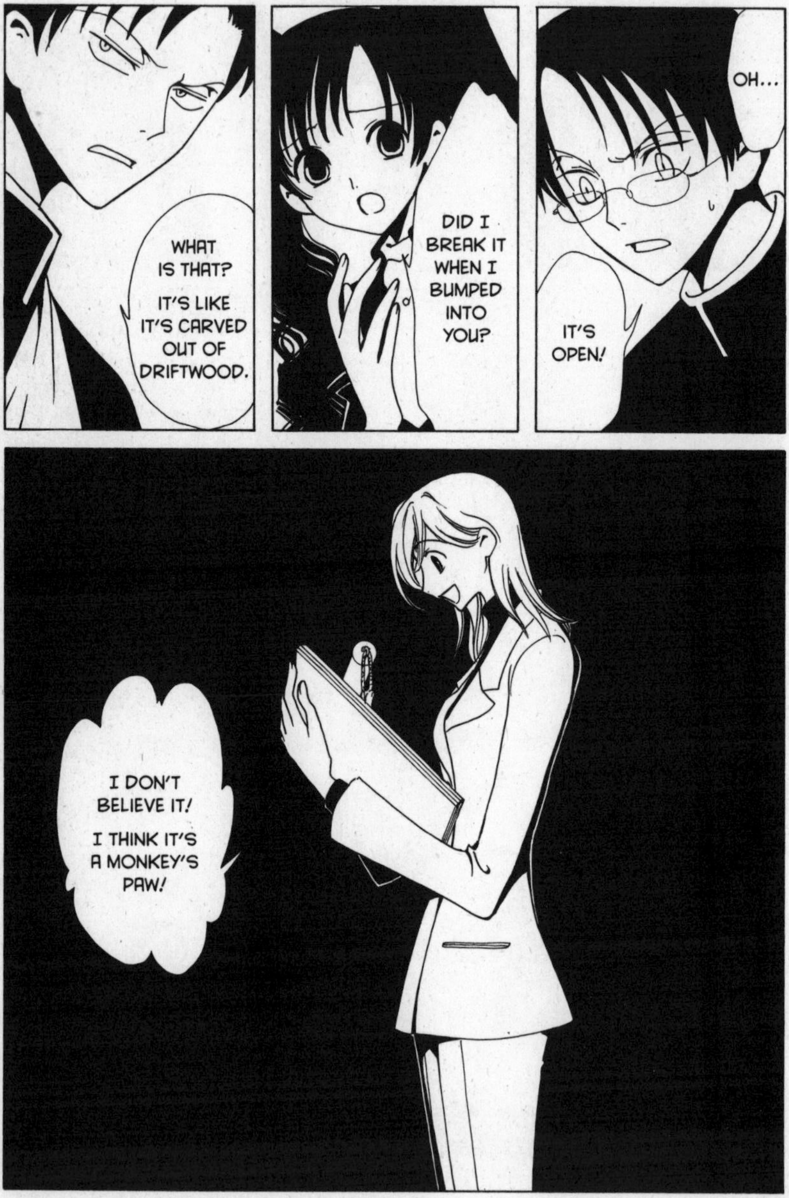
OH...
IT'S OPEN!
DID I BREAK IT WHEN I BUMPED INTO YOU?
WHAT IS THAT?
IT'S LIKE IT'S CARVED OUT OF DRIFTWOOD.
I DON'T BELIEVE IT!
I THINK IT'S A MONKEY'S PAW!

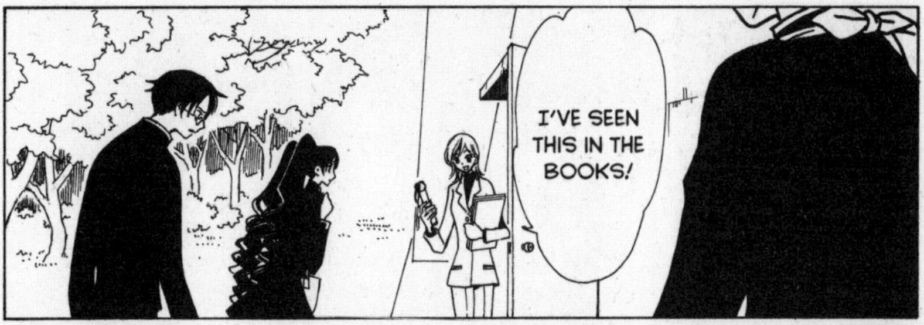
I'VE SEEN THIS IN THE BOOKS!
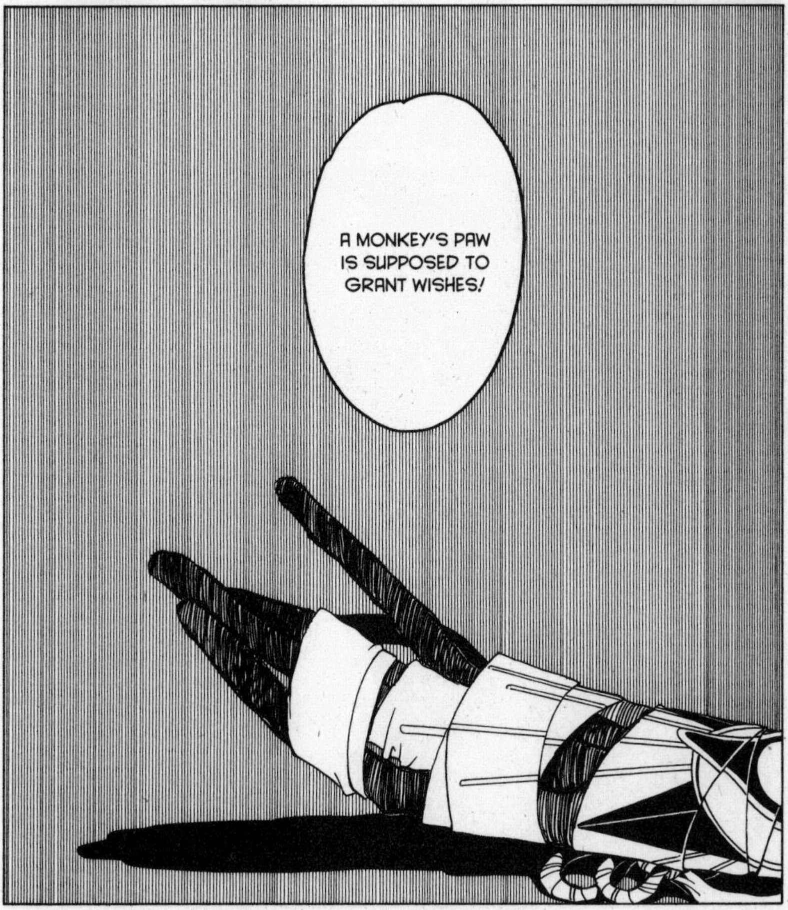
A MONKEY'S PAW IS SUPPOSED TO GRANT WISHES!

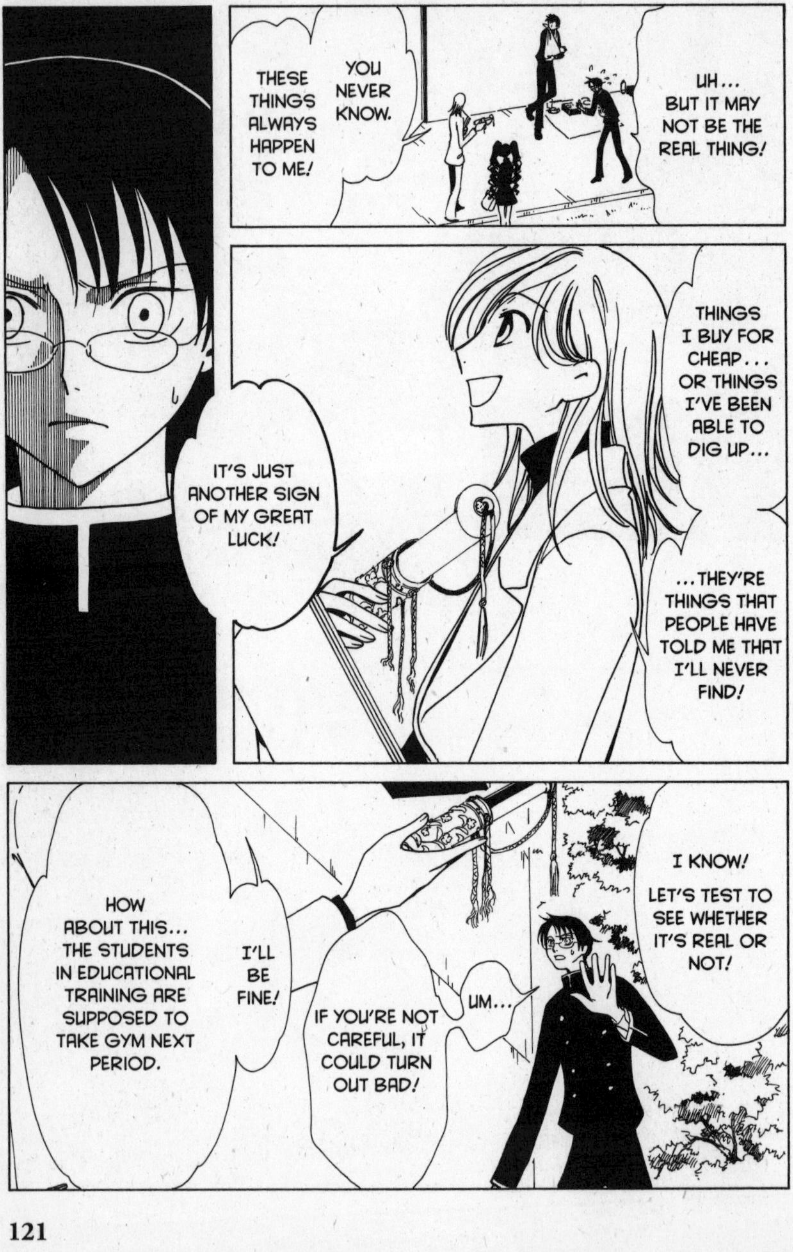
UH... BUT IT MAY NOT BE THE REAL THING!
YOU NEVER KNOW.
THESE THINGS ALWAYS HAPPEN TO ME!
THINGS I BUY FOR CHEAP... OR THINGS I'VE BEEN ABLE TO DIG UP...
...THEY'RE THINGS THAT PEOPLE HAVE TOLD ME THAT I'LL NEVER FIND!
IT'S JUST ANOTHER SIGN OF MY GREAT LUCK!
I KNOW!
LET'S TEST TO SEE WHETHER IT'S REAL OR NOT!
UM...
IF YOU'RE NOT CAREFUL, IT COULD TURN OUT BAD!
I'LL BE FINE!
HOW ABOUT THIS... THE STUDENTS IN EDUCATIONAL TRAINING ARE SUPPOSED TO TAKE GYM NEXT PERIOD.

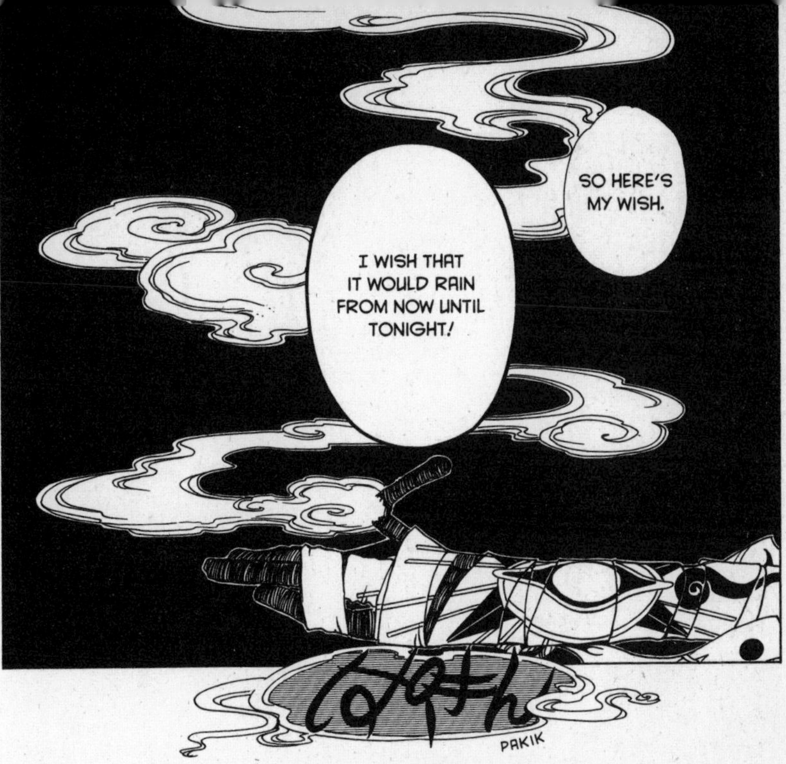
SO HERE'S MY WISH.
I WISH THAT IT WOULD RAIN FROM NOW UNTIL TONIGHT!
PAKIK

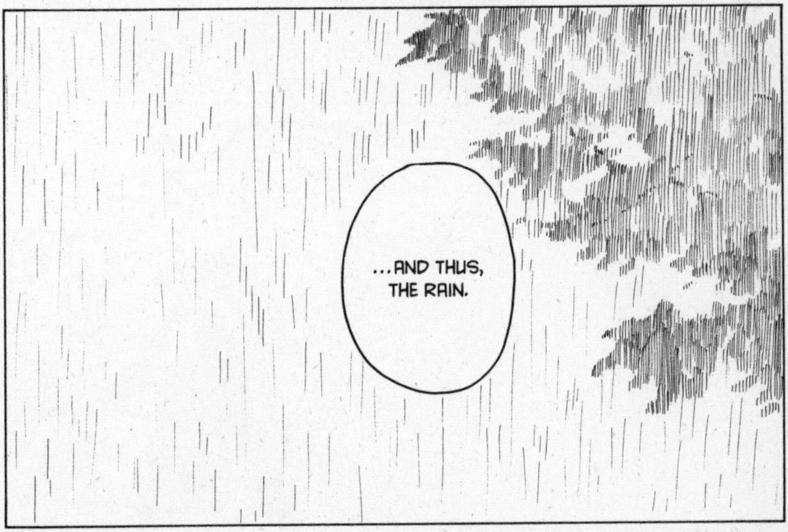
...AND THUS, THE RAIN.

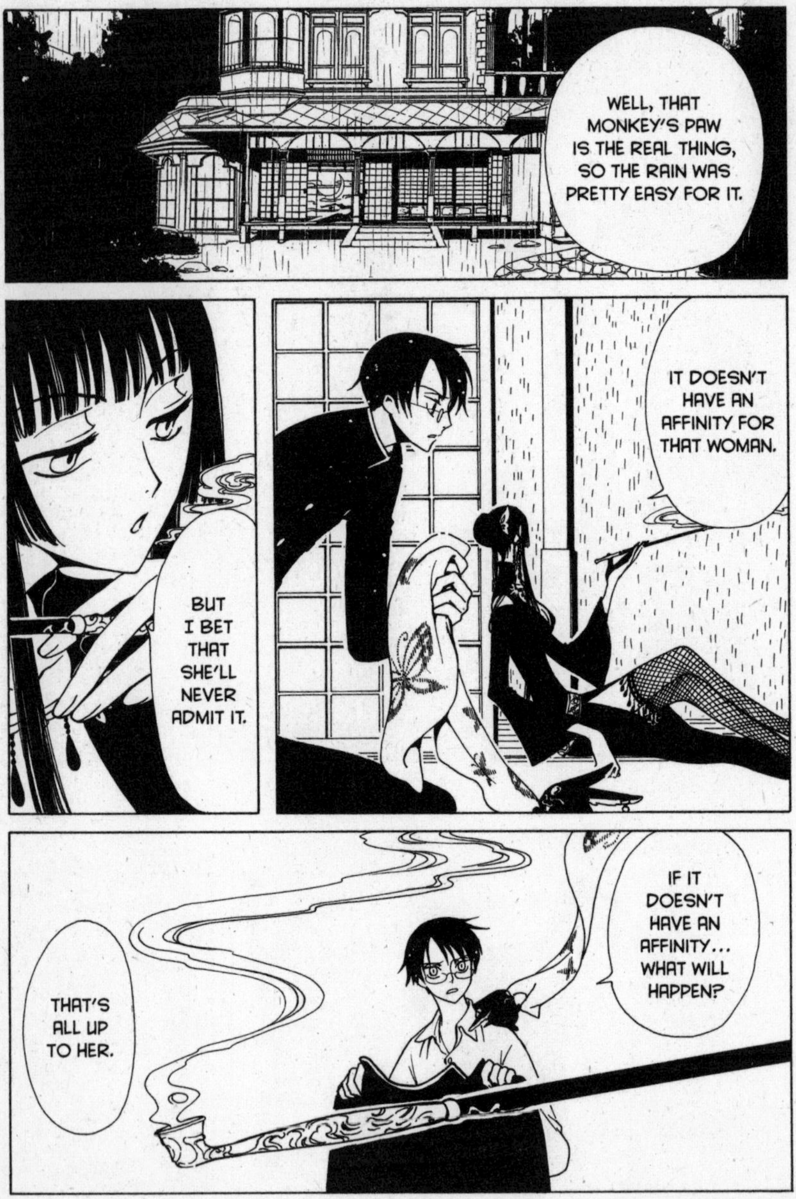
WELL, THAT MONKEY'S PAW IS THE REAL THING, SO THE RAIN WAS PRETTY EASY FOR IT.
IT DOESN'T HAVE AN AFFINITY FOR THAT WOMAN.
BUT I BET THAT SHE'LL NEVER ADMIT IT.
IF IT DOESN'T HAVE AN AFFINITY... WHAT WILL HAPPEN?
THAT'S ALL UP TO HER.

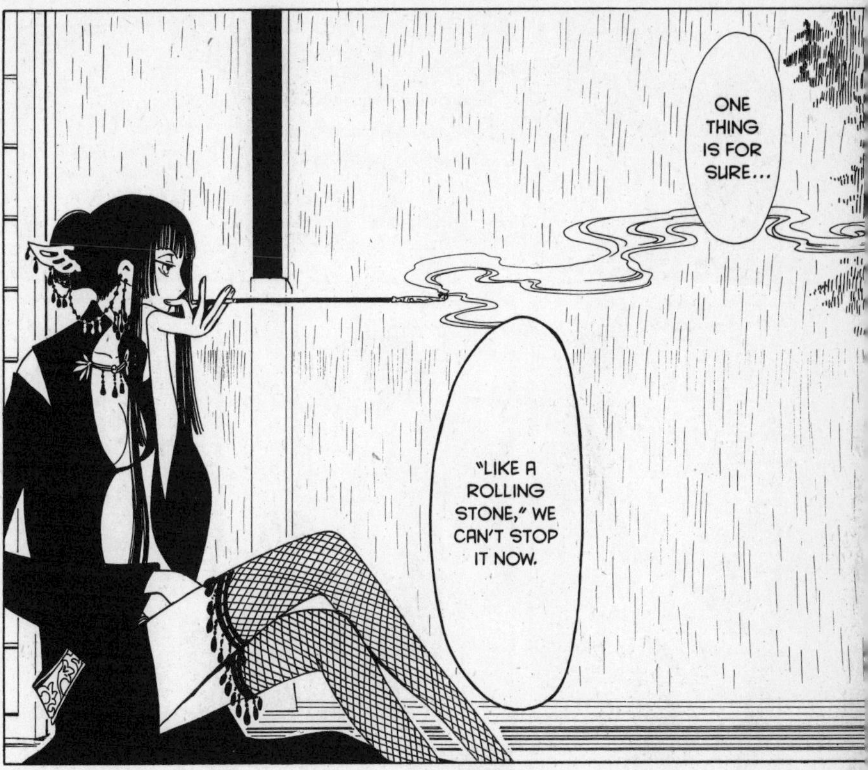
ONE THING IS FOR SURE...
"LIKE A ROLLING STONE," WE CAN'T STOP IT NOW.

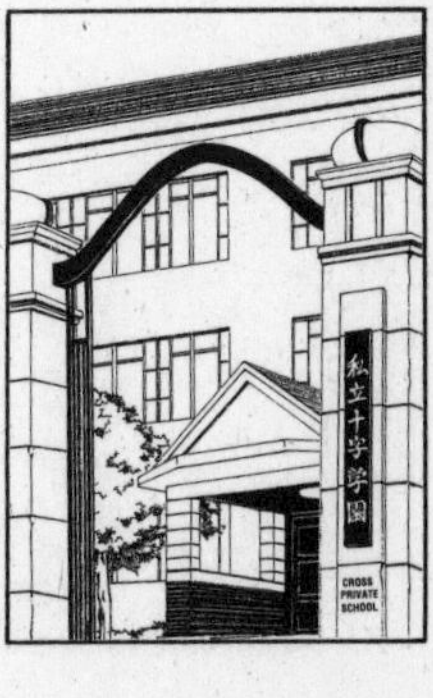
私立十字学園
CROSS PRIVATE SCHOOL

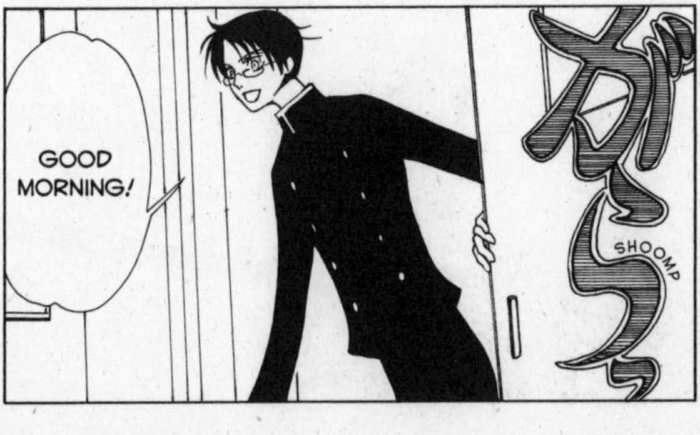
SHOOMP
GOOD MORNING!

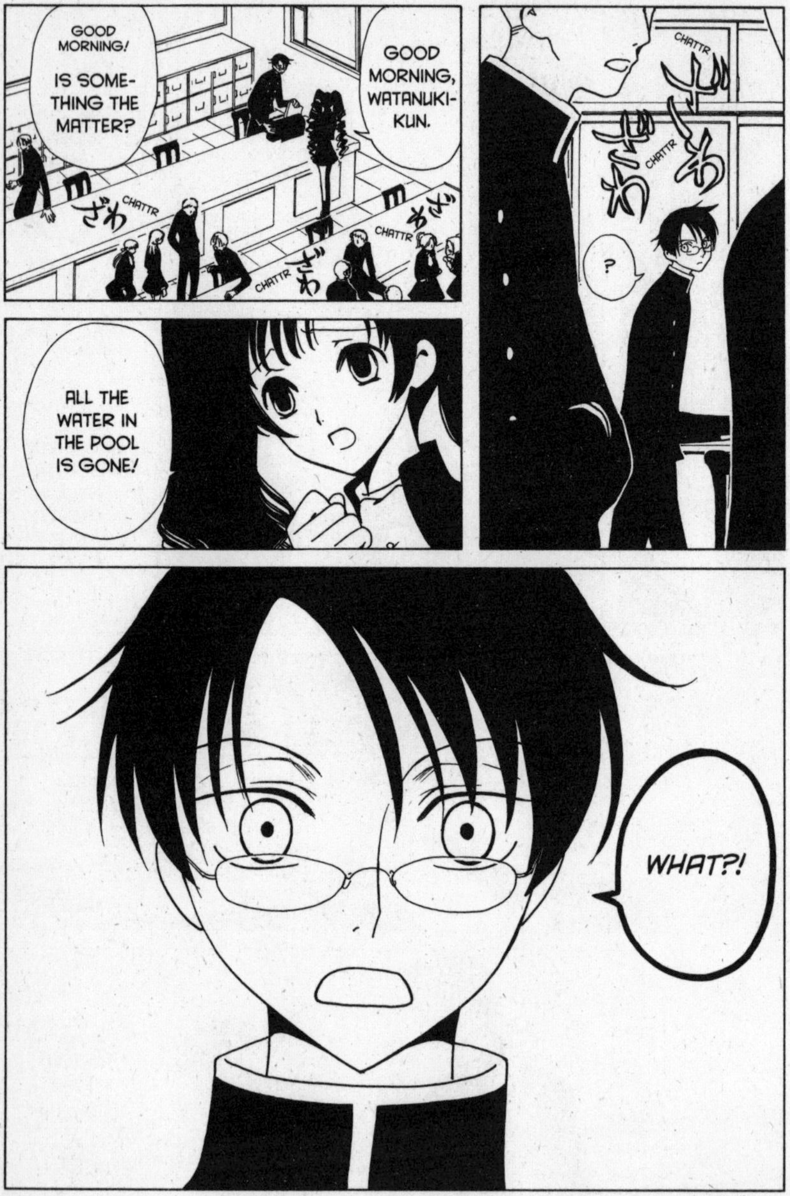
ざわ
CHATTR
ざわ
CHATTR
?
GOOD MORNING, WATANUKI-KUN.
GOOD MORNING! IS SOMETHING THE MATTER?
ざわ
CHATTR
ざわ
CHATTR
ざわ
CHATTR
ALL THE WATER IN THE POOL IS GONE!
WHAT?!

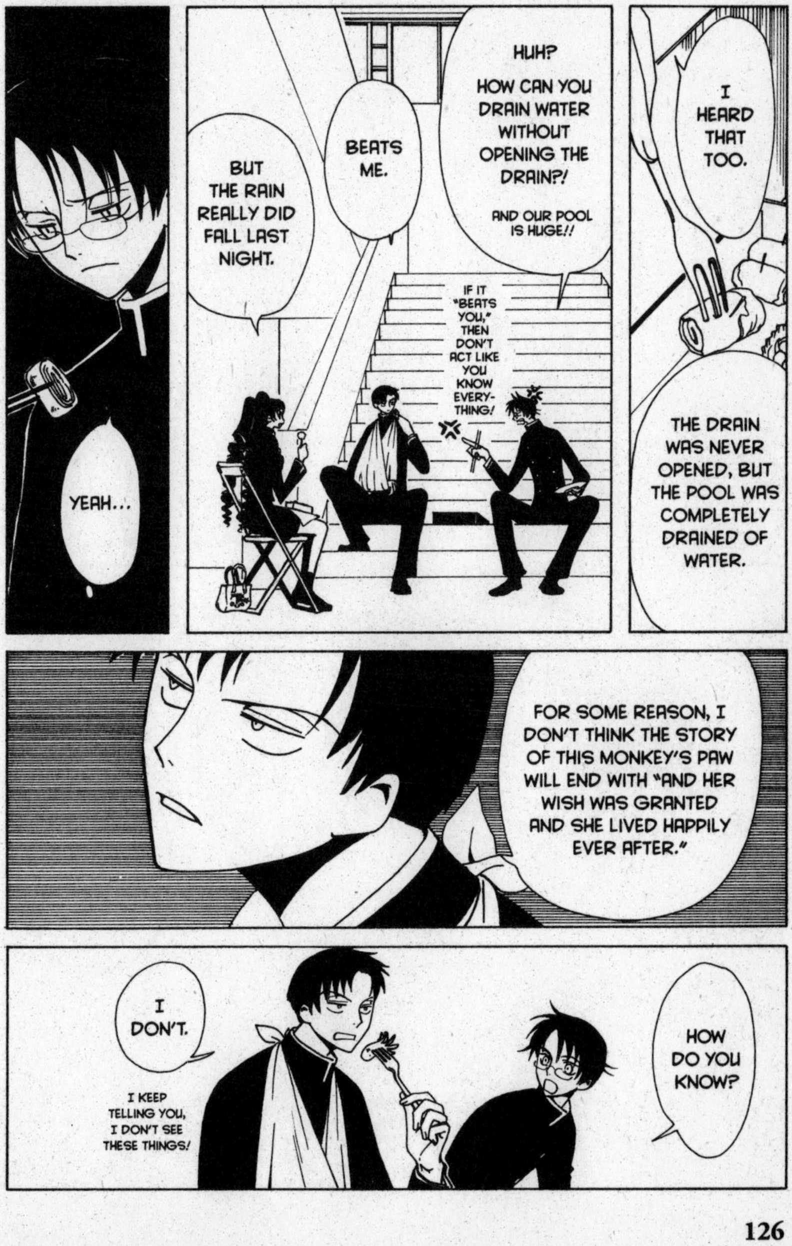
I HEARD THAT TOO.
THE DRAIN WAS NEVER OPENED, BUT THE POOL WAS COMPLETELY DRAINED OF WATER.
HUH? HOW CAN YOU DRAIN WATER WITHOUT OPENING THE DRAIN?!
AND OUR POOL IS HUGE!!
BEATS ME.
BUT THE RAIN REALLY DID FALL LAST NIGHT.
IF IT "BEATS YOU," THEN DON'T ACT LIKE YOU KNOW EVERY-THING!
YEAH...
FOR SOME REASON, I DON'T THINK THE STORY OF THIS MONKEY'S PAW WILL END WITH "AND HER WISH WAS GRANTED AND SHE LIVED HAPPILY EVER AFTER."
HOW DO YOU KNOW?
I DON'T.
I KEEP TELLING YOU, I DON'T SEE THESE THINGS!

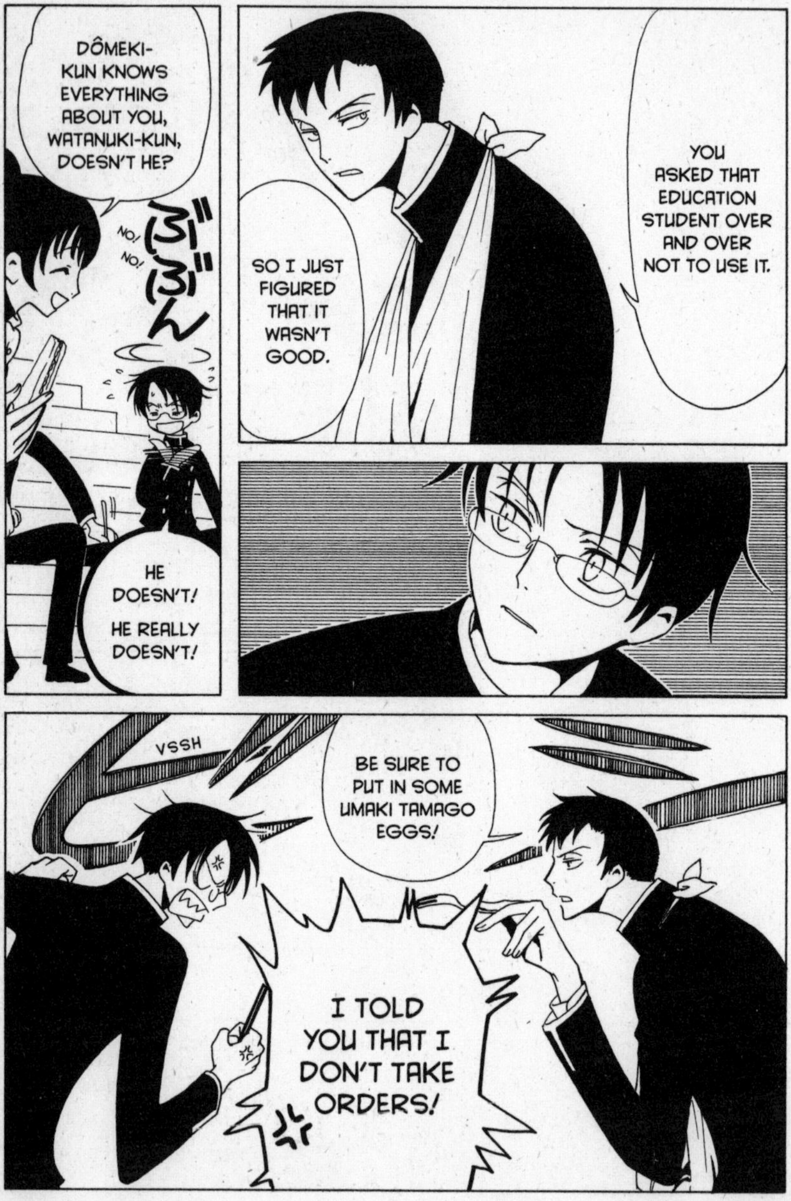

YOU ASKED THAT EDUCATION STUDENT OVER AND OVER NOT TO USE IT.
SO I JUST FIGURED THAT IT WASN'T GOOD.
DÔMEKI-KUN KNOWS EVERYTHING ABOUT YOU, WATANUKI-KUN, DOESN'T HE?
ぶぶん
NO! NO!
HE DOESN'T! HE REALLY DOESN'T!
BE SURE TO PUT IN SOME UMAKI TAMAGO EGGS!
VSSH
I TOLD YOU THAT I DON'T TAKE ORDERS!

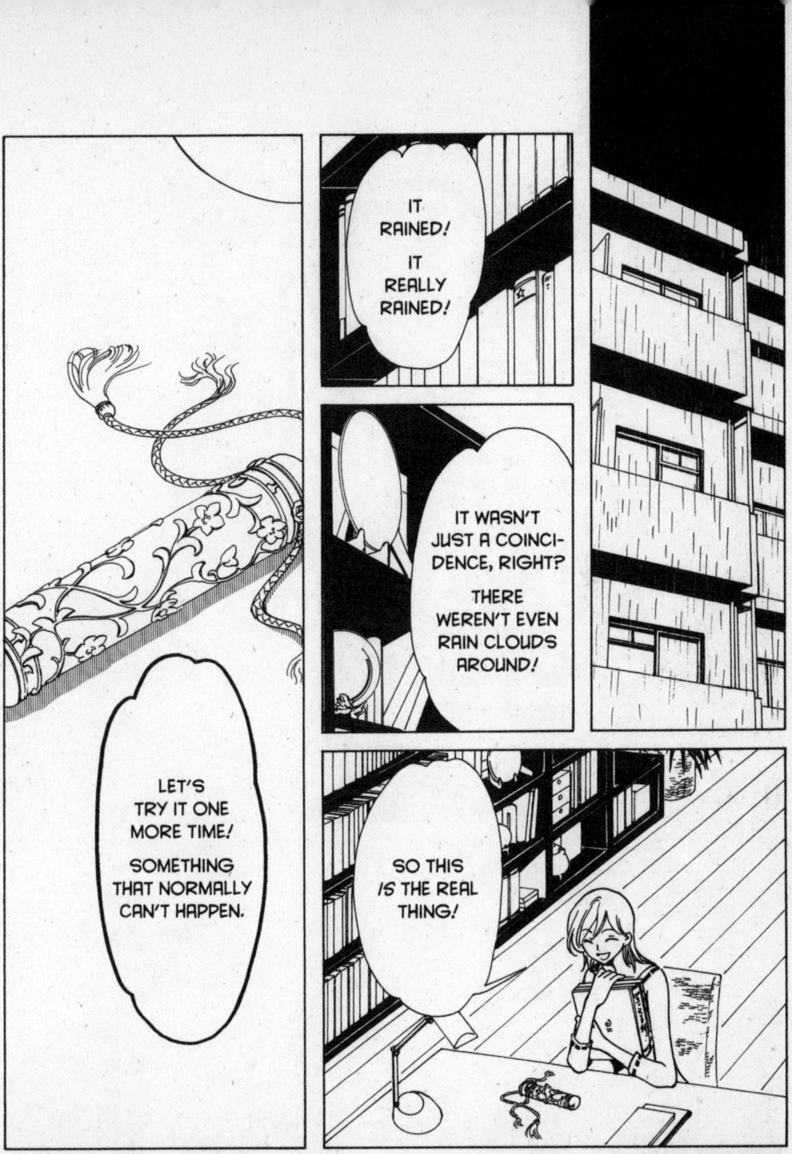
IT RAINED! IT REALLY RAINED!
IT WASN'T JUST A COINCIDENCE, RIGHT? THERE WEREN'T EVEN RAIN CLOUDS AROUND!
SO THIS *IS* THE REAL THING!
LET'S TRY IT ONE MORE TIME! SOMETHING THAT NORMALLY CAN'T HAPPEN.
I'VE GOT IT!

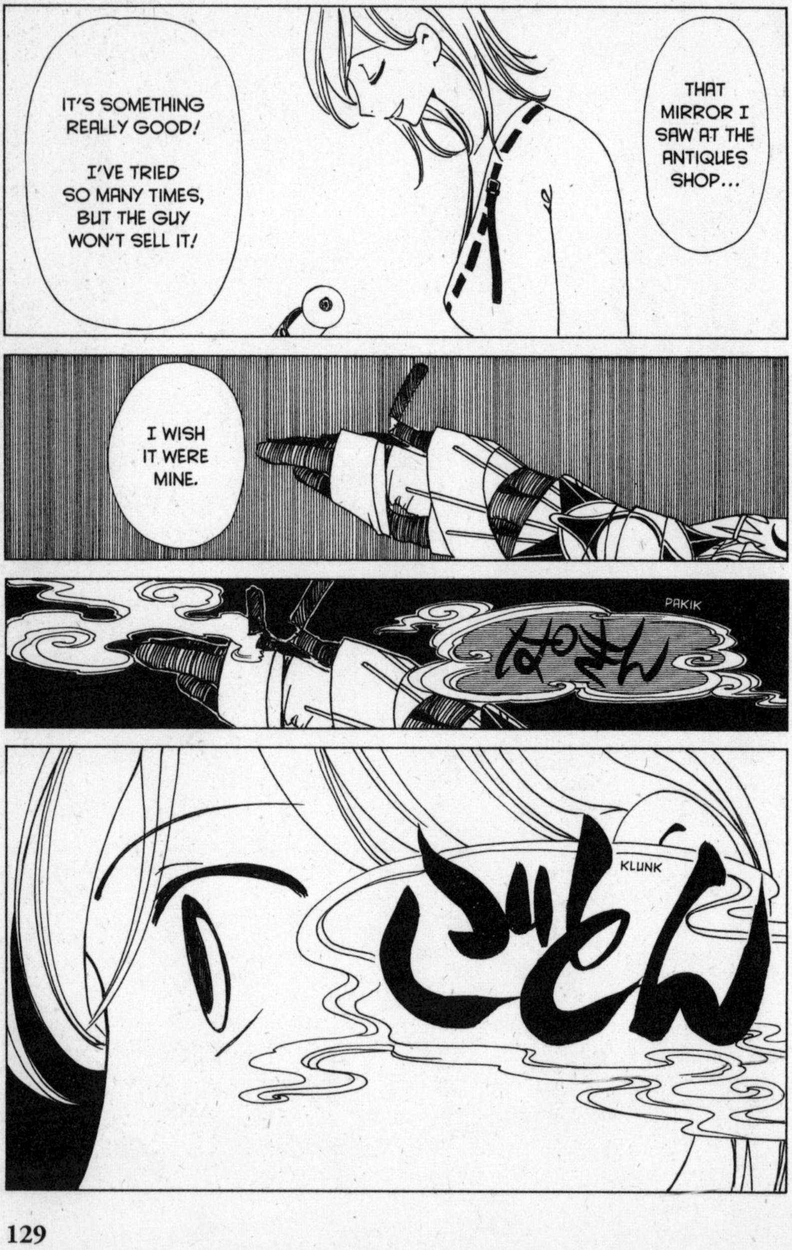
THAT MIRROR I SAW AT THE ANTIQUES SHOP...
IT'S SOMETHING REALLY GOOD!
I'VE TRIED SO MANY TIMES, BUT THE GUY WON'T SELL IT!
I WISH IT WERE MINE.
PAKIK
KLUNK

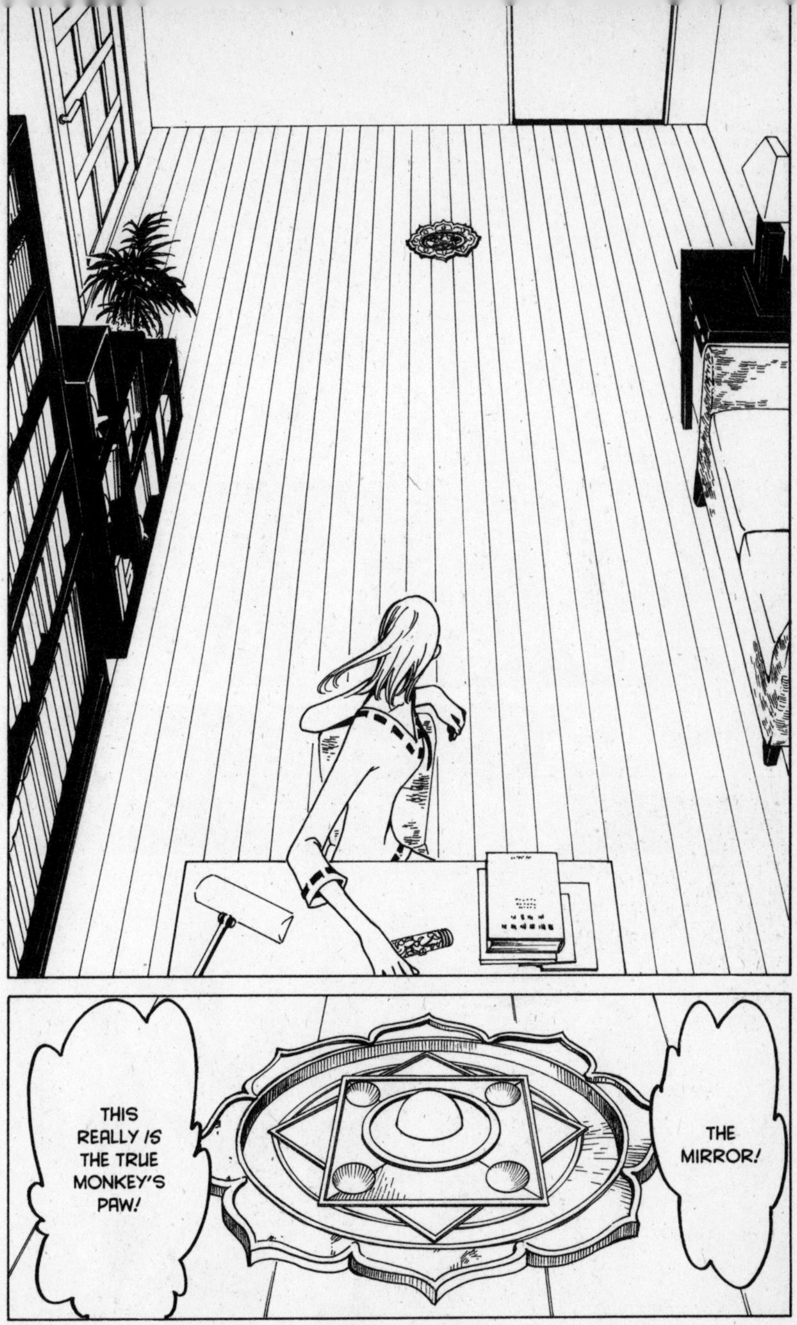
THE MIRROR!
THIS REALLY *IS* THE TRUE MONKEY'S PAW!

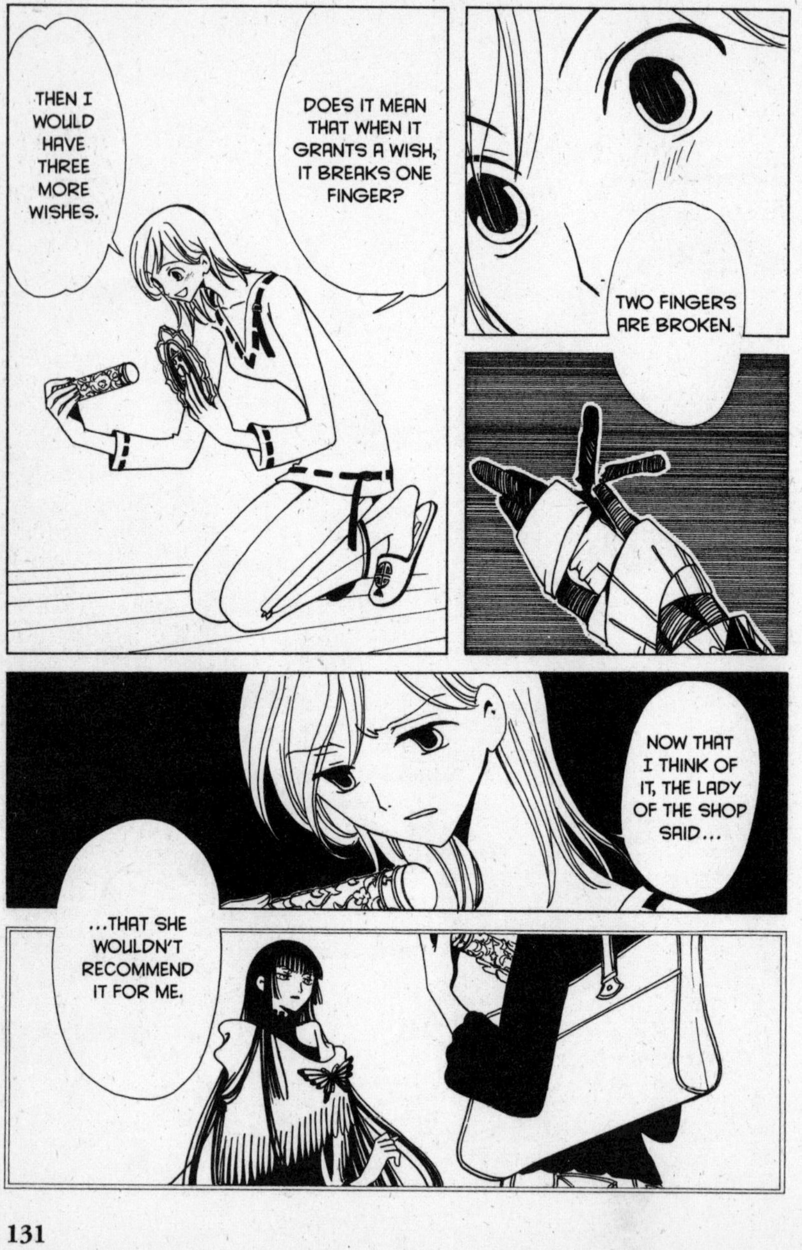
TWO FINGERS ARE BROKEN.
DOES IT MEAN THAT WHEN IT GRANTS A WISH, IT BREAKS ONE FINGER?
THEN I WOULD HAVE THREE MORE WISHES.
NOW THAT I THINK OF IT, THE LADY OF THE SHOP SAID...
...THAT SHE WOULDN'T RECOMMEND IT FOR ME.

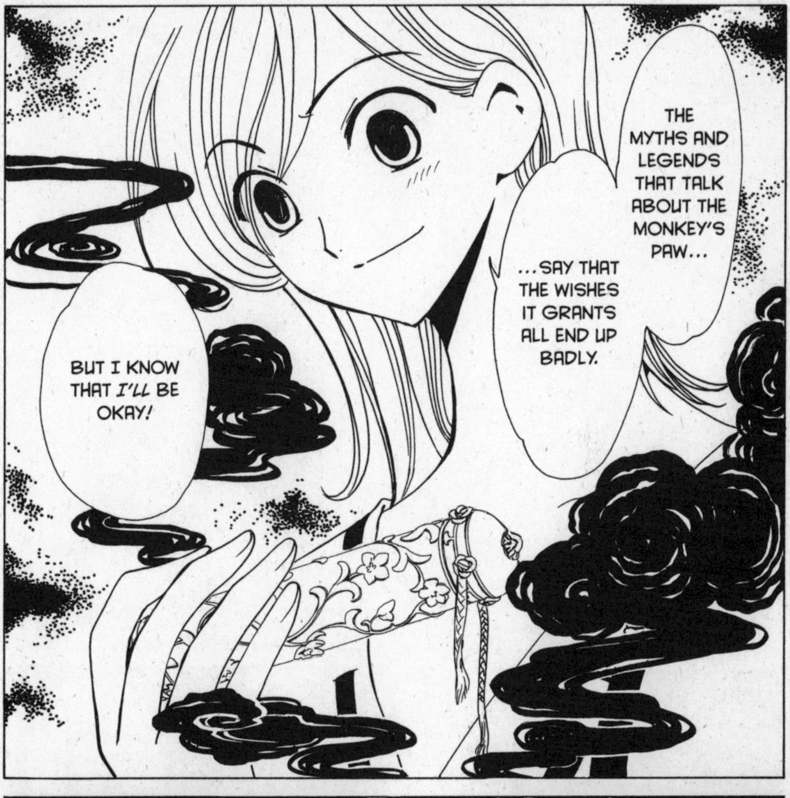
THE MYTHS AND LEGENDS THAT TALK ABOUT THE MONKEY'S PAW...
...SAY THAT THE WISHES IT GRANTS ALL END UP BADLY.
BUT I KNOW THAT *I'LL* BE OKAY!

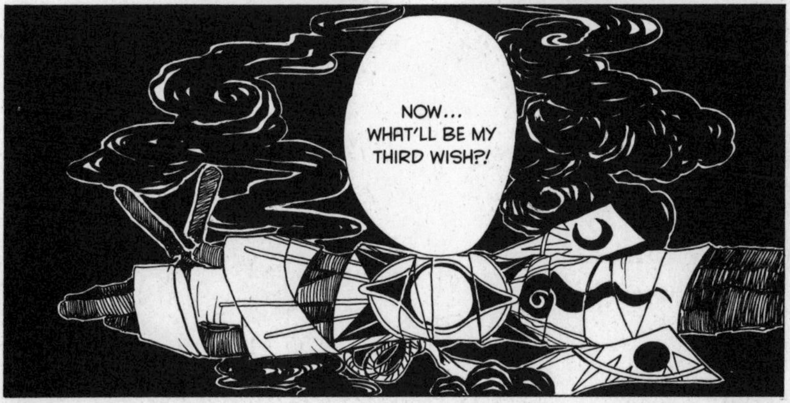
NOW... WHAT'LL BE MY THIRD WISH?!

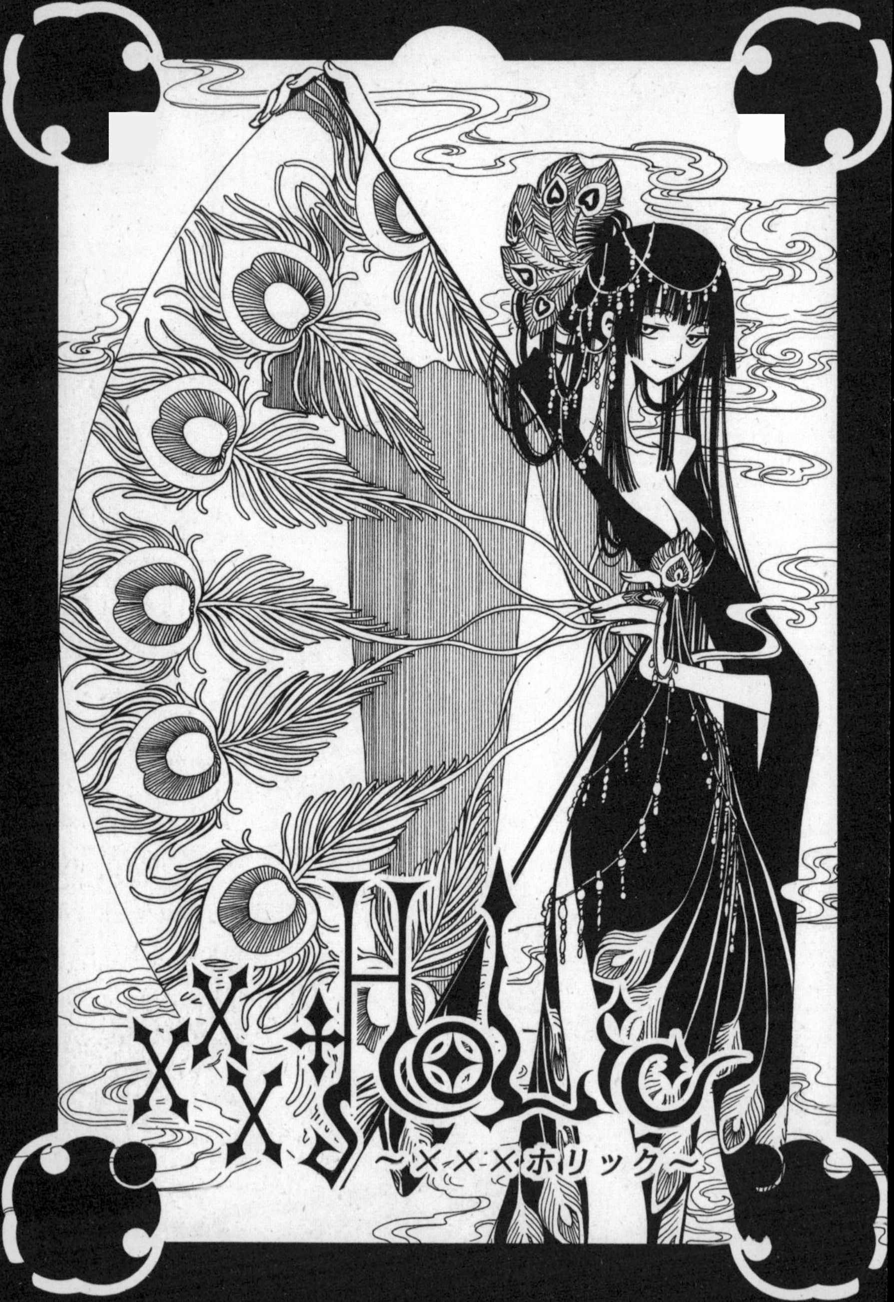
xxxHOLiC
～×××ホリック～

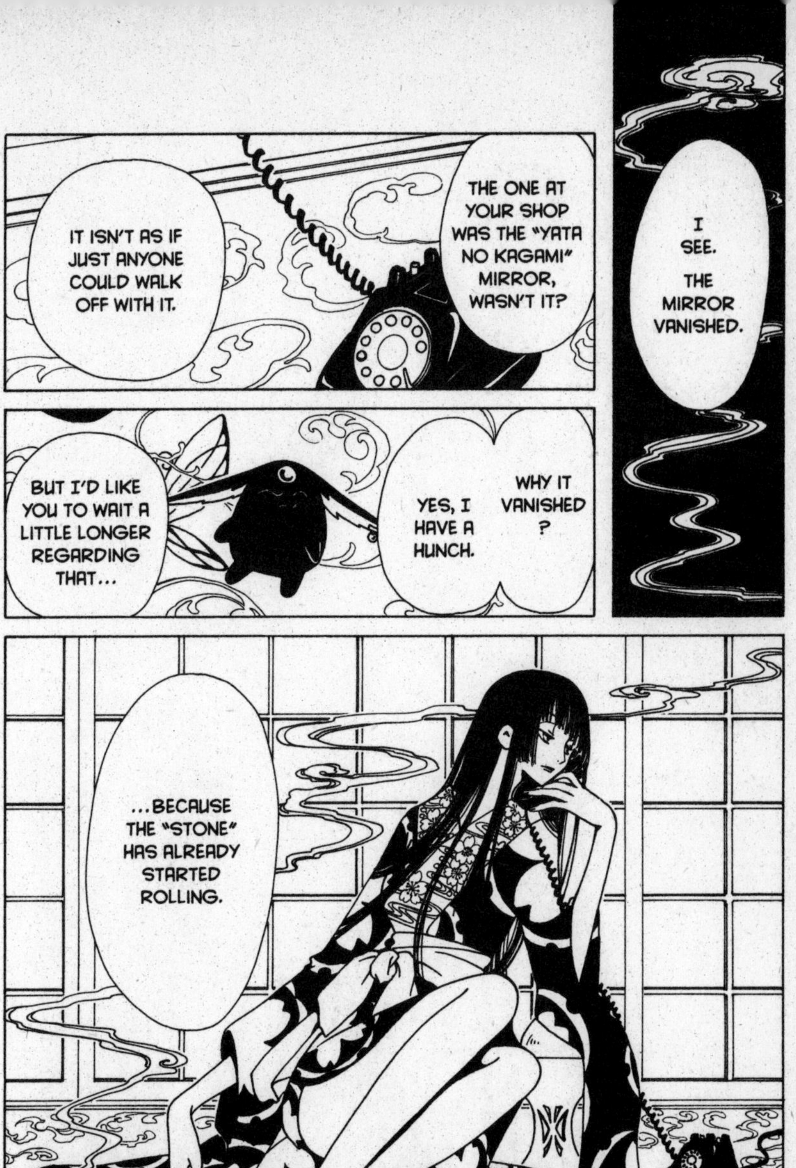
I SEE.
THE MIRROR VANISHED.
THE ONE AT YOUR SHOP WAS THE "YATA NO KAGAMI" MIRROR, WASN'T IT?
IT ISN'T AS IF JUST ANYONE COULD WALK OFF WITH IT.
WHY IT VANISHED ?
YES, I HAVE A HUNCH.
BUT I'D LIKE YOU TO WAIT A LITTLE LONGER REGARDING THAT...
...BECAUSE THE "STONE" HAS ALREADY STARTED ROLLING.

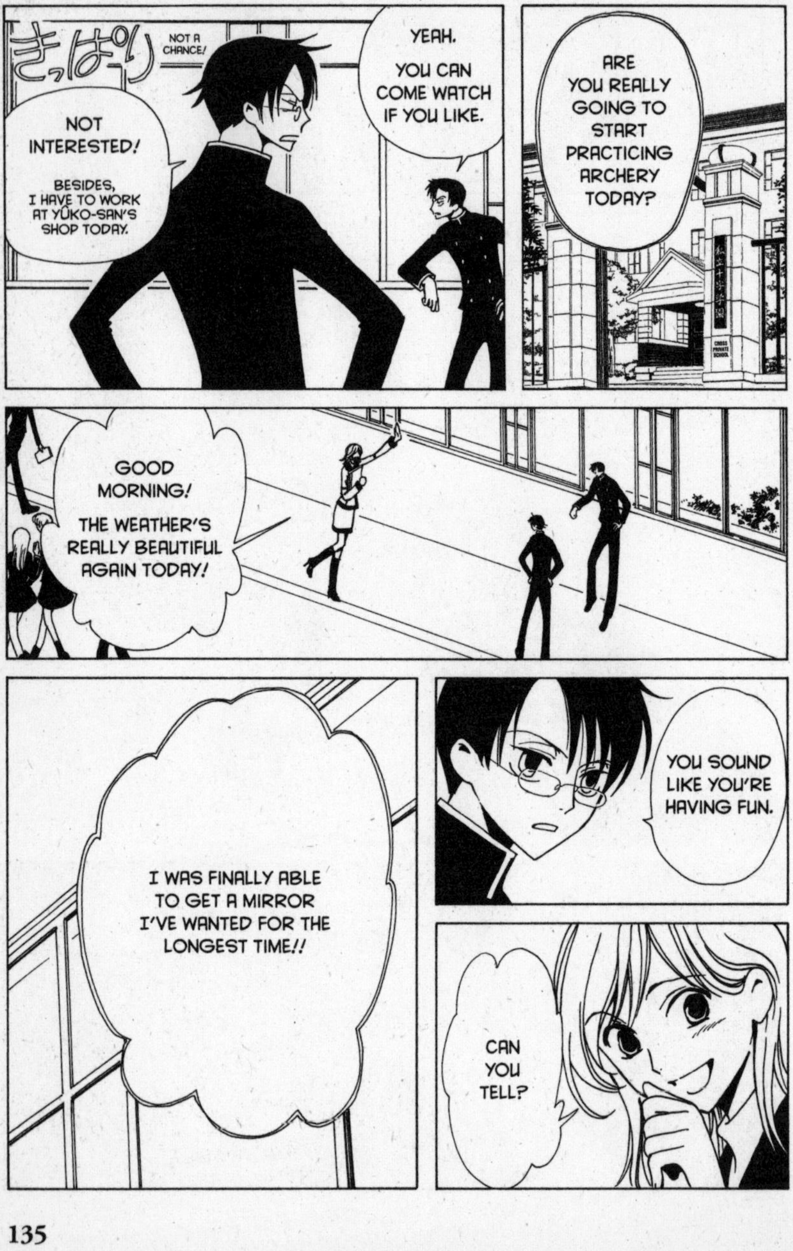
ARE YOU REALLY GOING TO START PRACTICING ARCHERY TODAY?
YEAH.
YOU CAN COME WATCH IF YOU LIKE.
きっぱり
NOT A CHANCE!
NOT INTERESTED!
BESIDES, I HAVE TO WORK AT YÛKO-SAN'S SHOP TODAY.
GOOD MORNING!
THE WEATHER'S REALLY BEAUTIFUL AGAIN TODAY!
YOU SOUND LIKE YOU'RE HAVING FUN.
CAN YOU TELL?
I WAS FINALLY ABLE TO GET A MIRROR I'VE WANTED FOR THE LONGEST TIME!!

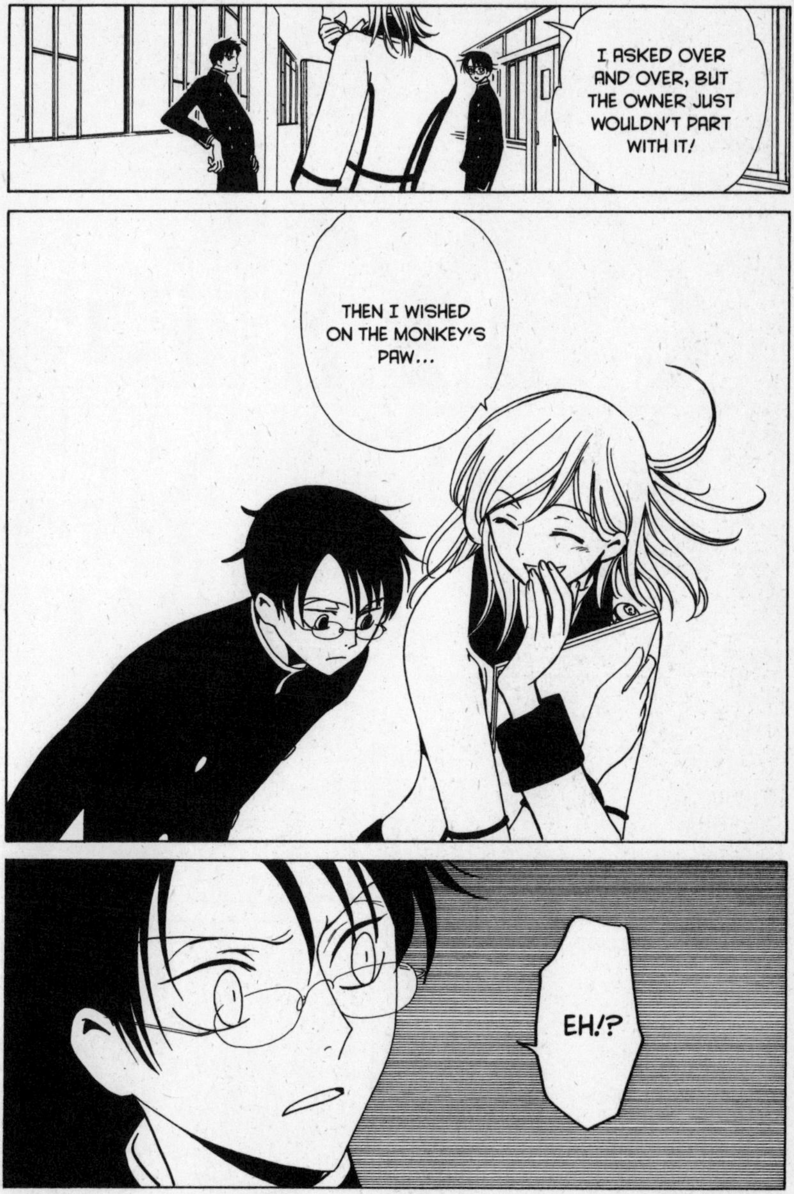
I ASKED OVER AND OVER, BUT THE OWNER JUST WOULDN'T PART WITH IT!
THEN I WISHED ON THE MONKEY'S PAW...
EH!?

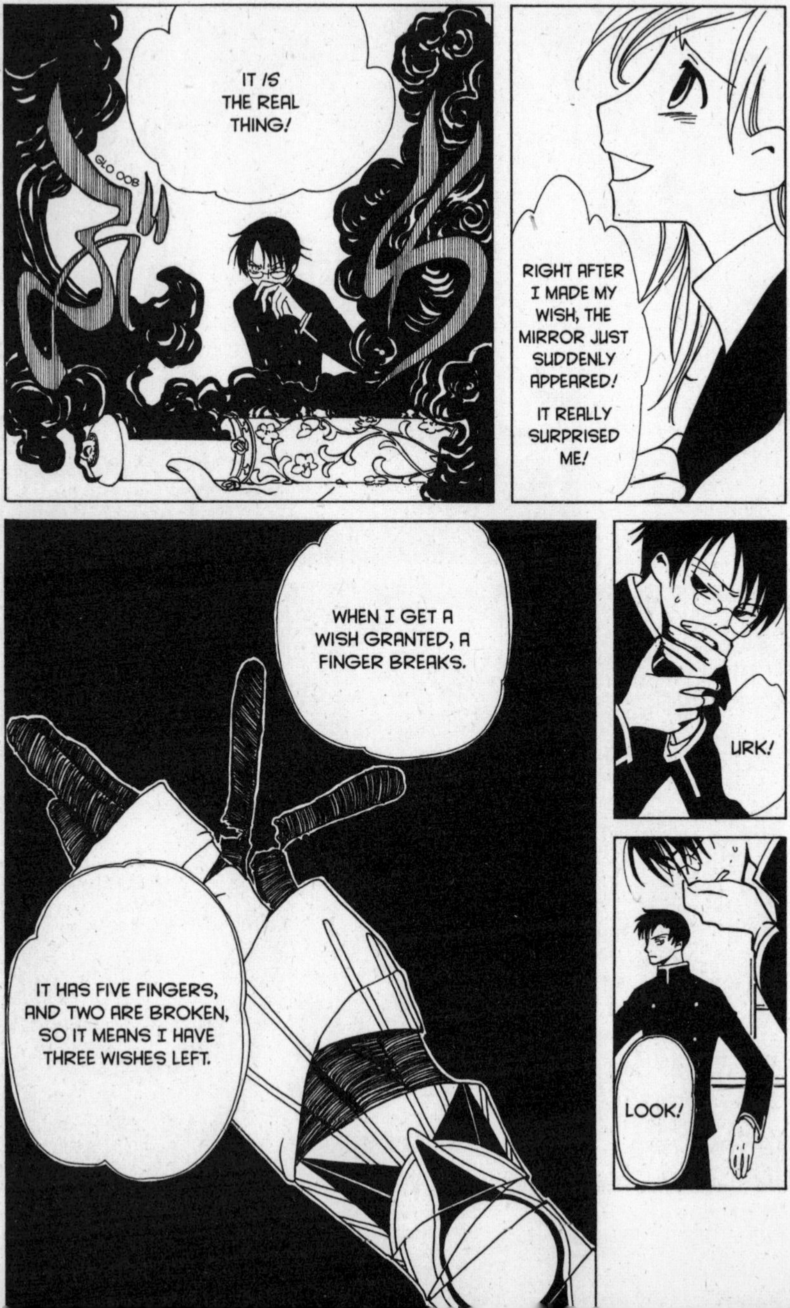
RIGHT AFTER I MADE MY WISH, THE MIRROR JUST SUDDENLY APPEARED!
IT REALLY SURPRISED ME!
IT IS THE REAL THING!
GLO OOB
URK!
LOOK!
WHEN I GET A WISH GRANTED, A FINGER BREAKS.
IT HAS FIVE FINGERS, AND TWO ARE BROKEN, SO IT MEANS I HAVE THREE WISHES LEFT.

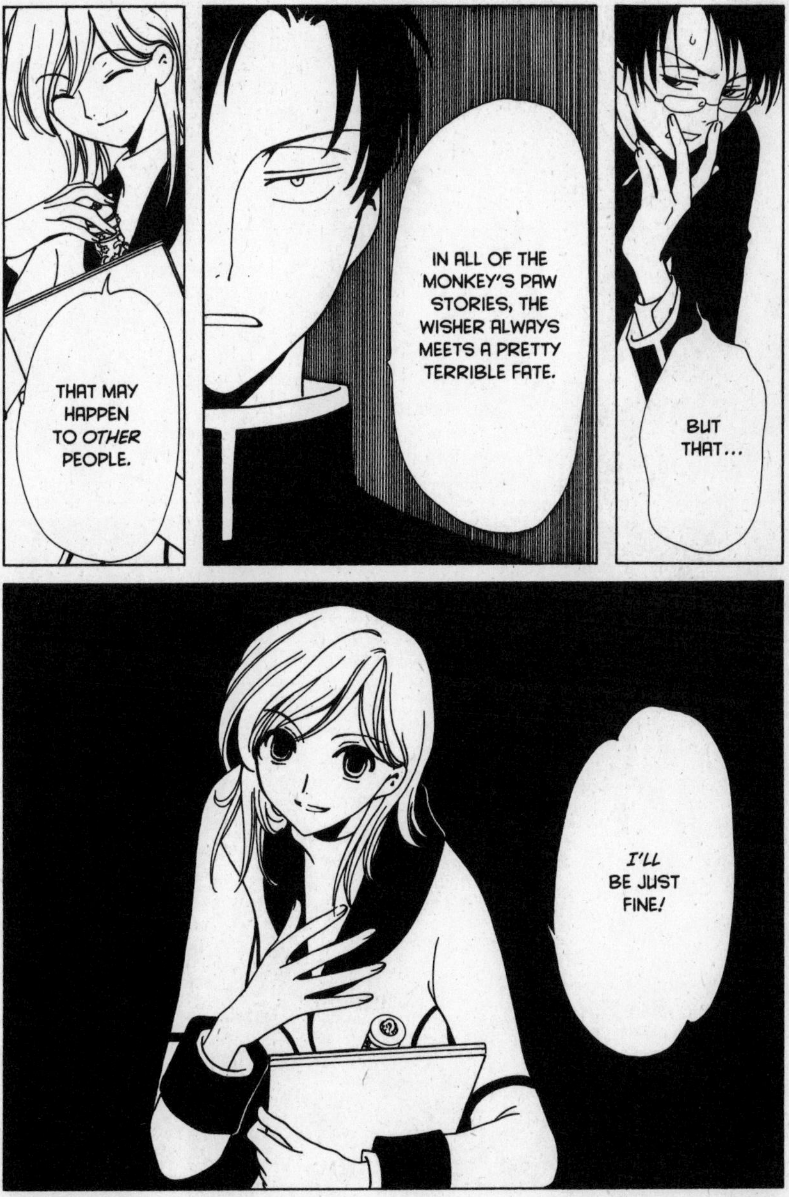
BUT THAT...
IN ALL OF THE MONKEY'S PAW STORIES, THE WISHER ALWAYS MEETS A PRETTY TERRIBLE FATE.
THAT MAY HAPPEN TO *OTHER* PEOPLE.
I'LL BE JUST FINE!

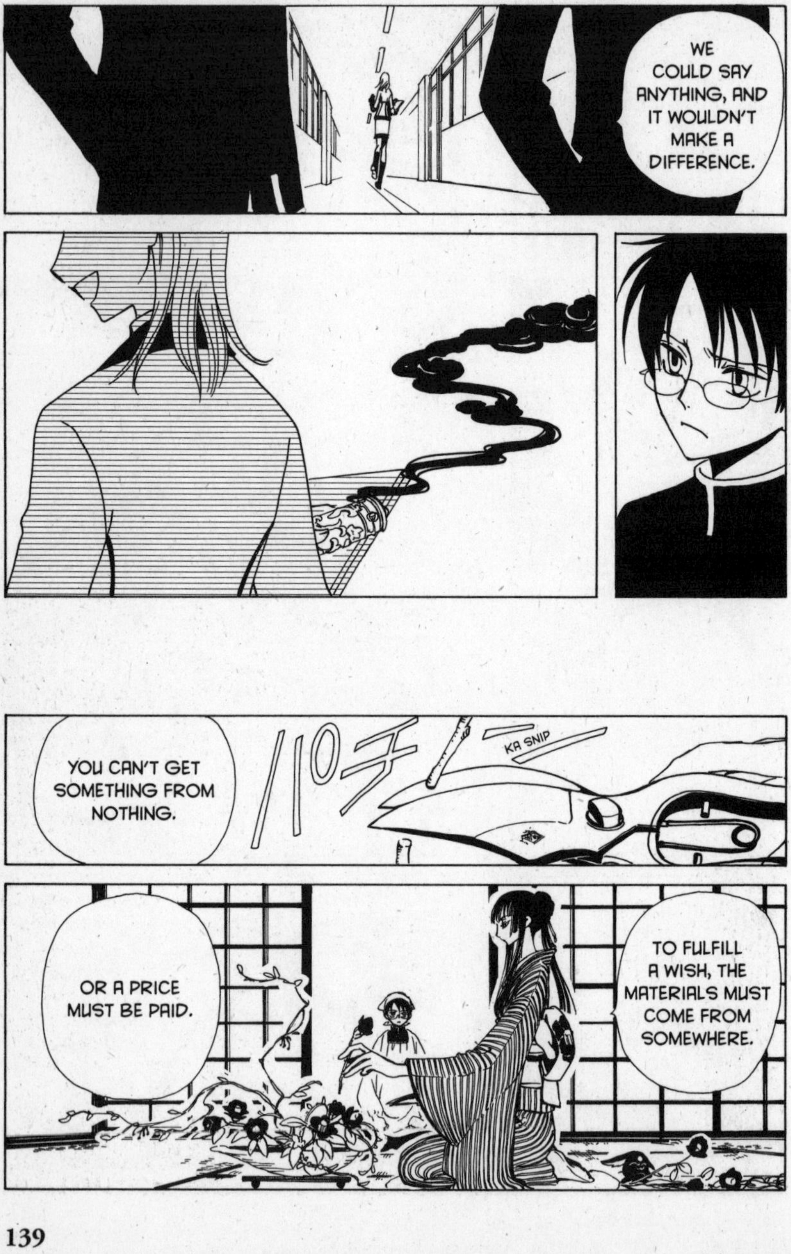
WE COULD SAY ANYTHING, AND IT WOULDN'T MAKE A DIFFERENCE.
KA SNIP
YOU CAN'T GET SOMETHING FROM NOTHING.
TO FULFILL A WISH, THE MATERIALS MUST COME FROM SOMEWHERE.
OR A PRICE MUST BE PAID.

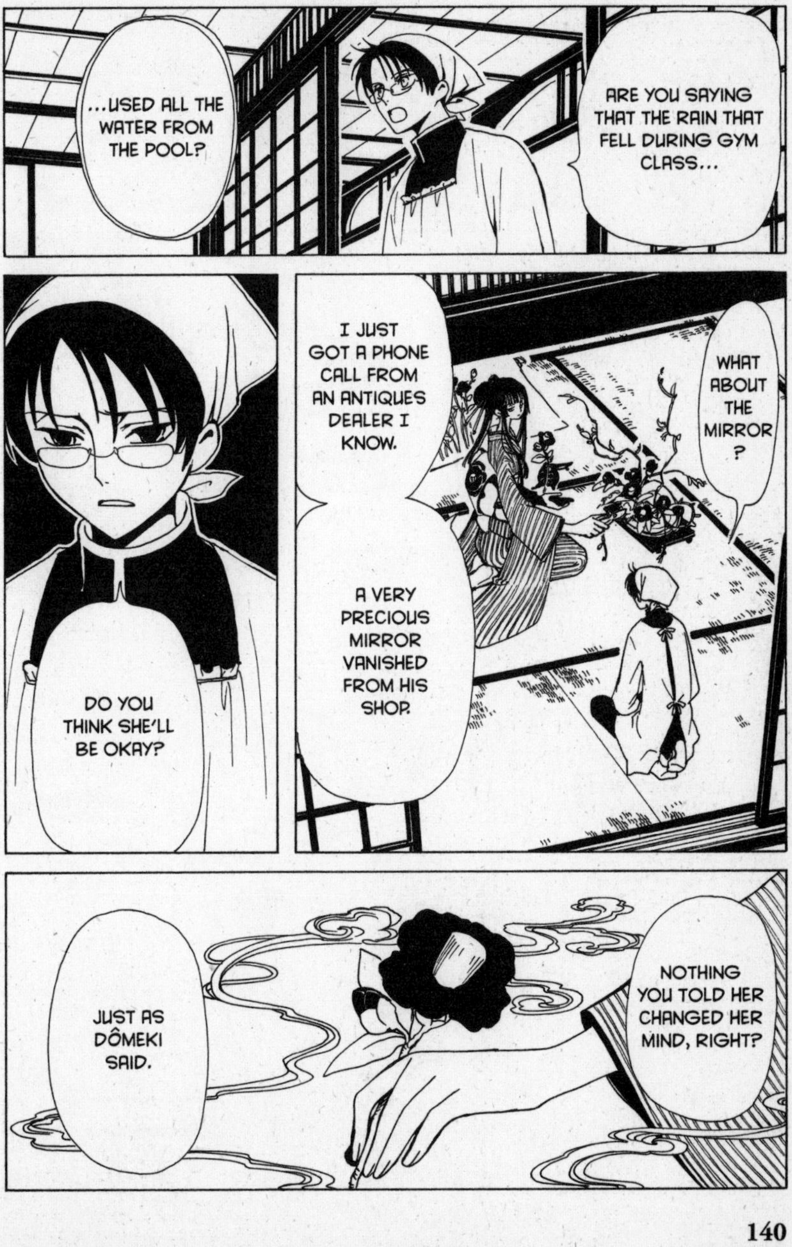
ARE YOU SAYING THAT THE RAIN THAT FELL DURING GYM CLASS...
...USED ALL THE WATER FROM THE POOL?
WHAT ABOUT THE MIRROR ?
I JUST GOT A PHONE CALL FROM AN ANTIQUES DEALER I KNOW.
A VERY PRECIOUS MIRROR VANISHED FROM HIS SHOP.
DO YOU THINK SHE'LL BE OKAY?
NOTHING YOU TOLD HER CHANGED HER MIND, RIGHT?
JUST AS DÔMEKI SAID.

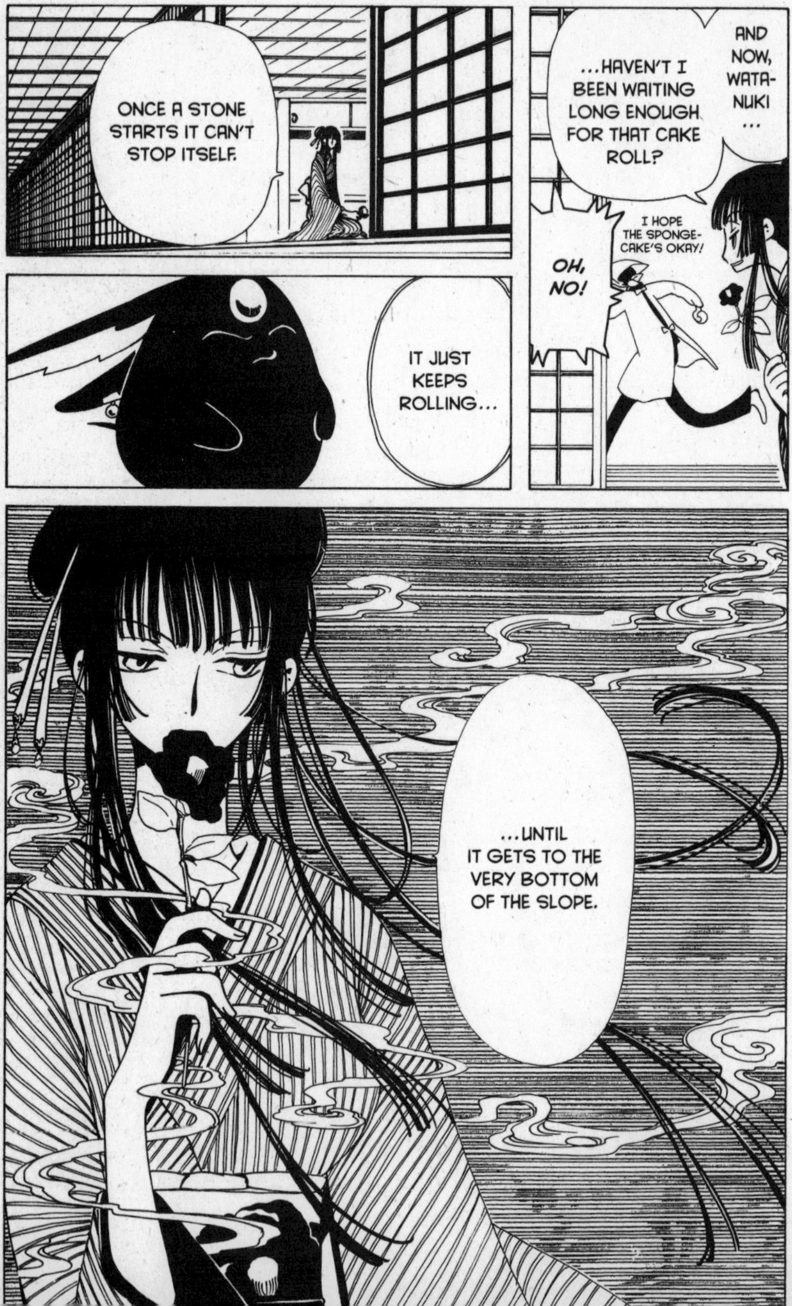
AND NOW, WATA-NUKI ...
...HAVEN'T I BEEN WAITING LONG ENOUGH FOR THAT CAKE ROLL?
I HOPE THE SPONGE-CAKE'S OKAY!
OH, NO!
ONCE A STONE STARTS IT CAN'T STOP ITSELF.
IT JUST KEEPS ROLLING...
...UNTIL IT GETS TO THE VERY BOTTOM OF THE SLOPE.

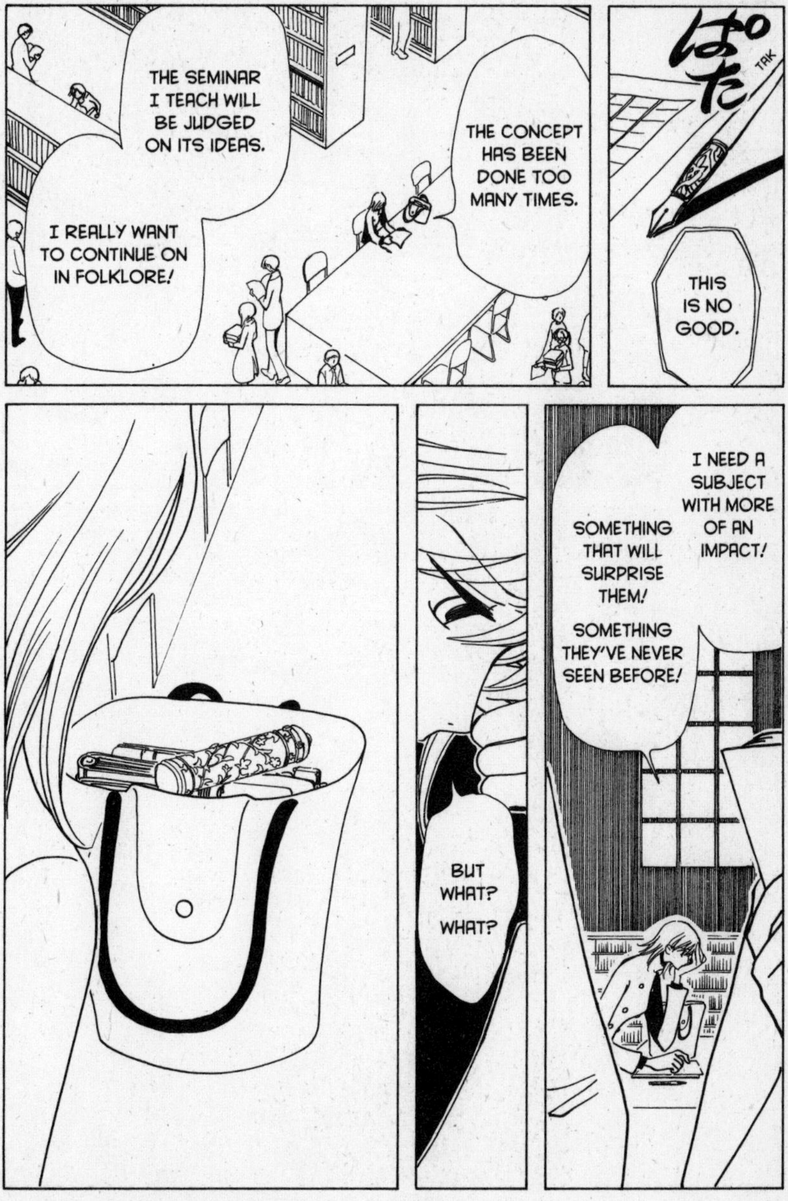
ぱた
TAK
THIS IS NO GOOD.
THE CONCEPT HAS BEEN DONE TOO MANY TIMES.
THE SEMINAR I TEACH WILL BE JUDGED ON ITS IDEAS.
I REALLY WANT TO CONTINUE ON IN FOLKLORE!
I NEED A SUBJECT WITH MORE OF AN IMPACT!
SOMETHING THAT WILL SURPRISE THEM!
SOMETHING THEY'VE NEVER SEEN BEFORE!
BUT WHAT?
WHAT?

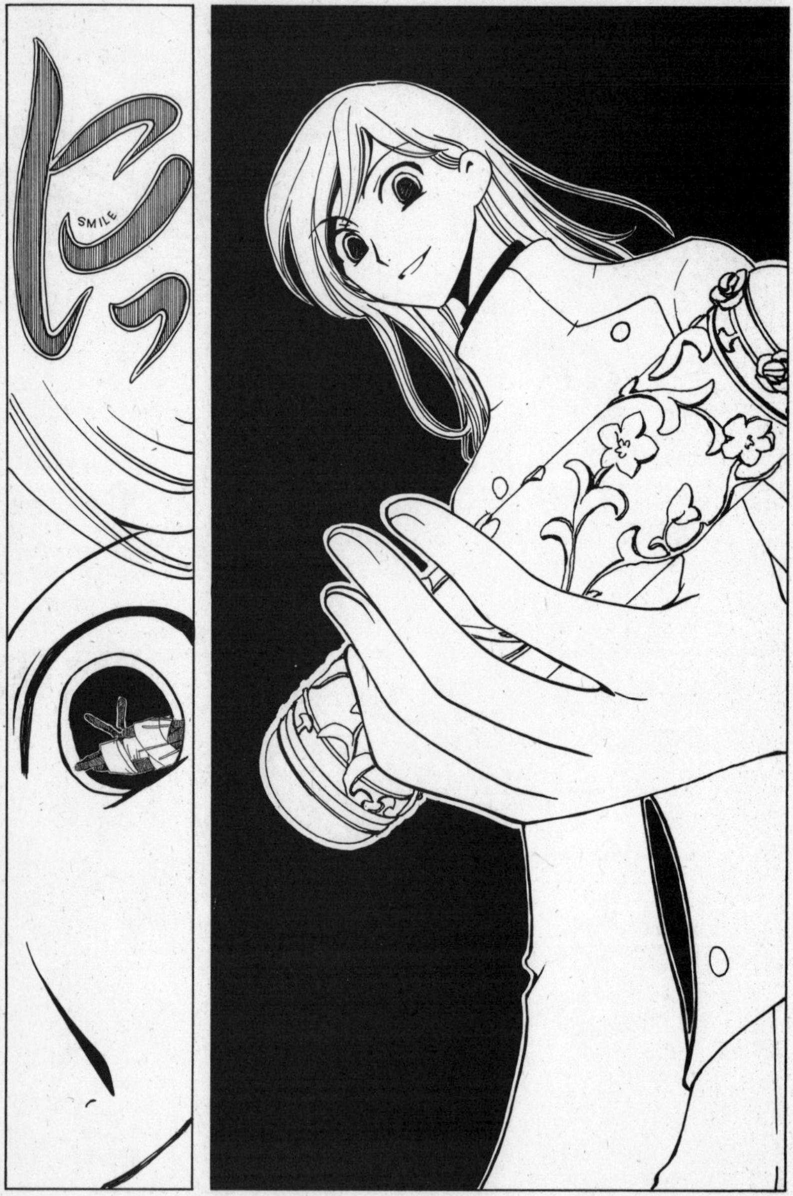
にこっ
SMILE

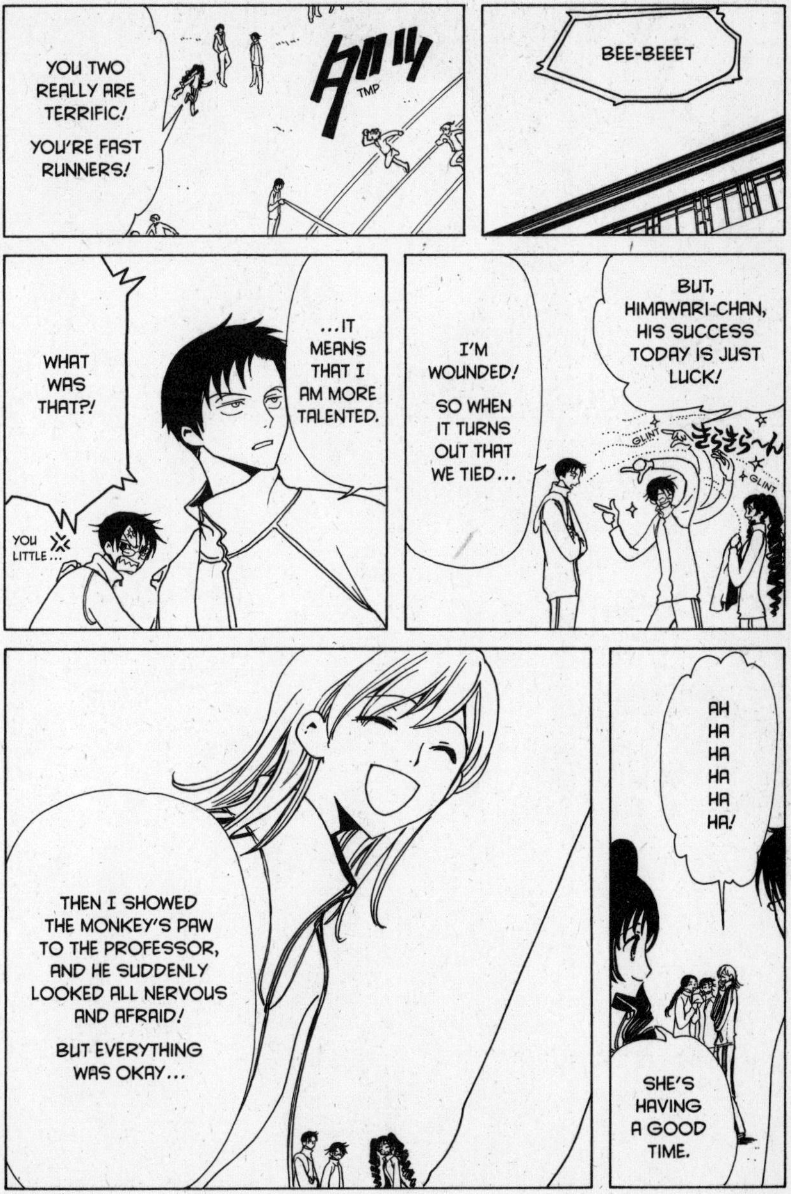
BEE-BEEET
YOU TWO REALLY ARE TERRIFIC!
YOU'RE FAST RUNNERS!
タッ
TMP
BUT, HIMAWARI-CHAN, HIS SUCCESS TODAY IS JUST LUCK!
GLINT
きらきら〜ん
GLINT
I'M WOUNDED!
SO WHEN IT TURNS OUT THAT WE TIED...
...IT MEANS THAT I AM MORE TALENTED.
WHAT WAS THAT?!
YOU LITTLE...
AH HA HA HA HA HA!
SHE'S HAVING A GOOD TIME.
THEN I SHOWED THE MONKEY'S PAW TO THE PROFESSOR, AND HE SUDDENLY LOOKED ALL NERVOUS AND AFRAID!
BUT EVERYTHING WAS OKAY...

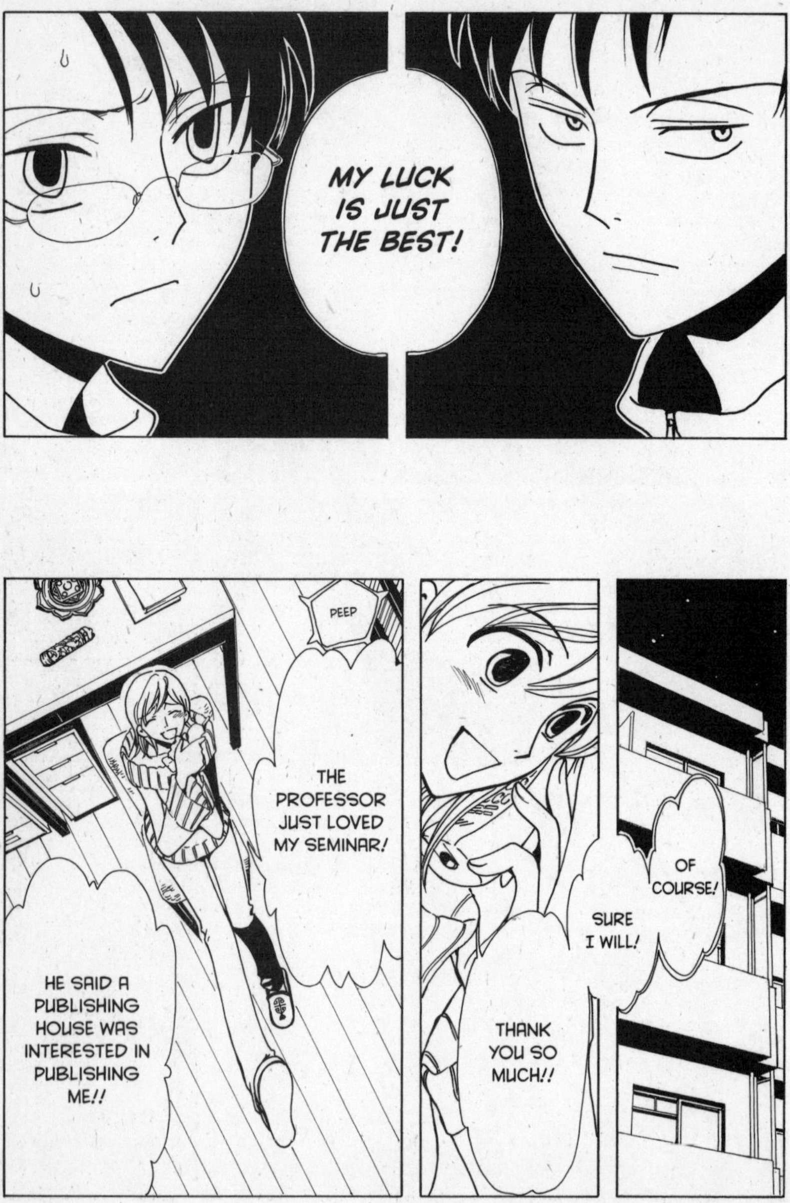
MY LUCK IS JUST THE BEST!
OF COURSE!
SURE I WILL!
THANK YOU SO MUCH!!
PEEP
THE PROFESSOR JUST LOVED MY SEMINAR!
HE SAID A PUBLISHING HOUSE WAS INTERESTED IN PUBLISHING ME!!

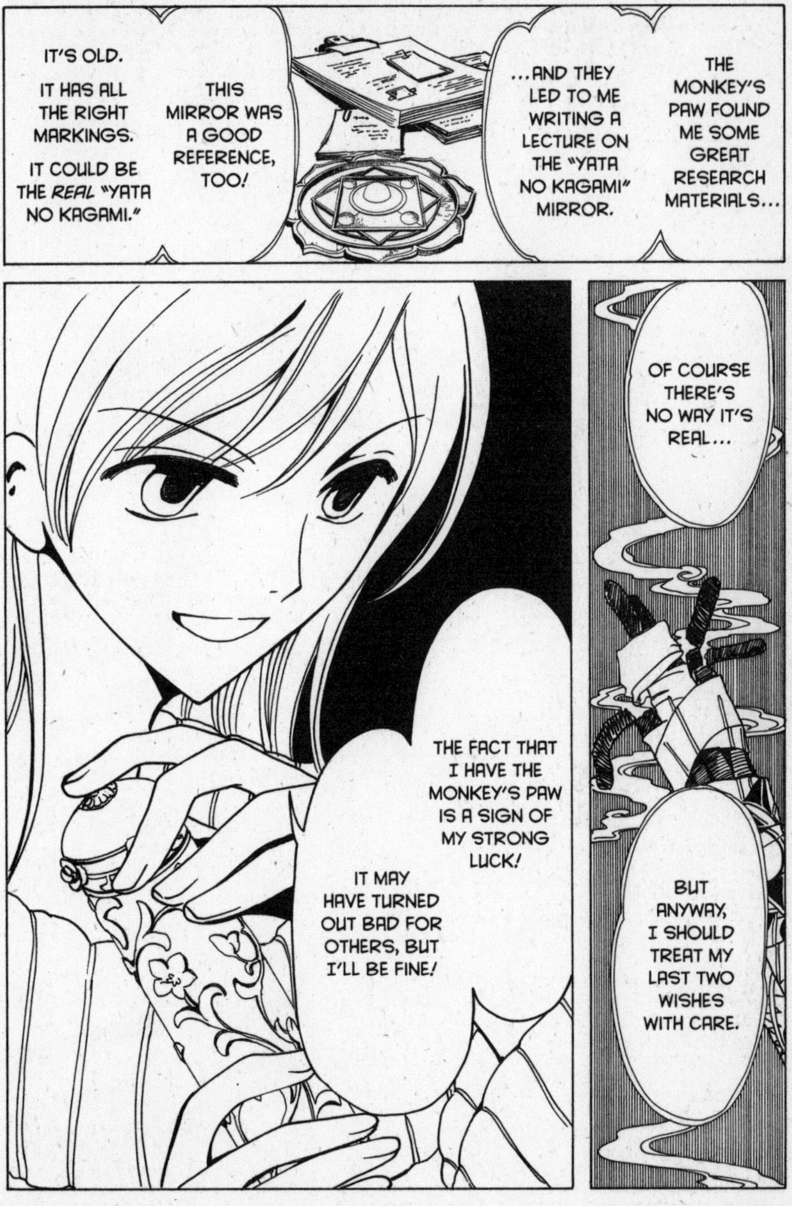
THE MONKEY'S PAW FOUND ME SOME GREAT RESEARCH MATERIALS...
...AND THEY LED TO ME WRITING A LECTURE ON THE "YATA NO KAGAMI" MIRROR.
THIS MIRROR WAS A GOOD REFERENCE, TOO!
IT'S OLD.
IT HAS ALL THE RIGHT MARKINGS.
IT COULD BE THE *REAL* "YATA NO KAGAMI."
OF COURSE THERE'S NO WAY IT'S REAL...
BUT ANYWAY, I SHOULD TREAT MY LAST TWO WISHES WITH CARE.
THE FACT THAT I HAVE THE MONKEY'S PAW IS A SIGN OF MY STRONG LUCK!
IT MAY HAVE TURNED OUT BAD FOR OTHERS, BUT I'LL BE FINE!

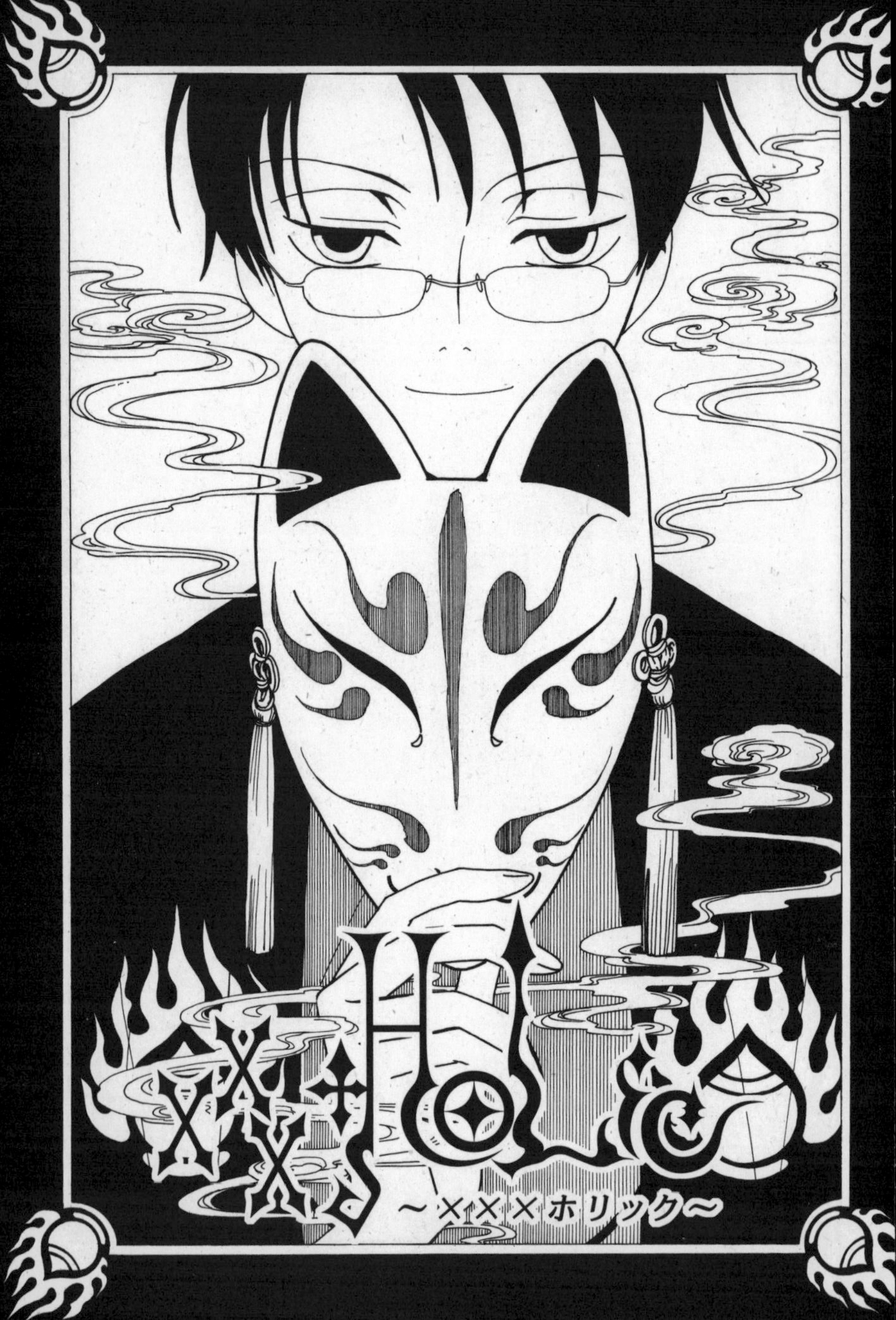
xxxHOLiC
~×××ホリック~

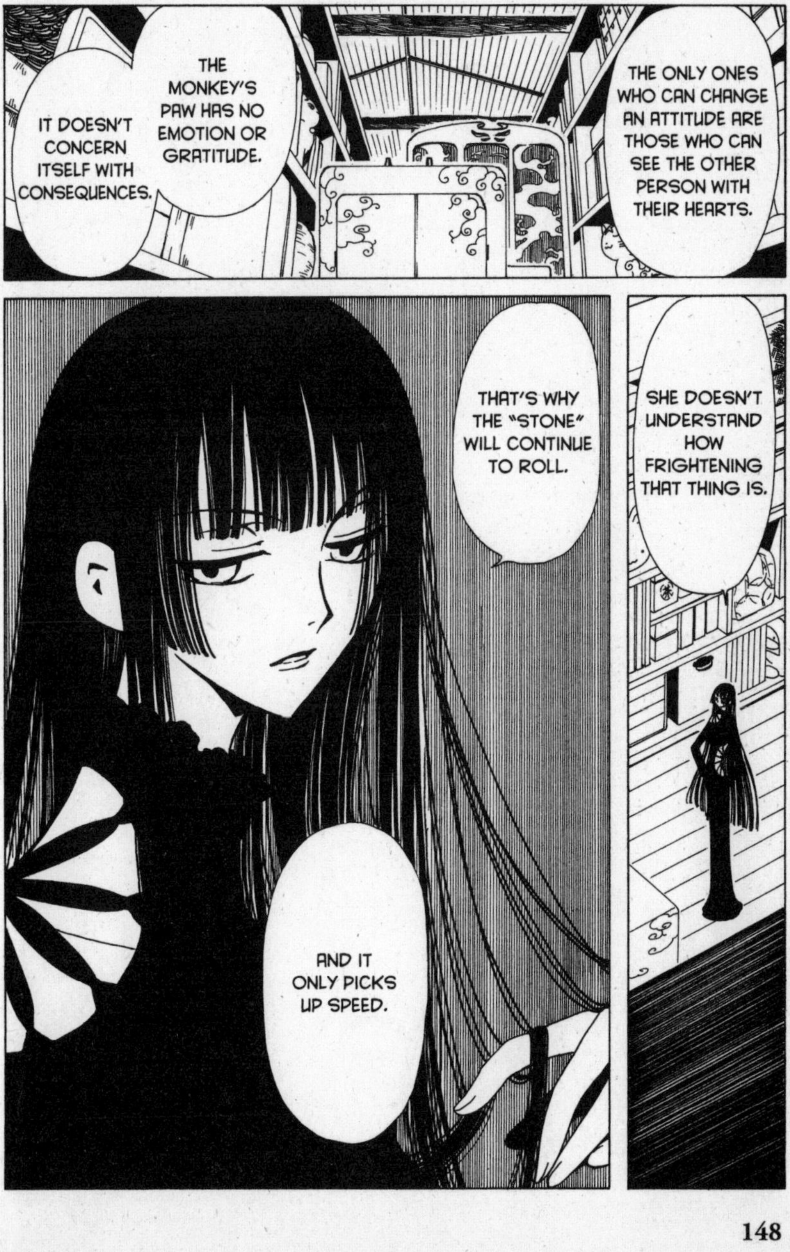
THE ONLY ONES WHO CAN CHANGE AN ATTITUDE ARE THOSE WHO CAN SEE THE OTHER PERSON WITH THEIR HEARTS.
THE MONKEY'S PAW HAS NO EMOTION OR GRATITUDE.
IT DOESN'T CONCERN ITSELF WITH CONSEQUENCES.
SHE DOESN'T UNDERSTAND HOW FRIGHTENING THAT THING IS.
THAT'S WHY THE "STONE" WILL CONTINUE TO ROLL.
AND IT ONLY PICKS UP SPEED.

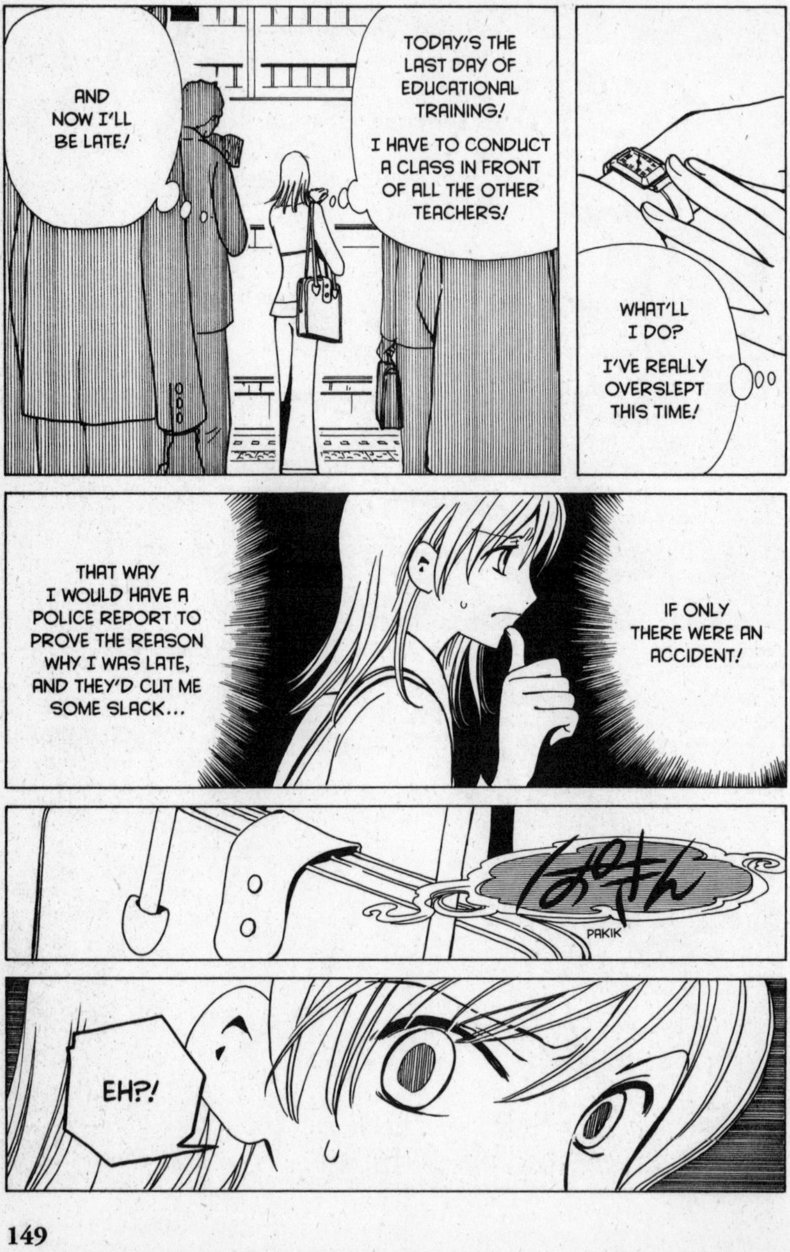

WHAT'LL I DO?
I'VE REALLY OVERSLEPT THIS TIME!
TODAY'S THE LAST DAY OF EDUCATIONAL TRAINING!
I HAVE TO CONDUCT A CLASS IN FRONT OF ALL THE OTHER TEACHERS!
AND NOW I'LL BE LATE!
IF ONLY THERE WERE AN ACCIDENT!
THAT WAY I WOULD HAVE A POLICE REPORT TO PROVE THE REASON WHY I WAS LATE, AND THEY'D CUT ME SOME SLACK...
PAKIK
EH?!

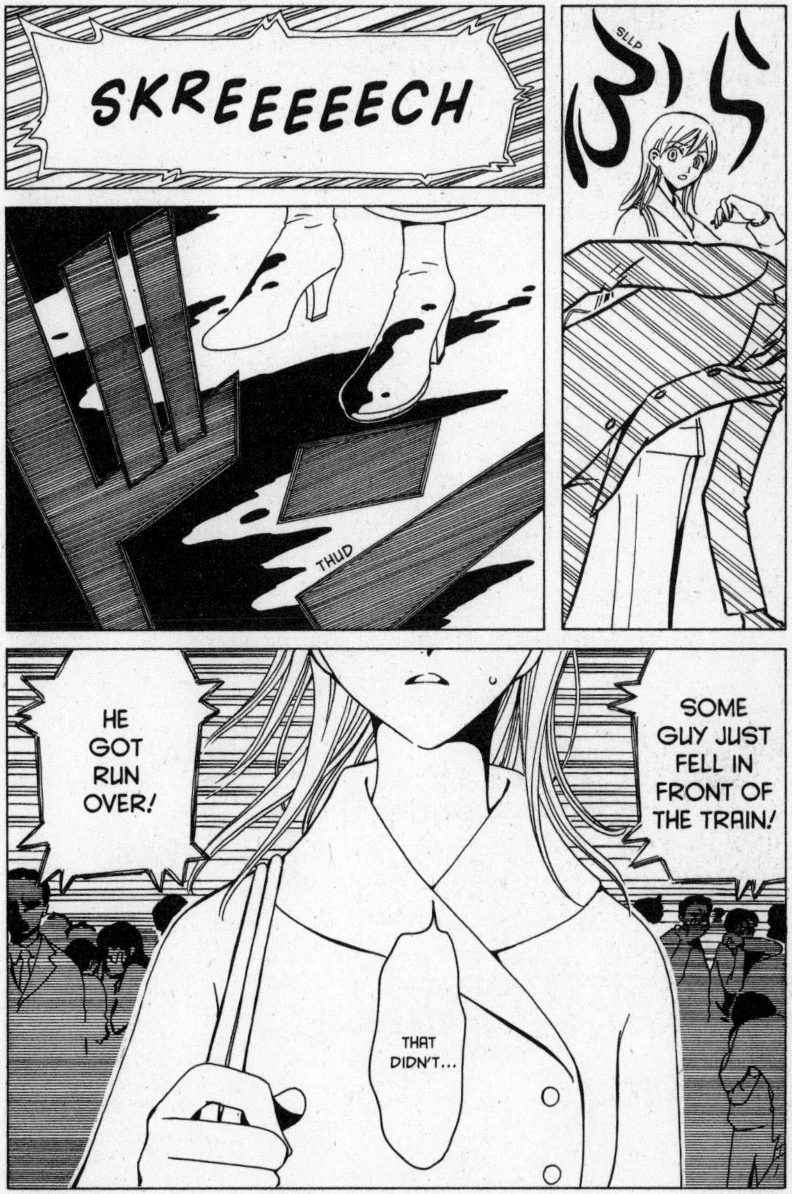
SLLP
ぶら
SKREEEEEECH
THUD
SOME GUY JUST FELL IN FRONT OF THE TRAIN!
HE GOT RUN OVER!
THAT DIDN'T...

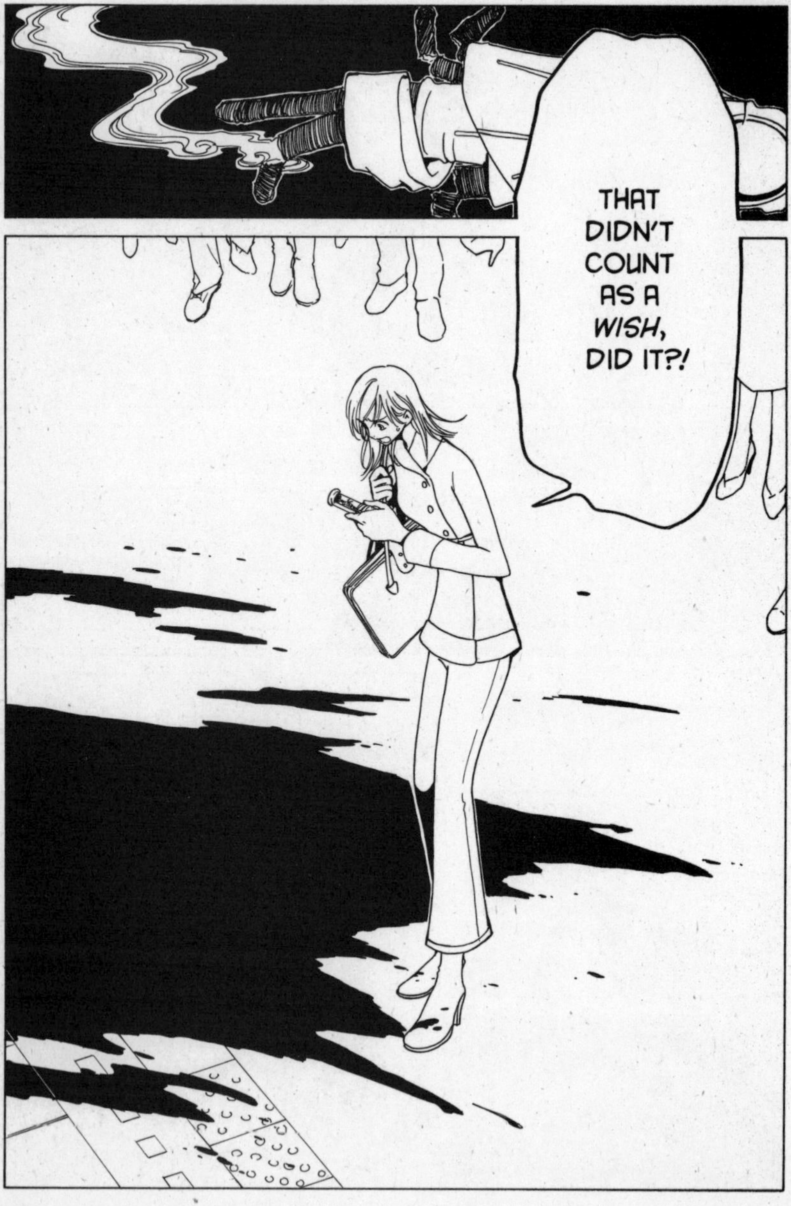
THAT DIDN'T COUNT AS A *WISH*, DID IT?!

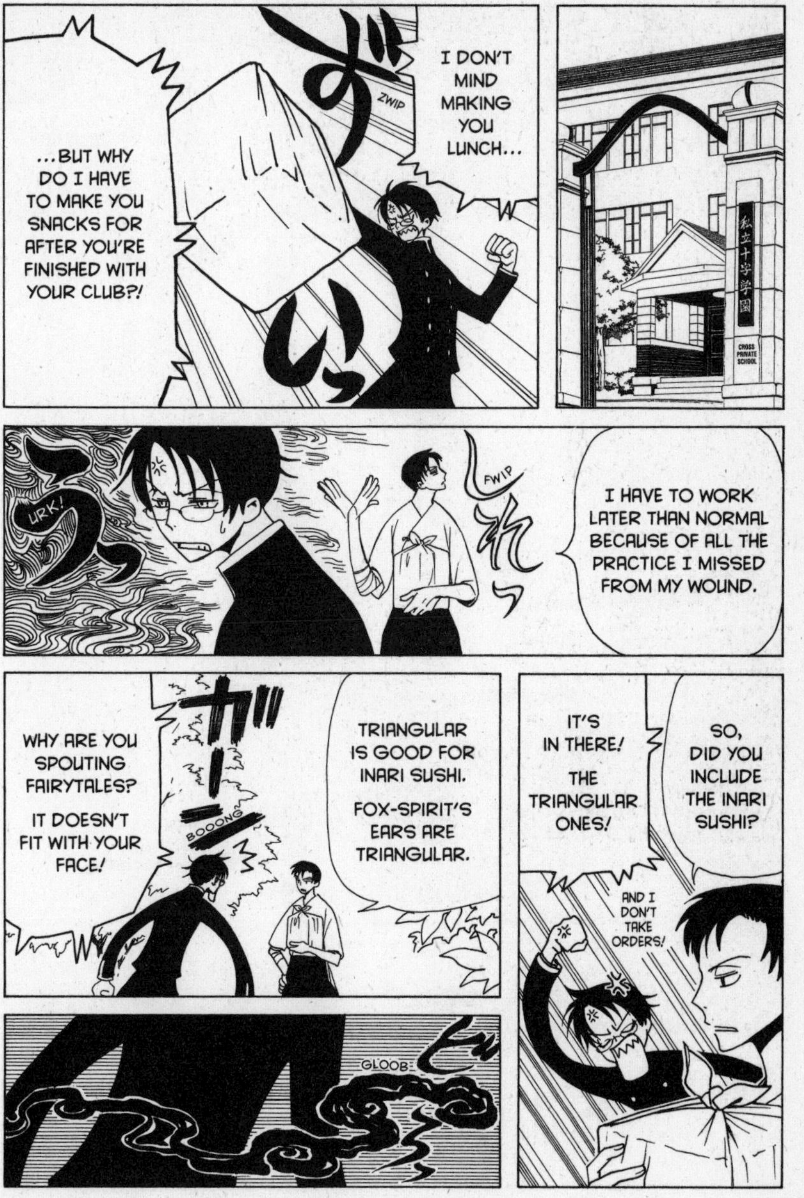
私立十字学園
CROSS PRIVATE SCHOOL
I DON'T MIND MAKING YOU LUNCH...
ZWIP
...BUT WHY DO I HAVE TO MAKE YOU SNACKS FOR AFTER YOU'RE FINISHED WITH YOUR CLUB?!
I HAVE TO WORK LATER THAN NORMAL BECAUSE OF ALL THE PRACTICE I MISSED FROM MY WOUND.
FWIP
URK!
SO, DID YOU INCLUDE THE INARI SUSHI?
IT'S IN THERE!
THE TRIANGULAR ONES!
AND I DON'T TAKE ORDERS!
TRIANGULAR IS GOOD FOR INARI SUSHI.
FOX-SPIRIT'S EARS ARE TRIANGULAR.
BOOONG
WHY ARE YOU SPOUTING FAIRYTALES?
IT DOESN'T FIT WITH YOUR FACE!
GLOOB

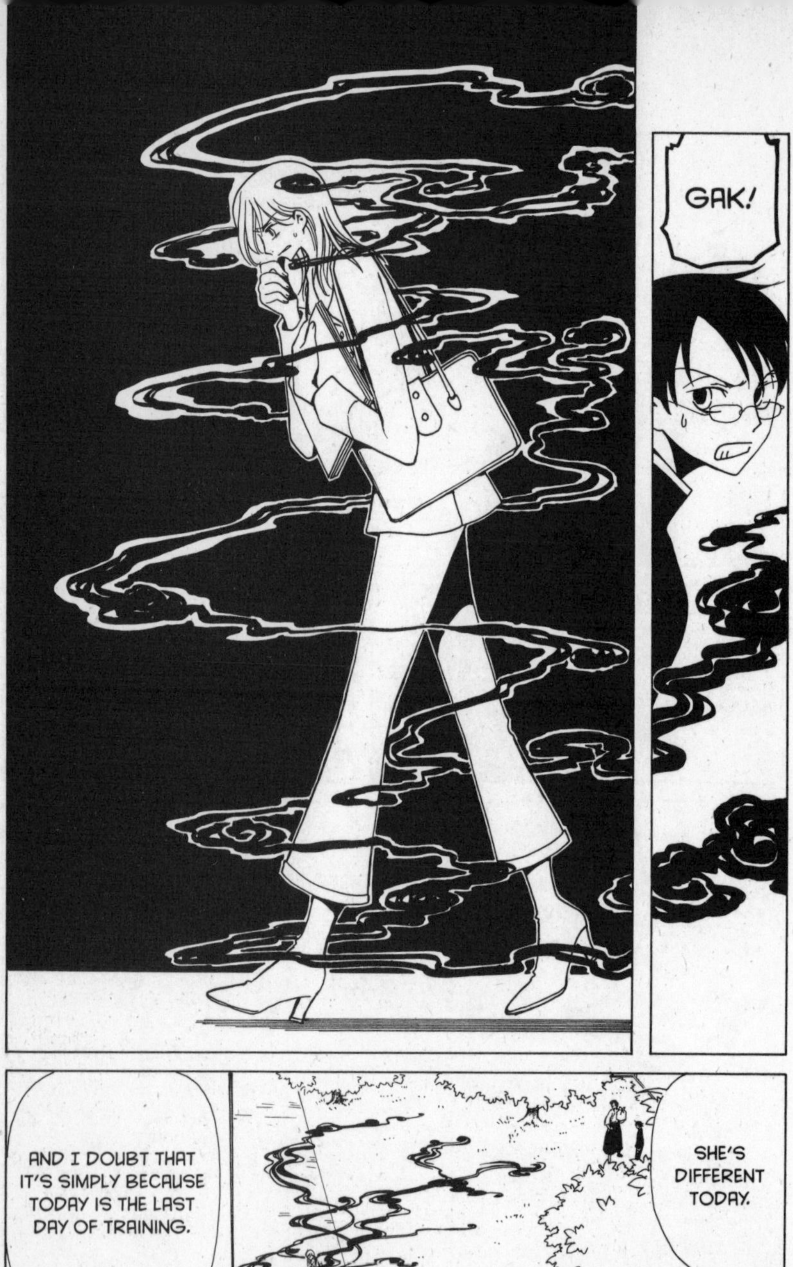
GAK!
SHE'S DIFFERENT TODAY.
AND I DOUBT THAT IT'S SIMPLY BECAUSE TODAY IS THE LAST DAY OF TRAINING.

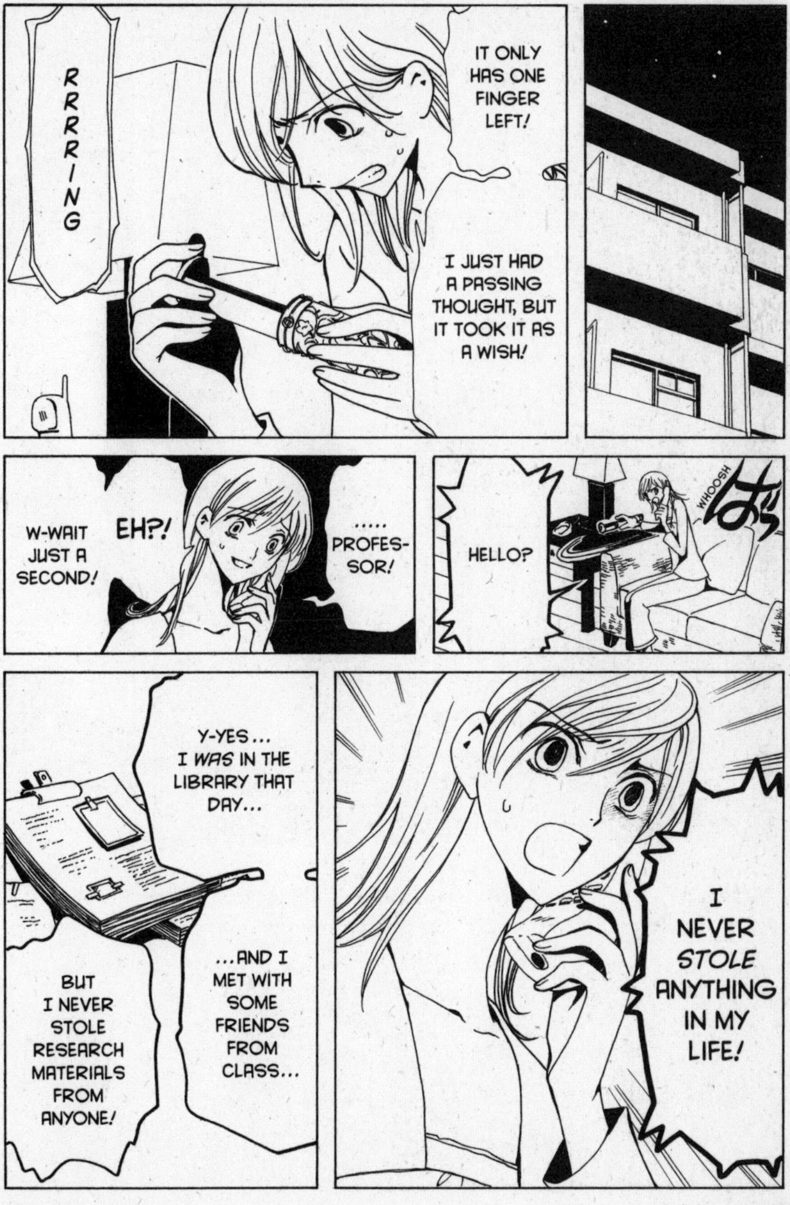
IT ONLY HAS ONE FINGER LEFT!
I JUST HAD A PASSING THOUGHT, BUT IT TOOK IT AS A WISH!
RRRRING
WHOOSH
HELLO?
..... PROFES-SOR!
EH?!
W-WAIT JUST A SECOND!
I NEVER *STOLE* ANYTHING IN MY LIFE!
Y-YES... I *WAS* IN THE LIBRARY THAT DAY...
...AND I MET WITH SOME FRIENDS FROM CLASS...
BUT I NEVER STOLE RESEARCH MATERIALS FROM ANYONE!

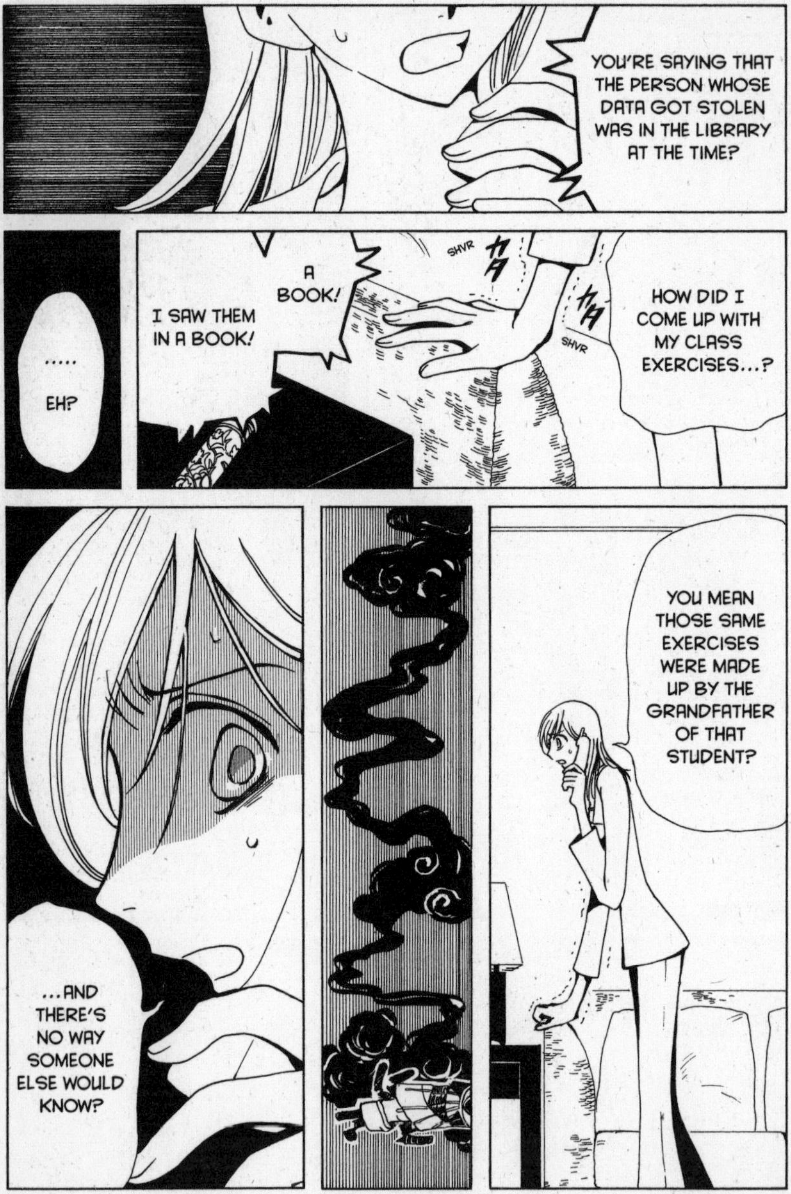
YOU'RE SAYING THAT THE PERSON WHOSE DATA GOT STOLEN WAS IN THE LIBRARY AT THE TIME?
HOW DID I COME UP WITH MY CLASS EXERCISES...?
SHVR
SHVR
A BOOK!
I SAW THEM IN A BOOK!
.....
EH?
YOU MEAN THOSE SAME EXERCISES WERE MADE UP BY THE GRANDFATHER OF THAT STUDENT?
...AND THERE'S NO WAY SOMEONE ELSE WOULD KNOW?

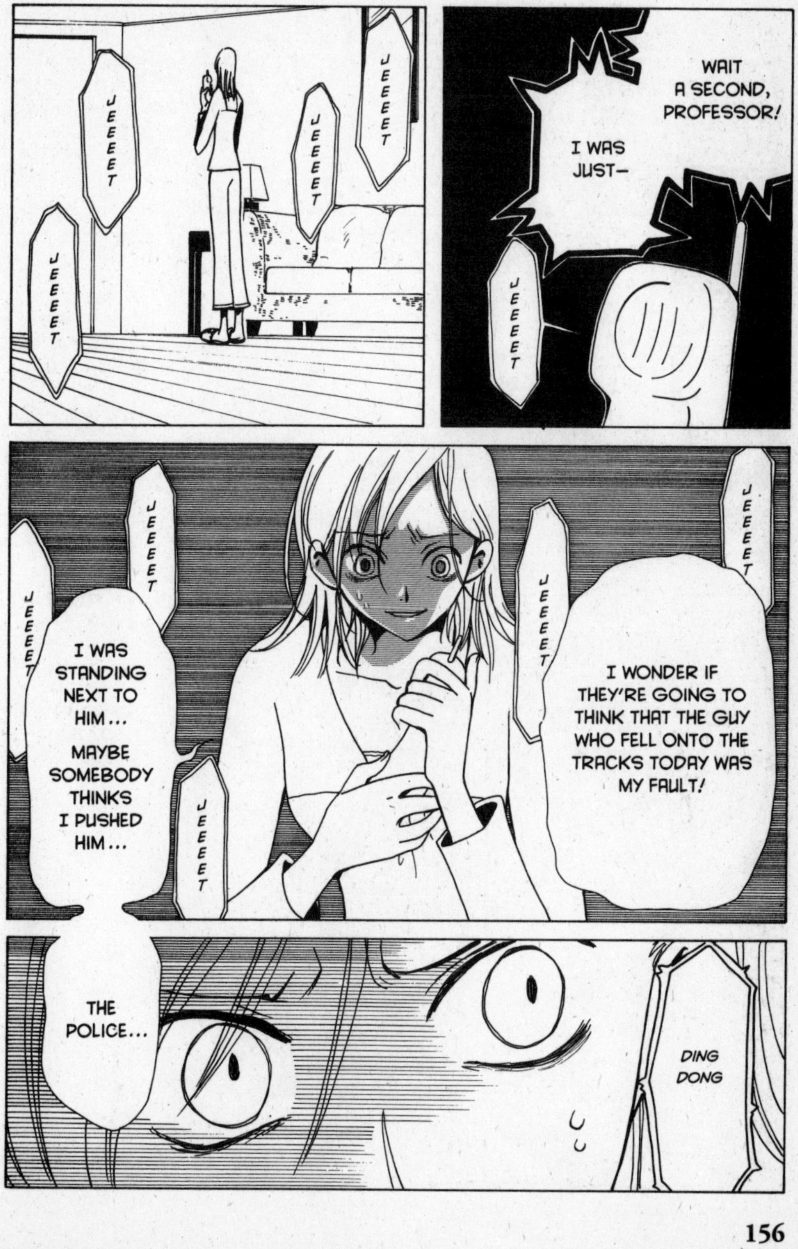
WAIT A SECOND, PROFESSOR!
I WAS JUST—
JEEEET
JEEEET
JEEEET
JEEEET
JEEEET
JEEEET
I WONDER IF THEY'RE GOING TO THINK THAT THE GUY WHO FELL ONTO THE TRACKS TODAY WAS MY FAULT!
JEEEET
JEEEET
JEEEET
I WAS STANDING NEXT TO HIM...
MAYBE SOMEBODY THINKS I PUSHED HIM...
JEEEET
DING DONG
THE POLICE...

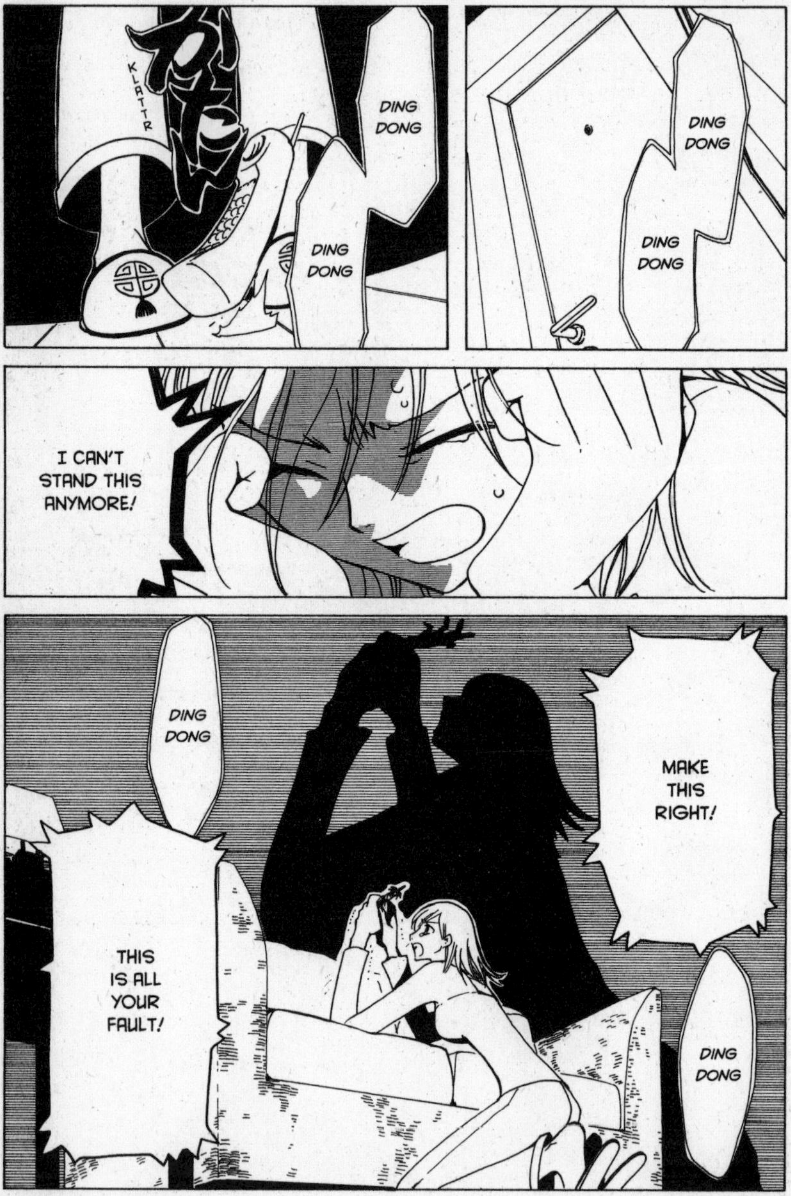
DING DONG
DING DONG
DING DONG
KLATTR
DING DONG
I CAN'T STAND THIS ANYMORE!
MAKE THIS RIGHT!
DING DONG
DING DONG
THIS IS ALL YOUR FAULT!

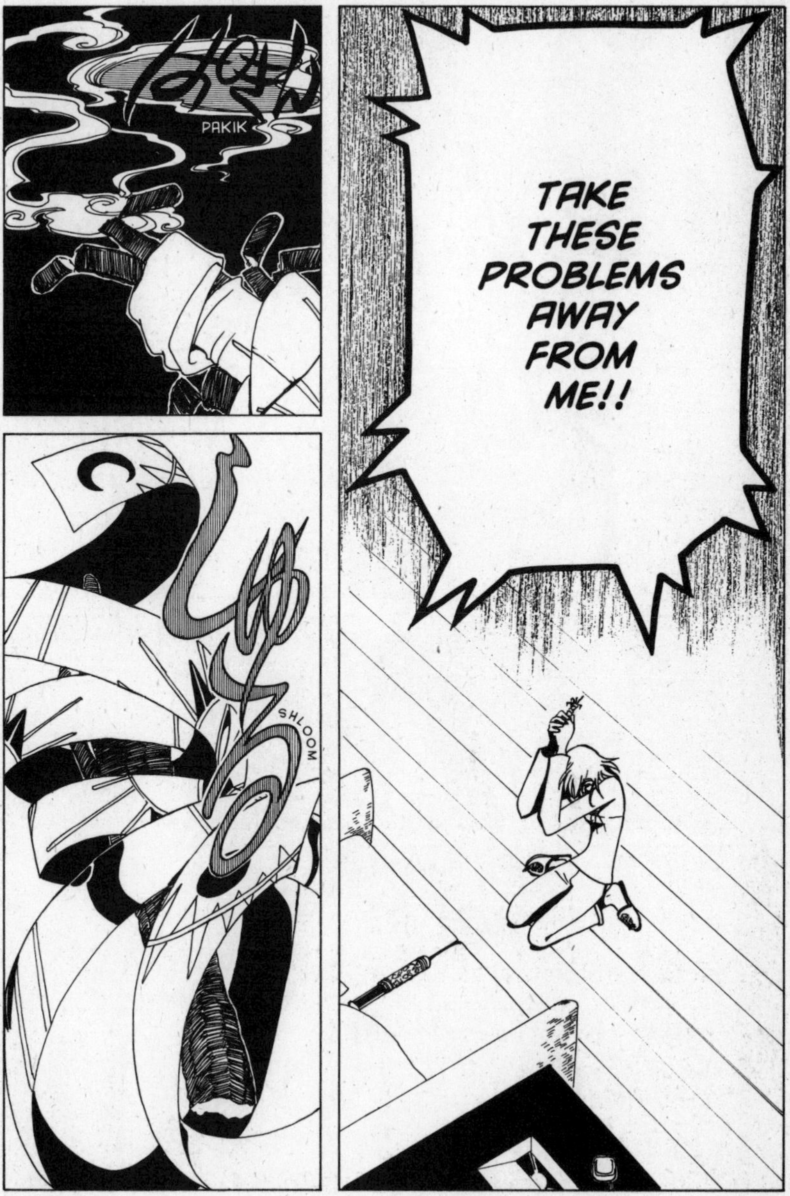
TAKE THESE PROBLEMS AWAY FROM ME!!
PAKIK
SHLOOM

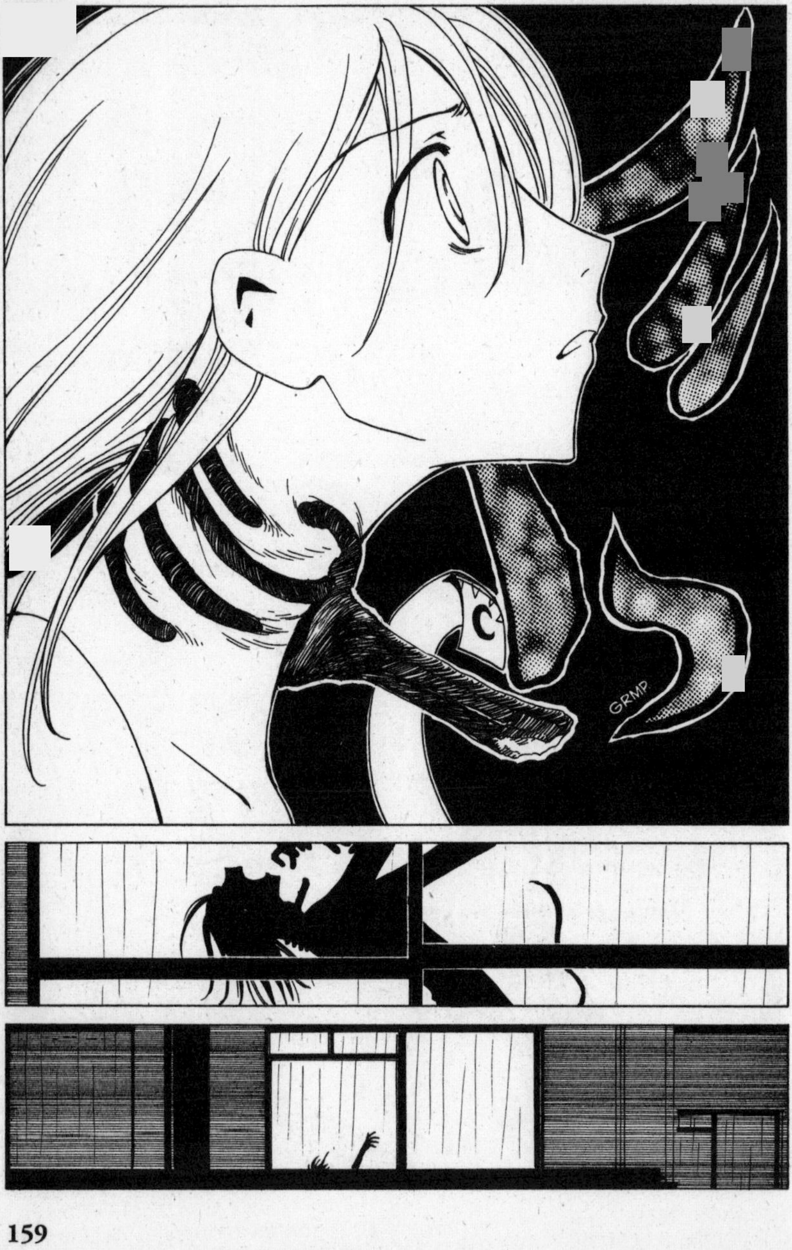
GRMP.

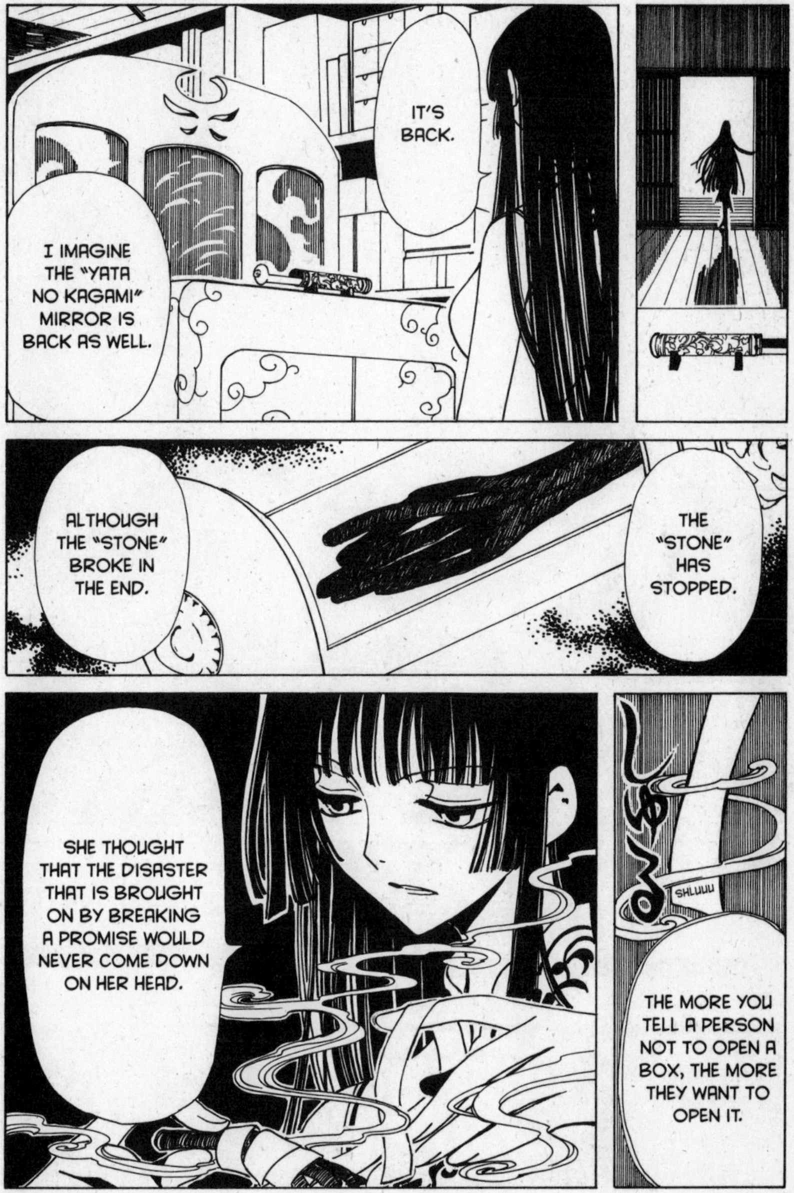
IT'S BACK.
I IMAGINE THE "YATA NO KAGAMI" MIRROR IS BACK AS WELL.
THE "STONE" HAS STOPPED.
ALTHOUGH THE "STONE" BROKE IN THE END.
SHLUUU
THE MORE YOU TELL A PERSON NOT TO OPEN A BOX, THE MORE THEY WANT TO OPEN IT.
SHE THOUGHT THAT THE DISASTER THAT IS BROUGHT ON BY BREAKING A PROMISE WOULD NEVER COME DOWN ON HER HEAD.

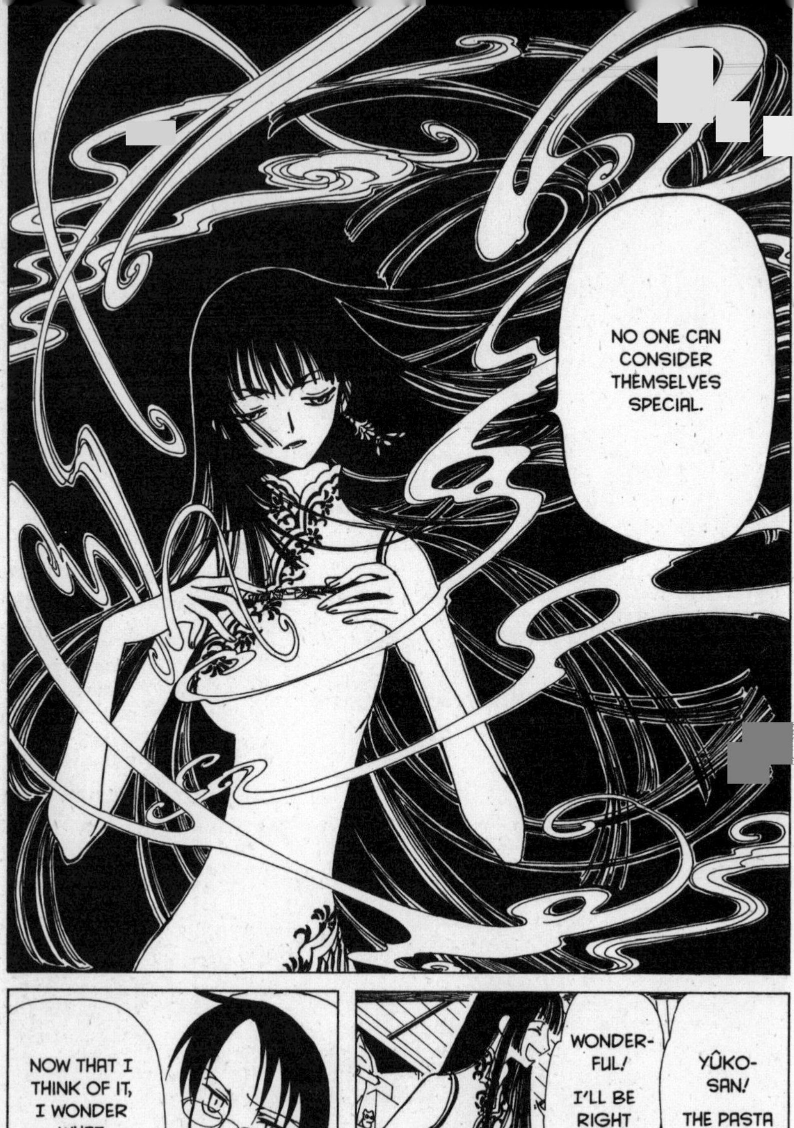
NO ONE CAN CONSIDER THEMSELVES SPECIAL.
YÛKO-SAN! THE PASTA IS READY!
AND THE WHITE WINE IS CHILLED!
WONDER-FUL! I'LL BE RIGHT THERE!
KLUNK
NOW THAT I THINK OF IT, I WONDER WHAT HAPPENED TO THAT EDUCATIONAL TRAINING STUDENT.

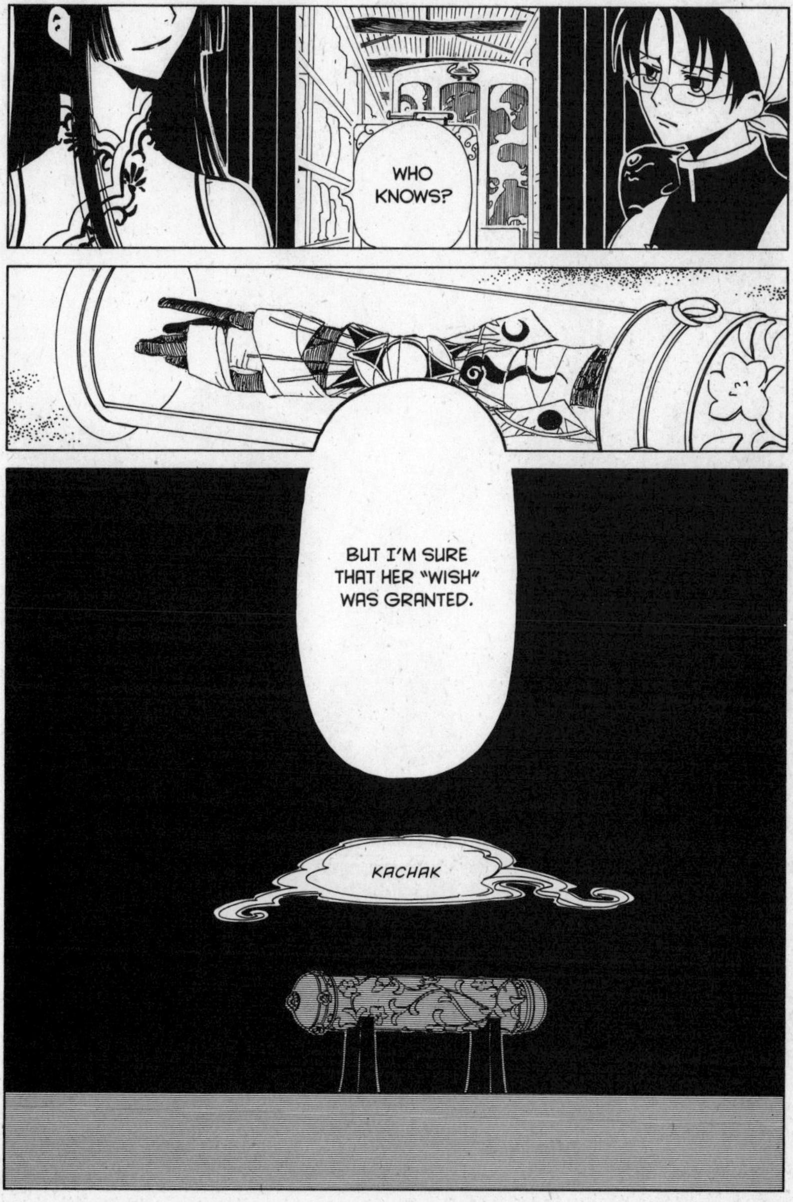
WHO KNOWS?
BUT I'M SURE THAT HER "WISH" WAS GRANTED.
KACHAK

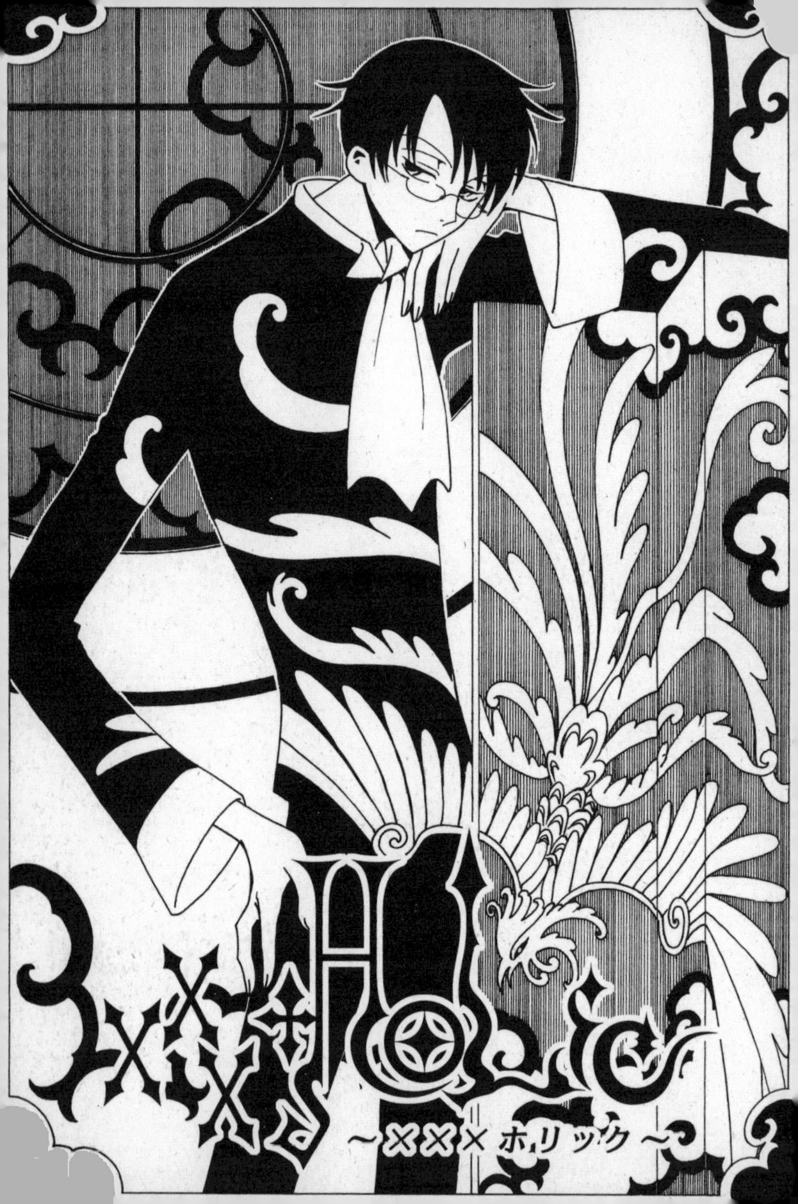
xxxHOLiC
~×××ホリック~

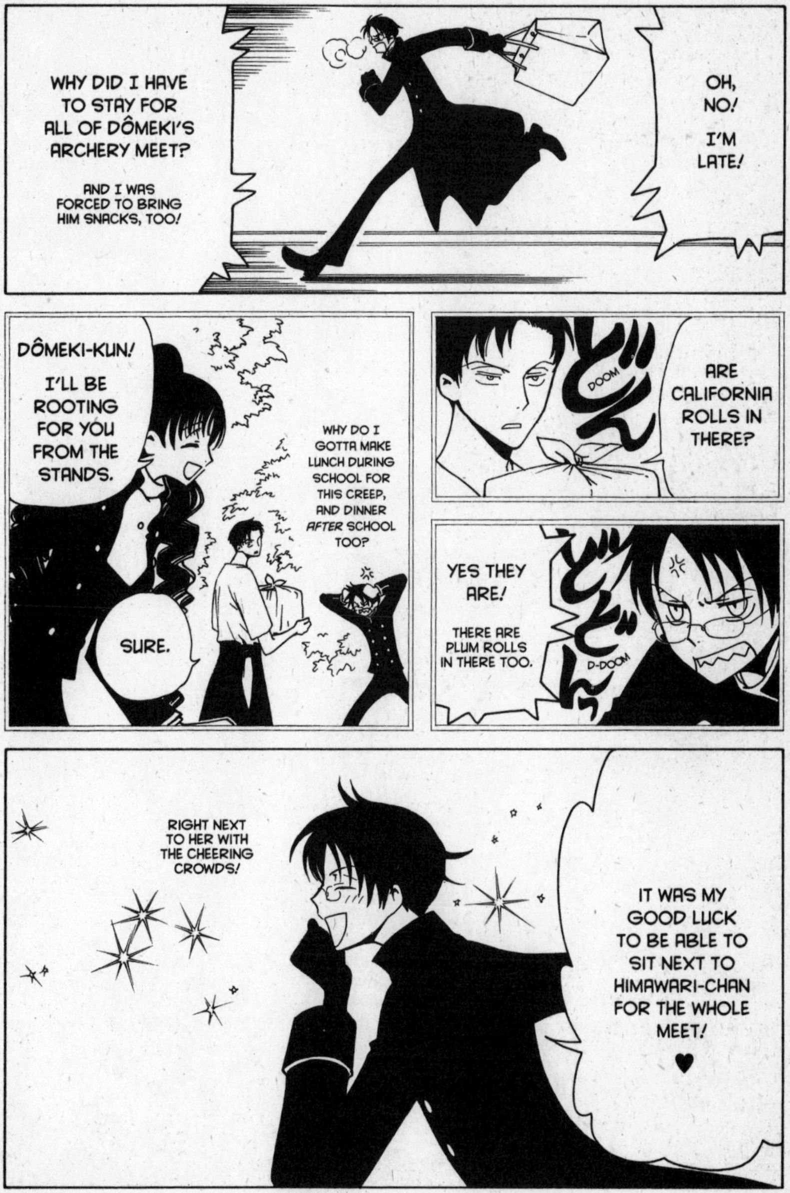
OH, NO! I'M LATE!
WHY DID I HAVE TO STAY FOR ALL OF DÔMEKI'S ARCHERY MEET?
AND I WAS FORCED TO BRING HIM SNACKS, TOO!
ARE CALIFORNIA ROLLS IN THERE?
DOOM
YES THEY ARE!
THERE ARE PLUM ROLLS IN THERE TOO.
D-DOOM
DÔMEKI-KUN! I'LL BE ROOTING FOR YOU FROM THE STANDS.
WHY DO I GOTTA MAKE LUNCH DURING SCHOOL FOR THIS CREEP, AND DINNER *AFTER* SCHOOL TOO?
SURE.
IT WAS MY GOOD LUCK TO BE ABLE TO SIT NEXT TO HIMAWARI-CHAN FOR THE WHOLE MEET! ♥
RIGHT NEXT TO HER WITH THE CHEERING CROWDS!

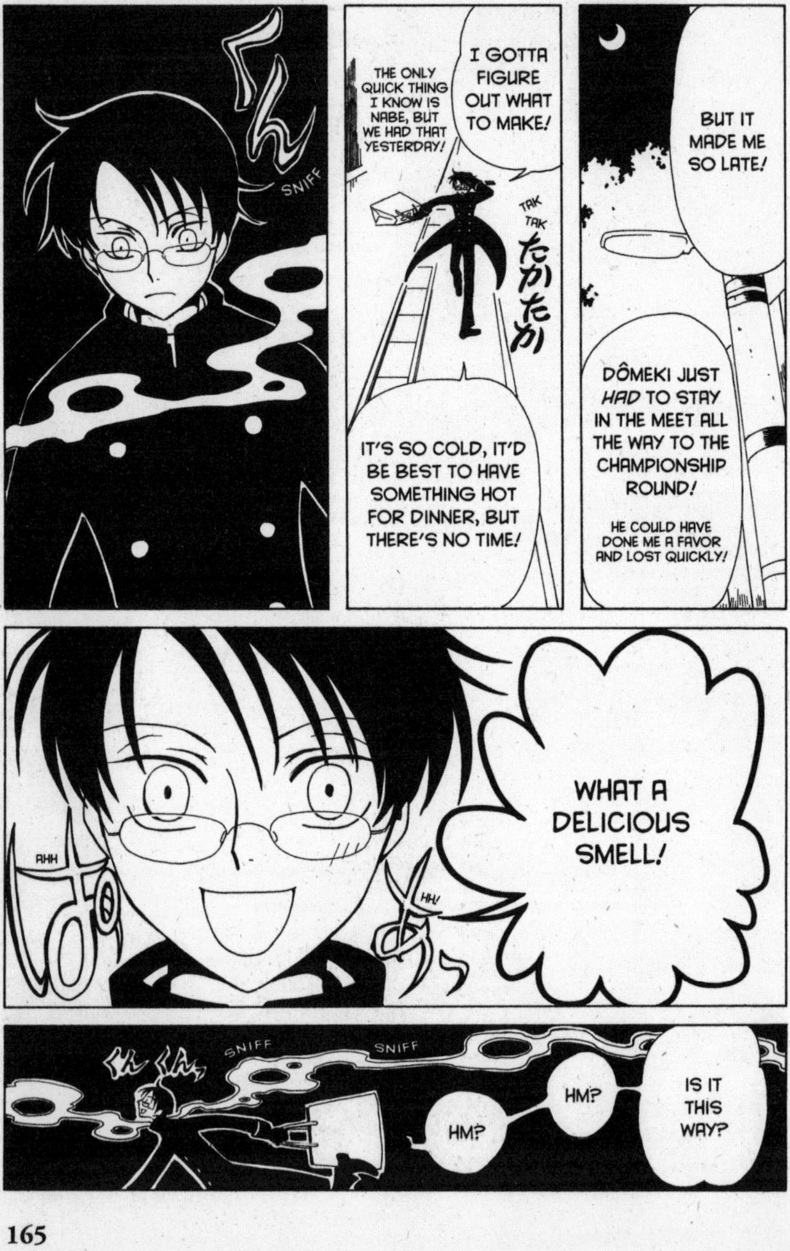
BUT IT MADE ME SO LATE!
DÔMEKI JUST *HAD* TO STAY IN THE MEET ALL THE WAY TO THE CHAMPIONSHIP ROUND!
HE COULD HAVE DONE ME A FAVOR AND LOST QUICKLY!
I GOTTA FIGURE OUT WHAT TO MAKE!
THE ONLY QUICK THING I KNOW IS NABE, BUT WE HAD THAT YESTERDAY!
TAK TAK
たかたか
IT'S SO COLD, IT'D BE BEST TO HAVE SOMETHING HOT FOR DINNER, BUT THERE'S NO TIME!
SNIFF
WHAT A DELICIOUS SMELL!
HH!
AHH
IS IT THIS WAY?
HM?
HM?
SNIFF
SNIFF
くんくん

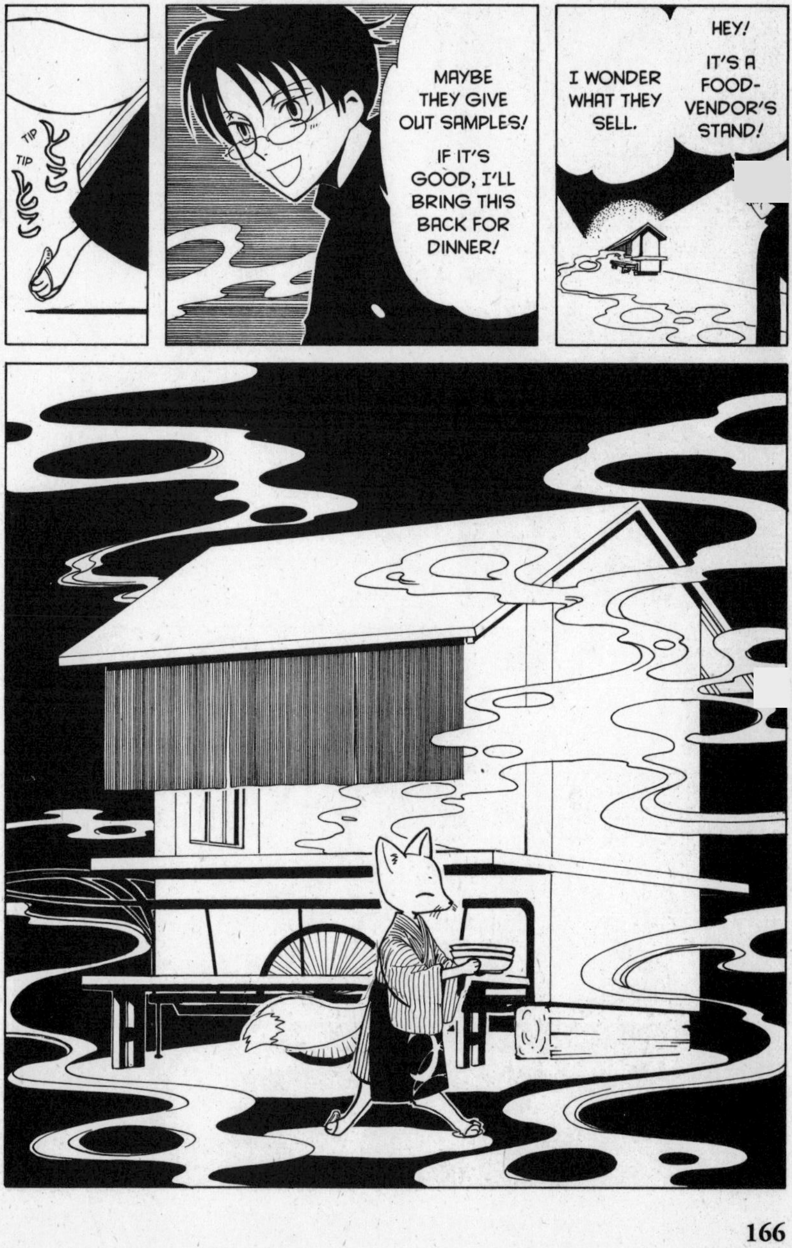
HEY!
IT'S A FOOD-VENDOR'S STAND!
I WONDER WHAT THEY SELL.
MAYBE THEY GIVE OUT SAMPLES!
IF IT'S GOOD, I'LL BRING THIS BACK FOR DINNER!
TIP
TIP

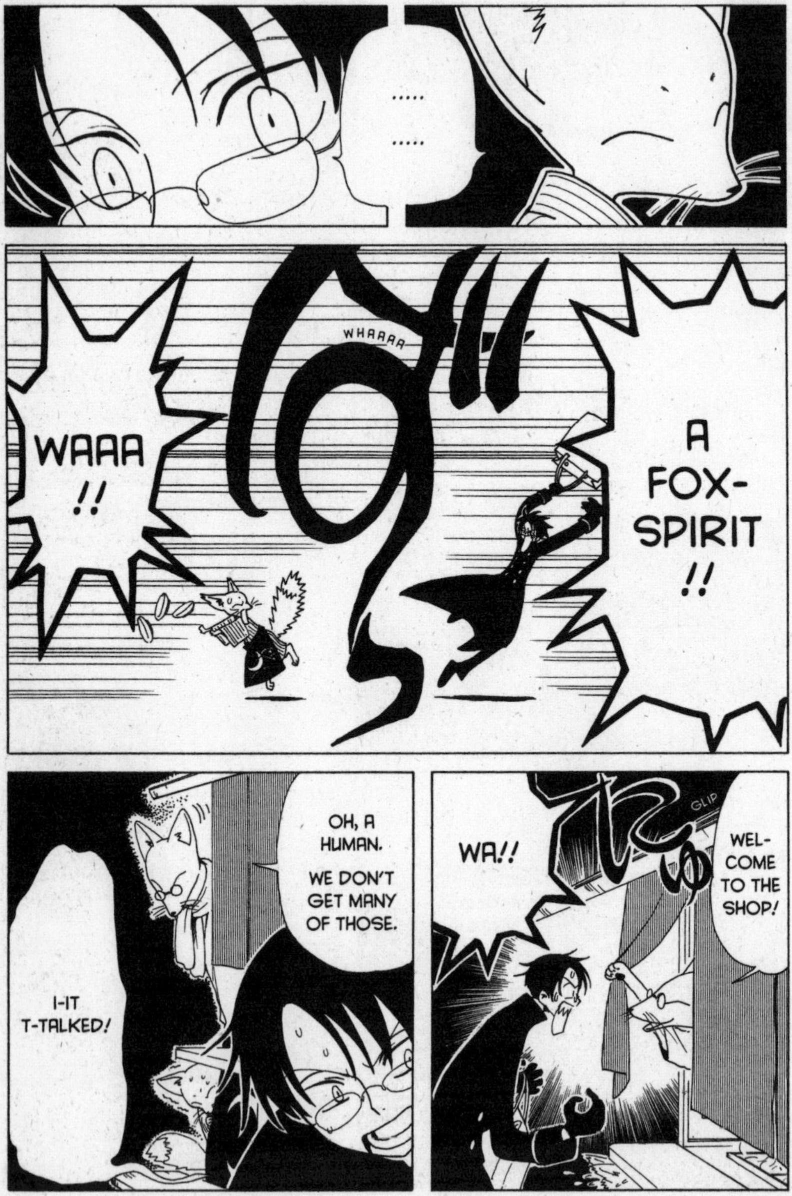
.....
.....
A FOX-SPIRIT!!
WHAAAAA
WAAA!!
WEL-COME TO THE SHOP!
GLIP
WA!!
OH, A HUMAN.
WE DON'T GET MANY OF THOSE.
I-IT T-TALKED!

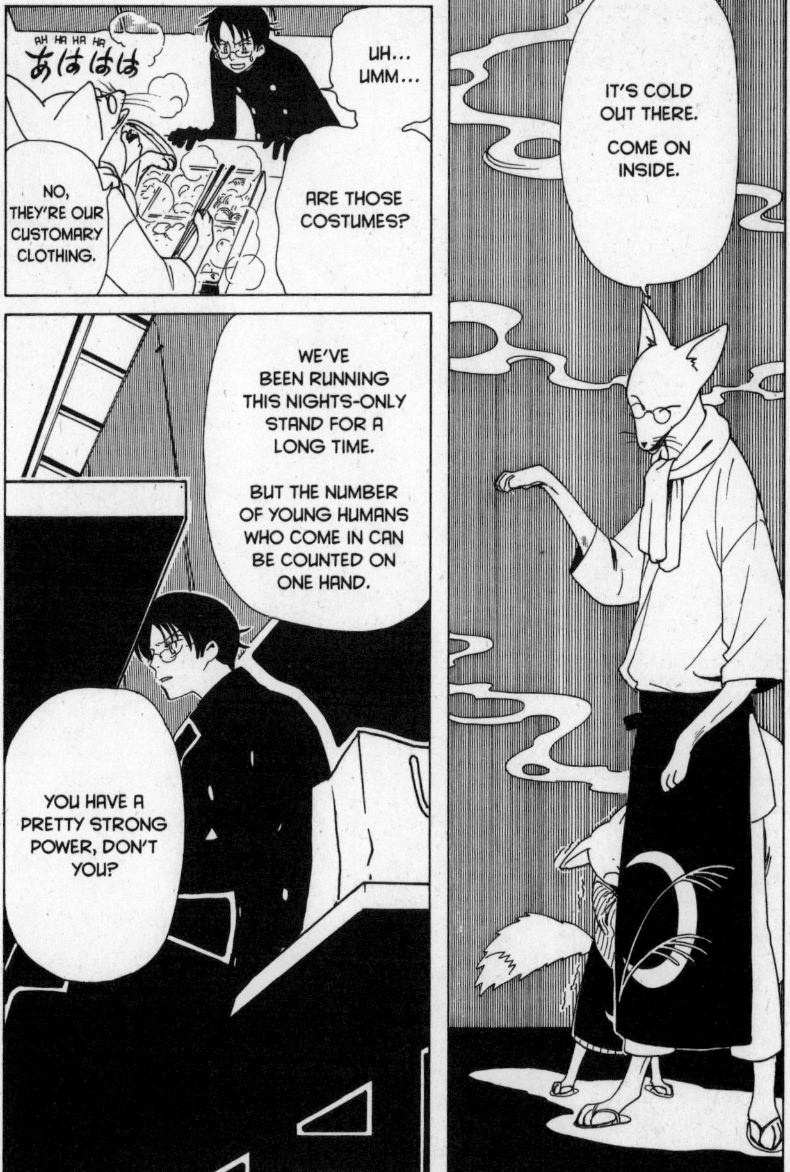
IT'S COLD OUT THERE.
COME ON INSIDE.
UH... UMM...
ARE THOSE COSTUMES?
AH HA HA HA
あははは
NO, THEY'RE OUR CUSTOMARY CLOTHING.
WE'VE BEEN RUNNING THIS NIGHTS-ONLY STAND FOR A LONG TIME.
BUT THE NUMBER OF YOUNG HUMANS WHO COME IN CAN BE COUNTED ON ONE HAND.
YOU HAVE A PRETTY STRONG POWER, DON'T YOU?

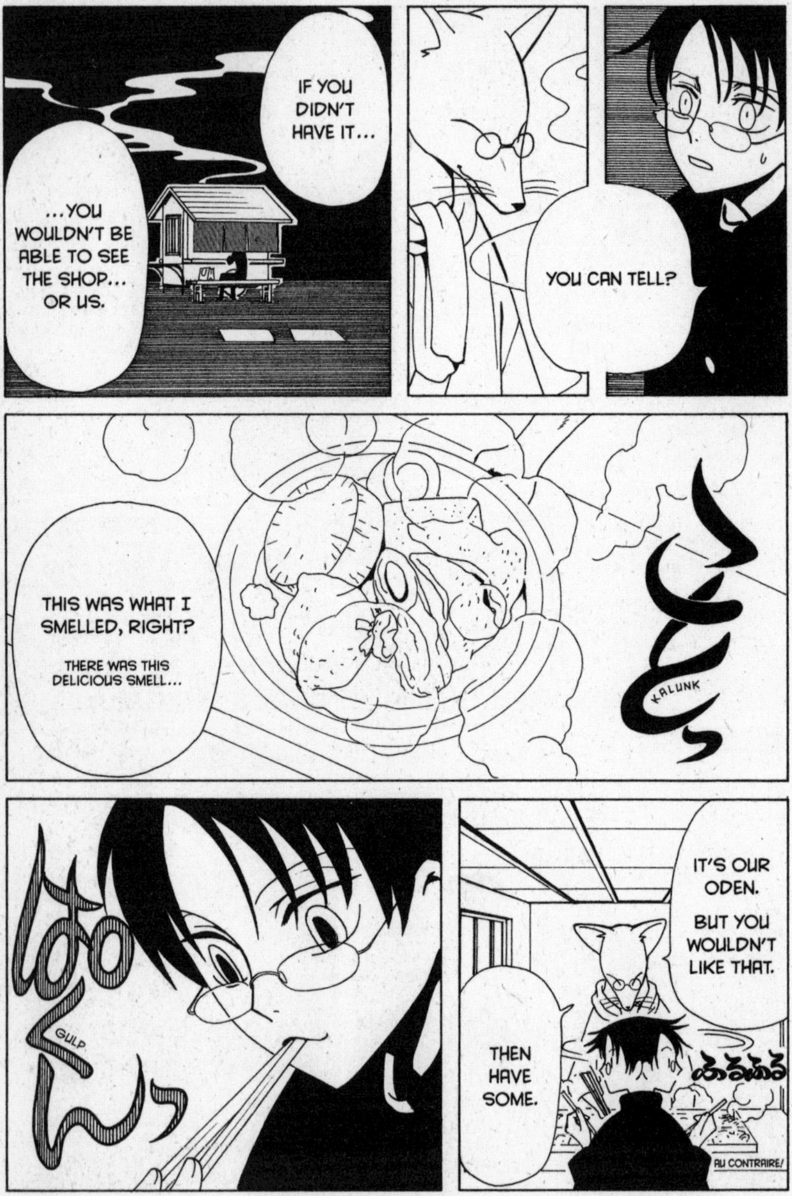
YOU CAN TELL?
IF YOU DIDN'T HAVE IT...
...YOU WOULDN'T BE ABLE TO SEE THE SHOP... OR US.
KALUNK
THIS WAS WHAT I SMELLED, RIGHT?
THERE WAS THIS DELICIOUS SMELL...
IT'S OUR ODEN.
BUT YOU WOULDN'T LIKE THAT.
THEN HAVE SOME.
AU CONTRAIRE!
GULP

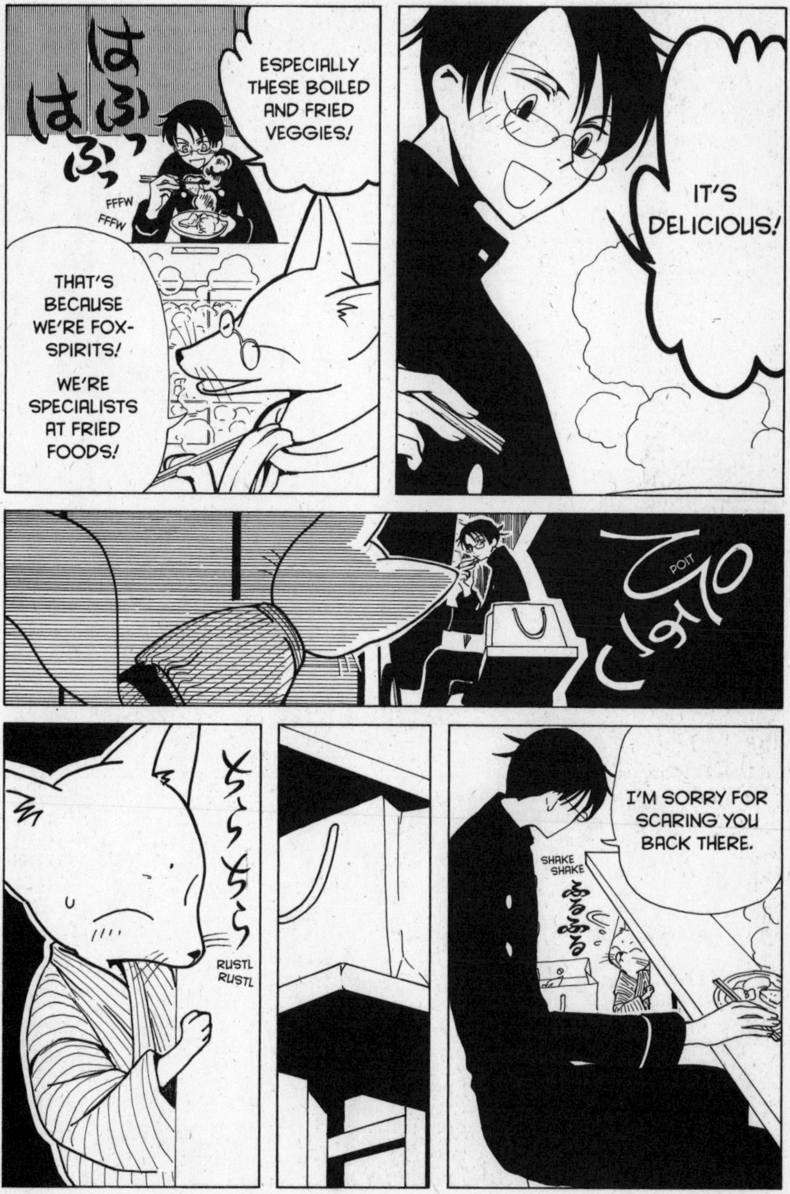
IT'S DELICIOUS!
ESPECIALLY THESE BOILED AND FRIED VEGGIES!
はふっはふっ
FFFW FFFW
THAT'S BECAUSE WE'RE FOX-SPIRITS!
WE'RE SPECIALISTS AT FRIED FOODS!
ぽいっ
POIT
I'M SORRY FOR SCARING YOU BACK THERE.
SHAKE SHAKE
ふるふる
ちらちら
RUSTL RUSTL

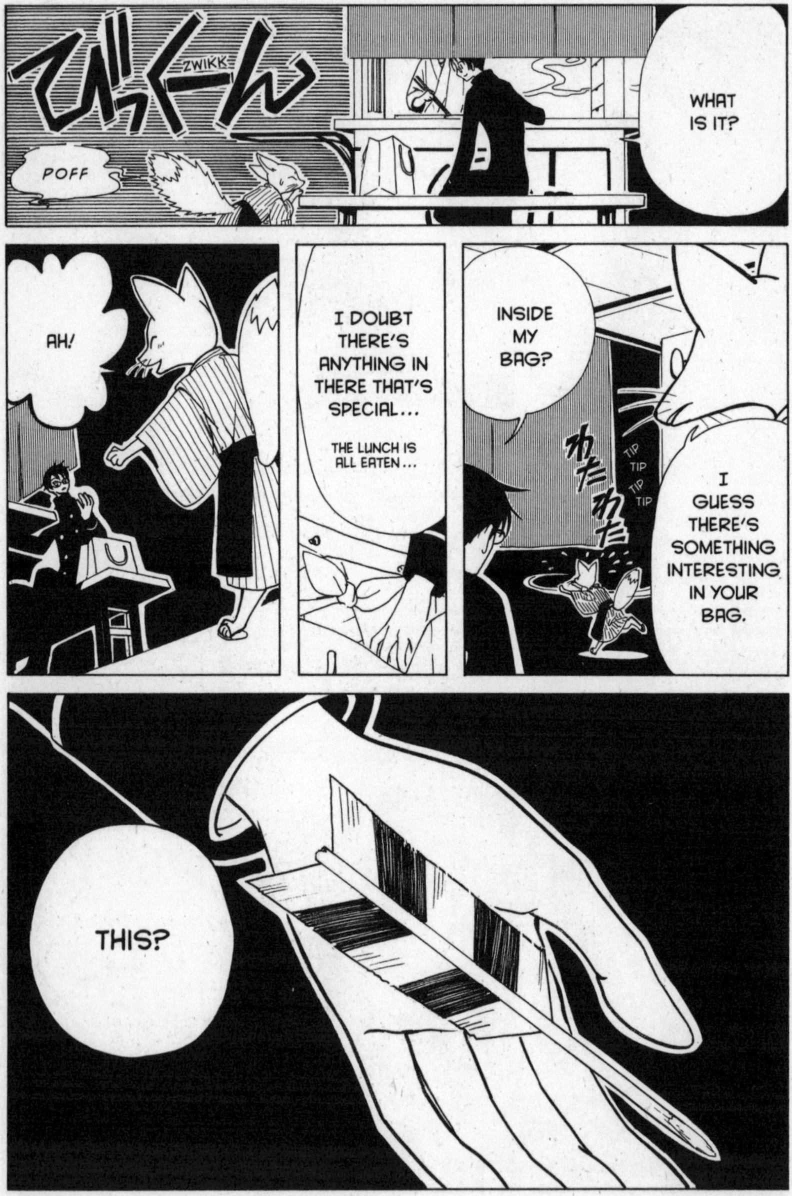
WHAT IS IT?
びっくーん
ZWIKK
POFF
I GUESS THERE'S SOMETHING INTERESTING IN YOUR BAG.
INSIDE MY BAG?
わたわた
TIP TIP TIP TIP
I DOUBT THERE'S ANYTHING IN THERE THAT'S SPECIAL...
THE LUNCH IS ALL EATEN...
AH!
THIS?

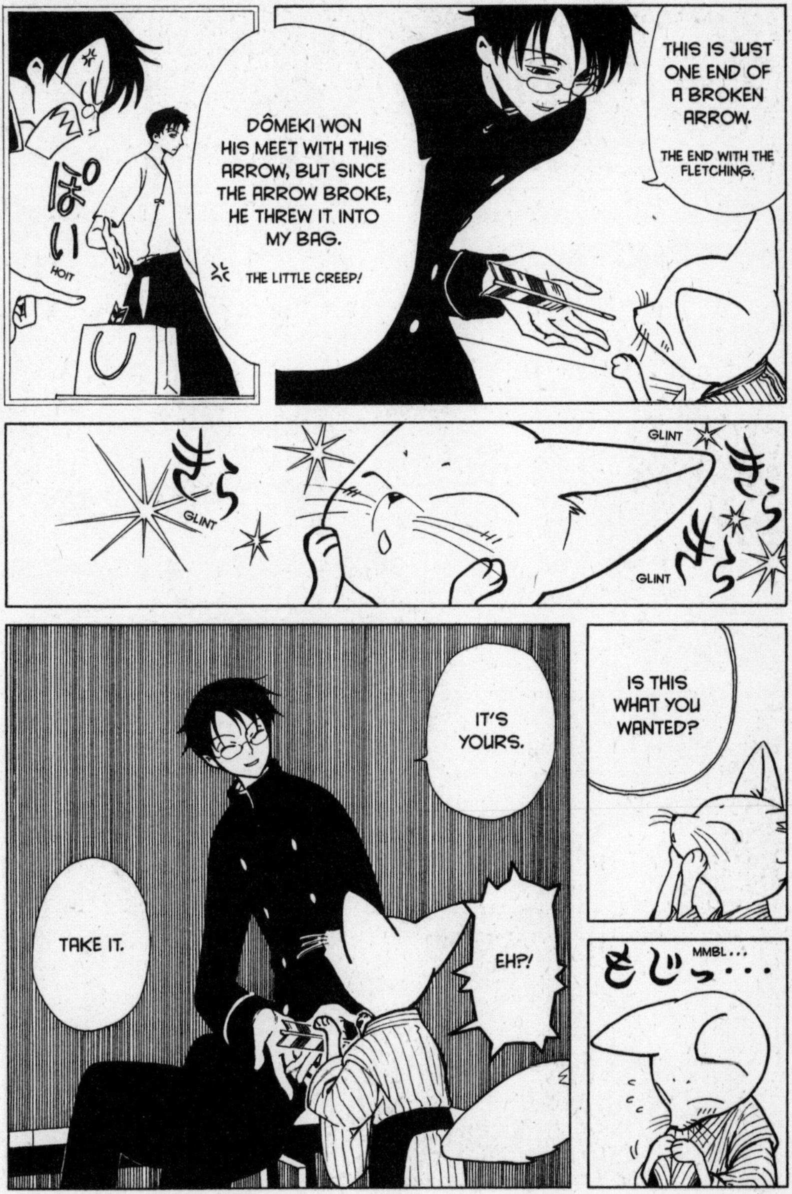
THIS IS JUST ONE END OF A BROKEN ARROW.
THE END WITH THE FLETCHING.
DÔMEKI WON HIS MEET WITH THIS ARROW, BUT SINCE THE ARROW BROKE, HE THREW IT INTO MY BAG.
THE LITTLE CREEP!
ぽい
HOIT
きら
GLINT
きら
GLINT
きら
GLINT
IS THIS WHAT YOU WANTED?
もじっ…
MMBL...
IT'S YOURS.
EH?!
TAKE IT.

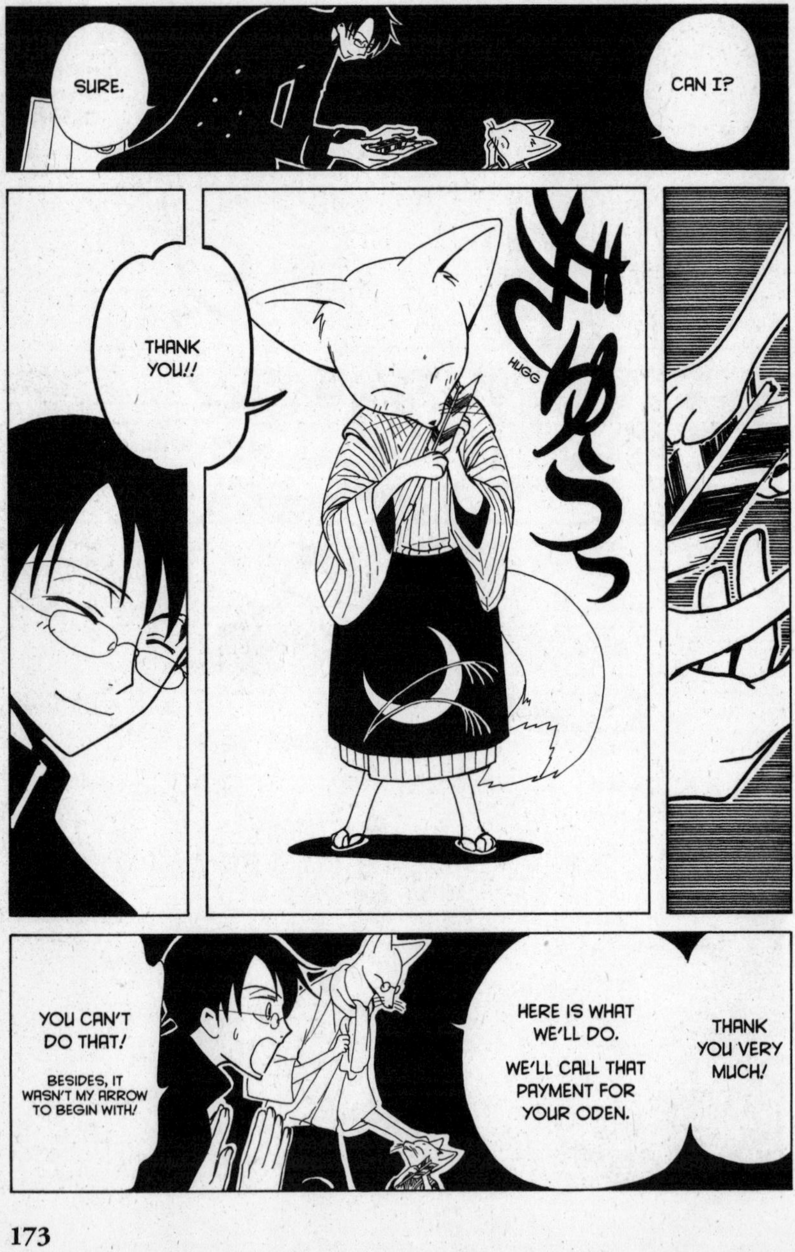
CAN I?
SURE.
HUGG
THANK YOU!!
THANK YOU VERY MUCH!
HERE IS WHAT WE'LL DO.
WE'LL CALL THAT PAYMENT FOR YOUR ODEN.
YOU CAN'T DO THAT!
BESIDES, IT WASN'T MY ARROW TO BEGIN WITH!

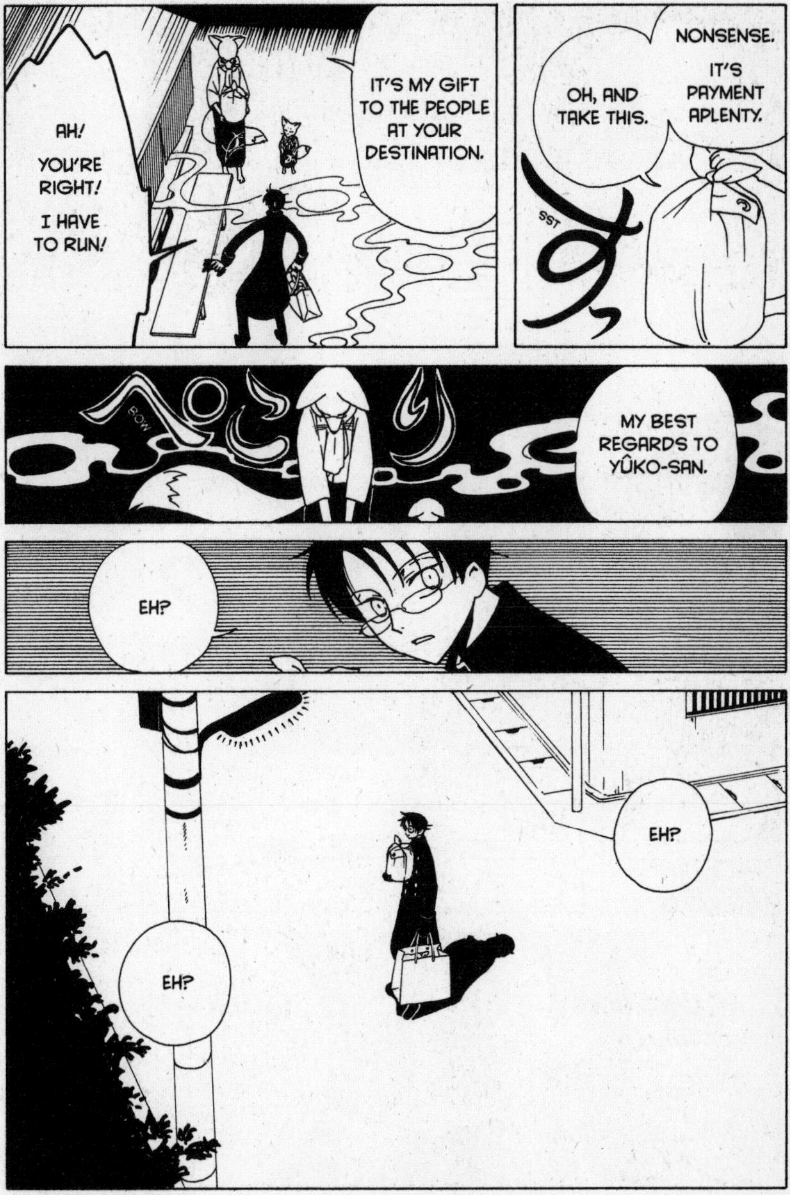
NONSENSE. IT'S PAYMENT APLENTY.
OH, AND TAKE THIS.
SST
IT'S MY GIFT TO THE PEOPLE AT YOUR DESTINATION.
AH! YOU'RE RIGHT! I HAVE TO RUN!
MY BEST REGARDS TO YÛKO-SAN.
BOW
EH?
EH?
EH?

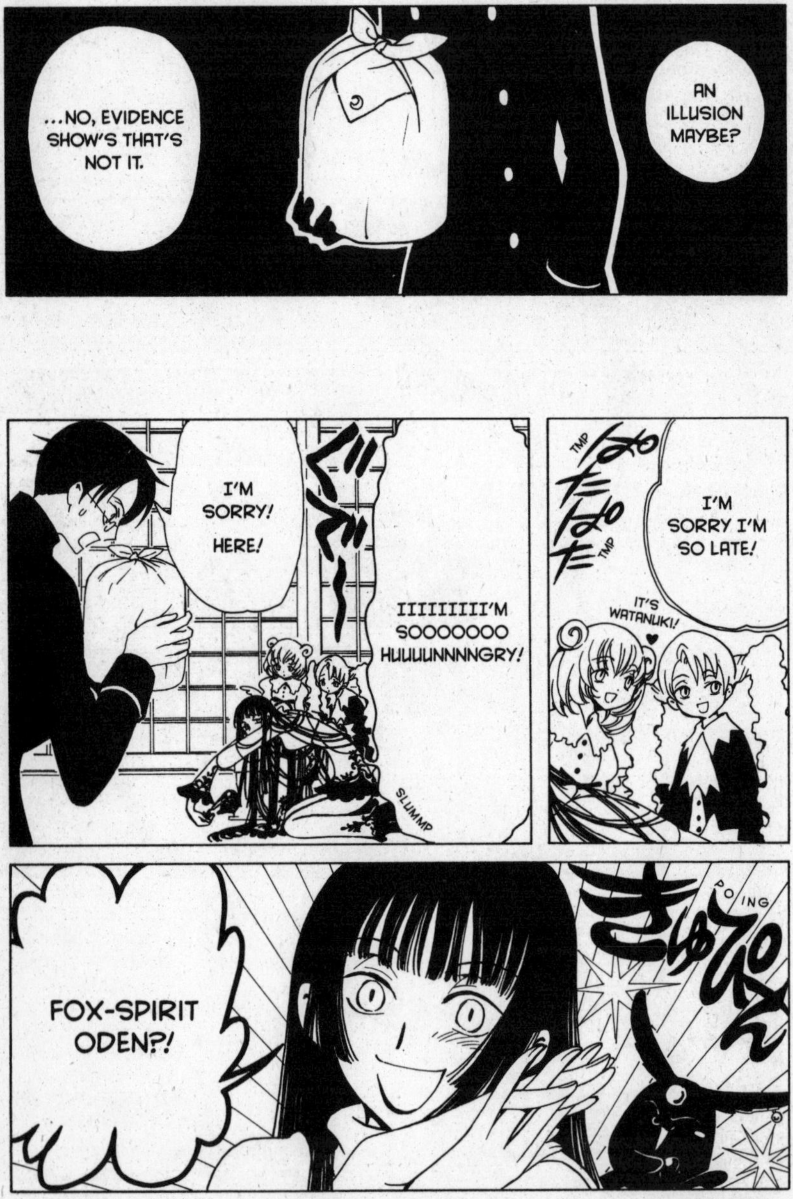
AN ILLUSION MAYBE?
...NO, EVIDENCE SHOW'S THAT'S NOT IT.
TMP
TMP
I'M SORRY I'M SO LATE!
IT'S WATANUKI!
IIIIIIIII'M SOOOOOOO HUUUUNNNNGRY!
I'M SORRY! HERE!
SLUMMP
POING
FOX-SPIRIT ODEN?!

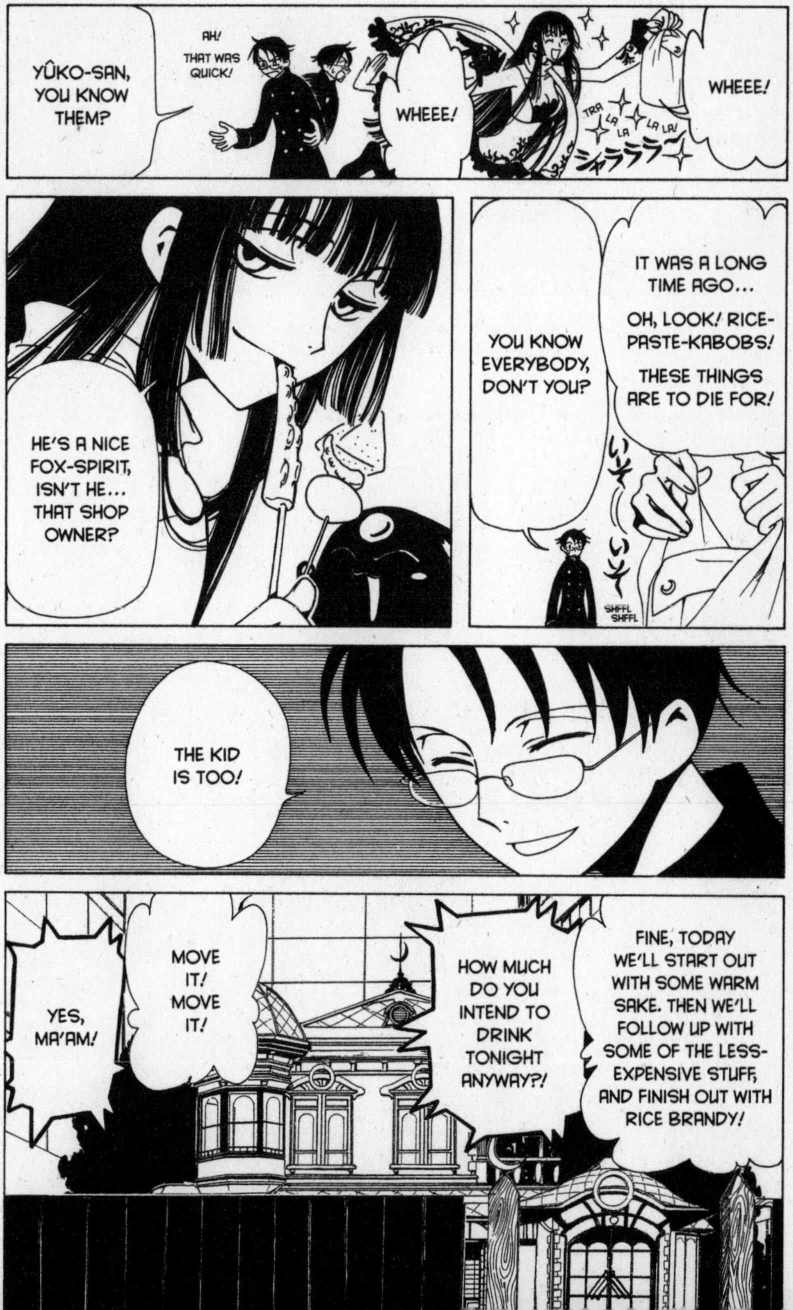
WHEEE!
TRA LA LA LA LA!
シャラララ
WHEEE!
AH! THAT WAS QUICK!
YÛKO-SAN, YOU KNOW THEM?
IT WAS A LONG TIME AGO...
OH, LOOK! RICE-PASTE-KABOBS!
THESE THINGS ARE TO DIE FOR!
YOU KNOW EVERYBODY, DON'T YOU?
いそいそ
SHFFL SHFFL
HE'S A NICE FOX-SPIRIT, ISN'T HE... THAT SHOP OWNER?
THE KID IS TOO!
FINE, TODAY WE'LL START OUT WITH SOME WARM SAKE. THEN WE'LL FOLLOW UP WITH SOME OF THE LESS-EXPENSIVE STUFF, AND FINISH OUT WITH RICE BRANDY!
HOW MUCH DO YOU INTEND TO DRINK TONIGHT ANYWAY?!
MOVE IT! MOVE IT!
YES, MA'AM!

✠ Continued ✠

in *xxxHOLiC* Volume 4

About the Creators

CLAMP is a group of four women who have become the most popular manga artists in America—Ageha Ohkawa, Mokona, Satsuki Igarashi, and Tsubaki Nekoi. They started out as doujinshi (fan comics) creators, but their skill and craft brought them to the attention of publishers very quickly. Their first work from a major publisher was *RG Veda*, but their first mass success was with *Magic Knight Rayearth*. From there, they went on to write many series, including *Cardcaptor Sakura* and *Chobits*, two of the most popular manga in the United States. Like many Japanese manga artists, they prefer to avoid the spotlight, and little is known about them personally.

CLAMP is currently publishing three series in Japan: *Tsubasa* and *xxxHOLiC* with Kodansha and *Gohou Drug* with Kadokawa.

Translation Notes

For your edification and reading pleasure, here are notes to help you understand some of the cultural and story references from our translation of *xxxHOLiC*.

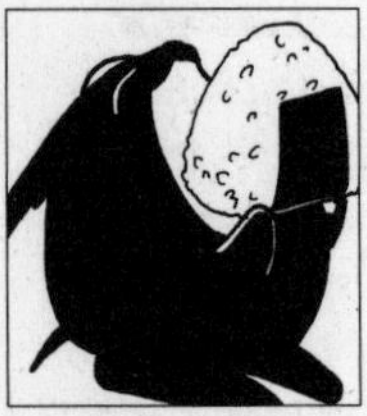

Onigiri (Rice balls)

In Japan, when you say lunch away from home, you say *onigiri*. Usually made by mother but available at any grocery store, convenience store, or food kiosk, this is as much a staple of the Japanese lunchbox as sandwiches in the United States. It is made from a triangle of sticky rice and a seaweed wrapper for holding, and although it may consist of just rice and seaweed, it sometimes includes a filling in the center such as grilled salmon or a sour pickled plum (*umeboshi*).

Star Wars

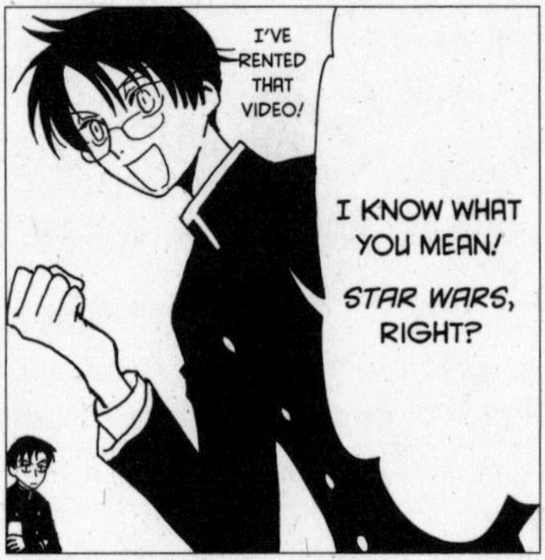
I'VE RENTED THAT VIDEO!
I KNOW WHAT YOU MEAN!
STAR WARS, RIGHT?

In the world of manga fandom, one of the biggest criticisms leveled at U.S. publishers of manga has to do with story adaptations. Unsurprisingly, since manga was originally published in Japan it often contains cultural references that may not make much sense to an American reader. Some publishers have therefore opted to change the references so that they make more sense here. The reason we bring this up is to make sure you know that this is not what we are doing here—in the original Japanese text, Kimihiro really is talking about *Star Wars*!

Casshern

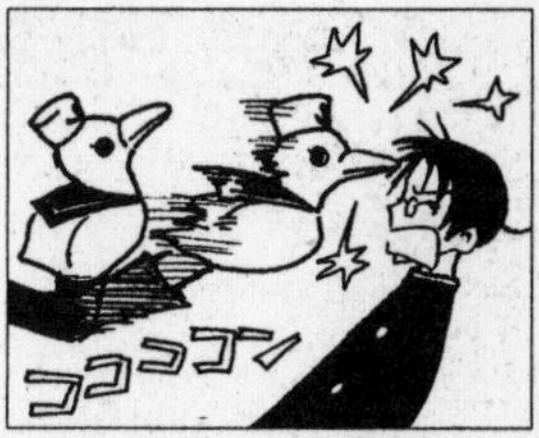

A popular 1973 TV anime show in which a scientist created a robot to clean up pollution. Unfortunately a lightning strike scrambled the brain of the powerful robot, turning it into a monomaniacal, robot-army-wielding menace. The scientist's son, Tetsuya, fuses himself with a robot to become the New Superhero Casshern, who fights the good fight against the robot army. By his side is his loyal bionic dog Friender (or Flender), and they are aided by a robot swan named Swanny, which contains the essence of Tetsuya's mother. If Kimihiro doesn't know about Casshern yet, he will soon because it looks like the Japanese special effects film of the same name (released recently in Japan) is a big hit.

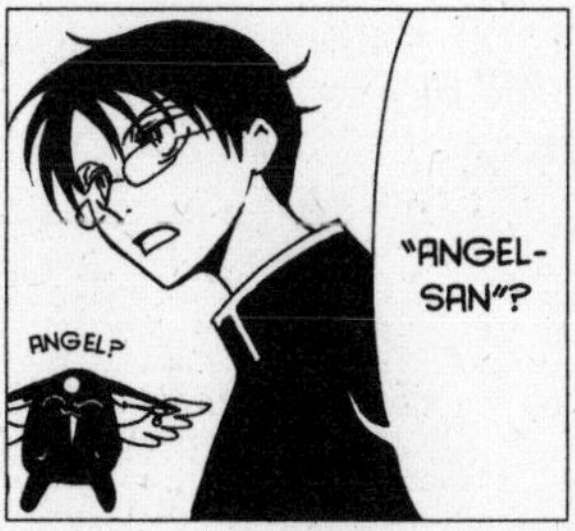
"ANGEL-SAN"?
ANGELP

Angel-san, Kokkuri-san ("Prophesy-san")

Anyone who has bought the Parker Brother's game, Ouija, and tried to get some questions answered will recognize what is going on with Himawari-chan's friend. However, it seems that Kokkuri-san is a cousin to its American counterpart only in that both are taken from a form of mysticism found in the mid-to-late 1800s called Table Tilting. It was a form of divination that became popular because it could be done without a medium (and we all know what Yûko-san would say about that!).

Chobits

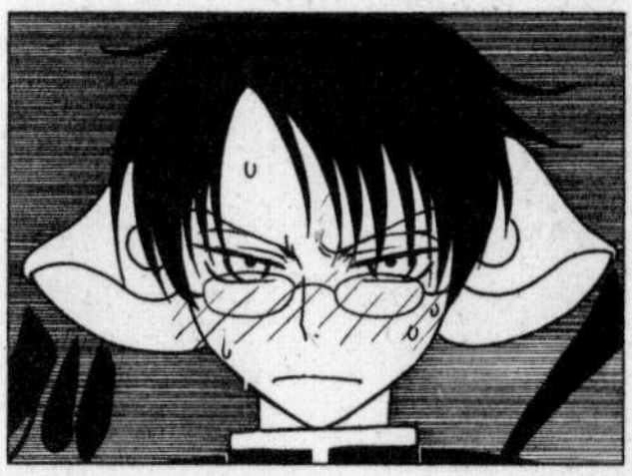

The ears, children's book, and Mokona's calling out of "Chi!" are all from the popular CLAMP manga *Chobits*.

...WE PRESENT THIS SACRIFICE...
...TO YOUR BRAVE AND HONORABLE SELVES!

Protective Spirits and Ancestor Worship

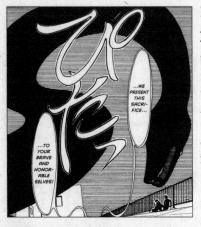

The Shinto religion is an animistic belief centering on spirits which imbue natural phenomena (rivers, trees, etc.) with a spiritual essence. Although they are commonly referred to as gods (*kami*), they aren't the same kind of all-powerful gods that can be found in western religions. The ubiquitous household Shinto shrines found in most homes are also dedicated to a family's ancestors who have become *kami*, and in the transformation are now dedicated to protecting the family in the spirit world. The snake that Kimihiro sees includes the natural kami and ancestors of the area combined to protect the neighborhood.

Bento Boxes

Some restaurants have taken the name of "bento" to describe any lunch that's packed up to-go, but the traditional lacquered, multi-level bento box, filled with sushi or other traditional foods, is a real treat!

Monkey's Paw

The legend of the Monkey's Paw appeared first in a short story written by William Wymark (W.W.) Jacobs in the magazine *Harper's Monthly* in 1902. Its many adaptations into movies, radio dramas, and TV programs have turned it from a turn-of-the-twentieth-century morality play regarding the dangers of the expansive British Empire into an occult myth. But who knows? W.W. Jacobs grew up on the docks of the port section of

London called Wapping and saw ships arrive from all parts of the world-spanning empire, so who can say what actual events may have inspired the story?

Kitsune Fox Spirits

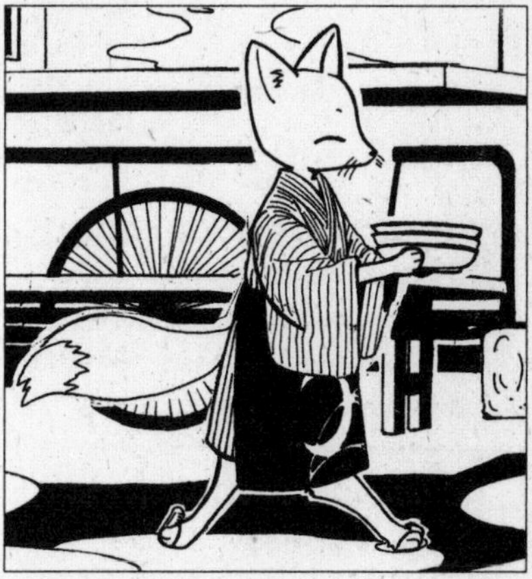

Like foxes in the west, fox spirits in Japan have been portrayed as both cute, sympathetic characters, and evil, mischievous characters in the many tales about them. Usually they have magic powers such as the ability to imitate any human, but they are generally portrayed as hardworking creatures that keep to themselves. The Fushimi Inari Shrine outside of Kyoto, a beautiful set of winding mountain paths under hundreds of red, Japanese arches leading to a shrine at the summit, is dedicated to the god Inari, the god of rice, and to the foxes who are his emissaries.

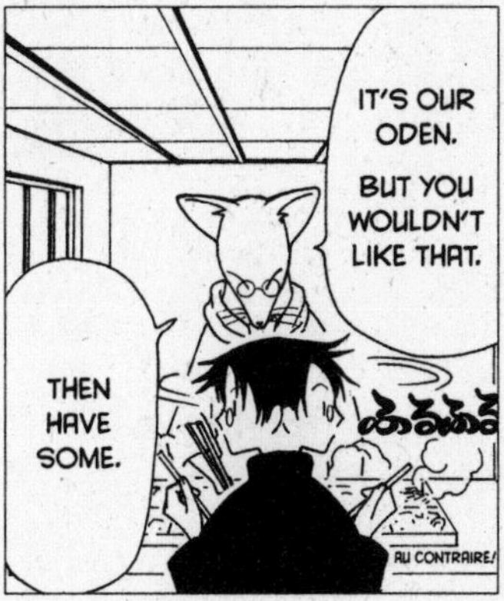
IT'S OUR ODEN.
BUT YOU WOULDN'T LIKE THAT.
THEN HAVE SOME.
AU CONTRAIRE!

Oden

An inexpensive stew, subtly flavored, can feature fish, tofu, squid, octopus, mochi (rice paste), seaweed, chicken, dumplings, eggs, radishes, potatoes, and other meats, vegetables, and concoctions. Although it is a stew, the elements (meat and veggies) are usually skewered on kaboblike sticks for easy access. Oden is served in restaurants, but the more common place to find it is in sidewalk stalls much like the fox spirit's stall in the episode.

xxxHOLiC

VOLUME 4

BY CLAMP

It's Valentine's Day—and while Domeki is showered with chocolates and cards from girls, Watanuki receives none. To make matters worse, he must also do the usual chores for Yûko, which includes making chocolate cake for her and Mokona, as well as the treats his boss wants to give away as gifts. But when Watanuki discovers he has a shy and secret admirer who is not quite human, he finds that chocolates can be more than just sweets.

Then, after seeing identical twin sisters pass by in the street, Yûko makes a curious remark: that there are chains that only humans can use to bind others. Watanuki meets the sisters and senses that the relationship between them is not what it seems. . . .

Volumes 1-6 are now available in bookstores.

 For more information and to sign up for Del Rey's manga e-newsletter, visit www.delreymanga.com

NEGIMA!

VOLUME 3

BY KEN AKAMATSU

There is a vampire stalking the night! Normally ten-year-old teacher/magician Negi Springfield would have no problem dispatching such a villain, but this vampire has a magic-enhancing partner, and worse, the vampire is a student in his own class! Now Nagi must find a partner of his own, but with a class full of beautiful girls all vying for the position, it won't be an easy task. Add in Negi's old friend, a skirt-chasing, wisecracking weasel from Wales, and the nice, orderly chaos of Negi's life turns into a hilarious melee of sirens and sorcery!

3
NEGIMA!
MAGISTER NEGI MAGI
by
KEN AKAMATSU
CREATOR OF *LOVE HINA!*

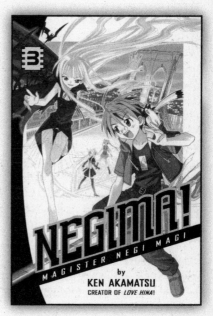

Volumes 1-7 are now available in bookstores.

DEL REY

For more information and to sign up for Del Rey's manga e-newsletter, visit www.delreymanga.com

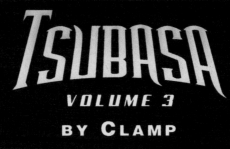

TSUBASA

VOLUME 3

BY CLAMP

Sakura is awake, but she remembers almost nothing—certainly not Syaoran, who has sacrificed everything to help her. Accompanied by the happy-go-lucky Fai, the intense Kurogane, and the strikingly odd creature Mokona Modoki, Sakura and Syaoran make their way into a new universe where a traveling magician has suddenly become frighteningly powerful and is terrorizing an entire town. Only a few independent-minded stragglers remain to battle for control of their own lives. Fai, the lone magician in the group, traded his magical powers to the dimension witch, xxxHOLiC's Yûko, before the journey started. Without a weapon with which to fight, can the extraordinary group of friends defeat a master magician who can control the Earth's elements?

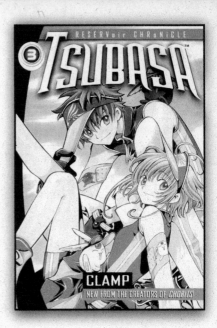

For more information and to sign up for Del Rey's manga e-newsletter, visit www.delreymanga.com

TOMARE!

[STOP!]

You're going the wrong way!

Manga is a completely different type of reading experience.

To start at the *beginning*, go to the *end*!

That's right! Authentic manga is read the traditional Japanese way— from right to left. Exactly the *opposite* of how American books are read. It's easy to follow: Just go to the other end of the book, and read each page—and each panel—from right side to left side, starting at the top right. Now you're experiencing manga as it was meant to be!

NE

4/12